ALMIGHTY ME

Robert Bausch

ALMIGHTY
ME

Houghton Mifflin Company

Boston

For information about permission to reproduce selections from
this book, write to Permissions, Houghton Mifflin Company,
2 Park Street, Boston, Massachusetts 02108.

Library of Congress Cataloging-in-Publication Data

Bausch, Robert.
Almighty me / Robert Bausch.
p.   cm.
ISBN 0-395-56266-X
I. Title.
PS3552.A847A79   1991   90-24775
813'.54 — dc20   CIP

Printed in the United States of America

BP 10 9 8 7 6 5 4 3 2

In memory of Alex Sztanko

1974–1990

For Denny, lovely in her bones
and by whom I measure time . . .

I form the light, and create darkness;
  I make peace, and create evil;
I the Lord do all these things.

> — Isaiah 45:7

It is better to dwell in the corner of the housetop
  than with a brawling woman and in a wide house.

> — Proverbs 25:24

She perceiveth that her merchandise is good:
  her candle goeth not out by night.

> — Proverbs 31:18

I

One cold night in November, three years ago, I was a normal person opening his mail. I was a very normal person. It was November seventh, a Tuesday. I don't see any reason why I should try to be modest about this: I was a very kind, nice sort of person. I never harmed anyone on purpose. I tried to smile all the time at old people, and I was patient with other people's children. I paid my bills on time, contributed to the National Arbor Day Foundation, Greenpeace, and Jerry's kids. I believed in God.

But I was not who I am now.

I did not think I would ever write this story. But at the end of that winter three years ago — the winter that began with that cold November evening when I first opened Chet's letter and discovered I had been awarded the power of God for one full year, no strings attached — I made a momentous decision, which has required that I set down this narrative. At present I see what I will write as the first step in a final attempt to break a terrible stalemate, a paralyzing stand-off between myself and God. The decision I spoke of was the most significant of my whole life. In truth, it may be epochal for just about everybody.

But I have leaped ahead too far.

I should get back to the beginning of my story and simply tell you, as accurately as I can, what happened. I'm more devoted to the truth now.

In fact, you can be sure that nothing I say here is anything but the cold, blasted truth. Trust me.

Up until that night in November — which seems so long ago now — the truth interested me only occasionally. I wasn't a liar or anything; the truth was very important to me on an abstract, nonemotional level. I just didn't think it was necessary unless you were in a personal crisis of some kind. You know, when the truth is *required*, the best people tell it. I was that sort of person. If it wasn't required and a lie would serve everybody better, I was good for the lie.

Perhaps I should explain: I'm pretty good at empathy. When I notice that a person is embarrassed or feeling out of place, I can feel that way too. Sometimes just watching somebody's face can change my mood. So I've always tried never to say anything that would make anyone feel bad, or uncomfortable, or awkward. Before all this started I was an automobile salesman — I sold Dodge cars and trucks — and I worked with different people every day. I had to force myself to be pleasant all the time, even when I found myself feeling insulted, or hurt, or, God forbid, hateful toward an errant customer. So I spent a lot of time ignoring bad behavior, making up stories to get out of invitations, and pretending to be amused when I was not.

Invitations were a real problem. I knew how I felt if I invited somebody to my house or out to lunch and he refused. It always seemed as though something about me was probably not likable — that I possessed some vaguely unpleasant trait people wanted to avoid. It embarrassed me. And I have to admit, when I turned down invitations, it was usually because the person inviting me was not very likable and had some vaguely unpleasant trait I wanted to avoid. (You just can't go to dinner with an eighty-five-year-old man who has just purchased a two-hundred-dollar piece of rust you thought would go to the junkyard. But what are you going to say? "No, thank you, I don't like eating dinner with real old men, and I'm afraid the car won't make it to the restaurant"?)

Being a salesman, I got asked to do a lot of things by people I wouldn't normally have anything to do with unless we ended up in the same hospital room, maybe. So I became an accomplished evader. I could invent a prior engagement that would be so specific, with such convincing names and places, that nobody ever doubted I was a very busy man socially.

2

Perhaps I wasn't really normal. I thought I was. I wanted to be kind and do good things. I dreamed everybody said what a wonderful person I was. It seems to me that if you work at being nice, people will generally like you, and the ones who don't will probably be evil, or have some terrible deficiency of character that you needn't concern yourself with.

On that night in November, I'm thirty-five. Married. It's a tattered marriage, but I'm holding on because in every sinew of my heart I still love my wife, and I have two girls for whom I would become anything. I mean it. They say, "Daddy, be our horsey," I'm down on all fours whinnying like a palomino.

My wife — her name is Dorothy — my wife has left me so many times in her dreams, she is now truly considering it, although she would never do it in November. She finds it hard to do cold things in cold months, and she has already admitted that leaving me would be a cold thing to do. She says that I'm driving her crazy, that she doesn't understand how anyone who loves her so much can be so blind to her needs. If you ask me, she's merely a victim of the times, of the women's movement. Everyone tells me the women's movement is over now and we've got to live with it. I keep hoping it isn't over, that it will never be over until we all understand how we're supposed to behave. Right now, I have no idea.

In the beginning of our marriage, I would have said I knew exactly what was expected of me. I always thought Dorothy loved me the same way I loved her. We were outside of the world and its events, learning to live well. We even talked about how short our lives are and how important it is to use our time together, to love each other above all things. After all, one of us might die. In this culture our chances of being murdered or crushed in an automobile are greater than in any other. The world is hostile, and indifferent to each of us. Thus, in the first few years of our marriage we coveted time with each other. She used to say, "Life is so short, darling. Every minute counts." And I'd hold her and think of our time together — of the terribly brief span of life. But there was evidence even then that she would not always feel that way. I should have known.

One Saturday early in our marriage, back when we were childless and we both worked, she came downstairs smelling like a peony, all dressed up, her hair blown dry and beautiful, silver earrings dangling

3

in the shadows of her gorgeous jaw. I was lying on the couch reading the newspaper, and she breezed by me into the kitchen.

"I thought you were still sleeping," I said.

"Have you seen my black belt?"

"Where are you going?"

"Didn't I tell you? I'm going to lunch with Suzanne."

Suzanne was this small, slightly spherical loan officer who had been very kind to Dorothy when she was a teller trainee at Heritage Savings and Loan. I did remember that she had been pestering Dorothy to come have lunch with her. But Dorothy always told me she was doing her level best to avoid it.

"You didn't tell me you were going anywhere today."

"Well, I meant to." She was rooting through the cupboards in the kitchen.

"You won't find your belt in there."

"I'm looking for a clean cup. I want some coffee before I go."

I couldn't believe she was blithely going to abandon our time together and go off and have lunch with a person she had already explicitly told me she didn't want to have lunch with, and I told her so.

"Please, darling, not now. Help me find my belt."

"You look fine without the belt," I said. "In fact, you look beautiful."

She stood still for a moment and looked at me. "Thank you."

"How come you're doing this?" I said.

"Doing what?"

"You know."

"You mean going out to lunch?"

"Yes."

She seemed puzzled.

"I just want to know."

"I thought it might be fun. Besides, Suzanne has asked me so many times." She pretended not to know what I was talking about.

Later that afternoon, when she returned from her excursion with her flabby friend, I pretended to be upset at having to share her. I believe she knew, though, what her willingness to absent herself meant to me in the grand scheme of things.

"I just went to lunch," she said, laughing. "I didn't do anything wrong."

4

"No, of course not." I held her in my arms and kissed her forehead. "I sure missed you, though."

"And I missed you." She nestled into my chest and I smelled her hair.

"It's just . . ." I stopped.

After a long embrace, she leaned back and looked into my eyes. "Just what?"

"What if something happens to one of us?"

"Don't," she said. "I don't want to think about that."

"We should use our time. *Use* it."

"Would you stop it?" She started tickling me. "Don't be so serious."

But you see what was going on there? What did she mean when she held me in the darkness and whispered, "I want to spend every second of my life with you" or "I never want to be away from you"? Was she only saying those things because she'd heard people say them in books and movies?

Was I wrong to take her at her word?

I didn't notice it much at the time — I mean, whenever she went to lunch with Suzanne or one of her other friends, which got to be fairly often, I tried not to ask myself what it revealed about her love. But if she was willing to give up even one minute with me for time with someone else, then somewhere along the line (just a day or so after we got married is about where I'd place it) her supply of time with me got to the surplus side of the scale. Either that or what she said when she expressed her passionate love was just not true.

I know I never wanted to be away from her. Not for a minute. Her love was an element so crucial to my existence that I worried every day about losing it. Sometimes I went to the bank during my lunch hour just so I could see her. I'd pull up to the drive-in window and send her a note that said, "I'm hopelessly in love with you."

She'd laugh and send back a piece of paper that said, "You're impossible. Your balance is currently zero."

In some ways we're all a little out of balance, aren't we? This is surely a very strange time. Women have changed what it means to be a woman — I guess that doesn't bother me so much. It's almost certainly a good thing. But they've also changed what it means to be a man. And they've made a certain kind of bigotry acceptable. "Most men are pathetic,"

5

my wife said recently. "They don't have any idea what to do with their feelings." You replace the word *men* with any other kind of person and what do you have? Put Jews in there, or Protestants, or New Yorkers. It's troublesome to me to be judged by my genes. And it is not just troublesome in an academic sense. It makes my spine ache.

Now, if you had asked me to tell you the difference between men and women before my time as acting deity, I would have told you the simple, unadorned truth. Here it is, in one sentence:

Men do not care overmuch about their hair and women do, while women do not care overmuch about multiple bed partners and men do, although both sexes spend more time than either would be willing to admit denying what they know is true about love and each other and at least part of that truth is that most men and women take their vision of themselves and love from television commercials, situation comedies, and the movies, even though no one has noticed very much that if anybody knows less than a monkey about what it means to be in love it's a Hollywood actor, since most Hollywood actors spend less time in love than the average person spends in quicksand, hence it is unfortunate and so profoundly ironic you might call it perverse that we learn the language of love from such people, and we learn what we should do when we are in love, how to kiss and where to hold each other and now, in some movies, even where *not* to touch, but that's not even close to what is really bothering everybody, because the real trouble is that the feminist movement originally wanted to deny sex as an attribute and an activity, when it is simply true that as an attribute, it is absolutely undeniable since you are either a man or a woman and although you can pretend to be one or the other, or even have surgery to bring it about, you are nonetheless one or the other and it is perhaps unfortunate that one of the attributes of sex and sexuality is desire, and desire in males has nothing whatever to do with equality or social responsibility or aesthetics or even morality, because for men, sex as an activity is far more important than family or stocks and bonds or sports or democracy or even disarmament, and sex is driven almost exclusively by what men believe they appreciate in the sexual attributes of each woman, and without those desired attributes sexual activity is extremely difficult, if not impossible, while for women, sexual activity is one of many transitory expressions of an infinitely mysterious feeling that can be expressed just as easily with a little hugging or a quiet candlelight dinner or even a brief conversation about what one might be thinking about, and in any case such expressions of love are far less messy and take less time than the activity of sex does, and since sexual activity is merely one in an arsenal of possible responses to men it almost never takes on the importance of a goal in life, while for men it is frequently the only possible end with women and not a response but a stimulus, and since a stimulus provides evidence of life, sex is the one true and pure goal of all existence.

That's what I would have said is the major nonanatomical difference between men and women. Isn't it simple?

I shouldn't intervene so much with the cold facts. At least not yet. I was telling you about that day in November. By that time in my marriage Dorothy still loved me. She loved the children. But she hated loving me and the children. This was not just an intellectual response to her role as wife and mother. It took years for her to realize that she hated her daily life. She often said that she felt incomplete. She threw herself into volunteer work for a while, cooking for homeless people, cutting out paper dolls for kindergarten teachers, arranging square dances for senior citizens. But even the most obvious successes only increased her awareness of the "void in her life," as she put it. Nothing drove her like going to school did. She had never dreamed that she might be a good student. What she found in school was praise and recognition for her work, for her skill with thought and ideas and the written word. She took to school as though it were a career in itself. It sure felt better than being somebody's servant, which is how she came to feel about her life at home.

A year or so before that night in November — she was in her second year of college — Dorothy refused to do any of the things other wives did. "I don't want to be just a wife anymore," she said. The tone of the word *wife* would more accurately fit the word *janitor*. She scorned doing the laundry, making beds, washing dishes, cleaning, and vacuuming. She'd help *me* do those things — sometimes, if she wasn't too tired, or busy making phone calls or studying or helping the kids with their homework. She definitely wouldn't cook. "That's not woman's work. It's servant's work," she said.

"We don't have a servant." I tried to be polite. "Besides, that's what you've always done."

"Right. I've taken care of everything up until now. The housework, the kids. Why can't it be your turn for a while?"

"I've got a full-time job."

"And I'm going to school."

"Fine," I said. "I'll do the chores."

"That's your choice."

She said things like that all the time, as if that made the whole thing acceptable. As long as everything was somebody's choice, it must be okay.

But I didn't see any point in arguing about it. I saw this period as the last stage in the transformation of our relationship into a post-children marriage. I say "post-children marriage" because the difference between marriage before children and marriage after is sort of like the difference between, say, the island of Jamaica and Greenland.

Don't get me wrong. I already told you I loved the children. I did and still do, and that's the truth. Actually, I think I loved the children more than Dorothy did. At least I was willing to clean up after them. Anyway, both girls were pretty much housebroken before Dorothy decided it was my turn to take over the job, so I didn't mind it that much, to tell you the truth.

Oh, I didn't do everything around the house. Dorothy helped me out once in a while. She was actually pretty sweet about it sometimes. I'd come home from work and there she'd be, a big roast chicken on the table, rice pilaf, white wine, fresh asparagus.

"I thought you might be hungry," she'd say.

I'd holler, "You sweetheart!"

Sometimes she'd do all the wash for me, although she never folded it and put it away. I guess she was just fed up with trying to find where to put all those little things the girls wore. I didn't blame her. It was a chore sometimes. When the girls were babies their socks were so little they all fit into a drinking glass. Still, sometimes Dorothy would do things like that for me and I'd feel loved.

But things really changed after she became a sophomore. She started smoking again, a habit she'd given up when she first got pregnant. She even looked different — got her hair boiled and coiled, dyed and stiffened. She started wearing Levi's so tight they left a pattern on her skin. I tried to tell her she was ten years behind the times. Hell, twenty years. She didn't care. "I'm an individual," she said.

8

"Well," I told her, "you ought to dress the way individuals dress these days, so you don't look foolish and so lots of other individuals don't laugh at you."

"No one laughs at me."

"Maybe they're being polite."

This sent her out of the room, her principal response to disagreements.

Now at the time this story began, the two girls, Jody Beth and Claire, were five and seven, respectively. Since they were not allowed to do much housework on their own, I had begun to wish I had a son. Or two sons. But I knew a man must love his own, even when his own refuse to be referred to in that way.

One time, just a few months before that fateful November, Dorothy and I were sitting on a long bench at Champaign Mall, eating the roast beef sandwiches I'd packed for our lunch, and we started talking about my "attitude" toward the girls. "You have to stop expecting them to wait on you all the time," Dorothy said.

"I just need some help around the house," I said.

"It's okay to ask them for help. You don't do that. You expect it, and when they don't do it, you order them to."

"I do not."

"I've heard you."

"Maybe we should have had sons," I said.

She sat back and looked at the bench behind us. Then she said, "That wouldn't make any difference. I wouldn't want to impose a role on them either."

"I'm just asking for help. That's all."

"There's a difference between responsibilities we teach and roles we impose."

"Sure," I said.

I have to admit I wasn't very calm, and she knew it. I chewed my food slowly and tried to pretend I wasn't getting angry.

"I'm sorry if I appear unreasonable," she said.

"*Appear!*" I guess you could say I shouted then. I couldn't believe it.

At the next bench I saw this man and woman in their early sixties maybe, sitting very close together. They were whispering to each other, but I caught them staring at Dorothy and me.

"Married?" I said.

They both smiled, nodded.

"How long?"

Dorothy looked up, a pained expression on her face.

"Thirty-five years," the man said. The woman nodded again and touched his hand.

I leaned back, trying to appear friendly. But I was pretty angry, and I wanted Dorothy to hear this conversation. "Still love each other, I bet, huh?"

"Good Lord," Dorothy said.

The old man said, "Of course."

"She cook for you? Wash dishes?" I heard Dorothy crumpling her lunch bag and gathering her things. She went out to the car and sat there while I politely listened to the story of the old man and his wife — how they met, how many children and grandchildren they had. I couldn't get away from them, not and be polite. As it turned out, they each had one of those wallets with a fifteen-foot folding section of small plastic-covered photos. I got a chance to look at each of their children, their grandchildren, their pets, their children's pets, their rose garden, and his World War II buddies. She was beginning to unfold her garden club when I pretended to notice an emergency in the distance and feigned a desire to save my wife from certain disaster. Dorothy thought it was so funny, she forgot what we were arguing about. Or she pretended to. Even so, I was still not allowed to tell my daughters that any household chore was their responsibility. All I could do was ask them to help me. I had to tell them each time what to do. But you know, kids that age, you have to tell them all the time what to do anyway. So I didn't see the point in fighting about it.

At dinner on that night in November three years ago, I told Dorothy it would be very sweet if she would stop studying for a little while and spend some time with the children, and she said, "I can't. Not tonight. I've got a paper due tomorrow and a ton of reading to do, and I'm so tired I know if I don't get started I'll fall asleep."

"Just take an hour with them."

"I've got too much to do. I'll take them somewhere tomorrow afternoon."

"You always have too much to do."

"Honey," she said. "Please don't."

"Don't what?"

"You're not giving me any space."

"Take all the space you need," I told her. "You want, I'll eat outside."

"That's not what I mean and you know it."

"Well, communicate then. Go ahead."

"I think I might begin to hate you."

"Now," I said, "nobody I know hates me."

"You need to let me be . . ." She turned over a lump of mashed potatoes with her fork.

"Be what?" I said.

She shook her lovely head. "I need things you can't give me. Don't you see, honey? You're not . . ." She paused, seemed to cast around in her head for a lost word. Then she said, "You're just *not*."

"I love you," I said.

She started crying, then ran out of the room waving her arms as if she had knocked into a beehive or something.

"What'd I say?"

She disappeared up the stairs — didn't hear me, or didn't want to hear me. That's communication, isn't it?

"Your mother's going through a phase," I told the children while I cleaned up the dinner table. "She may not be eating with us for a while."

It was after dinner that I discovered the mail on the table in the hall. It was mostly a lot of bills and a few catalogues, but one letter, in a light blue envelope with an official seal, compelled me in an odd sort of way. Something much more than curiosity led me to examine the envelope very closely. I think I was pleased by its design. There was no return address, just a picture in the corner of a sun, half set, or half risen, behind two perfect mountains. The mountains were a darker blue, and the lines that emanated from the faultless half-circle of the sun were as fine as any I'd seen printed anywhere. Across the front, in bright white letters above my address, was this:

GOODMAN CHARLES WIGGINS, SALESMAN

I thought it was some sort of church mail. A request from the Catholics or the Lutherans to help support a youth league or a senior citizens' swim meet or something like that. I almost threw it away. But when I tried to drop it in the kitchen trash, I couldn't let go of it. Not that it stuck to me or anything. I simply did not open my fingers when I intended to.

I sat down in the kitchen and opened it. It said:

November 8, 1988

Dear Goodman Wiggins:

Congratulations! You have been awarded God's power for one full year. That's right, Goodman Wiggins. God's great power is yours, at no obligation or cost to you. For one full year from the date printed at the top of this page, you will be allowed to exercise the deity's power free of charge.

Just think, Goodman Wiggins. Now you can play the piano better than Beethoven, write sonnets that surpass Shakespeare's, hit a baseball better than Babe Ruth, paint better than Renoir. You can do anything you want, and it's all absolutely free. All you have to do is say yes to this offer and it's all yours.

No salesman will contact you, but I myself or one of our representatives will be getting in touch with you soon to find out what your answer will be. This is a limited offer. If you should choose not to accept it, there will be no other offers like it.

Sincerely,

CHET R. BUSH
Official Remitter of Offers
The Heavens

There was nothing else in the envelope.

Of course I thought it was a fairly clever sales pitch for something — real estate or insurance — and the rest of the material had inadvertently been left out of the envelope. I remember thinking it was a pretty sacrilegious ad, even for Madison Avenue. I set it back on the hall table and figured I'd save it as a sort of conversation piece.

I went to bed late that night. I didn't want to have to hear Dorothy telling me I was "not." She had been doing her reading in bed and had fallen asleep, curled up under the blankets like an insect in a conch shell. I lay there next to her, looking at the ceiling and thinking.

I was a good salesman. I made between sixty-five and seventy thousand dollars a year, closer to seventy in good times. I was in control of how I did — the harder and longer I worked, the more I made. That particular November, I was winding up one of my better years. I thought about all the cars I'd sold and tried to count up the money I'd made.

I'd done pretty well for myself, considering I didn't have a college degree. I almost graduated from college, but I avoided that terrible fate. I was like James Dean playing chicken in *Rebel Without a Cause*. He jumped out of his car at the last minute, just before it hurled over the edge and down. Right before the final exams in my last two classes, in the last semester, I jumped out of college.

My friends were like the other guy in the movie — Buzz. They went over the edge. All my friends thought I'd lost myself to drugs or some horrible sexual secret. They couldn't understand why a man would go to school for four years and then drop out right before graduation.

But the truth of the matter is, I just didn't want to take those tests. We all have tolerances for things. You take a certain number of aspirin, you kill yourself. Your number is different from mine or anybody else's. Some people can take thirty and only fall asleep. Ten might kill me. It's that way with exams and tests. I'd had so many and just couldn't take any more.

Besides, I really did see it as an escape. I thought having a college degree might harm me — might make me one of those people who think talking about hermeneutics is a conversation, or who go around using words like *paradigm* and *moreover*.

So I escaped, as I said. I made a career in the auto business. A good career, where I was honest and willing to be just about anything people wanted me to be.

I bought a house in a new neighborhood, and like all my contemporaries, I avoided my neighbors as if I were a lone cavalry officer and they were Apache Indians. I didn't really belong in the suburbs. I kept telling myself that. I saw it as a temporary setback. The house was nice, but it wasn't on an acre of land away from all those other houses that looked just like it.

Don't get me wrong. I love people and have many truly good friends — all at least a half-hour's drive from where I live. I just don't know what to do about neighbors. The last thing I wanted was to be identified as a suburbanite, and I believed I could avoid that by simply ignoring anyone who was close enough for me to lob a rock into his yard from my front porch. I refused to join any block or community organizations, even if they served free orange juice and gave away helium balloons. And every winter I erected a snowman that stuck its fat white tongue out toward the street.

I agonized over the same thing about neighbors that everybody else probably does. I never knew if I should wave to them or not. Sometimes I'd do it and my neighbor would miss it, or he would wave to me and I'd catch sight of it just before he turned away so he'd miss *my* wave, and neither of us is ever sure that the other one is not avoiding him or slighting him in some way. And what do you do when you do wave to your neighbor, and he waves back as he walks around to the back of his house, and you walk around your own house, and then you see him coming around the other side? Do you wave again? I've never known. I am certain that most people spend a lot of time pretending they don't even see their neighbors and thereby spare themselves the problem.

When one of my neighbors spoke to me, I answered, of course. I could imagine how I'd feel if I tried to be friendly and got no answer. So I tried not to be seen by my neighbors most of the time. I'd drive my Dodge into the garage, enter the house from there. When somebody knocked on my door I didn't answer it, unless it was one of the little neighborhood kids asking for Claire or Jody Beth. I let the girls have all the friends they wanted, but I told them I wasn't interested in meeting anybody's mommy or daddy.

Dorothy didn't want to meet anybody either. "They're all housewives," she said. She had this expression on her face as if she were smelling something awful. "I'm not going to sit around and get fat talking about babies and Tupperware."

"I don't blame you."

"We're just here temporarily, anyway."

"Right."

"We *are* going to move, aren't we?"

"Soon as we can. Soon as the house increases a little in value."

She wiped her brow, relieved.

We had that conversation the year after the second girl was born, before Dorothy had decided to go to school. So we stayed longer than either one of us wanted to.

❊

I thought about all these things that night in November, and about how much I loved Dorothy, and about how sad it was, what was happening to us.

She was so lovely there, in her sleep, I just couldn't understand how William Blake could be more important to her than I was.

Dorothy moved under the covers. I saw her hand crawl out from under the sheet and curl up by my pillow.

And I knew, suddenly, that she would divorce me.

I felt a slight tremor of fear, but it subsided. I put my head back against the headboard, watched the shadows in the room, and tried not to think about the future. I made up my mind, as I had done many times in the last few years before that night, to live each day by itself.

Then I remembered the letter, the blue letter from heaven, and I felt a charge of something very much like electricity race across the dome of my skull. I sat up again, blinked my eyes. I thought I might be dying. You never know what a stroke feels like until it hits you, right? My ears buzzed, and the letter seemed to spin before me like a whirling dream. I lay back down and crossed my arms over my breast, just in case this really was death. There was a long pause while I felt the vibrations and currents dance around the top of my skull. I was absolutely terrified. I closed my eyes and tried not to see anything, but the blue envelope kept whirling in front of me. I turned on my side and cupped my hands over my face.

Then I went to sleep.

❋

All morning the next day I felt sort of insubstantial, as if I might not appear in the mirror. I don't think I'd dreamed, but some secret fold in my brain continued to broadcast the jitters. I believed it was all a disturbing sort of waking nightmare brought on by stress and deep-seated fears of loss and abandonment.

Dorothy got herself dressed for class, an operation I kept reminding myself I'd have to watch someday; it must be fairly aerobic getting into those tight jeans so early in the morning. But she did all her preparations in her bathroom. This is a small toilet and sink off our bedroom that used to be our bathroom. I made no complaint about this arrangement, since at least it was one room in the house I didn't have to clean.

15

I made breakfast for the girls: Froot Loops and toast. They ate the cereal, leaving almost all the milk in the bowl, and scattered the crusts all over the table. I remember thinking that if I really did have the power of God, I'd make it so children ate all their food and cleaned up after themselves.

Before they went out the door for school, Jody Beth said, "Is Mommy still in a phase, Daddy?"

"Oh, yes." I knelt in front of her, zipped her red jacket.

Claire said, "I hate phases."

"Me too," I said.

"Can't you stop phases?" Jody Beth asked.

"I wish I could." I kissed both of them and shooed them out the door.

Dorothy came down looking tired and irritable. "I worked on my paper most of the night," she said. "I've had two hours' sleep. And it's still not right." She seated herself at the table. "I guess I can try to finish it this morning in the library." Her voice seemed distant and ruined.

"You almost came down here a minute too soon," I said.

"Why?"

"You'd have seen the children."

She let out this puppyish sort of whimper and threw her arms up. "I quit, I just —"

"I was just kidding."

"I don't think you were."

"Well, it is kind of mean to avoid your own children."

"I'm not avoiding them."

"What would you call it? Giving them space?" I couldn't help myself. I knew my attitude would not be likely to entice her to stick around and work on our tottering marriage, but she said things sometimes, and in such a hateful tone of voice that it was almost impossible not to give it back to her.

"I don't want any breakfast." Her eyes looked like poppy seeds. She gathered up the strips of crust and threw them in the trash by the dishwasher. Then she went to the door and opened it.

"Be careful," I said. "They're out there."

She looked at me as if I'd smacked her with a broom handle. "This is cruelty," she said. "Mental cruelty."

"I don't mean it," I told her. "I just want you to see how all this might look from their point of view."

"The children know how much I love them. I'm dealing with my own point of view right now."

"Well," I said. I didn't want to argue with her, because I knew she was right. She needed to get in touch with herself — isn't that what all the therapists and feminists and counselors and zookeepers and encyclopedia salesmen say? Get in touch with yourself! As if you could pick up the phone and call — invite yourself over for a stir-fry and then rap for a while. Jesus.

I just hated seeing her hurt the children, and it didn't do me any good being hurt either. But hell, I loved her. It's the truth. Just before she went out the door, I told her I was sorry.

She paused there in the doorway, looking at me for a moment as if she were trying to decide whether I meant it.

"Listen," I said. "When you get in touch with yourself, say hello for me."

"You just won't . . ." She stopped, seemed to search the floor in front of her for the next word.

"Say hello for the girls, too. Remind yourself that they exist and need — they need —"

She slammed the door! Do you believe that? Here I was trying to let her know I missed her, maybe to get her to see at least a minute fraction of one other tiny, minuscule, infinitesimal, little bit of a point of view. But no. She nearly broke the glass, she slammed the door so hard.

I headed for the shower to cool off. I thought, "Boy, it would sure be nice to have the power of God. Just for a *day*."

Shortly after Dorothy left and I had showered, cleaned up the dishes, and dressed for work, the phone rang. I was standing in front of the hall mirror, adjusting my tie, and just as I picked up the phone I noticed the blue letter lying there on the hall table. I felt something leap up in my heart, and then this voice said, "Goodman Wiggins?"

"Yes."

"This is Chet."

I did not want to be rude, but I also did not want to listen to somebody's blasphemous sales pitch. "I really don't have time right now."

"It will be today," the voice said.

"What will be today?"

"The offer."

"What are you selling?" Since I was a salesman myself, I thought I might comment on the originality of Chet's approach.

"What I have for you is not for sale."

"Well, what is it, then?"

"You read the letter."

"Yes, I did."

"That's what I'm offering."

"Look," I said. "What's this about? A funeral plot? Insurance? What? I really don't have the time."

"There's nothing to be afraid of."

When he said that, I felt my head start to whirl again, and without meaning to I hung up the phone. I think I was afraid the sound of Chet's voice was producing the simmering terror I'd felt the night before. I felt real sorry for hanging up on him like that — every salesman deserves the opportunity to make his pitch. I hoped he would forgive me.

I didn't have to be at the dealership until eleven or so. I worked whatever hours I wanted because I was the top salesman in the place. Hardly anybody buys a car early in the morning, anyway.

I was well liked at Shale Motors. Even Mr. Shale liked me. In fact, I may have been the only person Mr. Shale liked. He had never married, he had no family, and five years before that fateful November he'd had a stroke that robbed him of speech. Or I should say it robbed him of the control of his speech. He could talk the same as you or I, but he couldn't say what was on his mind. Something didn't translate right. It was really very complex, the kind of thing a linguist would have a ball with. Mr. Shale would want to say "hello" and that's what he'd believe he was going to say, and when he opened his mouth he'd say something like "boot camp" or "ashtray." Nobody knew what he wanted unless he wrote it down, and even that wasn't easy, because his hand shook like it was working a salt shaker.

I got to be his translator, because in my attempts to please everybody I developed the skill of pretending I understood what a person was saying even when I wasn't listening. Mr. Shale would walk in and point to one of the cars on the showroom floor and say, "Put the fan in the headlight and mark it tooth canary."

And I'd say, "Move it? You want it moved, right?"

He'd shake his head, look at me.

"Get one of the boys to wash it?"

"Peanut," he'd say, which sounded in tone just like "Yes." And it was clear he was happy I got it. So it turned out to be not terribly hard reading what he wanted from his voice and his shaky hands when the voice failed him. I always counted it a victory, though, if he didn't have to write down what he wanted me to do.

Of course, he probably never tried to tell me anything truly important out loud. He was a shrewd businessman and wouldn't take a chance like that, even though he believed I always knew what he wanted. So most of the time he thought I understood him, even when I didn't have any idea and only pretended.

I felt sorry for him. I guess I was pretty embarrassed about him, too. Sometimes a customer would surprise him — you know, walk into the showroom looking like his wallet weighed four hundred pounds — and Mr. Shale would jump up and say, "Elastic band, sir?"

Most of the time it didn't even make sense. He'd say, "Tone variety satan?" or "Drool video?" But you know how people are when they go shopping for a car. They fear salesmen so much they don't hear what you say to them. They get jumpy and squeal something like "Just looking, just looking." Everybody seems to think that a salesman has some sort of power that he just turns on and the unwary consumer begins to salivate at the sight of chrome.

I remember one time, though, a beautiful, tall, black-haired, professional-looking woman pranced through the door. She had to be somebody's divorce lawyer, the way she was dressed. She wore this gray suit coat and a long gray skirt with little white pinstripes, black nylon stockings, and shiny black pumps. She carried her purse as if it were full of some important medical serum or something. She held her head back, her nostrils pointing at everybody, and she wore disdain on her face like makeup.

I just hate women like that, don't you? They always act like they were born with those clothes on and they'd have to look up perspiration in the dictionary if they ever heard the word. You just know their idea of a good time is sitting in a fancy leather chair, sipping white wine and listening to Lionel Ritchie on the stereo.

Anyway, she walked in right when I was showing off this station wagon and Mr. Shale was the only other person in the place. I told my customer — an old man who I knew would no more buy a station wagon than he would a school bus — I told him I'd be back in a minute, but before I could get over there, Mr. Shale stepped up in front of the tall woman and said, "Got fine cunt, sir?" Then he blinked and said, "Ma'am."

Her black eyes scanned the showroom as if she were looking for a good place to leave a bomb or something.

"He can't talk," I said when I got to her.

"Fresh cunt?" Mr. Shale said. "Gnat? Notary."

"I hear what he's saying!" She was, of course, insulted.

"Really," I said. "He had a stroke."

"Bliss trout and cunt," Mr. Shale said in a very apologetic voice. It was obvious he was sorry.

"He's trying to apologize," I said.

"Cashew snatch," said Mr. Shale.

"What is this?" She continued to search the room, clutching her purse as though we had just tried to grab it. "I want to speak to the manager."

I pointed at Mr. Shale. "Well, he's the owner."

Whimpering, Mr. Shale said, "Burned leaves." He stood there like a praying mantis in front of her, his hands up under his chin. "Burned leaves?" he said again. "Simple arithmetic?"

"What?" The woman held her bag up over her chest, a shield against what was now the steady advance of Mr. Shale.

"I'm terrible shad roe," he said, reaching for her. She leaned away from him, refusing to give ground. Then, withdrawing his hand, he said, "Aahh. No pest strip."

He might have taken hold of her if she hadn't turned like a ballet dancer and pushed her way back through the double glass doors.

"She probably wasn't going to buy a car anyway," I said.

He shook his head and reached for a piece of paper on one of the small desks by the door. I watched for fifteen minutes while he struggled with his hand to write "I hope she wasn't a lawyer."

"She looked like one," I said. I tried to get past it — you know, get him to shrug it off. But he started crying, right there in front of me.

"That's all right," I said. "Come on, now."

He shook his head, then walked quietly back to his office.

The other people who worked for Mr. Shale laughed behind his back most of the time, so I tried not to do that. I respected him, actually — he made Shale Motors go on running, even though he was starting to wind down, if you know what I mean. He must have been aware that he was nearing the end. When you have a stroke, it's sort of like when you were a kid and your parents opened the door to let you know how terribly cold it was outside. Then they started putting on your coat, mittens, and overshoes. You just knew you were going out there. In the meantime, there wasn't a lot you could do, all bundled up and so stiff with extra clothing you felt like a teddy bear.

If you consider it, there are a lot of things in life to remind us of what's up ahead and plenty of people who've gone ahead to show us what time can do to a person. I guess that's why we're all pretty much afraid of things we can't put a signature on or dress up to cover. It's better not to think about it.

I always tried not to. I concentrated on enjoying what I had at the moment and not planning too much for anything the next week. That's the life of a salesman, actually, since if he doesn't sell anything next week he might be out of a job.

Anyway, on that day in November, the day I had my first conversation with Chet, I got to work about eleven or so, and Mr. Shale greeted me at the door with a sheet of paper.

"Wheels are stamped," he said.

"For me?"

He handed me the paper. "Nail," he said.

I stood there, my hand shaking so badly I could barely read the name on the note. It said, "Chet called. He said he'd call back."

I followed Mr. Shale to his office. He seated himself behind his cluttered desk, then gave a start of surprise to see me there. "Nest?"

"Did you talk to —" I stopped, held the note up. "Did you take this message?"

"Fender." He shook his head. "Fen— fist." He took a deep breath and pointed to the cashier's office in back of the showroom. "Electric tape — attitudes — by lake."

"Dottie took it?"

He nodded. "Nipple."

Dottie was the daytime receptionist. She had blond hair, thick glasses, and very kind, almost colorless eyes. If she had been a man she would have been fairly attractive. I thought when I first saw her that her name ought to be Chuck or something like that. But when I got to know her, I found her to be as feminine as you could expect in this day and age — when the word *female* is changing its meaning so much. I mean, now it seems to mean "man-hating, antisexual militant," or something close to that. Dottie was truly feminine, though. I always felt that if I needed a person to talk to, she would listen. If I needed somebody to reload my musket for me while I fought off the Iroquois, she'd do that too. That kind of feminine. I didn't think she was helpless or anything, I just thought she would be the sort of person you could go through things with and she wouldn't be wondering all the time if you weren't getting a notion of what her breasts would feel like in the palm of your hand. You know what I mean? Anything I hate, it's a suspicious person.

"It was just a plain man's voice," Dottie said when I asked her about Chet's call. "I never heard him before."

"What did he say?"

"Just that he would see you today."

"He didn't give a last name?"

"He said, 'Tell Mr. Wiggins' — no, he said, 'Tell Goodman Wiggins that Chet called.' Really weird." The phone buzzed and she picked it up. "Shale Motors."

I started to go back to my desk, but she reached out her hand and stopped me. "Service, line two," she said into a microphone in front of her. I heard her voice echo back in the garage. Then she said to me, "What's got you so afraid?"

"I'm not. Do I look afraid?"

"You look like you saw a ghost."

"I'm fine."

"Let's have lunch today," she said. She was always asking me to have lunch with her, and I never took her up on it. I was nervous about what people might say — no reason to feed the rumor mills — so I was usually too busy, or I had an important customer to see, or I avoided her so she couldn't ask. (My skill at evading invitations served me well here.) But this time I could see she wanted to help me, so I said okay. You should have seen the look on her face. It was as if I'd told her she won the lottery.

"You really *are* in trouble, aren't you?"

"I don't know," I said. "I might be losing my mind."

She turned to her switchboard. "When a person loses his mind, he doesn't announce it like that."

"Well, I just feel like something's going to happen to me that I don't really want."

She got this puzzled look on her face, then went back to the buzzing phones. "Maybe you've got to be crazy to go out to lunch with me," she said.

I went over to my desk. I sat there and stared out the showroom window at cars and trucks going up the street, at the shops and signs across the boulevard. *Okay,* I thought. *You are a normal, good person. You never consciously hurt anyone, you work hard at what you do, and you genuinely care how people feel. You are intelligent — you got terrific grades in college. So,* I wondered, *why is this happening to me?*

I did not understand what I was afraid of. I knew it probably had to do with Dorothy's desire to leave me, but it struck me as particularly odd that the blue letter, all by itself, had produced such physical, dizzying fear. I could not say that I was consciously afraid of losing Dorothy — I knew it was probably going to happen and I hated it, but it did not induce terror. Only the letter, and now this persistent salesman named Chet, seemed able to do that.

I thought about how I had always wanted to do wonderful things, but I never had the money, or the skill, or — I had to admit it — the power. That's what I needed to do any significant good. I don't mean political power, either.

I remembered a conversation I had had with one of my daughters' friends — a little boy named Brad, who lived across the street and who hung around our house all the time as if he were waiting for us to throw out the trash so he could search for valuables or maybe even for food. He was a scrawny little fellow, about Claire's age — seven or eight. He was seven, because I remember I asked him how he liked being seven, and he said, "Fine."

"I like being seven too," Claire said.

"Wouldn't you rather be six?" I asked.

"No," they both said. They were emphatic about it.

"How about my age?"

"Your age," Claire said.

"Would you like to be my age?"

"I wouldn't," my daughter said.

"Why not?"

"Because then I'd have a shorter life."

We were sitting under a crab apple tree in our back yard. It was a cloudy summer afternoon, warm and a bit moist. I noticed Brad wasn't saying very much and worried that he felt left out, so I said to him, "You like life, do you?"

"It's okay," my daughter said. And Brad said at the same time, "No."

He was real serious about it. I couldn't believe a seven-year-old boy could feel that way, so I teased him. "You're only kidding, right?" I said. "You can't fool me."

He didn't smile, or even move his head. He stared into my eyes as if he held a gun and was about to squeeze off a round. "I don't like it," he said.

"You're only seven years old."

Claire said, "I think you stub your toes too much in life."

I laughed. She didn't know what was so funny, but I thought she hit the old nail with that one. I could tell Brad had stubbed his toes far too many times for a boy his age, and I was already trying to figure ways to keep him away from my daughters. At the same time, I wished I could just wave my hand and make his life as perfect as Beaver Cleaver's. I felt so sorry for him. If I had had the power . . .

That's what kept running through my mind as I sat at my desk and watched the traffic thicken and congeal and finally halt outside the windows of Shale Motors. It was nearing lunchtime, so naturally the city would be paralyzed for two hours or so while everybody tried to get to and then back from lunch. I figured Dottie and I would walk someplace. I couldn't wait to talk to her. I had pretty much concluded by lunchtime that I was about to stub my toe on something horrible.

2

Dottie and I went to Rick's, a little pizza parlor just down the street from Shale Motors. It was a pleasant walk, although Dottie spent the time, as she frequently did, marveling over the fact that she and my wife had the same name.

"It's a miracle," she said.

She thought all coincidences were miracles. I told her, once again, that my wife's name was not Dottie. "She'd put me in a frying pan with some butter and garlic and sauté me if she ever heard me call her that."

"You're so funny." Dottie laughed. It didn't seem too cold, but I could see her breath in the air. The sun had moved behind a ruglike cover of gray clouds by the time we reached the restaurant, and the wind started to rush around a bit.

"I bet it snows tonight," Dottie said.

We took seats by a window.

"You think it will snow?" Dottie asked. She fumbled in her purse for something. Women always do that, you know? As soon as a woman sits anywhere, she reaches inside her purse — as if she's turning on a little recording device, or checking to see if her gun is loaded.

"Well?" she said.

"I'm sorry. I wasn't listening."

She shrugged. "I was just talking about the weather."

"Oh."

"Stupid, I know."

"No."

"I never know how to make conversation." She put her hands on the table in front of her, looked out the window. I could see she was discomfited, and maybe feeling sort of awkward.

"You talk to me just fine," I lied.

"You really think so?" She looked at me, her face slightly flushed. I knew I had made her feel better.

"Yeah, you're a good kid," I told her. I figured she'd remember me saying that for the rest of her life. A person like her — they need somebody they truly admire to praise them a little bit. But it bothered me that she was so glad to be having lunch with me. Maybe I was being supersensitive, but I just didn't want her to get the wrong idea. I figured she was probably attracted to me.

"Well," she said, after a pause, "we were going to talk about some problem you're having."

"I don't know if you'd call it a problem. I'm just sort of insecure." I had to make up something.

"Isn't everyone?"

I held the menu up in front of my face. "What are you going to have?"

"Why don't we just get a pizza?" Dottie said.

"Can't do that." I studied the menu. There was no way I was going to order an item like that. We'd have to share it, and also, she'd see me eating something messy with my hands. It's always a bad idea to put yourself on the spot like that around women. Women are always noticing things about you that you hadn't realized — you know what I mean? You might say "um" every fourth word, or some linguistic thing like that, and then you go out with some observant woman and she points it out and after that you can't make a complete sentence. Pizza was out of the question.

Dottie got quiet, looked at her menu. "I guess I'll just have a salad," she said when the waitress came for our order.

I could tell Dottie was disappointed in how things were going. You can't look forward to a thing for more than a year and have it turn out the way you want when it finally happens. I was embarrassed that I wasn't living up to her expectations.

"I'll have a salami sandwich."

"Oh, that sounds good," said Dottie. "I think I'll have one too."

The waitress, a tall blond teenager with unbelievable acne around her chin and mouth — she looked like she'd been bobbing for apples in spaghetti sauce — started scratching out Dottie's order.

"Don't do that," I said.

"What?"

"I'll have her salad, and she can have my —"

"Oh, if you're having the salad, then I'll have it too," Dottie said.

"What's it going to be?" Like Queen Victoria, the waitress was not amused.

I didn't know what to say. I looked at Dottie, who folded her menu as if she'd just read me the world's most profound book, and then back at the waitress. "I guess I'll — I'll go ahead and have the sandwich, then."

"Me too," Dottie said.

"Two sandwiches."

"Right," I said.

"And to drink?"

"What are you having?" Dottie asked.

"Are you just going to order whatever I do?" I couldn't control my tone. She looked scolded.

"I'll have a Diet Coke," she said. It's amazing how fast a woman can get sad, isn't it?

"Oh, what the hell. I'll have the same," I said.

When the waitress was gone, Dottie said, "So how come you can't eat pizza?"

"Did I say I can't?"

"You said, 'Can't do that.'"

"I thought I said something else."

"What did you think you said?"

"I don't know."

"You can't remember?"

"No. I don't know."

She looked at her hands. "I'm sorry."

"You don't have to go around apologizing all the time."

"I know. I'm so stupid." She tried to laugh it off, but I probably hurt her feelings. Or maybe I insulted her. She didn't look very happy.

"Sometimes I behave in a certain way and I don't even realize it," she said in a toneless voice.

"What do you mean?"

"I'm just getting on your nerves."

"I can't eat pizza because it makes my face . . . it makes me look like our waitress," I said.

She smiled, fiddled a bit with her purse. Then she said, "So, are you feeling insecure because you think you're losing your mind?"

There was a long pause while I felt really stupid. I never should have agreed to this lunch. I couldn't tell her about Chet; she'd think I was crazy, and it would probably destroy her fragile sense of her own worth to have one of her major idols — the dark, handsome, star salesman at Shale Motors — turn out to be a loon. Don't get me wrong. I am not really so dark and handsome. At least not in the sense you are probably thinking. I have dark hair, all of it, though it's getting a bit thin on either side of my forehead. I am five feet eleven inches tall, but I have a rather long face that makes me appear taller than I am, and I'm lean. I used to tease Dorothy by putting on a deep southern accent and declaiming, "Texas tall and slim as a brandin' iron." Dorothy would say, "You're slim. You're not Texas tall." But she often said I was handsome. If Dorothy, who was the most beautiful woman I had ever looked upon, thought I was handsome, you can imagine what poor plain-and-chunky Dottie thought. How could I tell her anything about Chet without giving her the wrong impression? Anyhow, there didn't seem to be any way to express what I was feeling. You don't tell a normal person you got a blue letter in the mail that you felt compelled to open and ever since you opened it you've had these spinning sensations in your head and fear like a stone in your stuttering heart.

The waitress brought our drinks and told us the sandwiches would be right out.

When she was gone, Dottie said, "Is there a specific thing you're worried about?"

"By the time we get our food, we'll have finished the drinks."

She made this fake laugh. I felt sorry for her right then. I knew she'd probably be a lonely old woman later in life.

I told her I didn't like to talk and eat at the same time, so when our sandwiches came we ate quietly. I looked out the window and attempted to make up a good story to tell her. I knew I had to have a problem because I had to have a reason to be going out to lunch with her. If I told her there was nothing, she'd think she'd been too aggressive with me that morning and then she'd be worried that I thought of her as some sort of sexual threat or some silly thing like that. I toyed once again with the idea of telling her about Chet.

As I was thinking about what I might say, I saw a short man in a pinstriped suit, with a jaunty sort of umpire's walk, approach the front door of the restaurant. What struck me about him, though, was not the clothing he wore or the way he walked. I watched him cross the cold street, saw people all around him, passing in the street and on the sidewalk, and I could see puffs of steaming breath coming from every one of them except him.

I guess my heart beat a little faster when I noticed that. But I didn't realize it was Chet until he sat down at our table and fingered what was left of my sandwich.

※

Chet looked a little like Mickey Rooney, except he was black and there was absolutely no hair on his head. "I'm glad we could finally meet," he said. He didn't have to say his name.

"This is Chet," I said to Dottie.

"Oh, she can't make out what you're saying."

"She can't?"

"Everything's sort of . . . slowed down for a bit."

I looked around the room and realized that no one was moving. "You've got to be kidding."

"Nope."

"That's just — that's a cliché, for God's sake." I couldn't believe it.

"It is not." He seemed offended.

"It is too. Every horror movie and *Twilight Zone* episode in the world stops time. It's the most —"

"I didn't say it was stopped." He put both hands on the table and sat back like a man about to deal the cards. "You can't *stop* time."

I waved my fingers in front of Dottie's eyes, got up, leaned over the table, and pressed my nose against hers. "Dottie, wake up. You're in my nightmare."

"She will see that," Chet said.

I was still leaning over the table, but I turned my head toward him. "What do you mean?"

"As I said, I haven't stopped time." He was indignant. "I've merely speeded things up between you and me. She's still moving in time the way she always has."

I sat down, slowly.

"Watch her jaw," said Chet. He was amused now.

Sure enough, when I examined Dottie closely, I could see she was chewing her food — the movement was almost as slow as a plant growing, but it was a definite movement. Also her lids shifted slightly, and a low, deep sound began to escape her lips.

"What's happening?"

"She's going to say something to you."

"Will I understand it?"

"You've got time. It'll be about ten minutes before she gets out the first bilabial fricative."

"Ten minutes?"

"Not your minutes. My minutes."

"I don't believe this." I looked into Dottie's eyes, tried to concentrate only on her. "Dottie, help me, I'm having a nervous breakdown."

Dottie's lips moved, almost imperceptibly. She sounded like Johnny Cash.

"This is embarrassing," I said.

"Why?"

"Excuse me, but is this really happening?"

"Sort of."

Dottie's mouth seemed to erupt in slow motion, folds of skin peeling back and away from her teeth.

"I feel like I'm violating something." I tried not to look at her. Her lips opened like some sort of weird mushroom.

"She's going to say something innocuous," said Chet. "But she's wondering if she really saw you zip out of your chair and back again. And she's worried about what that was on her nose."

"Look, whatever you're going to do, get it over with."

He leaned forward. "This isn't a horror movie. You don't have to be frightened."

"I'm not."

"Yes, you are. You called this a nightmare."

"I don't want it."

"The power?"

"Whatever you call it. Whatever you're here for. I don't want it."

He stood up, a casual movement that did not reveal any response to what I said. It was as if he'd decided to go get a napkin.

"That's it?" I said.

"You don't want it, fine. That's fine."

He stood there while Dottie's voice grew louder and her mouth changed shape like a smoke ring.

"Well?" I said.

"If I leave, you'll think about it and change your mind."

"Try me."

"I know," he said. He put his hands on his hips and shook his head back and forth as if he were ashamed of me.

"Sure, I see. Trick me into it."

"No trick," he said. "I know it will happen. I know human nature better than you know the alphabet. But if you don't want it, I'm wondering if I should give it to you."

"I can't believe this." I felt stupid for saying that over and over, but what would you do?

"Just say, 'I'm turning down your offer,' and I'll leave," he said.

"I'm turning down your offer."

"You have to mean it." He frowned.

"I don't really know what you're offering me."

"The power of God for a year."

"And I can do anything I want?"

"Just about."

"How about a thirty-day trial?"

Chet seemed to slump a little bit. Dottie's tongue curled against her upper front teeth, and I thought of Dorothy leaving me. I remembered how close we came to bliss when we first fell in love, and I said, "Okay."

"It's yours." He turned and started for the door.

"WAIT!" I screamed.

"Yes?" His voice was absolutely serene, as smooth as any sound I ever heard anywhere. He could have been a funeral director asking for his check in the middle of a Mass.

"Is that it?"

"So far."

"What do I do?"

"Anything you want."

"Anything at all?"

"Anything at all." He held up a pink palm. "What you can't do you will learn."

"What I *can't* do?"

He came back to the table and leaned over so close to me I thought he was going to touch my nose the way I had touched Dottie's. "There are limits," he said.

"Limits."

He blinked. "You just going to repeat everything I say?"

"I'm real nervous," I said.

"There are limits. You will learn them."

"Will you teach me?"

He straightened up, moved again toward the door. "You have God's power, but not his wisdom."

"Oh."

"Don't make a mess we can't clean up." He stopped by the cash register. "You will learn a lot of it on your own. Some of it I will teach you."

"Should I quit my job?"

He laughed, raised his eyes to the ceiling.

"I thought knowledge was part of the power," I said.

"Your first lesson."

Dottie sounded like an electric lawn mower. She began a long, slow blink of her eyes. I thought she was falling asleep.

"Look at her," I said.

"You can learn whatever you want, do almost anything. But think," Chet said. *"Think."*

"Think?"

"Study consequences. Study them hard." He turned and walked to the door.

"Where are you going now?"

"I will be with you," he said. "Feel any different?"

"No."

32

"You have it," he said, still with that smile on his face. "You have it." Then he went out the door and Dottie's word seemed to speed up like a bad videotape until it became a sentence. She was saying, "What the hell was that?"

"What?"

"Something — something just . . . did you?" She looked at me carefully, as if she wanted to make sure I was real. "Something just pressed my nose — hard."

"Maybe they've got heavy flies in here."

"Did you sneeze?" She was terrified that I'd sneezed and left something on her nose.

"No." I picked up the last of my sandwich. "Why?"

She gave a nervous laugh. "I don't know what happened."

"Will you excuse me?" I got up and stood in front of her, waiting for an answer. She studied her sandwich, which she was just beginning to chew again. I could see she was considering the mystery. "I'll be right back," I said.

"You didn't — you weren't . . ." She stopped chewing. "I think there's something wrong with me."

She was absolutely terrified that she was just discovering the onset of some horrible brain dysfunction. When I realized this, it hit me that I knew with certainty how she was feeling.

"I've got to go to the men's room," I said. "I'll be right back."

When I got to the men's room I was very calm. I felt sort of regal, even in the presence of the urinals. I stood next to a very old man who was trying to get his bony white hands dry under an air dryer. His arthritis was so bad it was impossible for him to rub his hands together.

I made him feel better. I cured his arthritis; then, while he dried his hands there in the weak neon light, I gave him the cardiovascular system of a man twenty years old.

"Damn," he said.

"What's the matter?" I stood in front of one of the urinals, pretending to use it.

"Oh, uh . . . oh." He shook his head. I realized he mistook the sudden rush of youthful strength and deliverance from pain for the beginning of the end.

"You're going to be fine, old man," I told him. I made him believe it.

He straightened up, stretched as if he'd just risen from a long sleep. Then he looked at me, a glorious and triumphant smile on his face. "Nice day, ain't it?" he said.

"Boy, I'll say."

He swung the door open too hard on the way out, and it slammed against the blue tile. The whole time I was fixing him up I watched myself in the mirror, and you know what? There was no change. I was afraid that if I said something to invoke my power right there in Rick's Pizza Parlor, I might appear different — you know, like Spiderman or Superman — and then I'd have a lot of explaining to do. But I was just an ordinary man standing in front of one of the white urinals while the hot-air dryer echoed in the toilets.

"This is *really* going to be fun," I said to the mirror.

When I came back out I made Dottie forget she was afraid, and we finished our lunch. I didn't let her say anything that might embarrass her or make her feel awkward. I didn't let her ask why I wanted to have lunch with her, and I made sure she didn't misunderstand anything between us. I put her in the right frame of mind — just friends, that's what I put in her head. She and I were just friends. Also I made her feel terrific about herself, made her feel attractive — but to balance that I gave her a fairly strong sense of humility. As I said, I always liked her, so I wanted her to be truly happy. She skipped next to me like a ten-year-old on the way back to Shale Motors, talking the whole time about how much she loved snow, and the quiet trees all shrouded in white, and the lights in all the houses. "I do hope it snows," she said.

When we reached the sidewalk in front of Shale Motors, I was impossibly giddy, feeling so good about Dottie's mood and what I had done for her that I wanted to wave my hand right then and there and change the world into some sort of permanent terrestrial paradise.

"This has been fun." Dottie smiled. Her cheeks were pink, like a child's.

"You know what?"

"What?"

"I'm going to make it snow. Just for you." I waved my hand and willed snow. The first flakes drifted crazily down, whirling silently in the traffic. You should have seen the look on her face.

"How did you know it was going to do that?"

"I made it happen."

She was laughing. "You really are crazy." She turned to go in. It was just the right thing to do. I felt like we were in a very delightful movie. Boy, did she admire my timing. She told everyone in the dealership how I'd pretended to make it snow for her. And near the end of the day, before she went to her little melon-colored Dodge Colt and started home, she came up to me and whispered, "Make it snow all night."

"Hah," I laughed.

She squeezed my arm and twirled on her heels. It was the best day of her life — she felt healthy and confident, as if the world welcomed her in ways it never had before.

❋

As soon as I realized that I had recreated the circulatory system of the old man in the men's room and made it snow with a wave of my hand, I knew Mr. Shale's speech problems would soon be over. I toyed with the idea of just stepping up to him and announcing it. "Mr. Shale, I have returned you to the realm of normal speech." But then I opted for the cure from a distance. I didn't want to be in the same room with him when he realized he could talk again — I was afraid it might embarrass him. Also, I wanted to see if I could fix his speech just by thinking about it.

Mr. Shale had a private office above the showroom, and in the afternoons he went up there to work. When Dottie and I returned from lunch, he had already sequestered himself in there, so I sat down in one of the guest chairs in the showroom and concentrated on him, willing an end to his problem.

Then I settled in to wait for him to come down. I was very anxious — almost joyfully excited, but a little frightened as well. I couldn't be certain that what I had willed would come to pass. No amount of concentration would give that answer to me. I could believe it had worked, but I couldn't know it with certainty until I heard him talk.

I sat there for a long time, wondering if God had the same sort of problem with his creations.

Mr. Shale worked unusually late that day, so I ended up waiting around the showroom most of the afternoon and evening. The salesman on floor duty was a man named Matthews. Everybody called him

Cherry for a reason you can probably figure out. He was the youngest salesman on the staff and he lived alone in a small apartment near the dealership, but he worked like a man with a five-bedroom house and three children to support. Nevertheless, selling came hard to him. He could never bring himself to call people out of the blue and ask them if they wanted to buy a car. He got most of his business from his days on floor duty, so he was a little suspicious of me waiting around the showroom after dinnertime.

"You waiting for a customer of yours?" he asked me finally. I knew he'd been sitting there encouraging himself to go ahead and ask me what the hell I was doing there so late on *his* floor day. Salesmen are a distrustful lot, and when it's your floor day, the floor is yours. Anybody who walks through the door is a potential customer of *yours*.

"I'm waiting for Mr. Shale," I told him.

"I saw you out with Dottie today."

"We had lunch."

"You going to put the moves on her?"

I only looked at him.

"She's desperate, you know."

"No, I didn't know."

"Yeah. I gave her a charity screw when I first came to work here." He chuckled. "I've been avoiding her ever since."

I never liked Cherry very much. I thought I didn't like him because he was so bad around people, but I was beginning to realize that he suffered from a worse flaw: he couldn't make the world or any of its inhabitants have existence apart from his own conception of himself. I knew he was lying to me about Dottie, that he had never slept with her, but he had to have me believing that she was one of his throwaways.

He was quiet for a long time, watching me out of the corner of his eye. It was a slow night, so he didn't have much to do. Finally he sighed and said, "Why don't you go up and knock on Mr. Shale's door?"

"I want to wait."

"Don't you want to know what he might say?" He laughed, ducked his head down toward his chest. "Cartwheel plow. Motor food. Crowd funnel."

"I don't want to disturb him." I made a point of not showing the slightest amusement.

"Well, for Christ's sake," Cherry said, "it's silly to sit here and wait." He sat forward, placing his chin in his hands like a petulant child. He had a tremendous head of black hair, a perfect widow's peak, and blue eyes. His hands were very nearly perfect — manicured, smooth, lightly covered with fine hair, white and clean. You never saw such impeccably tailored suits. He was really not a bad-looking guy. But every time he opened his mouth he revealed what an empty husk he truly was.

After another pause he said, "You're just afraid to go up there." That was how *he* felt — he was afraid of Mr. Shale — so he was sure I felt the same way. I thought of Dottie, how happy she had been that afternoon, and I remembered the tone of Cherry's voice when he said, "She's desperate, you know," and suddenly I was very angry.

So I gave him diarrhea.

I didn't want to hurt him or anything — I'd never do that. But he just got on my nerves, and I figured a little illness might move him in the direction of a more charitable attitude toward the rest of the world. It's pretty hard to be obnoxious, self-centered, boorish, and leering when you are beating a path to the men's room.

While Cherry was gone, I got impatient waiting for Mr. Shale, so I decided to make him come down. I made him want to get up and go home.

But nothing happened.

I sat there watching the car lights inching forward in the darkness outside the showroom. I could picture Mr. Shale in his office working over his books, but I could not get him even to look at his watch.

Cherry came back and sat at the desk by the front door. His face was as white as an egg. I felt bad that I had made him sick. He looked up at me with this sad sort of baby-seal look on his face. "I got sick," he said.

I didn't answer him.

He let out this deep breath, stared out the windows. I waved my hand. "Feel better?"

He shook his head slowly. Then he looked down at himself, rubbed his stomach. "Yes . . . I guess I do."

"Probably something you ate."

"Yeah."

He was worried that he might be getting the flu and he'd have to leave work early.

"It's nothing," I said. "Something you ate."

"I guess."

"Don't worry about it." In spite of his faults, I felt sorry for him. People who think only of themselves are so lonely most of the time.

I was terribly disturbed that I couldn't know whether or not I had fixed Mr. Shale, and I did not seem to be able to get him to come downstairs. I waited for a long time, trying to think it — trying to create an image of the knowledge in my head — but nothing seemed to work. I could *think*, "You've done it." But the certainty wasn't there. And it didn't matter if I willed him to come downstairs. All I could do was make him want to do it. But he could resist; he could do something other than what he wanted.

This was perplexing. It seemed to me that if I really had the power of God, there wouldn't be any limit to what I could do. Unless I just didn't know the right words yet. I had to admit that that was a possibility. Maybe I just didn't yet know the language. Some things I could alter and know I'd altered them. But others, the bigger things, I had to learn the right words for, or the right hand movements or signals. Probably that was it. Also, I figured I'd have to learn the difference between those things that were bigger and those that were not. I didn't think God would have the same set of "bigs" and "littles" as everybody else.

I drove home that night in one of the worst snowstorms in the history of the state of Illinois. After an hour on the road, I was ready to make changes in more than the weather. The snow created a traffic tie-up so complete the entire interstate looked like an automobile graveyard. I don't know about you, but I hate traffic jams. They make me feel like a trapped animal.

I knew the snow was my doing. I had created it, on top of what was apparently already on the way. It was going to snow anyway, and I added to it by waving my hand. I did this to impress Dottie, mind you. Not exactly the sort of behavior one expects from the deity.

I probably could have made the snow stop, but I was worried about the consequences. I had made it snow on top of what nature was up to, and that had no effect on what nature intended: its snow came anyway, along with mine. I did not want to fiddle with nature again so soon.

I sat there in the thickening snow, feeling slightly inadequate, just like all the other cornered souls, and waited for the cars to inch forward far enough for me to get home.

3

Reading over these pages, I see I may have given the impression that the troubles between Dorothy and me were inherent and therefore inescapable. There may be some truth to that. I have often thought that perhaps Dorothy never truly understood my personality. There's simply no mystery to it: we are very different people.

This was not something I understood early in our relationship. In the beginning, we were so excited to be in each other's arms, so thrilled with ourselves, it was impossible to see each other clearly. We were quite certain that no single pair of human beings had ever loved each other so completely. We were the first true lovers in the whole biological and spiritual history of the race. And it was not something we wanted to keep secret. We talked about our famous love affair to anyone who would listen. It seemed such a miracle.

Although Dorothy moved at ease in love, I was shocked to find myself in such a state. I had been, since early manhood, fairly afraid of women, so I never thought I would ever be in love, much less have a wife. Trust me, this had nothing to do with my mother — I mean, she didn't bark at me too much, or chain me to a violin. She was as kind and loving as anybody's mother.

If I had to say why I was terrified of women, I'm not sure I could name one event or situation — although I might want to. There *was* a time, when I was working my first job, that a very old woman named

Miss Pym revealed herself to me in such a way that I felt pretty much discouraged about myself and women. But who's to say whether it was that one event or some other longer and more ongoing circumstance that burns in my psyche unbeknownst to me?

In any event, I do know that at the time, my experience with Miss Pym withered me like a charred orchid, and I believed it would set the hue, if not the tone, of all my relationships with women for the balance of my adult life. And if what happened didn't really shape my private reactions to people and events, it did afford me the luxury of a kind of benevolent cynicism concerning life and its ultimate meaning. Miss Pym showed me what we are all waiting for, even hoping for.

When I got out of high school I was lucky enough to get a job — my first — in the public library. I worked there for one summer, before I started college, and I still remember it as one of the more forgettable periods of my life. I was very young, and frightened about the world, and mistrustful of everyone I didn't know personally. I don't mean I was shy; I just didn't see myself as the gregarious, outgoing type. Some people know you for five minutes and they've already told you something private about themselves, information you don't really want — how much money they make, or how painful and large their hemorrhoids are. I just wasn't that kind of person.

I was hired by Mrs. Hills, a fat, stern woman who everybody said carried a heavy pistol in her purse. She wore gold wire-rimmed glasses attached to a gold chain around her neck. When she had the glasses on the bridge of her nose, if she looked at you from the right angle, the bifocals made her eyes look like tennis balls cut in half, with smaller tennis balls inside them. She wore immense dresses to disguise the fact that she looked like a huge upright compost barrel. Her eyebrows were as bushy as a commissar's and just as busy. When she spoke to me, I felt her words making grooves in my brain. I was terrified of her. After all, she gave me the job, and I knew she could take it away. Also, though I never did see it, I had heard about that pistol in her purse.

My job, originally, was to work behind the circulation desk. I put books on the shelves and checked them out to lines of patrons. Sometimes I'd help somebody find a book he was looking for. It was all very soothing at first, and easy to do. I had a wooden, waist-high counter between me and every patron, and the job allowed me to treat everybody exactly the same, without having to look at any one person in particular and actually see anybody. Thus I didn't feel as if anyone could see me. Back then I was so gangly, skinny, and awkward that being invisible seemed very desirable.

Then Mrs. Hills got the idea that my talents would best be put to use rounding up overdue books. Collecting these books was supposed to be easy, too. All I had to do was drive around visiting the homes of errant patrons who had neglected to return books that were in considerable demand, books on the reserve list.

"You'll be like a door-to-door salesman," Mrs. Hills said. "Only you'll be performing a service. People will like it when they don't have to bring the books back themselves. And we won't have to keep our other patrons waiting too long for books they've asked us to reserve."

I liked it in the library; I didn't want to go out and knock on doors. But I didn't have the nerve to tell Mrs. Hills that. I could see she was very excited about getting me some fresh air, and she was proud of her idea; it was a new idea.

Now, I already had this problem with my self-image that always made me feel like I was naked whenever I was around strangers (I think it's fairly amazing, even now, that I ended up a salesman, and a damned good one, too). Mrs. Hills actually wanted me to go out and *seek* strangers, knock on unfamiliar doors and actually talk to people I didn't know. No matter what I did, I couldn't shake the feeling that everybody I talked to would see me as a potential burglar or rapist.

The first time I went out, I couldn't muster the nerve to knock on a single door. I drove around the neighborhoods, watching wild, noisy children playing in green yards, until my time was up. Then I returned to the library and claimed bad luck.

"You didn't even get one book?" Mrs. Hills said.

"Nobody was home."

"Not anyone?"

"I couldn't get a single person to answer the door."

Mrs. Hills sat behind her desk, her glasses dangling around her neck. She wore a pink dress, pink earrings. Her face was bloated around the mouth, and her eyes seemed to peer over puffy cheeks. "I don't think you were knocking very hard."

"Perhaps not." I looked at the floor, noticed her bulging ankles under the desk.

"You've got to be more aggressive."

41

"Okay."

"Next time, come back with some books."

"People are so busy," I said. "It's very difficult —"

"Come back with some books, okay?" She sat back in her chair and placed her mushroom fingers together in a little temple on her breast. "Tomorrow I'll give you a new list, and you will improve on your efforts of this afternoon."

"Well," I said.

"I think you shall improve."

I knew it was an order. The tone of her voice was soft and cold and unmistakable. She gave orders with the high-pitched timbre of a Nazi field officer. She struggled to her feet, waddled around the desk, and put a heavy hand on my shoulder. Then she smiled and said, "Run along now."

After that the days were not so good. On foreign porches, greeted by odd cooking odors, I would bang on doors so forbidding that the sound I made frightened me. Each time I did it, I couldn't believe I had the nerve. When the door opened I would stammer, trying to say "Good afternoon" as pleasantly as an altar boy, but it always ended up sounding like I'd just asked to use the bathroom. Then I was lost. I had no identification to prove I was with the library, and most people reacted to me with downright suspicion. I wanted to say, "Believe it or not, I'm from the public library. Trust me, I'm not a serial killer. I have a list right here of the books you've checked out of the library." But I hated speaking in long paragraphs to people whose first impulse, I knew, was to slam the door and lock it. Don't get me wrong — I didn't look any different from most young men in those days. But I was intruding on people with a premise most of them found difficult to believe: I was out collecting overdue books. Also, some people got angry when I told them why I was there, as if I had accused them of trying to steal the books they'd borrowed. One man said, "I've only had it a month."

"I know."

"I'm aware of my responsibility."

"Yes," I said. "But —"

"It's only a week overdue."

"Right. But it's on reserve, and the demand is —"

"What's the deal?"

42

"Well, there's no deal, sir."

He closed the door slightly, let me stand there looking at him. I didn't know what to say. The television behind him boomed applause from some quiz show. He seemed to be watching my face, trying to read something in my expression.

Finally I said, "Is that *Jeopardy!?*"

"I'll bring the book back when I'm goddamned good and ready to," he said. Then he slammed the door.

Finally I wrote a speech and tried to memorize it: "Hello, I'm from the Champaign County Library and you have some books that are slightly overdue. Normally we would wait for you to bring them back, but since the books are in demand, I've been sent to retrieve them, if you don't mind."

It was impossible to recite, even in practice. I revised it to "Hello, I'm from the library, and you have some overdue books that we need now. Would you mind getting them for me?"

That didn't work either. The first time I tried to say it, I said, "Hello, I'm from the public and you have some overdue libraries that you won't mind getting?"

So I revised my speech again. It went like this: "I came from the library to get your overdue books."

The first time I went out armed with the new, shorter, more direct version of my speech, a woman in a red kimono, with eye makeup on one eye, hair teased into a vertical thicket on top of her head, and little white tufts of tissue between each red-painted toe, opened the door and said, "What's the matter? Did you run over my cat?"

My memory dropped away like something thrown out of an airplane.

"I'm here to get books," I said.

"What?"

"You got books?"

"Of course I've got books." She snapped a compact open, studied her face in it. "You selling something?"

"You have an overdue cat."

"What?"

I felt the blood draining out of my head. "I work for the library," I stammered. "You mind getting me your overdue books?"

When she finally figured it out, she disappeared into the house and returned with three plastic-covered books and eye makeup on both eyes. Also she had removed the tissue. She laughed. "I couldn't figure out what you wanted," she said.

"I hate this job."

As she closed the door, she said, "You'll get better at it."

The truth was, I did not want to get better at it.

When I returned to the library, Mrs. Hills's insistent waddle as she came from her office to greet me told me I had not done enough. The look of disappointment on her face as I handed over the books seemed to cloud her glasses. You'd think I had placed a dead infant in her arms.

"Well, three today." She placed the books on the counter, tapped them with chubby fingers. "Only three. Tsk." She was like a doctor examining a chancre.

"That's all."

"People still not answering doors?"

"One lady thought I ran over her cat."

"You'll do better next time." She frowned at the books, then pushed them toward me with disgust. "Won't you?"

I met Miss Pym the last time I went out. (I quit after Miss Pym.) Mrs. Hills sent me to Riverside, a community of old Victorian houses that occupied a vast green hill above the city. Bank presidents, state senators, and gubernatorial candidates lived there. They had the money to endow whole libraries. And I was going to ask them for their overdue books. I couldn't believe anyone who lived in those castles would do anything so common as check out a library book.

I had little success in the early part of the day, and I don't think I managed to speak to more than a few nannies and servants before I got to Miss Pym's. Her house was so large I could not find the front door. I crept up a stone walk to a great white side building with latticed windows all around. There were french doors open wide at the front and back, so the interior was like a great porch. I could have driven my Pontiac Le Mans into the front and directly out the back without disturbing an umbrella stand. It was late summer by then and the sun beamed in columns through the windowpanes onto the black-and-white marble floor, as if this were the lobby of some sort of celestial hotel. In the three corners of the room immediately visible to me were urns as tall as I was, each with a green palm that crowded the ceiling. I wanted desperately to run, but I was afraid somebody had seen me coming up the walk, and if I ran, they might think I had stolen something.

I could not discover a good place to knock. There were only window frames and wide-open spaces in front of me. The door frame was solid oak. I smacked it with the palm of my hand, but I hardly made a discernible noise in such a large room. I felt myself beginning to sweat, but my heart seemed to steady a bit. By knocking I had taken action, and once I was actually doing what I dreaded, a part of me gave up my fear. "Hello?" I said.

I knocked on the frame again. It was such hard wood, I might as well have knocked on concrete.

"Hello, anyone home?" My voice echoed in the room, seemed to move the leaves of the palm trees above me. "Excuse me."

I could not hear anything in the house. A sense of relief settled in the back of my mind. *I tried*, I told myself. As I was turning to leave — to escape — my eye caught something moving on the other side of the far doors, out in the sunlight on what appeared to be a giant patio. It might have been a gray ball, lying on the brick there, but it moved and made a noise like a deep cough. I realized, just as it said, "Come here," that I was looking at a head bobbing up and down in what was not a patio at all but a huge swimming pool.

I cut through the columns of sunlight in the marble room and walked toward the far doors, trying to remember what I was supposed to say. As I approached the pool, Miss Pym came up out of the water, rising like a body from a grave, her hair stone gray, her face rumpled as a cerebral cortex. She was the oldest living human being I had ever seen. Bent over slightly, she lurched and pitched toward me. There was something caught between her legs — a torn gray leaf, or even a large insect — and I had started to warn her about it when it hit me that it was not an insect or a leaf at all. I was staring at silver, curly, beaten hair.

"My God," I said. "You're naked."

She came up to me, her eyes rolling like a frog's eyes. "Yes, I am."

"Oh my Lord, I'm so sorry," I said. I couldn't get my breath.

She went past me and took up a towel. Her buttocks looked like the mouth of an old man. "Don't mind me," she said. "I don't give a goddamn anymore."

45

"I'm so awfully sorry," I said. "I didn't mean to look at your — I didn't realize . . ."

"It doesn't matter," she said.

She was the first naked woman I had ever seen in person. Her voice was full of pebbles, and there was not a note of music anywhere in it. She was clearly beyond living, as though waiting for an end to breathing the way some of us wait in a doctor's office for an appointment. "I'm ninety-one years old, for God's damn sake." She put the towel up over her head and rubbed the iron hair there. Her breasts shook like tiny, empty Christmas stockings. "What do you want?"

"I came for your overdue books."

"What books?"

"You have some overdue library books?" I tried not to look at her, but she stood there in front of me, rubbing herself with the towel.

"You needn't be so upset," she said.

"I'm just so embarrassed." I wiped my eyes.

"When you get to my age, it all wears away."

"It does?"

"Everything. It's all gone except the waking up every morning." She did not smile. "I don't read your books. My nephew gets them for me and they sit here." The towel was around her waist now.

"Do you mind if I — if I just take them —"

"I don't know where they are." She waved her hand and withdrew toward the open porch as if I weren't even there. "You'll have to call him."

I waited by the pool, not knowing if I should follow her or what. After a few minutes she returned, wearing a terry-cloth robe and carrying a pile of books in her arms.

"When you were born, I was already a very old woman," she said. Then the corner of her mouth moved slightly, and I had the feeling she was trying not to laugh. I think she was very amused at me and my provincial embarrassment.

I walked out of that house carrying her overdue books and a strong sense of the uselessness of just about everything. I could not escape the vision of her naked body coming at me like a lizard on hind legs. After Miss Pym, it was very difficult not to see every woman as an early version of her. I never got over the sensation that somehow Miss Pym was secretly laughing at me. She knew what she was doing, as most women do.

I've wondered all my adult life what she could have been thinking of — why she came at me like that. Since then, very often I've looked in a woman's eyes and felt a judgment going on there — an assessment. Miss Pym destroyed a kind of innocence, perhaps without knowing it. And she gave me a glimpse of a future most of us would like to ignore. I was not, and since then have not been, interested in any later versions of myself. All I wanted after that was to escape the world and take what I could of love off this planet.

❀

When I met Dorothy, I was just as uncomfortable around women as ever, so I did not expect, or seek, further contact. Things just evolved. I was already selling cars at Shale Motors when we met, and Dorothy bought a Dodge Challenger from me. We talked several times in the process of making the deal, and from that innocent beginning our incredible passion developed. You might even be inclined to say it developed naturally, though I see no reason to insist on the point.

Of course I was attracted to her. She was beautiful, and still is. To look upon her is to understand the need for ugliness. Otherwise, perfection such as hers makes the rest of us appear hideous. Back then, her hair was very long and soft — it glistened in the sunlight like a mixture of spun gold and red silk. Her skin was as smooth and perfect as polished glass, and her eyes glimmered like iridescent blue stones under dark brown brows. She had the sort of face that stunned people into silence. I know such things have no real depth or importance between people who must remain engaged intimately for all their lives, but even after more than a decade, I still loved just looking at her. It pleased me to watch her move the same way it might please another person to watch a riotous, cloud-spattered sunset.

The fact that she was attracted to me was enough to paralyze every muscle. I asked her once why she wanted me, and she paused for a moment, and then she said, "Because of your passions."

"My passions?"

"You're the sort of man who won't go halfway on anything."

"Except when I'm trying to be halfway decent," I said.

"And your sarcasm," she said. "Sometimes I like that."

"Well." I was so proud, I wanted to tell everyone I knew. I wanted to say, "You know I'm much more passionate than you are." If Dorothy had told me the world was square, I might have believed it.

In the beginning, we were so happy. We'd stand naked in a mountain stream and laugh at the minnows tickling our toes. We'd hold each other high up in a ski lift, dangling over white pines, and kiss like mating birds. We found reason to share the world without considering who gets what, without examining motive or intent. It was simply our earth.

I always thought it was perfectly all right with her that I had been born a male.

I did not think I could possibly love her more than I did at first, but once we were married and embarked on our life together, our family, something happened to my love that less passionate people might find alarming. I did not feel as if I existed unless Dorothy was with me. I truly did not want to act unless Dorothy was there to approve or disapprove. I would gladly have died for her, and once I understood that, life away from her became a great chore.

Of course, as my love grew, the great differences between us receded further and further into silence. If she had not returned to school, I might not ever have recognized how different we are.

And I'm not talking about differences between us because of our sex — although perhaps Dorothy would wish to do that. I'm talking about differences between us as people.

I am the sort of person who wouldn't mind having a job that requires only that you sit in the warm, benevolent sun in a pair of white shorts and a smooth pair of leather sandals. Every now and then, someone you like very much comes up to you, hands you a hose, and says, "Here, water the zinnias."

Dorothy wants to have the kind of work in which network anchormen stop you in the street and ask if you have any comment. One of the reasons she majored in English was so she would be eloquent whenever that happened. "Language is the key," she said. "It's about everything. Psychology, history, philosophy, art, and politics. It's about life itself."

"I always thought it was about punctuation and the bad habits of writers."

Dorothy thought when you said something was funny you meant it was fishy. She believed corruption was a pathological phenomenon, like influenza.

I understood that love is the most powerful and desirable of all human emotions — and the only earthly glimpse we will ever get of unfettered human bliss.

Dorothy had come to see it as positive reinforcement.

She majored in English so she would learn all the subtleties of the language through its literature. I had majored in English too. It was the shortest line at registration.

"Language is power," Dorothy said once. We were riding in the car, on our way out to dinner for the first time in several months. I had to beg her to give up studying for one night so we could have the time together. "It matters what words you choose to describe the world, because those words help to make the world what it is. And they help to *change* it. Change is what I'm talking about."

"Language makes the world, huh?"

"That's right. The words you use bring about change. That's why —"

"Which one of your professors said that?" I asked.

She didn't answer me.

After a long silence, I said, "I'm sorry. Let's not fight."

"Fine with me."

We were going to dinner at a place called the Slim Line Café, a restaurant near the college that Dorothy had recommended very highly. After another fairly long silence, in order to foster renewed conversation, I asked her where she'd heard of the place.

"Oh, I've eaten there," she said.

"You have?"

Then she said, "One of my classmates took me. I came here with a friend, and the food is wonderful."

"A friend?"

"You don't know him."

The word *him* dropped like an ice cube in my right ventricle. "You were on a date."

"Don't be silly. I had lunch with a classmate." She turned toward the window, set her jaw away from me.

"I'm sorry," I said. "But when you talk like that, casually, about being *taken* somewhere, by a *him*, it does something shitty to my heart."

"You're so possessive."

49

"Perhaps *possessive* is the wrong word."

"No, it isn't." Still gazing out the window, she seemed to speak to her reflection in the glass.

"You used to say I was passionate," I said. "You used to like to be possessed."

"Now it feels more like being owned."

"I want our marriage to mean something."

"It means something."

"I want it to count for both of us. I'm talking about an exclusive relationship." I felt her turn to me, but I watched the road. I knew I'd plunked a chord in her. I had used her own words against her. Early in our marriage she used to say how much she loved the fact that we truly had an exclusive relationship.

"What you're talking about," she said, "is ownership."

"Is that what you call it now?"

"That's what it is."

"I guess it depends on who's talking, doesn't it?"

She waved her hand in front of her face as if she were brushing away a cobweb. "It *is* what it *is*. Could we talk about something else?"

"I don't know what you think the word *marriage* means."

"It doesn't matter what I think it means."

"It matters to me," I said. "That's because I'm married to you."

She rolled her eyes.

"Should we call it marriage?" I said, a little too loudly. "Or maybe something else. We could call it quinsy, or morganatics. Or maybe gink. How'd that be? You and I are ginked."

"Call it what you want. It won't change how I feel about it."

"It won't *change* how you feel about it?"

"No." She arched her brow, turned her chin up.

I couldn't help being sarcastic. I leaned over to her and said, "Language is power. It changes the world. Right. Dig."

She clenched her teeth and gazed straight ahead.

I tried to control my anger. But I tell you, my worst fault is my temper and what happens to me when I lose it. I can feel myself heating up like an engine, and as soon as I'm revved, nothing can stop me. I get sarcastic, eloquently nasty, stubborn. And it became so easy for Dorothy to make me angry. I was deeply hurt that she now appeared to think so little of us — of what we meant in the scheme of things. She remained the most vital element of my existence. I truly did trace the arch of my life around my time with her.

After a short period of stewing, she said, "If language doesn't have power, why does it upset you so much?"

"*You* upset me. Not language."

She sank down in the seat and arranged herself in a final position of comfort that seemed to announce the last word on the subject. "It's power, all right." She wore a most satisfied and confident smile.

"It's nice to think so," I said. "But it isn't."

"It's power!"

"Okay," I said. "Make cancer go away with it, why don't you? Use it to pay for dinner tonight."

She didn't say anything else to me until we'd gotten to the restaurant and had our Cornish hens. In between those two events she slapped down menus and glasses and silverware as if she were testing them for durability and strength. It wasn't until the waitress was clearing our table and the wine glasses were empty that Dorothy finally said, "That was good."

I wiped my mouth with a brown napkin, set the napkin on the table in front of me, and smiled.

"I'm sorry we had our little disagreement," she said, returning the smile.

I couldn't believe it. She thought it was okay that she hadn't spoken to me through the entire meal — she was only sorry we had had a "disagreement." As if it were a flat tire, or some other act of God. I said, "It's too bad you were angry all evening over something I said."

"Forget it." She waved her hand as if to say, "No need to apologize."

But I was not going to apologize. I was circling in for the fatal stroke. "You must be right after all," I said.

"Skip it. Really."

"No. You're right, and I'm wrong."

"It's not important."

"Language *is* power," I said. "I can accept that now."

She looked at me with her head tilted a bit to the side. I could see that she wasn't quite sure if I was serious. Her hair gave off the most beautiful glow, and the candles in front of her eyes made a sharp pin of light on each pupil. She was still the most gorgeous person I'd ever looked at. And I knew I had her. I said, "I spoke a single sentence, not ten words, and I turned *you*, my little dear, I turned a fine human being like *you*, my darling, into a perfect bitch."

She threw her napkin down.

"Next time my *langwidge* creates a bitch like you, I hope I'm near a vet so I can get some indication of your pedigree."

"You're simply irrational now."

"No, I'm not!" I yelled.

"This has been fun," she sneered. "Thanks ever so much." She left the restaurant so fast, I think several tablecloths got swept along with her.

I sat there, all alone with my temper and nobody to complain to or yell at. I swear if I didn't love her so much, she probably wouldn't make me so furious.

Arguments like that had gradually increased between us, even before Dorothy went back to school and became an adversary. She just didn't appreciate my sense of humor. In fact, to tell the truth — the bald truth, which it hurts me to admit — I just don't think Dorothy appreciated appreciation. You know what I mean? She took everything personally, and never could stand off and look at a thing for the beauty of it, for its humor or its quality. She said once that she didn't think Woody Allen was very funny. Can you believe that? I told her that was like saying, "Jesus isn't very nice." Or "Santa Claus is pretty selfish and judgmental."

"It's just a matter of taste," she said.

"It is not."

"It is too."

"It is *not*."

"He's just one of your heroes."

"In the world of objective reality," I said, "the humor of Woody Allen is like one of the planets, or the law of cosines, or the sum of three sides of a triangle, or —"

About that time she threw her hands up. "I'm not going to argue with you." She went out of the room almost as fast as she had left the restaurant.

Perhaps you're getting some idea of how most of our discussions went.

She'd throw her hands in the air, or her napkin down, or her fork, or whatever she held in her hands at the time, and leave the room. We never truly finished an argument. Except the time I messed up and brought Yee home. Yee was our wonder dog. We finished *that* argument all right. And perhaps that one event, more than any other, illustrates most graphically the trouble between us.

※

It was Dorothy's idea to get a dog. I didn't want to have anything to do with it. I didn't want a cat, either, or any other pet except maybe a tropical fish or two. It's not that I don't like animals. I love animals. I just never understood how anybody could live with one. Most people wouldn't stay a fortnight with a human being who never brushed his teeth or used toilet paper when he was finished going to the bathroom, yet there are folks who live decades with some dog or cat, cleaning up after it the whole time, as if that weren't behaving like the animal's servant or personal valet. Anyone who's ever spent any time with dogs knows they all smell like a bag full of used coffee grounds; and if it killed a dog not to drool, they'd all be immortal.

But Dorothy got this idea she wanted a dog. This was only two or three years before Chet came to me. She'd been out running five miles, and she looked as if somebody had hosed her down before she left the street. She fixed herself a glass of mineral water and ice, then came back into the den, where I was stretched out on the couch.

"Did you hear me, honey?" she said. "I want a dog."

I told her I didn't want a dog. She sat on the coffee table right in front of me, still breathing heavily, sipping the mineral water. The ice rattled in the glass, making me thirsty.

"Come on," she said. "It will be fun."

"Look," I said, "we've got no place to keep livestock."

"We can use the spare room for it."

"And when your parents come to visit? They'll sleep in a room full of dog hair and fleas?"

"They like dogs."

"They like fleas?"

"We can keep it clean. Come on. The girls will —"

"We? *We* can keep it clean?"

53

"Me and the girls." She put the glass down, leaned over, and kissed me on the forehead. She transformed her voice into this half-whispering sort of breathy temptation. "I'll take care of it."

"No."

She put her hand on my stomach, smiling as if she were doing a screen test for a blue movie. "I'll take care of *you*."

You can guess what happened after that.

So, since she had positively reinforced me, she never let up about the dog. Everywhere we went, if she saw a dog, she'd ooh and aah over it as if it were an infant. It didn't matter if the dog looked like a hedge pig. She even began to act like a dog, following me around everywhere with eyes that must have been labeled BEG when the Lord took them off the shelf and installed them.

It was clear that she would not give up, though she claimed to several times. As much as I hated the fact of actually having to live with an animal, circumstances soon made it possible for me to do two good things at once: save the life of a dog and give Dorothy what she wanted.

I sold a pickup truck to a farmer named Angus, and while he was signing all the forms, he happened to mention that he had a dog for sale.

"It's a peaceful creature," he said. "Yessir."

I thought it was pretty close to an act of Providence that he should mention a dog he wanted to sell at the very time I was resisting buying one so vehemently, and I said so.

"Well," he said, "maybe the Lord wants you to reconsider."

"Heh." I handed him his keys. "Enjoy your new truck."

"It's too bad if I don't sell him, you know."

"Why?"

He folded the signed papers and stuffed them into the pocket of his coveralls. Then he looked at me with an expression as serious as a surgeon's. "I'm going to have to put him to sleep."

I didn't say anything.

"Yeah. Have to kill the old fellow."

"Why?"

"He's no use on the farm anymore. We don't keep them as pets, you know."

"What's wrong with the dog?"

"Ain't nothing wrong with Pressley except he's just old. Like me. Only ain't nobody around to put me to sleep, though." He winked, moved to the door.

"You wouldn't really kill it, would you?"

He came back toward me. "I'll tell you what. If you want to give the old boy a new home, I'll let you have him for nothing."

"Free?"

"Sure, why not? You gave me a good deal here."

"What kind of dog is it?"

"A big old sheepdog in mutt's clothing."

"What's that?"

He let out a brief baritone snort. "It's a mutt that acts like a sheepdog. Except he's too old to cut it anymore — the sheep bully the poor fellow so bad my wife's taken to praying for him."

So I brought Pressley home and renamed him. I got the idea for his name while riding in my Dodge station wagon with the dog breathing on the back of my neck and whimpering as if his feet bothered him terribly. His breath put condensation on my soul. Maybe he wasn't dead yet, but his insides had already moldered. I tried to get him away from me, and all I could do was let out this odd sound. I said, "Yee." I swear to God I just couldn't speak. Every time I tried to yell at him to please get *back*, this rush of decomposed air would take hold of me, my lungs would shrink and recoil from it, and the best I could do was let out this high, girlish sound "Yee."

Dorothy couldn't believe either the dog or his name.

"You can't be serious."

Jody Beth, my youngest, fell instantly in love with him. She crawled all over him and tried to get up on his back. Claire, who was just beginning her first year of sophisticated training at the Gerald R. Ford Grade School, was cooler and more aloof about the whole thing. She patted Yee on the head, rubbed his tattered ears, and then brushed his hair with my hairbrush.

Dorothy seemed a little breathless. She watched the girls assaulting and fumbling Yee like lion cubs around a dead antelope, and gradually her face grew more and more severe. She looked like she was making up her mind to blow up a nursery. "Why a full-grown — why did you?"

55

"He was free," I said. "Besides, we don't have to go to the trouble of training him." I thought she'd be happy to see I'd gotten her a dog, so I was a little shocked at her reaction.

"Oh, can we keep him?" Claire asked.

Dorothy tightened her jaw and moved her head slowly back and forth as if she were trying to hide some unbearable pain. "I've never seen such an ugly dog in my life."

"He's a gift — for the family." I said. "I thought you'd be surprised." I tried to pretend I didn't notice her displeasure, just on the off chance that she might regain her composure and feign appreciation for my thoughtfulness. After all, I had steadfastly refused to get a dog for the better part of a year, and now here I was, with a full-grown, already housebroken animal that the girls absolutely loved.

"I've never seen anything so ugly," Dorothy said. She looked very sad.

Yee *was* pretty bad. You wouldn't ever expect to see him with a blue ribbon on his collar and some woman who looked like him clipping hairs over his eyes. He had a coat of brownish fur that appeared to be two or three sizes too large, with odd yellow and orange flecks in it. There's really no way to describe him accurately, except to say he looked a little bit like garbage — like he just rose up one day out of a multi-colored pile of refuse and advanced into the world of animals like a new virus.

"Yee!" Dorothy said with disgust.

The dog barked. One loud syllable.

"Look," I said. "He knows his name."

"This isn't funny," Dorothy said.

Yee staggered into the kitchen, hit the front panel of the dishwasher head on, then dropped to the floor like furry sack of tools.

"Yee fell down, Daddy," Claire said.

"His hair's so long he can't even see," said Dorothy.

Yee barked again. It was several syllables this time, almost a howl, but it died down to a pitiful and diminishing cough.

"He barks every time I open my mouth." Dorothy looked like she'd eaten something rancid. "And what's that smell?"

"It might be his breath," I said. "Either that, or —"

Jody Beth patted him where he lay. "Dead dog," she said. "Dead doggy."

"He's not dead, honey," I said.

"Well, what's wrong with him?" Dorothy was turning red with anger.

"I don't know," I said. "Maybe he's blind."

"This is just not funny."

"You don't have to get loud." I was so ashamed, standing there in the malodorous, decayed fumes of my surprise gift, my love offering. It never occurred to me that Dorothy would be offended by him. I thought she would be ecstatic and throw her arms around my neck like she used to and say she loved me. I had never bought a dog before, so how was I to know this was a bad deal? He was free, for God's sake; I didn't think you could get swindled if it didn't cost you anything.

"It's a terrible, rotten thing to do." Dorothy's face dripped with contempt. I didn't know what displeased her more, the dog or me.

"You'll get used to him," I said. "He's an outdoor dog."

"I don't care what the girls want. I will not have that — that animal in this house."

"Maybe he'll grow on you," I said.

About this time I expected her hands to go up; then a quick, disgusted exit from the room. Instead, I saw her legs stiffen. She planted her feet as if she were on the deck of a ship and it was heaving to port. "NO!" It was an explosion. The girls jumped at the sound of it, and Yee moved his head back and let out another slight and distant-sounding cough.

"You scared the dog," I said. By this time, predictably, I was getting angry. "You don't have to be rude about it."

Jody Beth started to cry.

"I don't want that animal on our property." Dorothy tried to contain her rage, but her feet were definitely planted and she'd chosen that moment, I could see, for a siege.

"You wanted a dog," I said. And then I saw us all standing in the kitchen over this breathing, whimpering pile of oily rags, and I started to laugh. In spite of my hurt feelings, my gathering anger, the whole scene was hilariously funny.

Dorothy did not see the humor of it. She stepped up to me, her eyes fierce and frozen. "You — you."

"Come on," I said. "Where's your sense of humor?"

"You think I'll take anything, don't you?"

This last remark did not sit well with me. "Look, dammit, I haven't done *anything* on purpose. There's no intent here."

"No intent, my eye."

"I made a mistake. Okay? I admit it. I truly thought you'd —"

She positioned herself directly in front of me, grabbed my arms, and dug her nails in so fiercely I cried out like one of the girls. Then she punched me in the abdomen — a solid, short left hook that emptied my lungs.

She was drawing back to hit me again when I realized I was going to have to be the one to leave the room. Also, I knew it would be several months before I'd be getting any positive reinforcement.

Dorothy never got over Yee. It turned out that he was in fact blind. Angus said he couldn't believe it. A few days after I brought Yee home, the old farmer came back to pick up new tags for his truck and I told him all about "poor old Pressley."

"I swear to God I didn't know it," Angus said. "I feel sorry for him." He bent over and spit on the sidewalk. We were standing out in front of the showroom, and I had this deep fear somebody would see him sullying the grounds.

"You shouldn't do that," I said.

"Oh, I feel sorry for anything that goes blind. Don't you?"

"I wish I had known he was blind."

"It's a shock." He stepped closer to me. "That ain't all that's wrong with him, neither."

"What else?"

"Barks at anything makes a noise. Or he tries to, anyway."

"I know. I've heard him."

"Got some sort of lung disease."

I shook my head, tried to back away. I was afraid if we continued talking the dog would turn out to be contagious.

"Sounds awful when he barks, don't it?"

"It sure does," I said. I'd had the dog three days and I was already considering having him put to sleep.

"Like a crowd of old women drowning." Angus shuddered, wriggling his shoulders as if he were shaking off snow. "Made me sick to listen to it."

"Well," I said, "I guess we'll just have to have him put to sleep after all."

"I tried to kill him myself," Angus said. He seemed proud. He reached up and grabbed the lapels of his coat, then rocked back and forth like a candidate getting ready to claim a landslide victory. "The animal simply wouldn't abide by it."

"Maybe he —"

"I gave that dog a whole box of rat poison, and you know what? He didn't even fall asleep." Angus crossed his arms and considered for a second, then said, "You know, Wiggins, I don't think you could say he even become lazy."

"No kidding."

"A whole box, and it only made the dog happy."

"Well, the vet won't have any trouble killing it."

"I wish you luck," Angus said, moving to the door. "The best of luck."

"Thanks." If he hadn't been a customer I'd have really let him have it. I thought it was a pretty rotten thing to do, giving me a dying dog. But being a salesman at heart, I weighed my anger against the possibility that old man Angus might also buy his next truck from me, and it was easy to keep my mouth shut.

I never had the heart to have the old hound put to sleep. Yee lived almost a year, moving around the house like a great-grandmother on all fours. He moaned and groaned and farted his way through the days and barked halfheartedly all through every night. After a while it wasn't that bad, though. Near the end he could barely manage a deep-throated whimper. If the furnace came on, you couldn't hear him.

That was not the first time Dorothy ever misunderstood my intentions, but it was the first and only time she ever hit me. It became a hard thing to forget, even though she apologized for it later. She tried to be nice about it, said she could see that I had meant well and only suffered from poor judgment where animals are concerned. But the thing is, she never did see the humor of the whole episode, even when she realized she was standing on our front porch every evening hollering like a seventeenth-century town crier, "Here, Yee, here, Yee." What sort of person wouldn't appreciate the humor in that? I know I did.

4

On my first night as the acting deity, the night I created the big snowstorm, the girls were already in bed when I got home. The house was dark downstairs, and the faint light from our bedroom told me that Dorothy had pretty much quit for the night too. I figured she was in there reading some feminist propaganda, so I took off my boots, hung up my coat, and sat at the kitchen table to think about myself and what was happening to me. I couldn't understand what it was in my life that made me worthy of this gift. I wanted to know why I had been chosen, but when I concentrated on it, nothing presented itself. Even when I willed an answer, there wasn't one.

I was both excited and appalled at the notion that I could now be or do virtually anything I wanted. Chet had said there were limits, and I supposed I would discover them as I went along. But the initial feeling of the power, the unbelievable sense of newness it gave me, created an inexhaustible mixture of pride and humility. I could feel sorry for myself and love myself with the intensity of a new father — as if I were my own son.

While I thought about these things, my mind wandered into the realm of Dorothy and our marriage. I knew she was still awake upstairs, and I wondered if I should tell her about the gift. I could make her believe it very easily, and I wondered if it would make her see me in a different light. What would she do if I made an oak tree in our bedroom, or created a salamander out of a spool of thread?

First, I decided to make her very glad to see me. I knew I could have Beethoven's Third Symphony playing in her head when she saw me if I wanted to. I worried, however, whether this would be fair. Not that fairness was ever a truly crucial issue with me. It was just that I had the power — I could act with at least the same force as God. I wondered if I should try to imitate him in some specific way, try to act with similar motives.

But how could I know any motives but my own?

I got up and went to the refrigerator for a glass of cold milk, but there was only an empty carton sitting on a bare upper shelf. "Dammit," I said out loud. "This refrigerator's always empty."

Barely thinking, I put four quarts of two-percent milk on the shelf, two packages of cheddar cheese, a pound of bacon, and a half-gallon of orange juice. It was odd. They didn't just appear there, though I understand if that's what you were thinking. It was simply a change in the progression of things, so that what I observed when I first opened the refrigerator became what I had imagined I would see when I opened it, and what I put on the shelf with my will became what I found when I opened the door. Does that make any sense? I liked having the power, but I was beginning to realize that it wasn't always going to seem like power at all. You know what I mean?

Let's say you're a tennis player and you have a chance to hit a terrific overhead to the opposite side of the court from where your opponent is stretched out in midair like a dried deerskin. You know if you hit it right, you've got him. Half the time you miss overheads because you don't know how to hit them. But this time you don't think about anything; you close your eyes, swing the racket, and miraculously catch the ball right in the sweet spot — *wham!* It rips in a straight line to the corner, right where you wanted it to go. You know it was an accident; if the person you're playing with knows you and your game and is more intelligent than a rabbit, he knows it was an accident. He might say, "Nice shot," and you might thank him, but who *really* hit the ball? Who can take credit for it? It was an accident, you see. That's what it felt like sometimes when I used my power. I didn't think I could take credit for it, but since I had it, since God or Chet or somebody had given it to me, I didn't know who else should get the credit (or blame) for what I did with it. At the time, I never even considered who should get the credit (or blame) for what I *didn't* do with it.

Anyway, I drank my glass of cold milk and considered the plan of operations for that evening with Dorothy. I decided I wouldn't tell her or anyone about the power. If I did that, I'd stop being me. I'd be God, or somebody possessed by God. Nothing I did would be truly mine, and no action of mine would truly draw her to me. In fact, I was fairly certain that if I told her I was the acting deity, she would be in a lawyer's office within the hour. No, she'd never know. What I would do was use the power on her very indirectly, to bring her back to me.

I wouldn't press things too far the first night. A sudden change in her secret wishes and desires might make her distrust her own sanity, and I didn't want that. I didn't think it would be unreasonable if I pretended to be exhausted and made her want to rub my feet. Once I was close enough to her for my will to have the most intensity, I'd make her ache for me.

Imagine my surprise when I found her leaning over the bed, peering into a red suitcase, counting blouses.

"What are you doing?"

"I'm getting away for a while." She didn't look at me. The room seemed to go out of focus for a moment.

"There's a blizzard out there. You got snowshoes?"

She slammed the suitcase shut, seemed to search for something in the air around her. Then she said, "I can't stay here anymore."

"But it's November."

"So?"

"It's a cold month."

"I don't see what difference that makes."

"It's a cold thing to do."

"It's a necessary thing to do."

"You're still just pissed off about this morning."

"I'm not." Her voice was very weak. I could tell she was trying not to cry, so I weakened her resolve, and she started crying. What a surprise it was to her — the expression on her face was absolutely priceless. It was as if she had just discovered a worm in her mouth.

"You ought to wait until the snow has stopped," I said.

"I don't believe this."

"You don't have to go anywhere." I tried to be calm, but the tension in my chest was unbearable. I didn't care about caution or pushing things too fast. I was so frightened at the prospect of losing her, I had God's strength turned up to full candlepower. I was creating in her confused and tangled mind an unrelenting desire to be with me, to smash her gathering dreams and desires on the permanent and immutable anvil of her passionate, tender, perfect, and infinite love for me.

She stood there in front of the suitcase for a moment. Then she said, "No. I *have* to do this."

I couldn't believe her resistance. It didn't seem to matter what I made her want. I was really getting confused. Then I thought it might be her anger that was giving her strength.

"I know you're still angry." I said. I did know it.

She went to the bureau, opened a drawer, and started removing undergarments. She was wearing her tight jeans and a gray sweatshirt. Her hair seemed dirty, and she moved languidly, as if she were trying to emerge from sleep.

I knew what was working in her. It was a terrible conflict. I realized there was no way I was going to try to make her rub my feet. I didn't think I could take it if God's power didn't work. Anyway, it would just be too ridiculous for her to be suddenly grabbing at me as if I were Robert Redford. It's funny, sometimes, our devotion to logic, even in our fantasies. I've never fantasized about having sex in a library, because a library is just not ever possible. A fantasy is exciting when it is at least weakly possible, and I guess that's sort of what was working with me over Dorothy that evening.

"I want you to sit down and think about what you're doing," I said. "There's four feet of snow on the ground by now. It was still coming down when I —"

"It took me all day to make up my mind about this," she said.

"I'm not saying you have to change your mind." I sat on the bed, pushing the suitcase toward the headboard. "You just have to change your plans. You can't go anywhere tonight."

"I don't want to talk right now." She sighed, holding a bra in each hand as if she were weighing them. Her hands moved slightly, and I recognized the first shadow of regret and doubt.

I figured that making her want to stay was enough, but I couldn't be sure. Maybe I didn't have the right words. The episode that afternoon with Mr. Shale still haunted me. I had to be sure she would not leave while I slept. So I made the doors jam. There wasn't a door in the house that she or anyone else could open without tools. Then I gave Dorothy a terrible fit of laughter. She just started laughing hysterically, and I laughed with her. She fell on the bed, covered her face.

I figured once I'd had a good night's sleep — a thing I was a little surprised I still needed — I'd unjam the doors and think of some other way to keep her at home. In the meantime, I held on to her until she laughed herself out.

"We haven't laughed like that in a long time," I said.

She tried to catch her breath, wiping her eyes with the loose end of the pillowcase. "I don't know what was so funny."

"Ah," I said. "Maybe it was just our . . . just our situation."

I made her laugh a little more. She put her head down, and I caressed the hair by her ears. I was very sad when I thought about the struggle going on in her head right then, a struggle between what I was making her do and her will.

"If you really do have to leave me," I said, "I'll miss this."

That got her. With the full force of my power giving her the incredible desire to stay, she couldn't take any more. She started sobbing like somebody's new widow.

"There, there," I said while I patted the back of her head.

I waited for her to stop, then watched her curl up, still in her clothes, and fall asleep. I didn't have to help with that — between all that laughter and the tears, she was exhausted. Before I went to sleep myself, I raised the temperature outside to fifty degrees. If I had remembered anything at all about the weather, I never would have done such a thing. I just didn't worry about making mistakes, since I figured I could undo or cancel any problems I created.

Isn't that what you would have thought?

❉

The morning after the snowstorm, I was awakened by Dorothy's screams. The children were crying, and when I got downstairs, I nearly cried too. There were at least two inches of brown water in the dining

64

room, living room, and kitchen. Outside, rain pounded on the shrubs beside all the neat little houses in our neighborhood. Dorothy was crying because she was trying to get the girls out of the house and the doors were jammed.

"Do something!" she screamed when she saw me.

I made it stop raining.

"Do something!" Dorothy screamed again.

The girls cried and walked around in the water as if it were boiling hot.

"It's just water," I said. "Stop crying."

"I don't believe this." Dorothy pulled on the door.

"I'll get that," I said.

She stood back. I waded over to the door, took the brass knob in my hand, and pretended to have difficulty turning it. "It's got to be just as flooded outside as it is in here," I said.

"It's not so . . ." Dorothy looked at the girls. Her hair hung next to her face like huge wet leaves. "It's not so incongruous outside."

"What?"

"They — it's not so odd, the water outside. It's the creek in their living room they don't understand."

"That's what *you* don't understand," I said. "They're upset because of the way you're acting."

I don't think she heard me. She looked up and her expression changed — she suddenly looked as if she'd seen the Virgin Mary.

"What's the matter?"

"It's stopped."

I wanted so much to tell her it was I who stopped the rain. Instead, I told her to take the girls to her parents' house.

"Why?"

"I'll clean this up."

"You can't —"

"I said take them out of here." It was a command, expressed with all the force I possessed.

"Okay," she said. In this particular case, I probably didn't need God's power to make her go.

As I watched the three of them trudge up the flooded walk to the top of the hill at the end of our street and get into a waiting cab, I felt something drop down in my heart. I didn't know why a temporary separation should feel so much like a permanent loss.

Once they were gone, I waved my hand in each room of the house and everything went back to normal. (It was really fun watching that happen.) But it was considerably easier to clean up the mess in our house than the general chaos I'd created in the rest of the state. There was widespread flooding, and violent twisters had ripped through several small villages and trailer parks. The channel ten news said it was one of the most bizarre weather patterns in history: a blizzard crashing head-on into an enormous warm front. As long as they'd been keeping records, nothing like it had ever happened. You see, in order for the temperature outside to get to fifty degrees, it was necessary for a hot front to collide with the mass of cold air that was causing the snowstorm. The front that hit my snowstorm had a mass of air in the nineties. It was barely above fifteen degrees in the storm. "When they came together," the weatherman said, "it was like the wrath of God."

And then I heard that four people had died. Two men in Danville, a little town about forty miles east of Champaign, and a man and a woman who lived in a trailer park near Rantoul and Chanute Air Force Base. I was sick in my bones and sorely tempted to confess what I had done and reverse everything. But you see the problem I had, don't you? I couldn't very well announce to everybody I was the acting deity. I didn't think that was the way things were supposed to go. There didn't seem to be any sense in calling attention to myself like that. I knew the newshounds and cameramen and nighttime anchor personalities would descend on me like ants on a Good Humor stick. I did not want to be a celebrity, a freak. And if I merely brought the dead back to life without announcing myself, I'd be creating an inexplicable event. A public miracle ought to have some thematic or metaphorical value; it shouldn't be merely for show. God only knows what sort of mess would follow a multiple resurrection.

Even the small miracles I had performed privately worried me. I was afraid I would get careless and do something that would cause terrible horrors for the world — maybe ruin the environment, or foster murderous bacteria. The fact that I had unwittingly created tornadoes just about paralyzed me with apprehension. Something told me I was capable of making a fatal mistake. Fatal to me, or even, heaven forbid, fatal to everybody else. God might destroy me, or the world, in some decidedly unGodly way.

So it didn't take me long to understand that I had to accept the misfortunes I had caused. I prayed for the souls I'd sent spiraling toward heaven and tried to forgive myself for being so reckless. In spite of my power, though, I couldn't forget those four lost lives. I was frozen with fear that I might repeat the crime in a careless moment. Their faces haunted me. Maybe you know what I'm talking about. I felt like a hit-and-run driver.

Dorothy's parents lived in Dunkin, a small town only about thirty-five miles south of Champaign. There was very little weather damage there, perhaps because the town sits on a bluff overlooking what can fairly be described as a garden of coal mines. Except for the blackened faces of most of the residents and the terrific scars in the flat ground at the foot of its largest hill, Dunkin might be the subject of a Norman Rockwell painting. The houses are all Victorian or Colonial, white, with cedar roofs and blue or orange shutters. Dunkin is also one of the few towns in all of southern Illinois where the trees have escaped Dutch elm disease, which is to say there are trees there. Large, healthy, permanent-looking trees. The girls love it in Dunkin, and Dorothy finds it tolerable as well.

Since it's only a thirty-minute drive, I could cruise down there after work in the evenings to visit, then leave late at night and claim to be heading back to finish cleaning up the mess. I wanted Dorothy to think I was working very hard on the disaster back home, so I let things get drawn out a bit. I never intended for her to begin to see it as a sort of trial separation. But that's what she started to call it.

I called her one night to tell her I'd worked too late to drive down there. I wanted to tell her I loved her and hated being alone in the house. I might have intended to tell her the house was almost finished, but before I could say anything she told me this time apart was a good thing for her. I couldn't believe the woman's nerve. Here I was — or at least as far as she knew there I was — slaving like a migrant fruit picker every night after work, trying to get the house back in living condition, and she's thinking of the whole thing as an opportunity to "think things over," as she put it.

"What is there to think over?" I said. I was very polite about it.

"I just need a little time," she said.

"Some more of that space you were talking about."

She didn't say anything.

"Why don't you look into becoming an astronaut?" I said. "Then you can have all the space you want." I slammed the phone down. It didn't help any that I knew what she was thinking before she told me about it.

In spite of the pain it caused her, she wanted out of our marriage — out of the whole thing. Not just her relationship with me (what was left of it); she thought she might have to leave the girls as well, at least for a while. She did not want to leave them, but she had already surrendered a lot of her life to them and she did not want to surrender the rest. She feared resenting them if their needs forced her once again to put aside her own life, her own needs. When I challenged this thinking by pointing out that college should not be more important than your own children, she flew into a rage. "It isn't college," she said. "It's me. My *life*."

"When you're a mother," I said, "your children come first."

"They *are* first. But I can't truly love them — not properly — if I resent them, don't you see?"

"Yeah, I see all right. If you abandon us, you'll just be gone, and that's what they'll remember about your love."

"I didn't say I was going to abandon them. I don't know what I'm going to do." She burst into tears.

Her desire to leave didn't have a lot to do with me, really — otherwise I might have taken it personally. She still loved me. I saw to that. Whatever love might have existed before I increased it to full candle-power, I would not want to speculate. But on the night of the great weather disaster, I created storms of love in her. No, it had nothing to do with me. Or the girls. It had to do with her. What she believed she wanted — her freedom.

It may be true that people need to be free; I wouldn't want to debate the point. But what do people mean when they use that word? Especially in these times? Dorothy was not interested in political freedom. She didn't want to be free to worship a turnip or assemble in a public place with a lot of other extremists. I don't think she wanted to be free to *do* anything. I think she wanted to be free *from* certain things.

All I wanted was for her to need me the way I needed her. There was a time in our marriage when she did. What changed it? It was so ironic. I did not feel complete without her, and she felt incomplete with me and the children. Go figure. In spite of her love for me, in spite of her considerable doubt and guilt over abandoning the girls, she wanted out.

Against her conscious choice to strive for what she needed, my power seemed helpless. Either it was inadequate, and God's power was tremendously overrated, or women have unbelievable strength, and even God pales in the face of a woman's will. I didn't know which to believe. But I couldn't wait to talk to Chet, I'll tell you that.

❋

The first day after the storm, while Dorothy was on the way to Dunkin, I went in to see Mr. Shale. I'd made up my mind to try to get a leave of absence. I thought it might be an unfair advantage to be acting God *and* an automobile salesman. When I walked into Mr. Shale's office, he said, "Sit down."

"Thanks," I said.

He looked at me as if he'd just given me an explosive cigar and I was in the process of lighting it. "Well? What do you think?"

"About what?" Then it hit me that he was talking normally. I'd forgotten all about what I'd done the day before. "You're — you don't . . ." I pretended to be speechless.

"I wanted you to be the first to know," he said. He was beside himself with joy. If you've ever seen a man standing in front of a prison with a new suit, seventy-five dollars in his pocket, and a piece of paper in his hand saying he's done his time, that's what Mr. Shale looked like that day.

"How did it happen?" I asked. I wanted to see what he would say.

"Well, I've been working on it." He sat at his desk, folded his hands in front of him. "Every day I'd go home, or sit up here after we closed, and practice in front of the mirror."

He was lying. I knew he'd given up a long time ago, that he'd believed he would never hold a normal conversation again. Maybe if I had been just God, and not also human, it wouldn't have bothered me so much. But I thought he was pretty despicable, taking credit for what I had done.

"I started to have a breakthrough last month," he said. "It just started to get better."

"You don't say."

"I had the devil of a time keeping it from everybody."

"What a nice surprise."

He cracked his knuckles, let out a confident, heavy breath of air. "I was practicing the impediment after a while, just so I could keep a lid on this until I knew it was all the way back."

Even though he was lying, I liked it that he was inexpressibly happy. And I think he believed himself — he really did credit the change to his own positive attitude. Even though only forty-eight hours before, he had been ready to stick his head in an oven.

"Well, I'm certainly happy for you," I said.

There was a pause while we practiced not looking directly at each other. Then I said, "Well, I came in here for a reason."

"Before you say anything." He raised his hand and studied the desk pad in front of him. "I want to say something."

I sat back. He picked up a pen and started scribbling on the pad, watching the drawing that developed there with a critical eye while he talked. "No one else . . . I never had a more . . . a more loyal ser— . . . a better fr—" He looked at me. "You were more than efficient during my illness."

"Thank you." I felt vaguely humiliated, as if he were telling me I had bad breath.

He leaned toward me, placed his hands on the edge of the desk, and said, "Warmest personal regards, Wiggins."

"Well," I said. "Very truly yours, sir." I stood up. He jumped up as well, a movement that looked as if somebody had spilled coffee in his lap. I think he was more embarrassed at that moment than he was when he asked that tall legal-looking woman if she had a fine cunt.

"You wanted to talk to me about something?" he said.

"Oh, yes." I waited to see if he would sit back down, so there was this brief pause while he tapped his pen rapidly on the edge of the desk and avoided my eyes. Finally I whispered, "I need a leave of absence."

"I wanted to give you a raise."

We spoke at almost the same time.

"A raise?" I said.

"Absence?"

"What sort of raise?"

"You could call it a promotion."

"Well."

He sat back down at the desk and motioned for me to be seated too. "What sort of absence?"

"It was an idea I've been kicking around."

"The job I have in mind — you'd do a lot of the things I do around here."

"I might be interested in that." I remembered I was only going to have God's power for a year. I had to consider what I was going to do for a living when the time came for me to step down. I didn't want to jeopardize a possible career opportunity simply because I was on this temporary fellowship in the position of the deity, as it were.

"I've never had a general manager," Mr. Shale said.

"I know you always —"

"You're going to be my first."

I was astonished. Mr. Shale was the only man who could order cars for the inventory; I figured that was part of ownership. Here he was offering me a chance to do it. Not only that, I would be in charge of approving deals that other salesmen made.

"There will be bonuses, and a base salary."

"I'm so glad you've got your speech back, Mr. Shale."

He laughed, a hearty, loud belly laugh. You wouldn't expect to see a man who didn't smoke cigars laugh like that. Then he said, "Seventy-five thousand a year, not counting bonuses and commissions on what you sell. How's that grab you?"

What would you have done? I had this opportunity for my future. I wasn't sure I'd be able to arrange anything once the power was gone, nor was it certain that I'd even have a future. I'd never considered it. What I did know — and this was a function of my ability to know what Mr. Shale was thinking — presented me with a real dilemma. Mr. Shale would not make the offer again, and he would not like it if I needed time to think about it. What he admired had to do with my apparent decisiveness.

So I took the job. I thanked Mr. Shale and told him he would not regret it.

I couldn't wait to see Dorothy and tell her the good news. I figured it might impress her that I was smart enough to be promoted to general manager of one of the largest auto dealerships in the city of Champaign. And I knew that wasn't all I was going to do. Not by a long shot. I wanted to do wonderful, good things.

At the time I was not any more specific than that in my thinking, although I was very emphatic about being careful and deliberate in my efforts. I didn't see any reason why I couldn't work at being acting God part-time. Even a part-time God is a pretty formidable notion. In truth, I was slightly relieved at the idea, since I would be less likely to create some inadvertent evil, as I had already done. I did not know if I could carry the weight of any more innocent souls whirling above the clouds.

❊

You'd think a man with the power of God would be at least as intelligent as, say, a starfish. Right? So, you ask, how come I insisted that Dorothy go to her parents' barely six hours after I jammed all the doors to keep her home?

I asked myself that same question a million times, and there just didn't seem to be a logical explanation. To tell you the honest and untainted truth, I just did not know why I did some of the things I did. Creating the snowstorm was merely a whim — someone said she hoped it was going to snow that day, so I helped the weather along a bit. But I could not divine a reason for raising the temperature to fifty degrees. It was just something I did — you know, like when you suddenly realize you've been biting your fingernails. You don't really have a reason for doing it, you're just doing it.

Perhaps a part of me didn't like the idea that Dorothy loved me only because I willed it. I mean, you wouldn't want to trick somebody into loving you, would you?

What if you could get a pill, a capsule of some kind with a special drug in it, and whenever anybody took one, she instantly loved you. Loved you with disgusting passion. Would you use it? You'd be creating a person who loved you because of the drug, not because of you. So would you feel loved? Or, more accurately, would you feel lovable? Wouldn't drug-induced passion really be sort of fake?

But then again, love is love. It doesn't matter where it comes from,

72

right? For all we know, when a person falls in love with you it's because of some chemical in your sweat pores anyway — that's what a lot of scientists say these days. So what's the difference between a person's loving you because of your glands and her loving you because of some tiny time pill?

I wanted a particular Dorothy to love me. Not the Dorothy I was trying to deal with at that moment, the one who frizzed her hair and said things like "Mizz Wiggins. Call me Mizz Wiggins." Not the one who believed a uterus was equivalent to the Congressional Medal of Honor and who called a woman married more than once a flying ace. I wanted the Dorothy who liked cuddling up to me under the covers and didn't mind it when I held her in the crook of my arm and caressed her long, straight hair. The one who carried my daughters in her arms and gazed down on them like a Renaissance Madonna. I wanted the Dorothy who did not think the world is a prison camp and males are the guards.

If I could get her to behave like the old Dorothy, I might be able to decide if there was any difference between love I created and real love.

❧

The week after my promotion, when Dorothy was still only temporarily at her parents' and I was pretending to be cleaning up the terrible mess of the flood, I had my second meeting with Chet. I'd just returned from a place called the Campus Shoe Store in Urbana. I figured if I was going to be the general manager of Shale Motors I should have a pair of black wing-tip shoes. I was standing on my front porch, fiddling with my keys, and Chet opened the door.

I screamed and dropped the shoe box.

"It's just me."

"I didn't expect — you startled me."

"I gathered that." He pushed open the storm door. "Come on in."

I went inside and took the shoes right to my bedroom and placed them under the bed. I didn't want Chet to see them.

"You don't have to hide those," he said.

I didn't know he had followed me. "I'm not hiding —"

He stopped me with a knowing stare.

"They're just new shoes."

"So. You got promoted. Congratulations."

"I didn't know what else to do. I have to work when I'm not — when I don't have the power anymore." I sat on the bed and tried to figure out what to do with my hands. I felt as if I had a block of ice in my stomach. I just knew Chet was not happy with me.

"Well," he said. "It's what you do."

"That's right. My job."

He stood in front of me, shifting his weight from one leg to the other, his hands tucked in the pockets of his trousers. A farmer might stand like that on a Sunday morning after church, knowing that if he hangs around he's only going to have a conversation with the minister, and if he gets going it's just back to the dusty fields.

"How've you been?" I said.

"You haven't been paying attention to details," he said.

"It's not easy."

"You have the power."

"I don't have the knowledge," I said. "So I don't know what the details are."

"There's no plan."

"What do you mean about details, then?"

"Just the simple everyday stuff." He began to pace. "You should have known what would happen when you raised the temperature thirty-five degrees in a matter of minutes."

"I guess I did know it."

"Right. But you didn't pay attention to it." He stopped by the door, leaned on the brass knob. "You have to think. All the time."

"I will, I will."

"Weigh everything."

"It's pretty hard, you know. I've got problems of my own." I wasn't afraid anymore, and with the fear gone I began to feel a very slight sensation that I can only approximately describe as embryonic anger. I did not like my dilemma with Dorothy and her love, and I did not like the fact that Chet was watching me and apparently grading my performance. I guess if I were truthful with you, I would have to admit that I was a little disturbed with God as well. I didn't think it was fair to give me all that power and leave me to design or discover my own plan.

"Try not to think so much about your personal problems," Chet was saying. "You have greater responsibilities right now."

"I hope you'll forgive me, but I don't think there's any greater responsibility than my family." I stood up and moved close enough to him to violate his comfort space and set him to pacing again. "Maybe you picked the wrong guy," I said.

"I didn't pick you."

"Oh." There was no way I was going to suggest that God picked the wrong substitute. I knew that wasn't possible, or I hoped it wasn't. I worried about what sort of God he might be if he was a little deficient in his judgments concerning human nature.

After a long pause, during which Chet paced up and down slowly in front of me and I toyed with the frayed edge of one of Dorothy's robes, which hung on the back of our door, I said, "Why can't I get Dorothy to stay with me?"

"She doesn't want to."

"No — I made her want to."

"You have that power. You can make her desire you, force her to want you worse than air. But you can't make her act on that desire."

"I guess I knew that. That's not the question I'm asking."

"Well?" He stopped pacing again, this time in front of me. He rocked on his feet, his hands behind his back now, and it hit me he was waiting for something. I was not meeting some expectation of his. Perhaps I was not asking the right questions, or I had not said what I was supposed to say.

"Why can't I just create her doing what I want, make her behave in certain —"

"I just told you."

"No, I mean why can't I change whatever it is in her that makes her resist what she wants?"

"Her will? You want to get beyond that?"

"Oh," I said. "I see."

"The earth's not a machine. There's plenty of room for accident, for the routine of instinct, and for — well, you know. For creation and defiance."

"Seems hard to believe."

"It's not hard to observe, so how could it be hard to believe?"

"I see."

There was another pause. Chet tapped his foot there by the door, and then I noticed he had wing tips on.

75

"Nice shoes," I said.

"Look," he said, "while you have this power, you can do anything you want, as long as you don't violate one of the laws."

"Well, you see?" I couldn't resist asking him the obvious question. "I don't understand this part about the limits. If I have God's power, I have no limits, right?"

He smiled, shaking his head. "Look. What if you had absolute power and you said — you said — no, you *decreed* that no snowflake would ever land on a human hand and not melt."

"I guess that would be the case, then."

"But what if you changed your mind later? What if you wanted a snowflake to land on a human hand and remain exactly as it was?"

"I'd decree that."

"But you couldn't. Don't you see? Your first decree precludes the possibility of that ever happening." He put his hand on my shoulder and leaned very close to me. I felt a lot like a boy listening to his father. "If your power was absolute and you used it to set up a condition you did not want changed, ever, then once you created such a thing, your power would cease to be absolute."

"Why? Why couldn't I just —"

"Because in creating a thing that can never be changed, you would diminish your power by that one thing. The more of those you created, the more limited your power would be." A gust of wind slapped the window, and he straightened up, looked over his shoulder.

"It may snow again," I said.

He turned back to me. "Well, don't you fool with it."

"I made a mess, didn't I?"

"Yes, you did."

"I felt so sorry for those people I — for those people who were killed."

"It's the earth," Chet said. "That's the way of it."

I didn't know how to look him in the face, but I could feel his eyes on me as if they gave off heat. "I didn't think I would hurt anybody."

He waved his hand. "There was no intent there. Don't feel so bad."

"I wish I didn't."

Neither of us spoke for a time. Outside, the sky was losing its color, and I thought of time and change and endings. I think Chet could see I was on the brink of a fairly black mood.

"You want to see heaven?" he said.

I was afraid to answer him. I stood perfectly still in front of the window.

"I don't mean what you think," he said. His voice was soothing and calm.

"What do you mean?"

"A guided tour."

"You're not serious."

"Sure. Why not? It might help you."

"A real tour of heaven?"

"I can arrange it. At least I can arrange for you to see part of it."

"Not now," I said. I went back to the bed and sat down. The thought of visiting heaven actually nauseated me for some reason. I wondered if he knew it — I was so afraid I'd offend him. And I had unbelievable anxiety concerning the myriad ways I might be insulting his boss. "I would like a tour later, though. Sometime. I really would."

"I'll arrange it."

"I just don't feel very well right now."

"It's the flu season."

"I guess."

He started for the door.

I said, "Can I get sick?"

"If you wish."

"No, I mean is it possible?"

"If you wish," he said. Then he smiled.

"I guess this has been one of my lessons, then?"

"When I've arranged the tour," he said, "I'll let you know. There won't be much need for preparations or anything."

"Okay."

"And by the way, there *are* things more important than your family."

"Not if you're —"

"When you have the power, your family is . . ." He stopped in the doorway and looked at me with tiny black eyes — eyes like a gull's eyes. "Your family is nothing." He closed the door very quietly as he exited, as if I were a toddler and he'd just put me down for my nap.

And guess what I did?

I napped.

I stretched out on that bed and lost consciousness like a man having a stroke.

It must have truly disturbed me, what Chet said about my family, because I dreamed of a thousand different ways to lose all of them. I saw the two girls fall out of an airliner, watched Dorothy be consumed by a forest fire. I don't know how many smashed and burning automobiles I pulled their limp bodies out of. It was just awful.

When I woke up I had my finger in my mouth, and I was sucking on it like a bald, pink infant. I couldn't believe how frightened I was. I was like a person who finds a lump and starts praying for a wen or a boil. When I'd had a chance to get control of my senses and the initial terror subsided, I decided that I would use my power to make sure I never had dreams like that again. I didn't want even to begin to try to understand what the dreams meant. It was too frightening to consider. I mean, when you've got God's power, what's the difference between a dream and a vision? For all I knew, I might be going mad. Imagine a lunatic with that sort of power. I might do anything — might purposely create a disease worse than cancer, or cause earthquakes in large, peaceful cities, or even give the world a new and disgusting life form like a tick or a leech.

While I was preventing nightmares for myself, I decided to do the same thing for most of the people I knew (like I said in the beginning of this story, I'm big on empathy). I knew what that sort of dream felt like, and didn't see any reason why anyone I cared about should feel like that.

I went into the bathroom and looked in the mirror. I had just altered the dreams, or at least the pattern of dreams, of several persons. My children, Dorothy, Mr. Shale, Dottie, the rest of the people at the dealership. Even Cherry. I hadn't even paused to think about it.

Chet had said, "Think. Think all the time."

I couldn't make myself consider things before I did them. It wasn't in my personality, not before or after I had the power. I knew if I didn't learn to think first, though, I'd only incur the further dissatisfaction of Chet and his immediate supervisor. Worse, I'd run the risk every day of killing more people and creating more suffering.

You know, it's a terrible feeling to have your wife tell you she wants to leave and to know you've created death for a few people and probably aren't making the good Lord too happy either. I think I understand a little bit of what it must feel like to be the Fallen Angel.

It didn't help that my efforts to keep Dorothy with me seemed vaguely satanic. After all, I was trying to beguile her into coming home.

She told me finally that I could come get the children if I wanted but that she was going to stay at her folks' for a while and sort things out. This was during one of our few telephone conversations, about three weeks after I got my promotion and two weeks after the visit from Chet. (Dorothy was so happy about my promotion she couldn't contain herself. Her right eyebrow arched slightly, and she said, "That's nice.")

"I think you should just come home," I said. I felt as if I were in a play and I knew all the lines so well they came to my lips automatically, so I could be thinking about almost anything else while I was saying them.

"We've been over all this, darling."

"I don't think you should do that to the girls," I said.

"I know you don't. But it's not your choice."

"I think you're —"

"Honey!" She was angry, but I liked it that she called me "honey."

"Okay," I said. "Suit yourself."

"If only it were that simple."

I was sitting at my desk in the office at Shale Motors, so I couldn't very well get emotional over the phone. But that last thing Dorothy said really made me angry. I wanted to scream so loud it would make an imprint like a phonograph record in her brain, *That's all you want — to suit yourself!*

I said, very calmly, "But there are other people to think of."

"Goodbye," she said.

"I don't think you should confuse *selfish* with *selfhood*."

"Goodbye!"

"Don't hang up." I was too late. I was so angry, I think if I'd had time, I might have hoped that she'd break her hand when she put the phone down. Lord knows what might have resulted from that. Is there a difference between hoping for something and willing it? How could I learn to be so careful that nothing rushed unfiltered into my mind?

As it was, that was when I realized I was going to have to bring Dorothy back by some means other than the mere power of God. Oh, I would use the power, all right, but not in a direct way. I was going to have to let fate play a part.

As the first step, I found it necessary to create an emergency of some sort — an apparently serious condition that would unite all of us in mutual fear and hope. I approached the notion with extreme caution and thorough consideration, owing to my respect for my own insecurities and for what Chet expected of me, and I willed in advance that absolutely no one would be permanently hurt or damaged in any way by what I was about to do. Then I made Dorothy's father extremely ill. He was rushed to the hospital in a state of unconsciousness. It didn't look good for him at all.

Dorothy and I were fraught with worry.

5

O f course I didn't give Dorothy's father anything serious — just something that looked bad. A malady that, in the hands of a capable physician, would ultimately be curable. I didn't want him to suffer very much, either, although he and I had never really gotten along, and I wouldn't have minded if he had had a little bit of pain, simply because he was the sort of person who would benefit immensely from personal agony.

So I created a condition that caused a sudden increase in a hormone in his system. This produced an excess of certain enzymes in his stomach, which robbed his body of the necessary level of potassium. He collapsed like a man dropping through a trapdoor. Scared the living hell out of his wife.

Dorothy called me at the dealership, crying so hard she was incoherent. I thought it was wonderful that I was the first person she wanted to talk to in these circumstances.

"I'll be right there," I told her. "It will be all right."

"I think he was dead," she cried. "He was so limp when they put him in the ambulance."

"How's your mother?"

"They gave her a sedative."

"Stay with her," I said.

"I'm going to the hospital."

"Is someone going to stay —"

"Mother is coming with me."

"I'll meet you there," I said.

Even when I didn't have God's power, I was always good in a crisis. One of the things Dorothy had claimed to admire about me was my calm demeanor whenever the earth opened up and swallowed our plans and hopes. That was probably why she called me first.

Dorothy's father was an odd sort of fellow. His name was Eugene Herrmann, but everybody called him Norm. I never knew why, since he had no middle name. I figured some kid probably called him "Yewjeenerman," then "Oojeenerman," followed by "Jeenerman," and then finally just "Nerman." After that, some adult simply called him "Norm." He was generous, especially with money, but he never bought a thing in his life that wasn't old or used. He spent more time at garage sales, sidewalk closeouts, and used-car lots than a kidney patient spends on a dialysis machine. His week was ruined if he didn't get a few days "shopping for deals," as he put it. He bought things no one needed.

On the occasion of our marriage, Dorothy's father gave us a hundred and fifty dollars and two stainless steel toenail clippers — huge toenail clippers. When he handed them to me, still encased in the plastic container of the manufacturer, he said, "His and hers." He had a wry smile on his face, as if he were sharing a secret with me that no one else would ever know.

What do you say in a situation like that? I looked at them for a long time, and he waited there, watching me turn them over in my hand. Finally I said, "I was hoping we'd get something useful. What a practical gift."

But the worst thing about Norm was that he had the most extraordinary capacity to arouse nausea in me. Not that he was feral, or unclean. In some ways he was very refined. He loved to listen to Mahler and Chopin, Rossini, Mozart, and Bruckner. He visited art galleries on Saturdays when he was not chasing after the perfect garage sale. Books were a sort of sacrament for him — he looked forward to cold blue Sunday evenings in front of his fireplace with his pipe, a glass of red wine, and a good book. When he sat down to read, he'd say, "Got to visit some old friends." Then he'd let out this loud exhalation of air —

a sort of piggish grunt — as he sat down. That's what would get me feeling nauseous. He could expel the most unnatural noises. Bodily sounds and secretions seemed completely beyond his ability to perceive.

I remember the first day I met him I had seated myself at the table for breakfast. It was a cold, colorless Friday during the Christmas season. I was extremely hungry — Dorothy and I had been on a ski trip in Wisconsin all the week before, and we'd just driven the four hundred miles or so to Dunkin and her parents' house. Since I'd been driving almost all night, I woke up a bit late, and everyone else was fed and finished. I sat at the dining room table, wondering when I would get the chance to meet "the old man," as Dorothy called him. Just as Dorothy put a plate full of fried eggs and bacon in front of me I heard a toilet flush; the water made gagging noises as it cleared the bottom of the bowl. This made me think about — well, you can't help it sometimes where your mind takes you. But I fought it off. I had just gotten to where I thought I could put a bite of eggs in my mouth, had just washed the idea of the contents of that toilet from my mind, and this short, very round, heavy-jawed, unshaven man came around the corner and said, in a voice so deep it sounded almost like a fart, "I just shit my brains out!"

You can imagine the effect this had on me. I couldn't very well run to the bathroom, either, because he'd just come out of there. I don't want to be crude, but I figured I wouldn't be ready to go into that bathroom until Thursday or Friday of the following week. I found myself trying to convince him, at 9:35 in the morning, that I was going to a movie.

Virtually all the noises he made from then on reminded me of that first encounter. It didn't help that he was the sort of man who did not mind the sounds his body occasionally made without his permission.

When Dorothy and I were newly married and telling each other everything, I told her about my problem. "Your father makes me sick," I said.

"Why? What did he do?"

"No, it's nothing he did or didn't do. He just makes these noises and says these things that make me sick to my stomach."

Of course this hurt her feelings. I wouldn't have minded that so much — people get over hurt feelings — but she went and told her father that he nauseated me.

Things weren't much good between Norm and me after that. There was this awkwardness there — a vague feeling of disgrace all the time, as if one of us had done some overtly sexual thing to the other and neither of us wanted to examine the fabric of such an act.

The whole time Dorothy and I were married, he continued to buy us things we did not need, and in quantities that made it impossible to use them up. One year he got us three thousand rolls of toilet paper. All of them had gotten wet in some sort of flood and each roll was crushed fairly flat, so it was impossible to find the beginning of the roll and get it started. I used to sit in the bathroom for what seemed like hours picking at those rolls of paper, until it looked like I was making little white replicas of Christmas trees. I never could get one of them actually to unroll the way toilet paper is supposed to. It got so every time I went to the john, I'd curse Dorothy's father.

After Jody Beth was born, he bought me forty-six boxes of Trojan-Enz rubbers. There were 340 rubbers in each box. You figure out how many that is. I never bothered. I figured I had enough rubbers to supply New York's prostitution industry for several years. And of course Dorothy and I never used that method of birth control anyway. I think all of those boxes are still in our basement, unopened.

But think about it for a minute. What sort of gift *is* that? Why would a person who has no regard for bodily secretions and sounds buy so many things that have to do with hygiene? That's why I say Dorothy's father was an odd sort of fellow.

❉

When I arrived at the hospital, Dorothy had gotten better control of her emotions — I was sure she had talked to the doctor already — and I think she was a little bit sorry she had called me. Her mother seemed angry at me for something, even in her anxiety and grief.

"It's going to be okay," I said.

"How would you know?" she said through her tears.

Picture this: the waiting room was furnished like all of them are, with the coffee table, lamps, end tables, bookcases, and pictures on the walls, just like the sort of interior you might find in somebody's living room. And chairs like the shabby little torture racks you have to squirm in when you're forced to wait in the lobby of a bus station — plastic, short-backed, and riveted to the floor. Dorothy's mother twisted in her chair like an enormous snail trying to emerge from its shell. Dorothy paced back and forth in front of a broad window that looked out on the parking lot, and smoked cigarettes as if she were running a test for some toothpaste advertisement. I sat next to the snail and tried to be encouraging.

I always got along with Dorothy's mother. I sometimes jokingly called her Mizz Herrmann, although she insisted I call her by her first name, Herta. You ever known anybody named Herta? How about Herta Herrmann? If you say that name fast enough, you can clear your throat. I used to tease her about it. In fact, I teased her about almost everything. She was a pretty good sport as long as I didn't push her too far. If she came to visit and cleaned the refrigerator — all mothers clean something when they visit — I'd say, "How come you haven't done the windows, Mizz Herrmann?" or "You ought to get to those curtains soon, don't you think?" She usually thought I was pretty funny. So I couldn't understand why she seemed so antagonistic toward me at the hospital. I sat next to her and tried to grab her hand every now and then, but it was like trying to catch a child's hand. She kept pulling it away and moving it around when I reached for it.

By the time the doctor came to see us, I had pretty much given up. I wanted to understand what was wrong with her, but I couldn't think it, couldn't use the power to conjure her problem. Either she would not think about it or she was not angry with me at all, she was just being inscrutable, the way women can be when the moon's right.

The doctor's name was Beach. He had a slight blond beard around his chin and the corners of his mouth, pale eyes, and gold hair. He locked like a golf pro or a tennis coach. Very tanned skin, a burgundy Ban-Lon shirt under his white coat. I knew there was an alligator on that shirt. I could tell by looking at him that he probably jogged. He was a marathon man. One of those people who seem to trot even when they're standing still. You know the type.

"We're going to have to run some more tests," Beach said.

Dorothy went right to him. She got so close I thought she was going to try to smell his breath. Her eyes simply glittered in the light by that window. She had just finished crying — or fighting off tears. It was hard to tell. But Beach was hooked by her eyes, her soft voice.

"What sort of tests?" she said.

"I'd like to have a look at his arteries. Just some routine tests to see if . . ." He looked at Dorothy's hands, then took them into his own. "There's a possibility he's had a stroke. We want to run a CAT scan, look at his brain."

"Oh my God," Dorothy said.

Herta squeezed out of her chair and stepped quietly over to Dr. Beach. She looked like she might kneel down in front of him and receive holy communion. "Did my husband have a stroke?" she said.

"I don't think so." Dr. Beach still had Dorothy's hands. He was very gentle with her; his eyes were kind, and there was something irresistibly sensitive in his demeanor and tone of voice. Dorothy trusted him almost instantly, and I found myself struggling against a furious desire to create a debilitating disease in his pancreas. I resisted it, I'm proud to say. I knew I was simply jealous. He was only being a man, and Dorothy *was* wearing her jeans. She would not stop looking at him.

"This just doesn't behave like a stroke," he went on. "His blood pressure is normal, his eyes look fine, and there's no sign of cerebral disturbance, except for this sudden unconsciousness. But I want to rule out stroke, and the only way to do that for sure is to run the test."

"Do what you have to do," Dorothy said. She reached for her mother. I stepped up. "Excuse me, might I have a word with you, doctor, about a possible hormone imbalance?" I don't know what got into me. I guess I wanted to impress Dorothy so much, I forgot why I'd made her father sick to begin with.

He looked at me. First his eyes focused on mine, then for a brief fraction of a second they shifted down, as if I were naked and he didn't want to notice it. "What did you say?"

"It might be merely a hormone imbalance."

"Hmm," he said. Then he turned back to Dorothy. "I want you to know there's also a possibility of a lesion in his brain."

"I think you should look at his hormones."

Dorothy gripped his hands as if she were trying to get juice out of them. "Oh my God."

"Would you quit saying that?" I said.

"What?"

"Say something else."

Dr. Beach took his hands away from Dorothy and placed them into his neat white pockets. "He's stable right now, resting comfortably. You can go see him in a few minutes."

"It's the hormones, I'm sure," I said. "Check that." I wanted to make it a command; I almost turned the power on Mr. Hemoglobin.

"You don't know what you're talking about," Dorothy said when the doctor had retreated.

"Yes, I do," I said. "I know exactly what I'm talking about."

"I think you should go home," Herta said.

"I'm not going. You need me to —"

"You should go." Dorothy took her mother's arm.

"I want to see Norm," I said.

They walked sullenly in front of me, as if I'd taken them hostage and might execute one of them at any moment. Don't you think it's amazing that women can demonstrate how they're feeling simply by the way they walk? Something about their gait, and the way they carry themselves, I don't know. Maybe it's the angle of the head, or a slight bend in the neck. But you can always tell when a woman is feeling less than charitable by the way she walks. If I were a panhandler, I'd save myself a lot of time among the women, I'll tell you that.

"Anyway," I said, "you called me and asked me to come down here."

"It was sweet of you," Dorothy said, without turning around. "But I don't really need you now."

"I'm not a Kleenex," I said. "I'm not a damned emery board."

She stopped, still clutching her mother's arm as if she had to hold the old woman up. "That will be quite enough," she said.

"Shall we go see Norm?"

Herta shook her head as she walked. I came to see that she disapproved of me because she thought I had created the rupture in her daughter's marital bliss. She thought the whole separation was my fault, that I was forcing Dorothy to stay away. Can you imagine that?

What a sweet old bird Herta was. You have to admire family loyalty wherever you find it, you know? Even though I was the object of her scorn, I was tempted as we walked down that long white corridor to create some lasting joy for her. I debated between changing her circulatory system, as I had done with the old man in the men's room when

I first inherited God's power, and curing her arthritis. Some internal resistance to unfettered generosity would not let me do both. It's the damnedest thing what happens to your perspective when you have God's power and only human inclinations to use it. It was like there were two of me, the fellow with the power and the person who knew the fellow with the power. And one always had some bickering interest in the pursuits of the other. Not wanting to be redundant, I cured her arthritis.

Norm was asleep when we got to his room. He looked like a huge cigarette butt the way he was bent up in the bed, his reddish hair all blasted out on the pillow and the white gown stretched and twisted tight on him. Herta let out this weak, sad little broken blister of a sigh.

"He'll be all right," I said.

She stood by the bed and looked at him, funerals whirling in her mind. Nothing I said or did made any difference. I inserted the certain knowledge that he would be okay, that he would survive, return home, and continue to plague her with complaints of mismatched socks and overcooked pasta. But she simply refused to let herself believe it. She was afraid if she did, the fates would trick her and kill him anyway. She believed, in the same way that you and I believe the world is in fact round, that if she expected the worst, the fates would, as was their habit, go against what she expected and give her the best.

I understood her thinking completely. It was an odd sort of game she played all the time in her head. She believed in the power of negative thinking. Probably four fifths of the human population believes in it. Whatever you want real badly, if you expect to get it, you won't. You have to expect not to. Then all sorts of wonderful things might happen. Of course, if the fates are on to you, you have to get fairly complex. You have to expect to get what you want and say you expect not to, while secretly thinking you won't really get it and don't care one way or the other if you do. The fates work with what goes on in your head, not all the time with what you say, and you can confuse them pretty easily if you convolute everything with several layers of ambivalence and ambiguity. So sometimes you have to say, "I'm going to win" when you want to lose, but in the tiny, secret, nonverbal part of your mind you really want to win, even though you are truly expecting not to, so the fates will go against what you expect and let you win.

Anyway, take my word for it: if success were food, positive thinking might get you a candy bar. With negative thinking, you're in the realm of loaves and fishes.

Dorothy reached over and touched Norm on the head. She also expected to be wearing black soon. I watched her and her mother hovering over Norm as he slept, and I had this odd sensation in the back of my head, almost as if I were getting a radio signal in my brain. It was like the beginning of a dizzy spell, only there seemed to be noises in it — a spinning sensation of buzzing sound. I was afraid I might faint, so I said to Dorothy, "I'm going outside for a moment."

"You might as well go home," she said.

"I'll be right back, I just want to get some air." I put the thought in her mind that I might die of a heart attack. You should have seen her eyes widen. She came around the bed, put her hands on my arms.

She whispered, "Are you all right?"

"I'm fine," I said. "I just feel a little dizzy."

"It's okay if you want to go on home."

Herta mumbled something that sounded like "Hell, Murray, pull the drapes."

"What?" I said.

She didn't look at me but leaned over her husband and whispered, "Bessie dart's pal, among women."

"What is she saying?"

Dorothy took her hands away. "It's just a prayer."

Herta said, "Pay for 'is dinner, now win at the owlverdeth, amen."

"She ought not to mumble like that," I said.

"Just leave us alone for a while, okay?" said Dorothy.

I found my way to the cafeteria. I was going to get a cup of coffee, but the whirling, loud, buzzing noise rattled in my head. It was very similar to the feeling I had had the night I got the blue letter, and it made me so nervous I felt as if my heart were bathed in icewater. My head seemed to swell up with the noise in it. I didn't know where to go or what to do. If a doctor had passed me, he might have thought I was having some kind of attack. There was no men's room in sight. I stood in front of that cafeteria, a room with bright orange walls and yellow footprints painted on the floor to show everybody where to go, and prayed to myself. I asked for the riot in my head to stop. The noise intensified briefly, as though something in my mind wanted to explode

89

before I could stop it. I was afraid my eyes were going to pop out. I walked unsteadily into the cafeteria, bought myself a cup of coffee, and sat down in an orange chair.

I don't know if the prayers to myself had anything to do with it, but my skull quieted down gradually. It may have been because I willed it, or perhaps the malady just ran its course. I felt very cold and small. My hands were shaking. I realized it would be an exquisite irony if I were in the embryonic stages of some sort of fatal illness, and understanding that, I could not make myself trust that I was okay. I hated not knowing what was happening to my body while I was the acting deity. I realized it was entirely possible that God's power was carcinogenic, or bad for the arteries.

In spite of my gathering fears and an extraordinary sense of inner weakness, I still had this problem with Dorothy and what I had done to her father. My strategy was not working as well as I thought it might, and I knew that as long as I stayed in the cafeteria sipping weak coffee and staring at the walls, the crisis I had created was wasted. It took every ounce of strength I had left and most of God's will to get up and return to Norm's room.

When I got there, he was still asleep, and Dorothy was alone with him. She leaned over him like a priest, giving absolution.

"Where's your mother?" I whispered.

"She couldn't stand seeing him like this." Dorothy was crying. I felt terrible for causing her this worry. Although it was for a good reason. At least I thought it was a good reason. What could be more important than the preservation of a family? I knew I could keep anything evil from happening to the old man. I just wanted to create a crisis, a powerful incentive for Dorothy to reexamine her perspective. But good intentions are not always the best excuse. I know that.

Norm turned his head and took a deep breath. He was just sleeping there. He might have been on his couch, dozing during a football game.

"He's all right," I said.

"This is a terrible time, you know?" Dorothy looked at me, her eyes glistening like fine crystal. Her voice was so sweet I think I felt it in my heart.

"You're really very beautiful," I said.

"This is a terrible time of life."

"It's the best time. Our children are young, we're —"

"No." She was sure. Absolutely sure. "We have to lose our parents now. Our . . . our protection."

"Protection?"

"You know what I mean."

"I never felt like my parents were much protection."

"It's like that," she said. "They're between us and . . . between us and the end." Her voice was high and soft and fearful, like a child's voice. "I can't believe I'm going to lose him."

"You're not going to lose him," I said. I waved my hand and increased his potassium level to normal. I didn't want to take any chances. It was one of the most difficult things I've ever done not to tell Dorothy what I was doing. I felt so damned clumsy. Like a city boy with the milking bucket in his hands for the first time. I knew I was probably a lousy God. I didn't want to speculate about what sort of husband I had been.

"Dorothy?"

"Hmmm?" She was looking at her father as if she were afraid he might disappear.

"I'm sorry about everything."

"Me too."

"No," I said. "I want to . . . I'm sorry about some of the things I've said to you. Some of the things I've done."

She looked at me. "If that were all." Her eyes seemed to gaze at something far in the distance, as if she could see through walls and out into the diminishing afternoon. "If only that were all."

She was thinking about the ways in which I had failed her. She could not remember a single moment of our happiness. She envisioned a different life for herself, a different self. I could actually see a figure in her eyes, not quite her but another woman, possessing a sense of the world that subdued it a bit, that made the intricacies of daily life a worthy amalgam of labor and contentment, work and change. Somewhere in her vision, there I was, with a broad accepting smile and approving eyes, proud of her, and with my pride lending her power. She had carried this idea of what she wanted in a husband from her childhood, and only recently had she become convinced that it wasn't a hopeless illusion. It was something she might have if only I would allow it. She loved me so much, her heart ached every time she made the comparison between the real me and what she imagined. Here she was, in a hospital room, watching what she believed was her father's death, and she felt so profoundly sorry for me that she wept. She looked into her father's half-opened eyes and thought of me, at my end, alone. And she wished she did not have to leave me. I hated knowing what whirled in her mind.

"You don't have to leave me," I said.

She looked at her feet, then back at her father. "Sometimes . . ." Then she turned to me. "Sometimes you know me so well." There was a trace of a smile there.

"I know what you're thinking," I said. "I know I'm not everything you want." It took all my strength not to start crying. For the first time in a long time, I felt like something other than her adversary.

"Give me this time," she whispered.

"I wish you'd just come home."

"I need to think . . . I need to see if . . ."

She didn't say it, but I knew what it was. She almost told me she wanted to see if she could find her imagined soulmate, the picture-perfect, warm and sensitive carbon copy of her secret self.

"You want me to wait around in case you fail, is that it?"

"Shhh."

"I'm trying to understand," I said.

"I'm sorry," she whispered, again starting to cry.

"We'll work things out." I put my arms around her. She cried silently, her face in the hollow of my shoulder.

"I'm sorry," she said. "I'm so confused."

I caressed her hair, and came to understand with each stroke that she was going to stay away for a while. And I was going to have to let her.

*

Go figure. I have God's power. Me. I love my wife and family above all things. In my own way, I'm occasionally a bit of a rascal. I like a good practical joke. I'm a little selfish. No, maybe very selfish. I behave badly when things don't go my way. I majored in English in college. Cheated twice, both times on French exams. I think rules are like New Year's resolutions: we keep to them only by conscious will and effort. The rest of the time there's no reason to pay much attention to them. Following all the rules is like dieting.

I'm pretty smart. You can tell that by now. But I don't know a lot, and what I do know, I often don't remember. I talk a good game. People believe me. I had Mr. Shale convinced I could understand him.

As I told you once, I make a conscious effort to please everybody. I don't stand up to anyone but Dorothy and the children. I never learned how to say no to anyone. I never hurt anybody on purpose — until I became acting God. Since then I had given Cherry a virus and put Mr. Herrmann in the hospital. I had also killed four people, although that was just carelessness.

Imagine that.

A careless God.

What could possibly have been working in God's mind when he picked me?

On the way back to the dealership that afternoon, I went over everything in my mind, and I decided I was going to find out from Chet once and for all what was going on. I wanted to know if maybe it was the end of the world and that's why God gave his power to me. So much of it didn't make any sense. I could not make Dorothy do what I wanted, but I had cured Herta of arthritis, done the same thing for a complete stranger as well as renew his circulatory system, and fixed Mr. Shale. I had created a record-breaking snowstorm and several murderous tornadoes.

And Dorothy was going to stay away. In spite of how close we had seemed to get in Norm's room, my strategy had failed. Dorothy saw a potential end to life, and it only made her more intensely interested in extracting joy from it. Perhaps, in ways I had not perceived yet, the episode with Norm did more to harm my marriage than help it.

I felt like a small child alone in a terrifying amusement park.

Given my circumstances, I wondered if it was going to be possible for me to be a good acting deity. I'd had the power a little over three weeks, and I still didn't know what I could and couldn't do. Every time I used it I wasn't sure what the outcome would be. Hell, I wasn't even sure half the time *when* I would use the power. Sometimes it just happened before I had a chance to think about it. And it was absolutely useless in the face of Dorothy's will.

By the time I got back to Shale Motors, I had pretty much made up my mind that having God's power was not such a terrific thing. I felt sort of possessed.

I wondered what kind of priest I would need to have God exorcised.

6

Weeks passed and I didn't see or hear from Chet. I tried to conjure him several times. I even went to a church, knelt in the first pew, and begged him to come. But in spite of what I perceived to be a real need, and in spite of the full force of my will pressing him to appear, there was no response. In the meantime, I did not allow my predicament to impede me very often. I decided I could wait for Chet, be myself, and forget God for a while.

Norm made a complete recovery, came out of the hospital after a few days, and joined Herta, Dorothy, and me in a subdued celebration of his renewed health. He dragged me with him to several garage sales, looking for a good used cane or a neck brace. "I've had a glimpse of my future," he said. "I might as well prepare for it."

Christmas came and went, a very dull, cold series of days at Norm and Herta's place in Dunkin, where Dorothy sighed and twisted in her chair and the girls played with dolls and video games. The Christmas spirit was evident only in television commercials. Everybody in the house knew there was something wrong between Dorothy and me, but nobody wanted to admit it. The icy nights mirrored the mood in the house perfectly.

Norm slept through most of it, and Herta cooked and baked like the head chef in an army division. I gained five pounds, but I knew I could will them away when I returned to work.

I was comparatively happy on Christmas morning, watching the girls tear into boxes like sharks into a side of beef. I was also excited about the gifts I had gotten for Dorothy. I couldn't wait to see the joy on her face when she opened them. I got her a new leather purse, a pair of long johns, a new ten-speed bike, an aerobics tape, two silk nightgowns, and, most special of all, a new engagement ring — five small diamonds set in a bright fourteen-carat gold band. I think she knew what it was when she saw the little black felt box it came in. She opened it with trembling hands and touched the ring as if it gave off heat.

She didn't smile or gasp, but I knew she thought it was beautiful; she put it on, held it up to the light so the girls could admire it. Then she pulled back a bit, as if she suddenly remembered she was going to be electrocuted the next morning. She removed the ring from her finger and placed it back in the box.

"Thank you," she said.

She didn't say anything else or display any emotion, and I spent the rest of that day feeling sorry for myself. I might as well have gotten her a pair of socks and a box of soap flakes.

I was amused by Norm's gift. He got me a plastic trashcan full of charcoal. He didn't bother to wrap it but just taped a red ribbon to the lid.

"Where'd you get this?" I asked.

"At the market. I got a great deal on it."

Apparently several bags had gotten wet in a storm and dissolved, so the manager of the store had thrown the soggy charcoal into one of his trashcans and sold the whole thing to Norm.

"That'll last you several summers," Norm said with pride.

"If I can ever light any of it."

"Oh, it'll dry," he said. He didn't look at me. I think he was a little sad. I know it was probably tactless of me to point out that my gift was still wet. I suppose I should have been glad he didn't buy me a year's supply of Preparation H.

You want to know what Dorothy got me for Christmas?

A subscription to *National Geographic*.

I didn't know what to say. The subscription was printed on a small card, and I turned it over in my hand for a few seconds, desperate for words. Norm said, "What a thoughtful gift."

Claire said, "What is it?"

This gave me something to say. "It's a whole year's supply of a geography magazine, honey." I was glad she didn't ask me anything more about it, because I couldn't have told her. I had never read a single issue in my life.

"Gee," Claire said.

Nobody moved for a moment. It was very quiet. I sat down next to Dorothy, placing the card on an end table. "Thanks," I said. "I've always wanted to read one of those."

"Yes, the pictures are wonderful," Herta said.

"And *National Geographics* weigh so much," I said. "Those are not cheap magazines."

I was very happy when we packed up the decorations and threw away the tree.

After Christmas I hurled myself into the job at Shale Motors, and at night I spent every spare moment reading. I began what can only be described as a Renaissance curriculum. I read the great books of the western world, from Aristotle to Zola, in one month. Then I tackled the Near East, Japan, and China. You wouldn't believe how fast an acting God can read. I knew Chet would come to me eventually, and I wanted to get to know as much as I could about the world before our talk. I wanted to become wise, to make sure I knew as much as *can* be known before I let myself behave again in a Godly way. Until then, I was determined to be inactive. Except for the studying. And the hard work at Shale Motors. I admit, I also kept tabs on Dorothy. It was not hard to do that, although after her father got out of the hospital she almost never called me except to let me say hello to the girls or arrange a visit.

She could not decide what to do about the children. Every time we talked about that she'd start crying and so would I. A part of her believed it was probably best that I should have custody, so she found herself spending a lot of time with them, preparing for what she believed was the inevitable break between us. We agreed before Christmas to let the girls stay in Dunkin with her parents until I could get child care. Then they would move back with me and go back to school, and Dorothy would take the time she needed to decide whether she really wanted to be shed of us all. In some secret lee of her heart she believed I could sustain the loss of our marital bliss if I had the girls to comfort me. But she was not very aware of it. Mostly she was tortured over them. She feared doing the wrong thing, and could not settle on anything she believed would be right. She was like an animal with two limbs in a trap, trying to decide which one to gnaw off first.

She didn't know I knew it, and she resisted a clear awareness of it, but she had already decided she was leaving. She let me believe there was some doubt, in the sincere hope that after a period of time apart I would get used to the idea and it would not be so painful.

Also, Dr. Beach stubbornly pursued her. He sent her flowers — a half-dozen roses, with a note that said the florist was running low. He had one of his nurses send her a reminder to get a TB checkup, and in the margin he wrote, "TB stands for Try Beach." I was watching that situation very closely, in spite of my good intentions. I was terrified that I might do something extreme and cold-blooded if she did go out with him. Although I wanted to be a good acting deity, I did not know for sure that I would not inflict some permanent damage on the doctor. I might give him a delirious need to provide his services for nothing, or a permanent condition that would make him pant and slobber like a hound whenever he looked at a golf ball.

I willed myself to remember that the doctor was merely a human being, and he probably did considerable good — I mean real, tangible good — on this earth. Nonetheless, I could not let him near Dorothy. I felt like I was protecting divine interests there. I mean, you just can't have a deity being cuckolded by a blond neurosurgeon.

I mentioned the hard work at Shale Motors because even though I tried not to use God's power while I was managing the dealership, it was much more difficult than you'd think. Since I ordered all the floor-plan cars — cars for the lot and the showroom floor — I wanted to have a reputation for knowing what to order. A customer would come in and look at a chartreuse two-door sedan with air conditioning and no radio, and I'd create an intense desire in him to purchase a green car without a radio. Most of the time it worked. "I don't know why," one customer said, "but I'm just plain sick and tired of music." I guess not everybody had a will as strong as Dorothy's.

I ordered weird cars on purpose so it would seem like I was a genius, buying odd combinations of options that our customers clearly desired before they ordered them. So we sold more and more cars from our lot, and the special orders declined alarmingly. Mr. Shale liked special orders because that was future business, but sales of floor-plan cars tripled in the first few months I was on the job. It was hard for him to complain about that.

"You sure know your cars," he said.

"I know what people want," I told him.

He smiled approvingly. "I hope it keeps up like this, because we don't have a lot of orders."

"It'll keep up. I really do know what people want."

I created a desire to buy a new car in everybody who walked in the front door. This, too, had unexpected consequences. I was in the bathroom one day when one of Cherry's customers, a particularly mindless and susceptible fellow in his mid-twenties, came in to pick up his new van, a maroon Caravan. Cherry gave him the instruction manual, took his check, got him to sign his contract, patted him on the back, and sent him out the door without giving him the keys. I came out of the men's room just as he was coming back in. You can guess what happened. I manufactured a nearly sexual desire in him to buy a new metallic blue Caravan we'd just unloaded from the truck. I didn't know he was Cherry's customer (I thought I knew all of Cherry's customers, since he almost never sold a car without my special help). The poor fellow hadn't even started his new car, hadn't put an inch on the odometer, and he was crouching over Cherry's blue book trying to trade his "old" Caravan in on a new one. Cherry couldn't believe what was happening.

"But you've got a new one," he said.

"I don't want that one anymore."

"But — but —"

"I'm tired of that one."

"You haven't driven it yet."

"I want that blue one."

"Well, I can't just cancel our deal. We've signed all the papers. It's a done —"

"Did I say anything about canceling anything? I want to trade my van in." The man was in a hurry. He panted like a bridegroom listening through the bathroom door while his new wife removed her pantyhose. I let the unfortunate fellow go ahead and make the deal, even though it cost him eighteen hundred dollars, the difference between a new van and an old one, even if the old one hadn't been driven yet.

Of course, I understood that using my will in such a way wasn't fair. But business is business, as Mr. Shale always says, and my mother and father taught me at an early age that the world isn't fair. Not in any real sense of that word. I figured that at least a portion of being a good acting God had to include being like the God I knew and loved before I had the power, and there wasn't anything particularly fair about him. I'd hate to try and figure out God's version of fairness, to tell you the truth. Anyway, it didn't take long for me to accept the idea that occasionally I would behave in mysterious ways, no matter how much I wanted to be good.

I guess you could say there was more than one kind of good I wanted to be: I wanted to be a good acting deity, but I also needed to be a good general manager of Shale Motors. And that meant selling cars, lots of cars. I wanted to be a good husband and father. Not all those things fit under one idea of good. Anybody knows that. Sometimes you can't be a good husband and a good father. When I brought Yee home, the girls simply loved him. I made them happy, and I knew I was being a good father. But I shouldn't have to tell you what sort of husband I was being. And hell, I know Dorothy was a good student. She spent just about every waking hour studying her lessons and trying to excel in every subject. But this took her away from me and the children. So she was a good student but a less than outstanding wife and mother. Maybe you think I'm being extreme to describe her in that way. What would you call a woman who leaves her family and makes plans to give up her children? Even if she remained a weekend mother, she would not be there to care for the girls in all the most important ways. And she would not be a wife to me at all. But you just know there are sociologists and psychologists out there who would say this is what she needs and so it's good.

You can't be a good God and a good salesman at the same time, either — I guess I already proved that.

If there was only one idea of good it would be easy living life, wouldn't it? You wouldn't have to argue over wine, or the placement of a stick of furniture, or the timing of an egg. You'd just know what was good, and everybody else would know what was good, and that would be that. There'd be no reason for parliaments or schools or books or documentary films, or almost anything at all. Just a list of what's good. And maybe, conversely, a list of what's bad. You wouldn't need commercials or magazine ads or lawyers or judges or even congressmen and senators. You'd need teachers to show you how to read and somebody to keep the list up to date, since the world is always changing — when a person developed a new wine there'd have to be somebody to tell us if it went on the good list or the bad. Think about how easy life would be, though, if we had such a list, and if we really *knew* what was good and what was bad. I know there are pea-brained people out there who think the world really is like that, but that doesn't mean it's a crazy idea — it's only crazy to think that's the way things are. There's nothing wrong with the idea. It sure would make it easier to be acting God.

So while I waited to hear from Chet, I was becoming the best general manager in the history of the automobile business. Sales at Shale Motors doubled in the first five weeks I was on the job. At seven weeks they had tripled. I realized I'd have to slack off a little bit, get back to more realistic numbers. Otherwise, when God took his power back, I'd be in the position of having to duplicate sales figures no mere mortal could possibly match. The sudden decline in sales might look like I'd lost my touch. You can get fired under circumstances like that. In sales, just as in professional athletics, what owners want to know is "What have you done for me lately?"

But it was very difficult to cut back on sales. The idea got caught in my larynx and choked me. I spent a few days letting customers walk out; I let Cherry scare people into keeping their old car another five years. Then I suddenly remembered what Chet had said about absolute power and how it works. I knew if I wanted to, I could decree an unchangeable condition with the power, and then when God returned to the job, it would be one of those items he could not change. At least I thought I might be able to do that. I wasn't sure what would happen if I messed with God's power in that way, but I gave the command anyway. I created the greatest general manager in the history of the business world — me. I commanded that I would have that skill no matter what God did when he decided to come back from vacation and be himself again. Then, just to insure myself against failure, I willed an unlimited amount of cash into my attic. I figured that if I didn't need to spend it, it would serve as added insulation. I said a little prayer, hoping God didn't mind.

With that done, Shale Motors grew and prospered, and Mr. Shale became, in less than three months, a rich man. And of course, although my marriage was crumbling around my ears, I wasn't doing so badly myself.

❋

One day in the beginning of that third month, around noon, Dottie came into my office. She looked as if she'd just crawled out of a pile of dirty laundry. Her clothes were wrinkled and stale-looking, and her hair was scattered on top of her head like crabgrass.

"What happened to you?" I said.

"Hide me." She put her hand on her breast and took a deep gasping breath in what I thought was mock fear.

"I really don't have time, Dottie."

"Seriously."

"What?"

"I can't get him to stop." She seemed about to cry.

"What's the matter with you?"

Mr. Shale strolled up to the door behind her.

She smiled at him, then looked at me as if she'd noticed something awkward about him. She nodded, stepped out of the doorway, and leaned on my file cabinet, her hands rubbing her thighs like she was getting ready to try to leap through the opposite wall.

Mr. Shale winked at me and pointed his finger at her. "No flirting with the cuties, now. Back to worky-work. Ay?"

"What?"

He lifted his brows, grinning as if he'd just raked in a huge pot with a pat hand. "Heh-heh. Heh-heh-heh." Then he disappeared from the doorway.

Dottie shuddered. "He won't leave me alone."

"You?"

"Ever since he got his speech back." Her voice trembled. "He's . . . he . . . You've got to help me."

"Are you serious?"

101

She moved to the desk, whispering. "At first I thought it might be nice. I liked it that he —" She stopped, watching my eyes. I realized that she was trying to decide if she really could trust me, so I inserted that notion in her head. She looked at her feet. "Nobody ever expressed much interest in me."

"Oh," I said.

"He was the boss. He . . . I didn't know how to say no to him."

"Well, a bachelor like him —"

"I didn't want to say no at first. He was — he *liked* me. I couldn't get over the fact that he wanted me."

"He's a nice man." I felt completely stupid for saying that. But I was embarrassed that she was so open with me, and I felt truly helpless. I mean, I had given him speech, and in doing so I had apparently unleashed some sort of libertine or satyr. I knew what she was going to say before she said it, and I didn't want to hear it.

"I don't know how to tell you this." She clenched her hands in front of her.

"You don't have to tell me."

"You wouldn't believe — when he . . . when he . . ."

"It's okay. Don't tell me."

"I have to yell 'Touchdown!' right at the — when he's . . ." She stopped and put her hand over her mouth. "He makes me yell 'Touchdown!' when he's having his . . ."

"Good God," I said.

"I have to scream it."

"What'd you go to bed with him for?"

"I couldn't help it."

"You couldn't say no?"

She leaned on the desk. "He was interested in me."

"Why don't you start yelling 'Ball four!' Maybe that will throw him off."

She stopped, looked away.

"I'm sorry," I said. "That was uncalled for."

She sighed. "He forces me now."

"He forces you to yell touchdown?"

"No. He forces me to — to go to bed with him."

"How?"

"He makes these threats." She looked at me with wide-open eyes that seemed swollen and blue. "These insinuations about my job, and the future."

"That's awful."

"I don't know what to do."

"You want me to talk to him?"

She frowned. "Oh, no. He'd fire me for sure."

"I'll do something to fix it up," I said.

"Please, don't — don't do anything that —"

"You have nothing to fear."

"What are you going to do?"

"I'm going to try and find him a female referee with a whistle."

She didn't think it was funny.

"Come on," I said. "I'm just trying to cheer you up. I'll fix everything, I promise." I put my arm around her. I was sure surprised at old Mr. Shale, though. You just never can tell about people, even when you're almost God.

I didn't even know Mr. Shale was a football fan. When I had a chance to think about what Dottie was going through, I was very sad for her. She had such a good heart and she just didn't deserve most of the things that happened to her.

I guess you could also say I felt some guilt, since I had set Mr. Shale loose by giving him back the power of speech. Perhaps I should be blamed for what was happening to Dottie. Although that didn't seem very fair. I thought I was performing a wondrous, kind, human act: to give back the gift of articulate speech. A truly Christlike miracle, if you'll pardon the comparison. It never occurred to me that by tampering with Mr. Shale, I was making a source of anguish and suffering. I wondered if maybe miracles weren't always good — or if sometimes they only seemed good. I mean, what if one of those blind people Christ healed went on to become a serial killer or a child molester? You have to admit, with human beings, anything is possible. If one of them did go on to a chilling criminal career, who would be at fault? You ever thought about that? I didn't see how I could be held responsible for a thing Mr. Shale chose to do, even if he chose to do it because I had restored his sense of power by giving him back his voice. Maybe I was rationalizing everything to get myself out of the noose of responsibility, but it just didn't seem fair that my miracle turned out to be such a pernicious thing. I had enough to feel guilty about already. I hated the idea that even when I was trying to do something wonderful, it turned out badly. Perhaps there was a lesson in that. It was becoming obvious that as long as I didn't do anything at all, I was safe. Maybe that was how to be a good acting God.

I couldn't wait to talk to Chet.

In spite of my fears about actively playing God, I considered putting Mr. Shale back among the speech-impaired. But then I decided I might as well talk to him first, see if I could have any influence without the power. I was pretty important to Mr. Shale at that point, and I suppose a part of me wanted to test the currents of our relationship.

When I went to see him, it was near closing time and he was seated at his desk talking on the phone. He'd removed his suit coat and loosened his tie, and he was stretched back in his chair like the winning candidate on election night. "I'll be right with you," he said.

I sat down, trying to imagine what I'd say to him. Then I realized he was making a reservation for two at some fancy restaurant.

"I want the best wine," he said. "And I want the violinist to pay special attention to us."

Poor Dottie. I pictured her, with her clumsy anxiety, her fear of being embarrassed or saying the wrong thing, sitting in the shadow of some steamy Italian, watching him work the bow on a scarlet violin. One of the things I'd been learning in my reading was how inexpressibly patient women have had to be over the ages. You have to admit, a man can be a pretty odious, snouty thing when he's breathing heavily and craving after a woman. And most of the time, that's what men are doing. Even when a man doesn't want a woman, he'll take one if she looks right.

"That will be fine," Mr. Shale said. He put the phone back in its cradle and sat up to face me. "Well?"

"Going out to dinner, huh?"

He cleared his throat and moved some papers on his desk. "You made some good deals today."

"A long day." I sighed. I wanted to create some sort of camaraderie, a kind of executive fellowship. After all, we'd been constructing the most successful Dodge dealership in the Midwest, and I had been the major factor in its growth.

After a pause, Mr. Shale said, "So what did you want?"

"Well." I didn't know what to say. "I was going to tell you about this woman I know." I narrowed my eyes and presented him with a leering smile. "I mean a fantastic woman."

"Some other time." I think he was nervous. He thought I was going to tell him about one of my sexual experiences. This made him very reluctant to have his face where I could see it.

"She's interested in you."

"Who?" Now he could look at me.

"You don't know her yet. She's terrific — sexy, athletic. She loves football."

"Well," he said, spreading his arms, "set it up."

"It's got to be tonight."

I thought I had won. But he slowly shook his head, never taking his eyes off me. "Sorry, old sport. I've got plans tonight."

"She's real anxious to meet you."

"I don't ever go on blind dates, anyway. I'd have to meet her first."

There was a long, uncomfortable silence. Then I said, "You taking Dottie out? You have a dinner date with Dottie?"

"Yes."

"So you two are dating."

"We're just going to talk," he said. He stood up and stacked the papers on the corner of his desk. "She's good company."

"It's none of my business," I said. "I just heard you making some sort of reservation — you know."

"Ah."

"The part about the violin."

He took his jacket from the back of the chair. "I like music when I eat."

"It's not very good for talking."

He came around the desk, his jacket slung over his shoulder. He wore a yellow polka-dot tie that hung loosely over the bulge of his stomach. When he was directly in front of me, he said, "Well, if you'll excuse me."

"Don't you think it'd be too loud to talk, with a violin and all?"

He laughed. "You go ahead and arrange for me to meet this wonder woman you're talking about. Tell her I'm *very* interested." He waited in front of me. It was clear he wanted to get out of there and I was being rude. "Was there anything else?"

What could I say? "You've got to stop screwing Dottie"? He was my boss. I'd have to work for him long after God had his power back. I realized I had been foolish to think I could do anything on my own to help Dottie. She needed God.

I was sitting there in Mr. Shale's shadow, trying to think of what to say, when Dottie came in. "I filed all the invoices," she said to Mr. Shale. She was smiling, moving with utter resolve and confidence, until she saw the expression on my face. I must have looked like a dog that had had an accident on the rug. She knew I had failed. The bounce went out of her walk so suddenly you'd have thought she was stricken with a sudden pain. "You — are we . . ."

"Just having a chat with my general manager," Mr. Shale said. He reached his hand out as if to say, "Stand up here, boy, and let me pat your back." I stood up under his pudgy paw, and he squeezed me. "And what a general manager he is."

As we left the office, Dottie walked in front of us like a woman on her way to the gas chamber. In her mind, horrifying visions of the evening before her flickered like an old pornographic movie. I watched them get into Mr. Shale's huge customized van — the interior was designed to look like a master bedroom — and considered my options. I knew I could rob him of speech again. Or I could make him sick, like I did to Cherry that first night I was acting God. Or I might stiffen his back a bit, create muscle spasms that would put him down for a week or two. I didn't consider trying to get him to do the right thing by putting the right thing in his head. I was afraid that if Mr. Shale could overrule his feelings with his will, just like Dorothy, it would confirm something about *my* will, and God, that I didn't want to examine too closely. If I had God's power and I couldn't seem to make any human being do a thing he didn't choose to, maybe God, who had God's power, couldn't do anything either. I swear the only success I had had with people so far was to make lots of them go ahead and buy cars. But most of those left home wanting to buy one in the first place. All I ever did was mess with their taste a bit and then give them a bit of a shove.

I finally decided to try something completely different. Instead of fooling around with Mr. Shale's desires and values, I made it so whenever he looked at Dottie, he would be reminded of a rat or a hamster. She would suddenly seem so repulsive to him that he'd be afraid to touch her. I didn't see how that could do any harm to either of them, and it would sure solve the problem.

That done, I set out for a visit with the girls. And Dorothy.

❀

Dorothy was not glad to see me, but my daughters were. I came up the walk in front of the Herrmann house, and the girls came flying out to meet me. Dorothy stood at the top of the steps with one hand on the railing and the other on her hip. She looked like she was posing for *Soldier of Fortune* magazine. She wore heavy fatigues, a red scarf, a shiny black belt.

"Daddy, Daddy!" Jody Beth hollered.

Claire grabbed me around the knees and would not let go.

I glanced at Dorothy. "You look like you're going out to create some problems for a SWAT team."

"Just some old clothes I threw on."

"Old clothes, huh."

"Something of Dad's."

"I didn't know your father was in combat."

"Don't keep the girls out too late."

"Out," I said. "Out? Can't I come in?"

"We — I'm having company tonight."

"Grandma and Grandpa are going to the movies," Claire said.

My heart fell. It was very quiet for a moment. Claire hugged my knees and Jody Beth pulled on my fingers. Dorothy did not move, and in the gathering darkness it was hard to see her eyes clearly. I could not get a clear image of her thoughts.

"You're going out with Dr. Beach," I said.

"Nooo." She was embarrassed.

It was someone I didn't even know. She was planning to entertain a strange man in her parents' house — a house that was a sort of sanctuary to me, since it had always been one of the enclaves of my family life, and at the time my daughters were actually living there. For her to see another man there was such a complete violation of the private cat-acombs of my life, I was momentarily speechless.

"Daddy, let's go," Jody Beth said. "I'm cold."

"You're entertaining here?" I said. Though I was making a heroic effort to contain my rage, it must have shown in the vibrations of my voice.

"I'm not *entertaining*. I'm just having a school friend over." She let one of her hands drop.

"Do I know her?"

She wouldn't look at me. "It's just a friend."

"But not a her?"

"It's a friend."

"If it's a he, then it's a boyfriend!"

In a calm, almost disinterested voice, Claire said, "Daddy, look." She pointed to the house. From the upstairs window, black smoke un-furled toward the starless sky like a great dark cloth.

"Good Lord," I said. "The house is on fire."

Dorothy looked up and staggered back when she saw what was hap-pening.

I ran up the steps and grabbed her before she fell. "Who's in there?"

"It's on fire!"

"Are your parents in there?" I shook her.

The front door opened and Herta rushed out.

Dorothy screamed, "Mother!"

"Your father," the old woman gasped. "Your father is upstairs."

By the time I dragged Norm out, there was a wall of fire as high and hot as a sunspot. I did not have time to think or exercise my will or even inhale. In fact, I'm not sure I remember everything in its proper order. I know I took Dorothy by the shoulders and told her to stay with the children. Then I remember the smoke, how thick it was, and hot. It choked me before I hit the staircase in the living room. I crawled up the stairs and scooted on my belly to the old man's room. I don't know if he yelled or what. He wasn't in his room, and I was a bit confused about where to look. I remember lying on the carpet, sweating from the heat, my eyes boiling. Then I think he called out. The fire roared like an express train. I rolled on my back and kicked a door in, then Norm was on top of me, his face blackened and wide-eyed.

"My house!" he cried.

I think that's all he said. We literally tumbled down the stairs, then I picked him up and hauled him out of there. In all the smoke and noise, I never saw a single flame inside the house. But it was a spectacular blaze by the time the fire department got there.

I stood with the girls in the grass and watched the house curl up and fall into itself like a paper box. Norm kept thanking me for saving his life, and Dorothy came over and hugged me. She started to say something, but the smoke choked her.

I put my arms around her. "I'm sorry, honey," I said.

The girls crept up behind us, Jody Beth whining and Claire trying to comfort her.

"Why?" Dorothy said. "Why this? Why now?"

Norm came over, shaking his head. "Thirty-one years. Thirty-one goddamned years."

"It's all gone," Herta said. She wiped her eyes with the edge of her skirt, letting her slip blow in the cold breeze like a great flag of surrender and defeat. "Oh, Lord." She dropped down on her knees. I thought she was going to faint. But she stared at the ground in front of her and prayed there in the yellow light, her nylons rolled carelessly around her calves.

I wanted so badly to wave my hand and fix everything, put the house back with a grand miracle, and then smile benevolently on all of them and announce who I was. Of course there was no way I could do that.

It was disconcerting to discover that the earth was going on with its business whether I behaved like God or not. I suppose I knew things could happen without me, but it never occurred to me that things could happen *to* me. The fire blossomed so fast, I didn't have time to be anything more than a terrified, powerless man. If I hadn't been in good shape and moved quickly, I might have died in there. As it was I damn near choked to death on the smoke.

Ironically enough, the fire rescued me. If I had had time to remember the power at my disposal, I am certain I could have stopped it before it did too much damage. Still, Dorothy had intended to welcome another man, a man I did not even know, into that house. They would have been alone in there. I told Dorothy she was lucky the fire happened when it did and not a half-hour or so later.

I was just lucky it happened.

7

In the wake of disaster, one is always prone to introspection, especially when it turns out that one ultimately benefits from the calamity. I benefited far more resoundingly than I realized at first. Dorothy and her parents had to stay with me until they could "make some other arrangements," as Dorothy put it.

The children were coming home, and so was Dorothy.

Now, I had extraordinary empathy for Norm and Herta. I truly knew their pain over their loss. Gone were all those years of growth and change, all those memories bound up in what had been their sacred home. It made me reconsider ever again using the phrase "permanent address." Yet I loved having the children with me again. The sudden loud shouts of laughter and anger, the brief eruptions of intrigue and conflict between them, made the house seem like something other than shelter. I could put up with Norm, even though he still made noises that made me wish I wore a hearing aid. He had settled somewhat since his illness, and the fire sobered him. He talked less and seemed vaguely distracted, as if he were trying to solve some sort of mathematical problem in his head. He had considered death, had acquired the notion of his last day, and it changed him. Something of this filtered into his wife's vision of things: She talked about the past a lot — spent hours doing crossword puzzles and privately questioning the reason for existence.

Dorothy hated the idea of having to come back, and of dragging her parents with her. It was clearly not her idea of freedom and independence. But I found myself happy. My house was full of family, and it wasn't just for a weekend or a brief holiday. It was going to be for a long time. That realization alone was a revelation that heaped me with joy, although clearly it was not appropriate to go around announcing it to everybody in the midst of such anguish.

I did tell Dorothy how I felt. We were sitting in the dining room the night after everybody had settled in, and I said to her, "You can stay as long as you want. I know you don't want to be here, but maybe this will turn out to be good for us."

Her parents had just retreated in search of sleep. They had said goodnight and closed the guest-room door as if Dorothy and I were teenagers and we'd better behave ourselves. Herta believed we were going to set about making things up between us. But I could see by the look on Dorothy's face that there was no reason to be optimistic about our chances. She wasn't angry or nervous or anything, just extremely intense and focused. As if she were waiting for a doctor to come through the door and tell her the results of a biopsy.

"In spite of all that's happened," I said, "I'm glad to have your mom and dad here. Glad I can help. And I confess, in spite of everything, I'm happy you're here, too."

"Right." She puffed madly on a cigarette.

"Relax," I said. "I love you enough not to expect you'll want to stay."

She looked surprised.

"I mean it."

"I'm sorry," she said. "I'm a little mixed up these days."

I felt very contrite for being so happy about everything. So I knew what to say, what she needed to hear.

Sometimes I just wanted to make Dorothy happy, and it really didn't matter about me. That's the truth. Also, I was beginning to realize, oddly enough, how truly different and apart from me she had become. If I could only have gotten over the anger I felt for what she had put me through — for all the days and nights when I was trying to hold everything together and she was fighting me like some sort of spiritual terrorist — I might have found the benevolence to let her have what she thought she needed.

Then again, maybe I wouldn't have found any benevolence in my heart at all. When I thought about how early in our marriage she had turned from me — she left me long before she actually moved out — I felt less zealous about making her happy. In fact, it was easy to make myself feel uncharitable toward her. All I had to do was remember how I had felt during all those muttering nights when she had withdrawn from me as if I reeked with some sort of unbearable stench.

But anger is not the same thing as enmity, even if it feels like that. Sometimes I would look at Dorothy and feel such tenderness my heart ached.

"There are things I want in my life," she said, dousing the cigarette. "I don't know if I can explain it."

"If there was something I could do." I leaned toward her.

"You know, whenever we talk about this, I think I know what I want to say. It's all very clear in my mind. And I look at you, at your eyes, and I just know I can explain it to you, make you understand how I feel. But when I try to say it, I end up saying something else."

"There are things you can't say to me."

"Yes."

"Because you'll hurt me."

"I don't mean to." She reached across the table, put her hand on mine. "It's not your fault."

"What happened?" I said. "What happened to us?"

She stood up, suddenly agitated. "I don't know. I don't know."

"Do you love me?"

"I'm not happy."

We spoke at the same time. She looked at me and felt an exquisite pain in her chest — a mixture of sadness and joy, love and disdain. Then she whispered, "I'm going to bed." She was terrified that I'd want to sleep with her.

"I'll sleep in the den," I said. I uttered those words in the breathless tones of a dying man.

Later that night I was sitting in the kitchen consoling Herta, who could not sleep for fear she would dream about the fire. She could not get it out of her mind: she kept picturing herself in burning nylons, running through her neighbors' yards and screaming. I was trying to convince her that she definitely would not have such a dream, that she wouldn't have a bad dream ever again, when Chet came to the back door and knocked.

"My God," Herta said. "There's a black man at the door."

"It's all right."

"No!" This was a whispered cry.

"What's wrong with you?"

"What's he doing here?"

"He's — there's nothing —"

"And dressed up, too." You'd have thought someone held a gun to her head. "Oh, my God."

"It's all right."

Chet knocked again and tried to peer through the glass. I went to the door and opened it. "Well," I said, "it's been a long time since I saw you."

He went by me into the kitchen. "Been busy."

"With what?"

"Arranging your visit."

I shut the door, wondering what he was talking about. Herta still had that frozen look on her face. "Is she — did you mess up the time again?"

She and Chet said at the same time, "What?"

"Nothing." I sat down.

"Good evening," Chet said to Herta.

"This is Chet. He's a friend of mine," I said.

"Oh." She stood up. "Oh, I see."

"We're just going to have a brief talk," said Chet.

"Excuse me," Herta said, wiping her nose with a napkin. She cleared her throat. "I'll just . . ." She moved around as if she couldn't find her way out, then went into the living room.

"Nice old woman," Chet said.

"I think she thought you were going to kill us."

"I know," he said.

"She's afraid of black people."

"No," he said. "Not really. She's afraid of *any* stranger on the back porch at two o'clock in the morning."

"So what's this about a visit?" I asked.

He seemed to slump a little bit. Then he sat down across from me. "Let's have some coffee."

113

"You really want coffee?"

He frowned, shook his head. It was as if we were bridge partners and I had once again thrown the wrong card. "Of course I want coffee."

I waved my hand and two cups of steaming coffee appeared on the table. "They're both cream and sugar," I said.

He was very disappointed. "I don't want miracle coffee. I hate miracle coffee."

"What?"

"I want real coffee."

"What's the difference?"

"Can't I just have brewed coffee?" He planted his hands in front of him like a child preparing for a siege. "I don't want this stuff."

There was a long pause. I wondered if he could see what I was thinking. It amazed me that he seemed so petulant and human. "Please," he said.

"Oh, what the hell." I went ahead and made fresh coffee. When I was done and we were seated again, across from one another, sipping loudly, I said, "This tastes exactly the same as the miracle stuff."

"It's not the same."

"Okay." I didn't see the point in arguing with him.

After a while he said, "You're going to see heaven."

"Now?"

"Soon."

"I need some advance notice — like a week or so."

He laughed, a slight sound in the back of his throat.

"Should I pack anything?"

"No."

"Nothing at all?"

He shook his head and rolled his eyes. "This is a spiritual journey. What would you pack?"

"How about a camera?"

"You won't need anything."

"Will I be gone long?"

"No. It's a very brief departure."

The word *departure* stabbed something in my chest and I was suddenly very frightened. "I'm coming back, right?"

This really amused him. His laugh was clear and loud, and there was something in it that gave me the most complete sense of satisfaction. Whenever I made him laugh it seemed like a personal triumph, even when I didn't mean to do it. "You probably won't want to stay there," he said.

"I won't?"

"You'll see." He fished a handkerchief out of his pocket and wiped his mouth. "It's not like anything you've heard or imagined."

"Well," I said, "I suppose I could imagine it *now*. Now that I'm —"

"No, you couldn't." He folded the handkerchief neatly on the table in front of him like a tiny bedsheet. "Thanks for the coffee."

"You know, I'm a little surprised that you need to eat and drink."

"I don't. But I like to."

He stood up. I thought he was just going to leave, but he came over to me, put his hand on my shoulder, and said something that stopped my heart. He said, "That fire. That was your doing. You know that."

"What?"

"You started it."

"I did not!" I think I shouted. The inside of my head came to a boil.

"Hey." He put his other hand on my cheek. "Calm down."

"It wasn't me. I know it wasn't."

"You don't know anything," he said.

⁂

You know, I was beginning to see that I had learned more than I wanted to in the brief time that I had been the acting deity. You come to the world as an adult with a certain broad platform of right and wrong upon which, finally, everything you experience comes to be judged. You may not ever put it into words, but it is there nonetheless. In my reading I had listened to the three-thousand-year conversation man has had with himself, and I came to it with my own mind, my own perspective. I learned about love and goodness with an idea of love and goodness in my heart already. Because of that, I came away from my reading without truly understanding either one. You cannot come to a rainbow without understanding what color is. It was only when I applied the power of God to the problem, when I observed my own poor command of love and goodness, that I began to see what almost everyone has refused to see from the beginning.

115

It is true that the world spins with a lot of wonderful things — or at least that's how we see it. We like to identify what's wonderful for ourselves — that's why we create art, make histories, keep old artifacts and objects. It's all an attempt to preserve what we believe is wonderful. Of course, you could have all the wonderful things in the world, every possible ecstasy, rolled up for you at the same moment in time, and every last bit of it would be canceled by only one of the world's significant agonies. Try it if you think I'm wrong. Wait until you are experiencing the greatest joy, the most exquisite pleasure, and then have somebody put a hatpin in one of your eyes. See how long the pleasure lasts. See how long you remember it up against what your eye feels like. And you know it doesn't work the other way around. Once the hatpin's lodged in there, no pleasure or joy in the world will make you forget it.

That's the way with all wonderful things, finally.

You want to know what I learned about love, once I truly examined it? I'll tell you, in one sentence.

LOVE: Love is the most wonderful of all things, and it is because of love that human beings can live day to day and face the gales of pain and suffering the world has to offer, so love enriches existence because it lends it meaning and significance, and people who have never experienced love are truly deprived and no more alive or human than an animal — although animals themselves sometimes experience a thing very much like love — but we are not talking about the same thing for everybody when we say love anyway, since love between brothers and sisters or between a man and his Labrador retriever is different from love between, say, a man and his mistress or his new bride or even sometimes his old bride, though it is nearly impossible to convince anybody that a man in his eighties loves a woman near the same age who he's lived with for half a century, since if you live with any human being long enough you start to get used to her and once that happens, how can you say about what people feel for one another, when they're sitting around predicting each other's behavior and shaking their heads about their partner's old bad habits and annoying traits, that that's love or anything like love, thus even when you have love you don't have it for any permanent length of time since it is destined to end one way or the other, although it is true that some people actually believe they will love their spouse even after they die, forgetting as they do that sometimes a man dies thirty years before his wife and when he does get to see her in eternity he will be young and vibrant and new and handsome and she will be eighty, so it isn't immediately apparent whether or not love lasts longer than our breathing, but even if it doesn't last that long the idea

116

that it might causes people to perpetrate more evil than any other single thing, human or animal, in the universe, and the sad truth is, if we had no love we might live more peaceful lives even though we'd feel like existence was empty and meaningless and we'd never ever speak because there wouldn't be anything to say.

That's what I learned about love.

This is what I learned about goodness:

GOODNESS: Goodness is the opposite of things that cause pain, suffering, decay, destruction, disaster, disease, or great sadness, and since almost everything in the world — love and all other human institutions, ideas, and dreams — causes some sort of suffering or pain or sadness or disease or destruction or decay or disaster at some point or other in the creases of time, goodness is when everybody alive is sleeping and all institutions are closed for the evening, except that some institutions, when they are not doing evil, help alleviate the agony caused by other institutions, and if they were all closed probably some pain and suffering would result, even though only God knows why we need institutions in the first place, since if there were no evil there would be no need for hospitals or orphanages or schools or charities or nursing homes or even perhaps the post office, although goodness certainly ought to include more than a notion of the mere comfort of an absence of evil, by which I mean it should at least involve some ecstasy, if not physical at least spiritual, but ecstasy only enhances the absence of it and creates perhaps another kind of suffering, since when people experience no ecstasy they get fairly irritable and make everybody else's life miserable, or they fear that somebody *is* experiencing ecstasy and do everything in their power to stop it right this instant and in the process create an even better argument for the idea that goodness is most likely to take place when everybody is asleep, so perhaps goodness is diminished by each person who's awake, unless that person is contributing to the welfare of himself or others —making sure that that contribution is life-enhancing and produces only aesthetic, abstract, nonphysical things, such as art, or a good book, or maybe a symphony, since if there is any other type of contribution it is bound to include either some suffering or some other sort of evil because any action has reverberations in the stream of things and you can't offer a chicken leg to a starving man without increasing his awareness of what he has not got and without therefore increasing his suffering in the very act of presenting him with succor, not to mention the fact that somebody had to kill a chicken in order for you to have the leg to offer in the first place, although most people would agree it's okay to kill animals as long as it is done humanely, with a view toward goodness, since goodness is desirable and the goal of all reasonable men and women although none of them can agree on what goodness is, since most of the world's great evil is done by people who mean well, and only one human being in a million would be willing to admit that he or she is opposed to goodness even when they prove to everyone around them except themselves that they are pernicious and greedy little roaches who think goodness is what they could have if only they had enough cash.

Finally and sadly, I am a human being. I love my wife and family. I want to be good and do wonderful things. And unbeknownst to me, my will — my id — took up arms against a sea of troubles. In the process, who was to blame for the great fire? I ask you. Who was to blame?

I sold a car years ago to a former prisoner of war. He told me something I've never forgotten. He said that when he was married the first time, he and his wife used to make Christmas a sort of sacrament for their love. Upon the altar of bright lights, decorations, cakes and pies and family visits, they would consecrate their marriage. Each year he and his wife made a huge paper chain out of brightly colored construction paper and hung it around the ceiling of their family room. It was always the first step they would take toward Christmas, so eventually it took on the significance of a religious ceremony.

They had been married for eight years when he was sent to Vietnam, and six months after he left her he was shot down over Hanoi. He was imprisoned for five years.

"You know," he said, "whenever Christmas came, it was worse torture than anything the VC did to me. I've never felt such pain — it hurt inside and out." He was almost in tears when he told me this. "I missed my wife so much. Then, the last year I was there, they started feeding us better. I knew I was going home. About two weeks before Christmas that last year, I got the first mail from the States. The first contact in almost six years. My wife had divorced me."

He started crying and I shuffled papers, mortified that this man who had suffered so much was grieving publicly. We were at the front desk of the showroom, and I don't even remember how we came to be talking about this. Maybe it was because he had seen the yellow paper chain Mr. Shale puts up every year. Anyway, he wiped his face with a tissue I gave him, then he went on. He said, "That last year, they let us have a Christmas dinner, and you know what they had hung up around the ceiling? A goddamned paper chain. Everybody else was so happy to be eating real food for once, but I couldn't take my eyes off that paper chain. It hurt me physically to look at it."

Now, I ask you. Was anything that happened to him good? How could a thing so simple as a paper chain be evil? But you see, it caused him unbearable pain just to look at it. Does it matter how he felt when he and his wife put up their chain, kissed under it, and drank eggnog to celebrate their joy in each other if the memory of that joy became the source of ineluctable and lasting agony?

I ask you.

8

I suppose it must be fairly easy for you to see by now that being acting God means knowing some truths we'd perhaps rather not think about. It must sound as if I'm a very bitter, if not downright cynical, man. I trust there is no amount of generosity, even in the best soul, that can obviate the fact that my text to this point has seemed to emphasize the negative — as if one has a choice in the number and variety of truths he uncovers. I know I have a choice concerning what I reveal. Make no mistake, I have anguished over the issue considerably. It is not easy acting like God, and that's the truth, strange as it may seem. But if I painted a picture less accurate than the one I perceived when I had God's power, what sort of acting God would I be? And who can doubt the perceptions of a man with God's power? I certainly didn't.

After Chet left that night, I sat in the kitchen listening to the refrigerator snick on and off until dawn. When the sun began to leak over the blue sill of the window above the sink, I went in the den and lay down on the couch in there. I felt empty and terribly alone. The mere fact of sight, of my ability to see the far wall or the ceiling, nauseated me. I knew I wouldn't sleep, but I closed my eyes anyway.

I could not get my mind off what I had done. Nor could I escape the colossal irony of the whole thing. I had God's power and no control over it. Can you possibly imagine how powerless you would feel in such a case?

As I lay there pondering my predicament, I came to know what had happened to Dottie and Mr. Shale on their ill-fated dinner date. All I had to do was think of them, and their entire evening played before my tired eyes like a three-dimensional movie. As you've probably guessed by now, their date didn't go very well. I wouldn't call it a tragedy, but it *was* a disaster.

Mr. Shale tried to overcome the fact that Dottie looked like a rodent. He thought he was just getting to know her better, beginning to see her in a different light, as most of use eventually do with people we get close to. It probably helped that he couldn't really identify what particular rodent she looked like. It was just an odd sort of feeling he had when he looked at her face that made him want to avoid kissing her. He thought he might kiss her in the dark, but not anywhere where he could actually see her tiny beady eyes and little snout of a nose. He found himself concentrating on her body, which he liked very much.

Dottie looked forward to the dinner with roughly as much enthusiasm as you and I might greet the news that we are going to need gall bladder surgery. So she suggested they go somewhere first. She knew there was always the possibility that fate would intervene and a car accident or a mugging might save her. She suggested a movie.

"I've already made reservations at the restaurant." Mr. Shale was nearly whining.

"They won't care. That place is never crowded anyway."

"I don't like movies."

"Everybody likes movies."

They were in Mr. Shale's van, waiting at a very long red light. Cars passed like electrical currents in front of them. Mr. Shale leaned over, his eyes still focused on the light, and said, "I like football."

Dottie felt her heart skip. "Why don't we go bowling?"

"Bowling?"

"That would be fun."

The light changed. As the van inched forward in traffic, Mr. Shale considered Dottie at a bowling alley, in the bright lights, jumping up and down like a ferret in front of the teetering pins. "Nah. I don't want to go bowling."

"Well, let's do something."

"You're really not hungry?" he said.

"I had a late lunch."

There was a pause while both of them watched the road, the passing signs and neon arrows. Then Dottie said, "What did you like to do when you were a boy?"

"I liked to play football."

"What else?"

"Pinball. Pool."

"You had an active childhood." She could not help the sarcastic tone of her voice, but she was reasonably certain that Mr. Shale missed it. He smiled at the road and appeared to caress the steering wheel.

"That was all a long time ago," he said.

"Yes."

"I went roller-skating once."

"Well, let's do that. I love to roller-skate."

"You do?"

Dottie was truly excited. She thought roller-skating was the best idea since relativity. For this night at least, he would be so exhausted, so bruised from the tumbles he was sure to take, that she would escape his hands. There was something else behind her excitement, though, and it made me sad to realize it. She hoped that if she and Mr. Shale did something other than sleep together, it might bring him to like her truly. If he saw her as a person and cared for her, she thought she could tolerate his odd sexual tastes and perhaps even come to feel a certain affection for him as well. After all, he did actually want her, and as far as she knew no one else ever had.

So they went to the Champaign-Urbana roller rink, a round, flat building in the middle of a cornfield. The place was crowded with the sort of people you see in roller rinks: one or two attractive young girls, a thousand pockmarked teenagers of both sexes, all of whom looked as if they were the product of five centuries of inbreeding, and more than a few middle-aged people in checked clothing, who appeared to have insisted that somebody push their pants up into the crack of their ass before they left home.

Dottie rented skates for the two of them, and before long Mr. Shale was clutching her arm, begging her not to let go and trying to keep from flying backwards to the floor. They stayed to the outside of the rink, where beginners clung to the rails and walked on their skates.

They made it all the way around to the opening in the railing, where Mr. Shale let go of Dottie, went through, and stopped himself against a brick pillar. Dottie almost went past, but she caught the railing.

"Well, gee," Mr. Shale said. "That was fun."

Dottie didn't say anything. She noticed sweat on his forehead. He concentrated on keeping his knees locked in place. He was certain that if he didn't move either leg, he would remain standing.

"What a thrill," Mr. Shale said.

"You're not going to quit, now."

"I shouldn't overdo it," he said. "I've had a stroke, you know."

"Oh," she said. "I'm sorry. I forgot your age."

"Well, it's not my age," he said, insulted. He pushed off and moved unsteadily to the railing on the other side of her. "I guess I can go around one more time." He hated himself instantly for saying that. He wanted to stop skating. He did not want to skate ever again. As soon as he had stood up with the wheels under his feet he had known he did not like it and he would never like it. He did not know what was a polite and reasonable time to skate, so he could not look forward to a courteous exit. Nor could he put his life in Dottie's hands for an indefinite period. He needed to know how long he was going to have to endure this peril.

"Only one more time around?" Dottie said, feigning disappointment. She was already trying to think of something else to do for the rest of the evening.

The problem was, of course, that Dottie wasn't much better at this than Mr. Shale. She had lied to him about knowing how to skate and now she was busy facing the consequences. She was afraid that if he noticed what a bad skater she was, he would know she was only stalling against his gridiron advances, and she would once again face the dilemma of choosing between unemployment and football with the boss.

"How many times do you normally go around?" Mr. Shale said.

"You don't usually count. You just skate."

"Well, once or twice should about do it, don't you think?"

So they stumbled and tramped and stalled around the rink while Billy Joel music assaulted the walls. Dottie gained more and more confidence on her wheels, but Mr. Shale most definitely did not. The second time around he said, "I'm keeping you from having any fun."

"No, you're doing fine."

"Don't let me fall," he said.

"I won't."

"I really don't want to fall."

Just as he said that, Mr. Shale's feet left the floor. He was in the air for what seemed like a very long time. When his soft, prosperous rump came down like a great bag of peat, his tongue popped out and a sound like an infant's sneeze escaped his throat.

"Did you hurt yourself?" Dottie asked.

"I bit my tongue."

He struggled to his feet, the skates scurrying back and forth under him. "Is it bleeding?"

"Let me see." She reached for his flailing arms.

"I hope I'm not bleeding." His voice shook. Then he went down again, this time on his stomach. In Dottie's efforts to stop him, she got too close, and when he landed at her feet she accidentally skated over a small pinch of flesh on his thigh.

"Ouch! Jesus Christ!" he shouted.

"I'm so sorry." Dottie felt as though she had attacked him. "Let me help you."

"This is dangerous." He got to his knees and took a deep breath. People skated awkwardly around him. He was like a big stone in a small stream.

"Need some help?" somebody asked as he went past.

"We're fine," Dottie said.

"Why don't you do something else with your hair?" Mr. Shale said.

"Pardon?"

"With it fixed that way you look like a hamster." He struggled to his feet, grabbed the railing again, and steadied himself. He didn't care about much of anything just then.

Dottie left him there and skated smoothly to the other side of the rink. The hell with him, she thought. She would skate by herself, and when he was gone she'd call a taxi and go home.

Mr. Shale felt terrible for saying that about her hair. When the pain in his leg subsided, he worked his way around the rink to her and took hold of her arm again.

"I'm sorry."

She didn't say anything.

"We'll skate a while longer," he said, thinking that would placate her.

Gradually they regained their composure. Mr. Shale still clutched her arm, but except for the fact that he didn't think his hips would stay correctly joined, he actually began to feel less threatened by the hard floor beneath him. By the time they were skating arm in arm with some confidence, Dottie realized that she had to go to the bathroom.

This particular establishment had bathrooms right off the rink. You skated in to take care of business, and when you were done you skated back out. Unfortunately, the bathrooms were at the far end of a long, wide hall. Dottie and Mr. Shale passed the hall several times before Dottie got the nerve to ask if they might sally down the corridor. "I've got to go down this hall," she said, pulling gently on Mr. Shale's arm.

He resisted at first; then, fearful of losing his footing, he turned with all his weight and headed in the direction of the hall. He swung his outside foot forward and leaned into it. Dottie went with him.

There was a very slight incline toward the bathrooms. Dottie and Mr. Shale clung to each other, side by side, so they looked like a happy couple having their picture taken, except the whole scene was moving at about thirty miles an hour.

The back wall came at them, two doors getting larger, faster and faster.

Dottie yelled, "I have to go to the ladies' room!"

Mr. Shale said, "What?"

"The ladies' room!"

"Which one is it?" Mr. Shale screamed. He could not bring himself to let go of Dottie, so he veered to the left and they both disappeared through the left-hand door.

Unfortunately for Dottie, they were in the men's room. Clutching each other and out of control, they sped past six or seven men standing at the urinals and zoomed toward the back wall.

"Push off!" Mr. Shale hollered.

They hit the wall doing at least thirty-five miles an hour, so it was not very easy to reverse direction. Dottie twisted her little finger and bruised her elbow. Mr. Shale cut his lip, cracked a rib, and jammed three fingers on his left hand. But they stayed up. Together they ricocheted off and started back the way they had come. As they passed the urinals for the second time, the men there cheered.

When they got outside, Dottie was so humiliated that she pushed herself away from Mr. Shale. As he grabbed for her, his eyes tiny with fear and red as a pig's, he disappeared backward through the other door.

"Nooooooooooooooooooooooo!" he screamed. It sounded as though he'd been thrown down a mine shaft.

Dottie found him lying on his back in the midst of a crowd of indignant women, waving his arms and legs like an insect.

After that, Mr. Shale did not think it would be discourteous to take Dottie home and call it a night. It was a horrible date for both of them, to be sure. But I figured it must have served its purpose. It didn't seem likely that Mr. Shale would want to go out with Dottie ever again.

⁂

The following Monday, two days after my visit from Chet, I dragged myself off to work like a man going to his own execution. I did not sleep all day Sunday, and in spite of the apparent concern of everyone, including Dorothy, I could not force myself to eat. I tried to concentrate on what I decided was the one good thing in this life: my family. I had made up my mind I was simply not going to act like God anymore. Even so, I was terrified about what my unconscious mind might be up to.

I arrived at Shale Motors expecting to see Dottie in a pretty miserable state. I was prepared to console her by mentioning that Mr. Shale would probably leave her alone from now on. When I arrived, however, Dottie wasn't there.

You wouldn't expect that a person with God's power could be surprised so many times by so many things.

"She quit," said Mr. Shale.

"What?"

"Saturday night, after our da— after our talk." He limped toward his office.

"What happened?" I said. I knew I was going to have to pretend I was hearing everything for the first time.

"We went to the restaurant, and outside —" He turned to face me, his hand pushing on his hip as if he'd just set down a huge basket of laundry. "We were mugged outside the restaurant."

126

"You were?"

"I fought them off, but it frightened Dottie so." He shook his head.

"You fought them off."

He held up his swollen left hand, pointed to the cut lip. "It was a hell of a fight."

I couldn't help myself. I said, "You didn't go roller-skating?"

The skin on his face tightened. "What?"

"I thought you went roller-skating."

"You've talked to Dottie?"

There was a pause. The look of panic on his face was so pathetic, I let him off the hook. "She mentioned something about trying to get you to go."

I could tell he was terribly disturbed. A part of him disliked the notion that Dottie had been planning all along to go roller-skating. He had believed it was his suggestion and had felt immeasurable guilt because of the trouble he'd caused.

"She didn't mention roller-skating," he said. "After I ran off the muggers, she started crying."

"She must have been upset."

"She said she was going to move back to Mattoon or someplace like that."

"And she quit, just like that?"

"Just like that." He opened the door to his office. "We've got lots of work to do, young man."

"You want me to talk to her?"

"No," he said, too loud. "She quit without notice and that's that."

"I liked her."

"Run an ad," he said. "Do that."

"Maybe —"

He leaned toward me, his voice very low and almost threatening. "Run an ad."

"Okay," I said. "I'll run an ad."

Now, what would you do? I liked Dottie, and you and I both know what she would have been doing if I hadn't given Mr. Shale back his speech: answering the phones at Shale Motors and bothering me about lunch. This was truly one of my creations. I knew I had to do something for her. I made up my mind I was going to fix Mr. Shale, too.

So there I was, only hours after resolving never to use the power again, preparing to mess around with circumstances once more. I felt like a man about to jump off a twenty-story building.

But I had to do something. This was my fault.

If I was going to fix everything, I knew I needed to be extremely careful. Remembering Chet's warning about consequences, I tried to consider all of the possible permutations of the options open to me. I made a list.

Option I: Make Mr. Shale and Dottie forget their date.

Necessary actions:
1. Fix various broken bones, bruises, and abrasions.
2. Reinvent Saturday's date so that it included things Dottie could stand.
3. Do something (I wasn't sure what) about all the people who saw the roller-skating fiasco, including everyone those people told about it. (It didn't seem safe not to consider this action. I was fairly certain that the story had reached the suburbs of Cleveland by Sunday.)
4. Either create muggers who actually attacked Mr. Shale or do something about the two or three hundred people Mr. Shale had probably already told about his heroics.
5. Reduce the receipts at the roller rink by at least two tickets. Change the numbers, by two digits, on all the tickets sold after Dottie and Mr. Shale arrived at the rink. Reduce the receipts on the skate rentals by two.
6. Invent tickets or receipts (or some such thing) for whatever activity I invented as a stand-in for roller-skating.

Possible complications:
1. I'd miss somebody who saw it or someone who heard about it. (Even though the odds were thirty-five million to one Dottie and Mr. Shale would never run into such a person, I was fairly certain that with my luck they would. Someone might even have a home video of the entire calamity.)
2. Although Dottie and Mr. Shale would forget what happened, the whole event would lodge in their subconscious mind and cause untold anxieties and subliminal agonies. (They might develop warts in the most unnatural places, or inexplicable terror of tiny wheels. Maybe they'd project their hostility toward roller skates and form a fringe group whose mission is to oppose the automobile, railroad, busing, and trucking industries.)
3. I would be uncreating an event, so it would then become something that did not happen. The story would continue to be told

128

by those who had seen it, and since it hadn't really happened, they would be lying. Thus, the story would eventually grow into an urban myth which would get told and retold for generations, and I would make a significant contribution to the vast horde of lies that already governed the earth.

I know you might think that eyewitnesses who recounted the event wouldn't really be lying, since they had actually seen it happen. But what is a lie but a thing people believe that just isn't true? There are people all over this country who say Elvis is alive. The truth is he's dead and buried. But if it ever came to light that he actually was alive, then there would instantly be people all over this country who believe he is really dead. It doesn't matter what people have seen or not seen, or even what they say or don't say. What matters is how much people need a lie to believe in.

Option II: Make Mr. Shale love Dottie and give up his curious sexual predilections. Make Dottie willing to give him another chance.

Necessary actions:
1. Put the power to the test. Use it at full throttle on both of them. Make Mr. Shale see a young Elizabeth Taylor when he looks at Dottie; make Dottie see a youthful Paul Newman. Give Mr. Shale a genetic need to hear Dottie's laughter.
2. Make Mr. Shale willing to forget the episode at the skating rink and admit that he lied a little bit about what really happened.
3. Make Dottie want to save Mr. Shale from himself. Give her a sense of her own worth for giving him one more chance to be human.
4. Give Mr. Shale a personality.

Possible complications:

Well, maybe you know what I'm going to say. The only real complication was, of course, that I had no way of knowing if the power would work under those circumstances. After all, I had made Dorothy love me so much it gave her heartburn, but she still wanted to leave me. She still wished to date other men, explore the fine new world of an independent, self-actualized woman. I knew I'd be taking a hell of a chance if I messed around with what Dottie or Mr. Shale *wanted*. You might say my whole history as acting God, up to that point, had been spent trying to make one damn human being do what I wanted. Except for starting big fires, making people sick, accidentally killing them, and making them buy cars, I was a pretty poor substitute for an all-powerful deity, I can tell you that.

❋

A few weeks later I came home, still worrying about Dottie and what I might do to help her, and Norm was sitting in my favorite black leather reclining chair, reading George Garrett's *Death of the Fox.*

"That's a great book," I said.

"I know." He put it down next to him in the chair. "I've been waiting to talk with you."

"What's the matter?"

"I think we should settle something."

"Okay."

"About rent."

"Oh, forget that —" I said, and at the same time he said, "I've given you a lot of things."

I didn't have the heart to tell him that not one of the things he had given me was usable and that some of them had still been wet when I got them.

"I think it would be unfair of you to require us to pay rent."

"I don't require it," I said.

There was a pause. He had the ability to recognize a great book when he saw one, but it didn't help him any to be reading it. He had virtually no consciousness of how others feel. Nor would he ever forget that I had told Dorothy that he made me sick.

"I never expected that you'd pay rent," I said.

He picked up the book, an officious frown on his face, and found his place in it. Then he settled back and cleared his throat.

"Where's Dorothy?" I asked.

"It's not my turn to watch her." He didn't look up from the book.

"Hey," I said.

He turned a page.

"You might try and be a little more polite."

"This is a great book," he said. "My second time through it. I recommend it to you."

"Thanks," I said. I went up the stairs, trying to control my anger. It was rude of him, but disliking him as I did, I didn't think it would be very Godlike to remind him whose house he was festering in.

I could not find Dorothy or the children anywhere. Herta was stretched on her bed snoring. I stood in the doorway and listened. There was a slight whistle to it, as if she held a little toy siren between her teeth. I felt sorry for her. She had to live with Norm and try to maintain some sort of dignity. It exhausted her. She might as well have been married to a German shepherd.

I went to my room and lay down on the bed. I needed to collect myself, get some sort of inventory of my circumstances. In spite of my apparent options and the brief catalogue of possible outcomes and problems, I was as confused as ever. I knew I could recall past events; I had no idea if I could change them. My apprehension increased as the days turned into weeks and the event receded further into the past.

You have to admit it's a fair idea to believe that God could change events if he wanted to, right? What with all that power and the world being his apple. But I was so afraid to do anything. I didn't have as firm a stage presence as God, I guess.

I don't know how long I lay there considering my problem. I might have dozed off a bit. But gradually I became aware of a noise out in the hall. It wouldn't have bothered me, except it was the sort of furtive noise you sometimes hear on the stairs when you know somebody is sneaking up or down. One of the steps squeaked, and then it was very quiet.

Herta's chirping snore continued down the hall. I got off the bed, tiptoed to the door, and cracked it open very slightly.

There, his shoes in his hands, creeping up the stairs like a late-returning husband, was Norm. He headed for Herta's room, taking infinite care not to wake her. From where I stood, I could not see him once he went in there, so I had to concentrate on it and bring the picture to my imagination. When he was finally next to her, he paused, watching her sleep. He blinked his eyes, put the shoes down on the floor by the bed, then very carefully sat down next to her. I thought he might start to cry, the way his eyes looked. He reached out a bony, crumpled hand and placed it on her shoulder, very gently, as if he were afraid the touch might break it. Then he said, "I love you, honey."

Her snoring continued with the same rhythm and intensity.

You know, people would probably be happier if they just said such things to each other when they were both awake. Norm settled down next to his wife and fell asleep.

I went and lay down on the bed again. It occurred to me that perhaps I had not told Dorothy how much I loved her. Oh, I'd said it often enough, but maybe I'd never convinced her. Maybe I'd never been clear about what I meant. I remembered all the times I'd lain awake, watching her face as she slept. I'd break down crying, I was so happy to have her there next to me. And later, after our troubles began, I'd wake up and touch her hand in the darkness to reassure myself that she was still with me. Then I'd weep with sadness at the thought of losing her, though I still felt profoundly lucky to be there next to her, even feeling pain as I did. Maybe a part of my rage came from a secret belief that she was somehow aware of all those veiled moments in the dark while she slept. How could she have known how much being with her meant to me? I don't think she ever understood when I tried to tell her. She just believed I was jealous. But it wasn't jealousy, it was desire. I don't mean passion, although that too was always on my mind. I mean *need*. I needed to be with her. I loved her with all my heart. I didn't want her to stay home and not have any fun. I didn't want her to refuse friend-ships and opportunities I'd have myself. I wanted her to refuse those things because *I* refused them. I had no real friends. I had no thrilling life away from home. My life *was* home and the children and Dorothy. Work was just a way of putting food in our mouths and allowing for survival, so we could be together and enjoy our love as much as possi-ble in the terribly brief time we had on this earth. How could love be anything less?

When Norm leaned over and put his hand on Herta's shoulder and said he loved her, it meant nothing, because she was sound asleep and snorting like a water buffalo. That expression of love was for himself, not for her. And now Dorothy was looking to express herself. She was going to forget me and perhaps even the children — she was willing to give up her sense of *us* — and explore the big world without her fam-ily. That was, finally and sadly, what she was up to.

Why didn't that entitle me to a little rage?

※

132

Just before dinner, Dorothy came back with Jody Beth and Claire. I had given up thinking about what to do, so I was in the kitchen cutting up carrots and mushrooms.

"Where'd you go?" I asked when the girls finished squeezing my neck.

"Out," Dorothy said. There was a discernible note of reluctance in her tone, as if I were a prying neighbor.

"Where?"

"Just out."

"Where out?"

"We saw a doctor, Daddy." Claire was very excited.

Jody Beth said, "He had a white coat."

"One of the children sick?" I said.

"Look," Dorothy said. "I couldn't get my father to stay with them, and Mother was sleeping."

"Who's sick?"

"Nobody's sick."

"Oh," I said. It was all there in my mind after that — my wife, my two daughters, and Dr. Beach.

"I couldn't get out of it," Dorothy said. She sat down at the table and lit a cigarette.

"Go in the other room and play," I said to the children.

Claire turned to go, but Jody Beth said, "I don't want to."

So naturally Claire said, "Me either."

"Well, go to your room, then." I admit the tone of my voice was not very kind.

"You don't have to take it out on them," Dorothy said.

I leaned down and looked into Claire's eyes. "Go upstairs and wake Grandpa, okay?"

"Okay." They both ran out of the room.

I turned to Dorothy and said, "So it was a date."

"It was coffee. That's all."

"With good old Bart the wonder doctor."

"His name is not Bart."

"That's what I call him."

"Anyway, it wasn't a date."

"With *my* children!"

It was as if Dorothy wanted to drag my whole family into her crisis — take the children, too, on her freedom ride. Leave me completely alone.

"You know," she said, "I feel like your daughter sometimes. You're so parental." She waved her hand with the cigarette, looked out the kitchen window.

"You know what I am?" I moved over next to her. My heart was beating so fast I thought it might explode. "Do you want to know what I am?"

She started to say something, but I froze her, I stopped her cold. Her face was turned up to me, her eyes wide, and I turned the power on her. I took away her capacity for speech.

She reached up and placed her hand on her throat.

"Do you know what I am?" I was very loud.

She slowly nodded, terror in her eyes. I loved her so much, I hated myself for making her fear me. It did something to me to see her so frightened. If it hadn't been for that, I might have told her I was God. I might have announced I was the deity and then created some sort of blight in her bowels, I was so angry. But I gave her her speech back, wiped away any fear, and walked out of the room. You just can't let anybody see God in tears, you know?

I went up to the bedroom — our bedroom. I had not slept well in a long time. I was pretty well sick of being human, much less acting God. I might have thought seriously about getting off the world altogether, except I loved my family too much to do that. I fell on the bed and slept through dinner.

I was surprised to see Dorothy standing over me when I woke up later that night. The light was on and she was in her robe, sipping a cup of coffee.

"What's the matter?" I said.

"You didn't come down to dinner."

"I'm surprised it got made. I know you wouldn't do it." I sat up.

"Mother made it. She says you cut the carrots wrong."

I rubbed my eyes, trying to clear my mind.

"You were very angry tonight," Dorothy said.

I looked up at her. She passed the cup to me and I took a sip.

"I'm sorry." She paused. I sipped the coffee, listening to the faint drone of the TV downstairs. Then she said, "About today."

134

"You're sorry?"

"Yes. It won't happen again."

I know my face must have changed colors. I was so glad to hear her say that. "You mean we're finally going to get through with all this?" I set the coffee on the nightstand and moved toward her with open arms. I was beginning to cry. "I've just been holding on here, honey," I said.

Before I was completely off the bed, she put her hands up. "I won't take the girls along. That's what I meant."

I stopped, one foot on the floor, the other trailing behind me on the bed. I must have looked absolutely foolish.

"I'm sorry if you misunderstood," she said. Her voice was so tender and so tinged with sadness, I couldn't hold back my tears.

There was a long silence while I stood there as if she'd just finished stuffing me and would make up her mind about where to hang me in the morning. She stared at her hands, and I came to understand that she was waiting for me to leave the room so she could go to bed.

Let me tell you, they call it a broken heart for a good reason. I hurt in the center of everything I've ever known.

※

I know you might think I was short on understanding. After all, with God's power I should have demonstrated at least some largeness of spirit, the humble ability to consider things from a point of view other than my own. A person looking at the situation from the outside might say that Dorothy and I were simply not compatible, that fulfillment and happiness for her were not possible as long as she remained in a claustrophobic relationship that threatened to, as she put it, "choke off her potential."

I can see things now in a different light, but back then I believed I was truly defending my family, my happiness, my survival. I didn't think of life without Dorothy. It was not an idea I could muster on my most sensitive days. What good would my life be if I let her out of it? And why should I let her put my children through that?

If somebody came up to you and said, "Excuse me, I'd like to cause your children the most significant pain of their young lives and create for them a traumatic experience that will shackle them until the day they leave the planet," what would you say to that person? "Go with it; I hope it's a growing experience and they find their niche"? I don't know anybody who ever enjoyed divorce. Do you? I mean, it's called a broken home, not a divested one. The fact is, divorce is one of life's cruelties, and we bring it on ourselves. It's a choice we make, and it seems to me we've begun to make it without very much provocation. I mean, it's gotten to the point where a person might burn the toast and end up in court. People have trial separations these days the way they used to have cookouts. And they talk about fulfillment as if it were some sort of mail-order gadget they sent for when they were born, and if it doesn't come soon they're going to sue.

I don't know what I might have done about Dorothy if I hadn't been acting God. It didn't seem to make much difference about the power, to tell the truth. Except for causing her considerable anguish and fear, as well as a modest amount of confusion, I'd had no effect on Dorothy whatever. I might as well have been a dead body trying to interrupt my own funeral. Besides, I was beginning to wonder if there wasn't at least a tiny bit of hurt pride involved in the extreme nature of my anger and resentment when I discovered that she'd been out with Dr. Beach. It just didn't seem right to have the power of the deity and have to work hard to keep track of an errant wife.

I pictured myself taking her by the shoulders and shaking her furiously, begging her to stop and think. That seemed the only avenue left open to me, and it was a distinctly human one at that. I was reduced to helplessness in spite of my power.

Then it hit me. As though a voice spoke in the center of my mind, I came to see that anger, even God's wrath, was no way to keep her. She needed to experience once again the great joy of family life. She needed to see me as she once had — as a loving husband and sensitive father. That was something I knew she had admired and longed for in the beginning of our relationship. She had only lost sight of her need for such things because in our gathering troubles we had given them up. The children had become a nuisance because we could not talk about our problems in their presence.

We used to go on picnics on weekday afternoons when the park was empty. Sometimes we'd take the girls on "educational" excursions, long drives up into Wisconsin to tour a dairy farm or a cheese distributorship. One time we took everybody, even Norm and Herta, to Chicago to watch one of the hog butchers make hot dogs. You don't want to know what that looks like. I didn't think I'd be ready to eat again for at least a year or two. When we came out, Norm was furious. "I used to love hot dogs," he said. "I wish I hadn't seen that." I told him that I was sorry but that I was glad the girls had seen it. Claire said, "Daddy, I don't ever, ever, ever, ever want to watch them make hot dogs again."

Claire and Jody Beth were average students in school. But they were not as naive as many children their age are.

Such outings and vacations had become secondary to the paralysis between Dorothy and me. We'd even given up our late summer canoe trips in the cool lakes and swift rivers of Minnesota. We had just gotten used to being a suburban family with personal problems.

I could have kicked myself for not thinking of this before. I would arrange the most perfect family outing God could muster. Dorothy would be overwhelmed with bliss, pure bliss. How could any human being turn that down?

When I knew what I would do, I was elated. As happy as new parents holding their washed, fragrant infant for the first time. Maybe I wouldn't have to fix Bart the wonder blond and his wandering stethoscope. I was definitely back in the God business again — and I was surprised at my fearlessness.

The next day I left early for work. I got out of the house before the children had pushed their covers back and slapped the cold floor with their bare feet. I decided that Dorothy and her mother could get the girls ready for school, fed, and out the door. I was going to be busy getting ready to perform a very useful miracle.

I'd just backed my car out of the garage when I saw Brad, the little boy who lived across the street and who had hung around the house so much early the summer before. He stood on the curb in front of his house, stamping his feet one at a time like a horse.

I remembered how, before I was acting God, I had wished for the wherewithal to make Brad's life as fine as Beaver Cleaver's, and I realized that it was within my power now to do that. As I drove by him I waved, and unbeknownst to him I granted him a blissful, painless childhood. I gave him love and imagination and innocence.

When I got to work, Mr. Shale was not there yet. I sat at the front desk, studied the little cubicle in which Dottie had answered the phones, and felt a brief storm of the old anxiety. I still didn't know what I would do about her. But I was much less anxious about using the power. Just a glimpse of Brad had set me off. Maybe I was feeling my oats because my new determination to give Dorothy a renewed sense of family life had come to me with very much the flavor and character of a revelation.

I spent most of the morning doing paperwork. I was going to get everything done so I could take Friday afternoon off and set up my miracle family outing.

Mr. Shale came in around eleven-thirty. By that time the place was crowded with potential buyers and I was pretty busy. Cherry sold four cars by noon. He kept bringing me the deals and asking for approval — deals so good he didn't need to show them to me. I realized he wanted to impress me with how well he was doing, holding eleven and twelve hundred on each deal. He thought it was because of him that we were moving inventory out of there, that he was closing sales like a Bible salesman at a Baptist hanging. I felt sincere compassion for him when I realized what sort of tumble his career would take once I was no longer the acting deity.

The phone rang incurably. Every time it did I thought of Dottie. It had been almost three weeks, and Mr. Shale still had not hired someone to sit there behind the glass and answer the phone, so people from the service department, salesmen, even Mr. Shale and I, answered it whenever it rang too long.

Around one or so, Mr. Shale had had enough. "We're losing business," he said. He went back to the garage, got a mechanic named Curly — an extremely tall twenty-year-old with greasy black hair, a five o'clock shadow from his temples to his dimpled chin, and a silver front tooth — and told him to man the phones until closing.

Curly said, "I don't know how to operate this thing."

"It's a goddamned telephone," Mr. Shale said.

"It ain't just a phone."

"Just answer it when it rings. Take a message."

Curly sat in the tiny twirling chair on wheels.

Mr. Shale turned to me and said, "Come with me."

I followed him up to his office as if he were going to scold me. When we were inside and he had shut the door, he went around his desk and sat down with a great exhalation of air. "Damn, what a day."

138

I sat in the chair across from him.

It was quiet for a moment, while he cast around in his mind for what to say. I did not think this would be a good time to tell him I wanted Friday afternoon off. He wore an odd expression, a sort of glimmer of mischief and expectation around the eyes, as if he'd slipped me a Mickey Finn and expected me to drop to the floor. "What a day," he said again.

He raised his brows and searched through the papers on his desk.

"Well, we're making money."

"Right." He found what he was looking for: an envelope. "Heard from Dottie."

"You have?"

"A letter. She must have put it in my box this morning."

I had this vision of her creeping up to his mailbox early in the morning, the pink early sunlight washing out the darkness. Poor Dottie. She'd probably changed her mind and was now desperate to get her job back, in spite of her bruised dignity. She might have loved Mr. Shale on some level deep in her frightened, lonely soul.

"She hates me," Mr. Shale said. "Calls me a pig."

"What?"

He threw the letter across the desk at me. "Read it."

It was very short. She wrote:

> Mr. Shale:
> You are a pig. I never want to see you again.
> Dottie

"You suppose there's any way I can get her into trouble for that?" Mr. Shale's eyes were flat and black like a rag doll's. "You suppose?"

"I'll be damned," I said. I was truly shocked. I had been wrong again. So wrong I was beginning to wonder if I might have to use the power to insure being right at least once in the coming decade. "She's just angry," I said. "That's all."

"I want to get her for this."

"Why?"

"I want to sue her, maybe. Something."

"She's just hurt."

"A goddamned employee sends me a letter like that."

"She's not an employee anymore."

139

He shook his head. "She wasn't even that good."

I gave the envelope and its contents back to him. "Forget it."

"I can tell you now," he said. "I was sleeping with her."

"No." I couldn't look at him directly.

"She wasn't a bad piece of ass."

The floor in front of his desk was dull and filthy.

"Not a great looker or anything." He laughed to himself, making a ticking noise with his tongue on his teeth. "She looked a lot like a . . . like some sort of — a sort of rodent, you know?"

"I didn't notice."

I felt so sorry for Dottie. All she wanted was somebody to care about her. Is that too much to ask? Somebody to love her for what she was.

"I don't think you need to pursue this," I said. "She'll probably apologize for it tomorrow, anyway."

"Figure women out," he said, leaning back in his chair. "I saved her life. Now I'm a pig."

"Yeah." He *was* a pig. But he didn't notice that I was agreeing with him on that point.

"I mean, I risked my life. I could have been killed."

"Lucky thing you weren't." I stood up.

He shook his head. "I sent them running."

"Yeah."

"Did I tell you there was four of them?"

I nodded. "And you sent them running."

"I saved her life."

I looked at him, letting his eyes fix on mine; then I turned the power on full blast. I made him love Dottie so much it cost him appetite and regularity. It was purely spontaneous. I didn't even have time to give a name to what I was doing. Somehow, I knew he would act on his love. He'd had a rather compelling intimation of death — a stroke is aptly named — and this had made him aware of his loneliness. At that point in his life, he needed to be loved so badly that he might have acted on it if I had turned him on to Mother Teresa.

He blinked, then sat back in the chair again and looked through the office windows, which opened onto the showroom floor below.

"Are you all right?" I said.

"I'm just tired." His voice was suddenly very distant, almost wistful. He wanted me to leave.

"I have to take off early Friday," I said, moving toward the door.

I wish you could have seen his face. It was so touching. He could not figure out what was happening to him. He believed he would never see Dottie again, and that made him profoundly sad.

"I've told Cherry to keep an eye on things," I said. "Can you lock up tonight?"

He nodded.

"If you can't, I can hang around." I stood there with my hand on the doorknob, watching love take hold of a man and nearly strangle him in only a matter of minutes. It was very moving.

He waved his hand. "I'll be here. Go ahead."

I closed the door to his office very softly. I can't explain this, but by the time I got downstairs, I felt absolutely wonderful. I wanted to grab Cherry and kiss him on the forehead. As it was, when I passed him in the hall between the showroom and the service department, I told him, "You'll full gross one this afternoon."

He thought I was *predicting* he'd close a deal at full profit. But I was *willing* it. I wanted to hold on to my newfound confidence. It was an extraordinary sensation to uncover what would save Dorothy from herself, then to heal Brad's life, and then to watch the power work on Mr. Shale and create love. I wanted to give up the idea of consequences altogether. Consequences only confused me. So did guilt.

I had been God nearly five months, and I figured it was about time I started acting like it. I had knowledge and I had experience, and now things were going to go right.

9

I knew it would take more than one family outing to rekindle Dorothy's interest, but I was going to begin that very weekend and I wanted
the weather to cooperate. That Friday morning as I unlocked the dealership and opened all the doors for the day's business, I created one of
the most beautiful days in the history of March in Illinois. It was already fairly warm for that time of year — it would have gotten to about
forty-five degrees by noon — so I just willed a bit more sun and a grad-
ual increase of about fifteen degrees. The day had begun wet and misty,
with a cool northwestern breeze, but with my work, by early afternoon
it was nearing sixty. I toned down the breeze and let the warmer air
work on the clouds. They would begin to rise and break up by the time
we all got to the park.

I felt so certain and infallible, I was not prepared for what happened
to me on the way home. As I was driving past the hospital, thinking
about surprising my daughters with a trip to the park and planning what
I would say to Dorothy, I felt once again a turbulent spinning sensation
in the core of my brain. I shook my head and tried to concentrate, but
it seemed to increase.

I came to a stop sign and pulled the car over to the curb. I was across
from the emergency room of the hospital, so I thought I'd wait there
for a moment in case anything bad was happening to me. I watched a

few cars pass, and I thought about the injuries, sudden illnesses, and maladies that populated this little space of earth.

A hospital is a sort of concentrated area of suffering. A place where souls come into the world and leave it with greater regularity than any other. It is also a place where people find themselves praying very hard — even people who have not prayed in decades. So perhaps it should not have been a shock to me when gradually I came to recognize that an extraordinary mixture of fear, anxiety, pain, and frustration had broken into my mind like a hemorrhage. I was being implored by thousands of voices, voices that spun in my brain so powerfully that they deafened imagination. I was beginning to let the prayers of thousands enter my consciousness. Not just the people sweating in the waiting rooms and corridors of the hospital, or mumbling incantations over loved ones as Herta had done over Norm, but people everywhere. I heard the secret pleadings of the human race, in all of its languages.

I wish I could describe the horror of that experience. The world sounded like a tremendous, loud, riotous beehive. Think of that. Imagine your head is a great beehive with millions of loud bees, and you can understand what they're saying. It was the most painful thing I have ever experienced. I grabbed my throat and commanded the voices to stop. If anyone had been watching, they would have thought I was threatening to strangle myself. Perhaps they'd have been right. I think if I had not managed to shut down the voices I might simply have choked myself to death — anything to stop all those sad, buzzing, hopeless prayers that implored God to grant things he has never allowed: an end to war, poverty, disease, suffering.

Once I had stopped the voices, I was exhausted and soaked with sweat. It was like a seizure, and I had no idea what had caused it, although I did notice that I'd been close to a hospital each time I'd suffered symptoms. I realized that the dizzying, anxious sensation I had felt when I opened Chet's letter that November day so long ago had been the first augury of my affliction. Only now the voices had broken through. Something had failed me, because I had not willed it. I would never will such a thing. In fact, I was absolutely terrified that the voices might break through again. I hoped with all my heart that I might escape the sad praise and puny requests of the human race, even though I could not find it in my heart to will that either. I mean, you can't have a deity who completely eliminates the possibility of ever hearing a prayer.

Because of the brief, painful episode near the hospital, when I got home I found myself struggling to regain my sense of power and happiness. My daughters were home from school, riding their bikes up and down the sidewalk in front of the house. Their small voices echoed under the bare trees and between the houses. Although it was still a fairly damp late March afternoon, the sun had begun to emerge and make weak shadows. Black birds scattered above the eaves of the house, and it hit me how terrifying and wondrous my life had become. I was the father of these two gorgeous creatures, my daughters, who raced to meet me with pink faces and wild, wind-blown blond hair. I owned and loved this house, which seemed more and more like a quiet harbor away from a riotous and tottering world.

And here I was, the acting deity, beginning to act. I had wanted it to be warmer that day and I was getting that. I had wanted a clear, beautiful sky and I would get that, too. I told myself that I might be able to get anything I wanted. I was fairly certain that nothing could permanently harm me or my family.

Nothing except Dorothy.

Against my will I saw everything gone — the girls, my marriage, the house. I felt myself sinking into a spasm of panic. I took a deep breath and shook my head as though I needed to shake off a dizzy spell. I made myself remember the power, the majesty of all its possibilities, and this miraculously contained my fear. I granted myself confidence, equanimity, and belief that I would not fail. This day would be the first step, the beginning.

I knelt on the sidewalk and hugged Jody Beth and Claire. The fragrance of their hair, of their cold, bright skin, intoxicated me. I hoped Dorothy was watching me out the front window.

"You're home early," Claire said.

"I couldn't stay away from you guys any longer."

Jody Beth tugged at my suit coat. "Get your bike, Daddy."

"No," I said. "We're going somewhere."

My initial goal was to get Dorothy to agree to an afternoon of walking in the park and then maybe an early cookout in the back yard. I didn't think I would have to overcome any obstacle besides her will to study, but I soon discovered different. In fact Dorothy was no obstacle at all.

When I walked into the house she was in the kitchen, heating a pot of coffee. Her eyes met mine, and then she looked away. There was an awkward moment, but I came up to her, put my hands on her shoulders, and said, "Let's take the kids to Crystal Lake and hike around the park."

"Good idea," she said with a bright smile. "I've been reading Blake criticism all day."

The major obstacle came from a different quarter. Norm, who was sitting in the black chair perusing the *OED* with a magnifying glass, looked up and winked at me. "That's a splendid idea. I'll get Herta and we'll all go."

I tried to put a look of sincere disappointment on my face, but he didn't notice it.

"I've got to go up and change first," Dorothy said.

"You can go like that," I said.

Herta came down the stairs. "What are you doing home?"

"I took the afternoon off," I said.

"I'll just be a minute," Dorothy said, and she ran past Herta up the stairs.

"We're all going to the park," Norm said.

I had to think fast. Instantly I created a powerful desire not to go in Herta.

She groaned. "It's too wet out."

Norm put his magnifying glass down and closed the book. "For Christ's sake."

"What?" Herta said.

"You never want to do anything. All you do is snore on that bed upstairs." He got up and slipped his white feet into a pair of slippers. "I'm going," he muttered.

"I'd go if it weren't so damp out. It hurts my bones."

"Your arthritis hasn't bothered you in weeks."

"I've been taking care of it," Herta said. She noticed Norm's white ankles. "Wear shoes and socks."

"The sun's out," Norm said. "It's damn near a spring day. I'll do what I want. You do what you want."

"It's just a little family outing," I said, more to Norm than to Herta. I wanted him to stay home and I didn't think he would go without his wife.

"She may as well be dead," Norm said.

"Oh, okay. I'll go," Herta said.

"Don't go on my account," Norm said.

"I'm not going on your account."

I made Norm want to stay home. He looked at Herta, raised both arms in exasperation, then sat back down. "Forget it."

Herta got loud. "Forget what?" She moved into position in front of him. I thought she might lift him out of the chair and shake him. "Forget what?"

"Forget it," he said. "I'm not going."

"You're not staying home because of me!"

"You're shouting," Norm said.

Herta looked at me. "He's always doing things like this to me."

"Doing what to you?" Norm said. Now he was loud.

From the top of the stairs Dorothy said, "Will you two just cut it out?"

"The girls are waiting outside," I said.

Herta cursed under her breath and went by me. Norm sat in the chair, staring at his feet. His jaw was set, and I knew he would not move now even if I willed it. When he made up his mind, he was tougher than the Red Sea.

Herta did not want to go, but she went. She went to spite Norm.

These circumstances dampened my enthusiasm a bit. I hated it that Herta was going to tag along. I figured I'd need God's power to help her waddle along most of the rocky trails in Crystal Lake Park. I wanted to concentrate on Dorothy. I pictured an idyllic, sunny spring afternoon. We'd stroll together, watching our children and talking to each other about what was very fine in them, as we had done many times before, back when our family was the only thing that mattered to both of us.

I was determined not to let anything get in the way of this ideal afternoon. The sky turned a deep blue, and white clouds, puffy and perfect, dispersed over the bony tops of the black trees. It was warmer now, and the forest seemed to welcome us.

I didn't put any pressure on Dorothy. We talked affectionately about the girls. We laughed about the first few years with each child. Dorothy asked me to tell her about the various plants we encountered along the path. At one point I showed her the buds on a pignut hickory tree. Herta said, "Spring's just around the corner."

I put my arm around Dorothy and said, "It's already here."

She didn't meet my gaze, but she smiled.

Then I said, "I love you so much in spring. *You* are blooming, as everything else is."

She absolutely loved it when I said that.

We walked along a bike path down to the lake. Jody Beth and Claire held hands for a while. I asked Dorothy what she was thinking about, and she looked at me very seriously for a second. Then she put her hand on Jody Beth's head and said, "I was just remembering how it felt to comb their hair when they were babies."

"It's fun to comb it now."

"I know." She didn't sound convinced.

"You know, someday years from now you'll be thinking about them at this age and feeling as though you missed something."

She smiled, watching the path in front of us. Her smile was very close to a smirk, but not quite.

"I mean no criticism," I said.

Herta, walking in the grass off the path, reached out and grabbed my arm. "I almost fell down."

"I've got you." I tried to guide her back onto the path, but she pulled away.

"I'm all right," she gasped.

"Why don't you walk in front of us, Mother?"

Herta shook her head. She didn't have the breath to speak.

"We should slow down," I said.

Dorothy put her arm in mine. "Sometimes your thoughtfulness is . . ." She stopped.

"It's what?" I didn't know what she was going to say, because she didn't know.

"Sometimes it's a very good thing."

"I would think being thoughtful is always a good thing."

"I know. I know you think that."

I put my arm around her. She walked very slowly, as though she wanted the afternoon to go on and on. There were times, even early in our marriage, when I would put my arm around Dorothy and feel the

147

weight of it, as though it were too heavy and I was conscious of the effort it took to hold it up. But my arm felt light and supple across Dorothy's shoulders that day. She seemed to like it there, although she didn't lean into me the way she used to. She walked with her arms folded in front of her, watching our daughters as they discovered once again the early buds of spring.

"You know," I said, "this is very close to perfect bliss."

Herta coughed behind me.

Dorothy gazed at the ground in front of us.

"There's nothing troubling us on a day like this," I said.

Dorothy shook her head. She was thinking of Blake's "Tyger." She was certain her exam would require her to discuss why he spelled it with a *y* instead of an *i*.

"Aren't you happy?" I said.

"What?" She didn't hear me.

"Look at us. We're with our children. They're healthy and so are we. I don't have any regrets or grief. Right now I'm happy. I'm as close to bliss as any human ever gets on earth."

"Bliss is such a funny word," Dorothy said.

"Nothing's perfect," Herta said. Her eyes were sad, and in spite of the cool air she was sweating.

"Aren't you having fun?" I asked.

"It's too humid," she said.

The girls started to run and Dorothy moved away from me to catch up. She caught Claire by the arm. "Don't get too far ahead of us."

"We were just skipping," Claire said.

Dorothy leaned down and brushed back the hair on her brow. In the columns of shade under the trees she was a beautiful vision. It was like a painting of motherhood, a moment of tenderness that seemed to calm all that was fretful and sad.

There was one episode later in the day that might have ruined things if I had let it.

We were sitting by the lake watching people feed the ducks. Behind us a jogging path wound its way through the park and back up toward the entrance. The sun had crept down far enough to lengthen all the shadows and cool things off a bit. Because it was late in the day and most people had gotten off work, the park had filled. I had just put my arm around Dorothy, and she reached up and covered my hand with hers. I squeezed her shoulder, and she squeezed my hand. Then I heard a man say, "Dot!"

Dorothy turned and moved from under my arm.

There on the jogging path behind us, sweating in a pair of blue running shorts and a T-shirt with four-inch letters that spelled TOD across the front, was a very good-looking young man. He had a thick growth of black hair on his head and a dense black beard.

"Tod," Dorothy said.

Herta turned to me. "Who's that?"

"It's Tod," I said.

The kid came over. He panted like a dog. He was jumping up and down to keep his legs limber. "What are you doing here?"

"I'm taking a break from Blake." Dorothy laughed. She stood with her arms folded under her breasts, her legs slightly bent.

Tod looked at me. "Hello."

Dorothy said, "I'm sorry. This is Charlie."

"I'm her husband," I said.

He smiled, offered me his hand. It felt like a dead carp.

"I'd rather read Whitman," I said. "Wouldn't you?"

"I was just running," he said. He had a slight British accent.

"This is Herta," I said.

Herta squinted at him briefly, then put her hand on my shoulder to balance herself, crossed her leg in front of her, and removed her shoe.

Tod watched her. He thought she was going to tell him something about her foot, or perhaps the shoe, which she held in front of her face now, examining it closely.

"So," Dorothy said to Tod. "What are you up to?"

"About page one-seventy-five," Tod said, laughing.

Herta held the shoe up to my face and said, "Can you tell if this is dog shit?"

I leaned back.

"Smell it." She tried to get it under my nose. "Is it?"

"How do I know?" She kept coming at me with it. I pushed her arm away. "Are you crazy?"

Tod stepped back, eying her warily. I think he was afraid she was going to head for him with the shoe.

"You don't have to be impolite," she said.

149

"Mother," Dorothy said, "go wipe it in the grass."

Properly scolded, Herta shuffled off toward the lake. She looked like a sad bear.

Tod turned to Dorothy and said something about an exam.

"I'm still studying for it." She tilted her head toward me and said, "Just a short break."

"That's me," I said. "Shortbreak. You can call me Short for short."

Tod was at least ten years younger than Dorothy. And he had these moments with her that I was not privy to. Not that I couldn't conjure them; if I'd wanted to, I could have played every minute they had spent together in a matter of seconds. But I knew there was nothing there. Nothing of any romantic significance. She had not slept with him, although she might have been interested.

What bothered me is difficult, even now, to put into words. It had something to do with a feeling of exclusion. Of being outside a major and important part of Dorothy's life. I was reduced to an attribute of her existence, a thing she might comment on or wish to avoid or even forget. I felt as though I had turned very suddenly and finally into a statue in the presence of this young man and his friend "Dot."

In spite of my gathering sense of estrangement, I used God's power to compel myself to behave. I didn't want to ruin the rest of the afternoon. But I couldn't resist pointing out that Dorothy's name was not Dot.

"Oh," Dorothy said, "a lot of the kids call me that."

I was so happy that she referred to Tod as a kid. He looked surprised. "You don't want to be called Dot?"

"It's okay." She reached out and touched his flat stomach.

"Dot and Tod," I said. "Just think, if you two ever got together you'd be a palindrome."

"What's that?" Tod said.

Dorothy said, "Very funny."

"Dot 'n' Tod," I said. "Get it?"

He nodded slightly, his mouth hanging open. He wasn't sure what to make of me. It bothered him to stand in front of me in his running shorts with his legs starting to feel cold.

"It's good seeing you," Dot said.

When he was gone, I put my arm around Dorothy and walked her back to the edge of the lake. Herta was sitting on a bench there, scraping her shoe with a Popsicle stick and watching the girls chase the ducks. "We should be going," Dorothy said.

I told her I thought Tod seemed like a very nice young man.

"He's not that young," she said.

"Well. He's a good ten . . ." I stopped.

"A good ten what?"

"How old is he?"

"He's a few years younger than we are."

"Nah. He's just a kid."

"We're just kids," she said. She smiled and pulled away. Then she said, "Thanks for not embarrassing me."

All in all, the trip to the park went pretty well. I knew it was the right way to work on Dorothy. She and I enjoyed our walk, and Claire and Jody Beth cavorted in front of us, as happy children ought to. Ironically, I was glad Herta came along. Until she came at me with her shoe, she kept pretty much to herself, and I think perhaps she understood that Dorothy and I needed this time together. She kept the girls amused whenever they threatened to erupt into combat or wander too far from the path, and she maintained a reasonable distance from us as we walked along.

Mostly, though, I was proud of myself for not behaving like a jealous husband when Tod jogged onto the scene. I thought I had done myself some real good there. Dorothy put her arm around me and thanked me. She was feeling close to me right then. I knew it. And that fed my elation like gasoline feeds a fire.

My plans for a cookout later in the evening were thwarted by Norm, who greeted us when we got home with boiled ham and sauerkraut. The house smelled like a dirty sock.

"Jesus," I said. "What's that?"

He stood at the dining room table, a sleeveless undershirt sagging over his ample chest. "Dinner. Wash your hands."

"It smells like I should wash the food."

Dorothy brushed by me and said, "I'll be upstairs, studying."

I smiled but she didn't see it.

Claire and Jody Beth were despondent over the sauerkraut. "What's that grassy stuff?" Claire asked.

"Don't mouth off," Norm said. The silver hair on his chest looked like swirling smoke.

"You don't have to eat it," I said. The girls ran to the bathroom to wash their hands.

"I was going to cook hot dogs on the grill," I explained.

Norm's face contorted a bit. Then he said, "Goddamned kids."

"They're my children, and they're not goddamned."

He looked at me, his mouth slightly ajar. "No offense."

"You shouldn't say such things."

"Okay."

"Even kidding."

"I wasn't kidding."

"Perhaps you'd like to stay in a motel." I couldn't help myself. He didn't have any right to complain about the girls, and I wanted to make sure he knew that.

He didn't answer me. I watched him set the table, his hands shaking. He seemed to be in a hurry, except I could tell he was fighting some sort of emotional storm. I'd hit him where it hurt. His jowls appeared to swell and turn red with each passing moment, and when he brushed past me it was with the sort of squeamish distaste one reserves for rotting corpses.

"I'm sorry," I said. "We have to get along."

"Yes."

"What family doesn't have its squabbles?"

"I made dinner," he said. "I was hungry, and I made dinner for everyone."

"Good." I wanted to say: "And you made what *you* like for everyone." But I managed to restrain myself.

There was another pause. Then he said, in a quiet, almost apologetic voice, "I've already talked to a real estate agent. It only takes getting the insurance money."

"It's okay."

He sat down, putting his hand on his forehead. "We won't be here much longer." He sounded as if he were whispering into a telephone.

"Stay as long as you like." I was afraid he'd start crying, but he only let out a long and apparently satisfying exhalation of air. Or at least I think that's what it was. It might have been from either end of him. He knew I didn't really want him to stay much longer, and I didn't have it

152

in me to disabuse him of that notion. Some things even a good acting God can't do.

I felt bad that it gave me such satisfaction to know that he believed he was imposing terribly on me. But I realized that it gave me such satisfaction because he was imposing on me so terribly. I was beginning to see that the only reason I put up with him and his bovine spouse was that I'd burned their beautiful house to the ground.

Dorothy did not come down to dinner. I knocked on her door and she hollered, "Blake exam!"

"You want me to bring something up to you?"

"No thanks. That smells like fried gym shorts."

I laughed. "Don't you want anything, dear?"

"No thanks. And tell Dad to stay out of the kitchen."

I wasn't angry or anything, but when I touched the door, I considered knocking it down — I could do that, with God's power. I could create a pile of hinges and toothpicks if I wanted to. A part of me needed to impress her so much. And I didn't want to let this evening get away from me; things had gone so well. I said, "Why don't you open the door?"

"You've studied Blake, haven't you? I need to concentrate."

"You could at least stop to talk to a person." I waited for an answer, gazing at the texture of the wood in front of me. The door opened a crack, and Dorothy peeked out into the hall.

"Look. This is important — I can't stop just now."

"It's Friday night. Come on down and we'll cook something on the grill together."

She considered it, her head tilted a little bit, as if she were asking me to photograph her good side.

"I have eleven poems to study. I've got notes to read. You wouldn't believe —"

"It's just a half-hour to eat with the family."

"I'm sorry."

There was a pause. She did not want to look directly at me, so her eyes wandered to the floor, then down the hall. She put her hand in front of her face and looked at her fingernails. The silence might have blossomed into uneasiness, and to avoid that I said, "This used to be my room, too."

Then she did look at me. I felt my face turning red.

"Do you want me to study somewhere else?" she said.

"I want you to have dinner with us."

"I'm sorry. I just can't right now."

"Well, we can have a cookout tomorrow. How'd that be?"

She started to close the door, then she stopped. "Oh, I can't. I promised Mom and Dad I'd help them look for a new house."

"How about next Friday, then?"

She smiled. "We might do that."

I said, "The kids had a great time today. We should take them to the park more often."

"It *was* fun."

"I felt happy again," I said.

She waved her hand back toward her books. "I really needed to get away from this for a while. I needed to give my mind a rest. I can get back to it now with a clear head."

"I think *we* needed today," I said, but she had already closed the door.

❊

I was really looking forward to our cookout, but Dorothy did so well on her Blake exam that she called me late the following Friday to tell me she was going out with some friends to celebrate.

"We're all just going to College House. It's a pub on campus," she said.

"I know where that is." I hoped she would include me, since in my own way I had helped. "It's a good thing I talked you into taking a break when I did," I told her. "You probably needed to relax for a bit to solidify what you were learning."

"I won't be too late." She was going to hang up.

"The children," I said, a bit too loudly. There was a pause, then I said, "The children and I will have a little celebration of our own."

"What do you mean?"

"The cookout. Remember?"

"What cookout?"

"You said we'd have our cookout tonight."

She tried to say something about how exhausted she was, but I pretended not to hear it and hung up the phone.

What kind of person is it, I wondered, who finds great joy and satis-

154

faction in something and then doesn't even think of sharing it with the one person with whom everything should be shared? I had shared everything in my life — except becoming the acting deity — with her. She was my life, the whole of it. She animated everything I ever cherished or hoped for or mourned the loss of.

I hated it that large portions of her life were completely foreign to me. She knew people I didn't know and had private conversations with them. She might talk about me. I couldn't picture Dorothy saying anything positive if I was the subject of discussion, so what would these strange people know? Something private and *bad* about me. Worse, she might say something about herself, disclose some attribute of her soul that I would never see. It would be a secret between her and somebody outside our family. Think of it. Some person I might never meet would know things about my wife that I didn't know.

It just didn't seem fair.

My whole life with her seemed public and knavish and not intimate.

So now I had developed a hole in my sense of well-being and power, and it grew with every passing minute as I waited in the living room that night for Dorothy to come home. I pretended to be reading so I wouldn't have to talk to Norm, but even so, I could hear him snuffling and grunting in his corner of the room.

Herta went to bed early. She stood up and seemed to totter a bit. Then she looked at me and said, "I'm so tired."

She'd been sitting in my living room most of the day, watching soap operas, then situation comedies, then a few game shows. She watched the news while I fed the girls and cleaned up the dishes. She and Norm sent out for a large pizza, and when it arrived they put the box on the coffee table and ate over it. They devoured the entire pizza during a rerun of *Barney Miller*. You should have seen them hovering over their segments of the pie, as if protecting them from light and air. I thought they might eat the box when they were done.

Jody Beth asked for a piece of pizza and Norm said no with his mouth full. If I had not been acting God, I think I might have punched the bastard right then. Jody Beth came back to me, whining for the pizza. I put my arms around her and held her against my breast. The poor kid didn't understand that I was fighting tears myself, waiting for her mother to come home.

All evening I watched the front windows, almost praying for a car to pull in the driveway. I might have exerted the power to bring Dorothy home, but I was afraid again — afraid of what device the power might find to bring about my wife's early return. I did not feel like contriving anything, or at least that is what I told myself.

What I did decide to do had nothing to do with my power. I put the girls in bed, told Norm I was going out, and drove over to the College House Pub.

Dorothy was sitting at a long table with six other students. There were only two males, but Tod was one of them, and he sat directly across from her. He was wearing a University of the Pacific sweatshirt. His hair was combed back and polished. He looked clean. He looked like one of Christ's disciples.

The other male had thin brown hair that he wore over his ears. He was losing it in the middle of his head, and it would not be long before he could put on a pair of wire-rims and give a fair imitation of Ben Franklin. He was probably younger than Tod.

I went over to the bar. One of the girls at the table noticed me, but she didn't know who I was. Dorothy hadn't seen me yet.

I ordered a beer and sat at the end of the bar sipping it. I didn't know if I should just let Dorothy see me and wait for her invitation or walk over there and say hello. She might believe I was spying on her if she saw me sitting at the bar. But I felt so awkward. I didn't know anyone in the room but my wife, and apparently she knew them all. She probably knew the bartender.

I sipped my beer briefly, then took a deep breath, got off the stool, and turned toward the table. Dorothy's eyes met mine just as I was taking the first tentative steps toward her. I held up my beer and said, "Congratulations, darling."

Everybody looked at me.

"Surprise," I said. "I thought I'd join you." I walked around the table and tapped the shoulder of a young girl who sat next to Dorothy. "Excuse me."

The girl got up hurriedly and moved to another seat.

"What are you doing here?" Dorothy said.

I sat down next to her. "I was so impossibly happy for you I couldn't wait to see you."

156

She smiled and turned her head slowly to face the rest of the table. "This," she said, "is Charlie."

"I'm Dorothy's husband."

They all nodded and grinned. I heard one of them say, "Ohhh, muh-god."

There was an awkward couple of minutes. I took huge gulps of my beer. My face felt alternately cold and hot.

Then Dorothy introduced me to everybody. When she got to Tod, I said, "I remember you."

"Right. Your mother wanted you to smell dog shit."

Everybody laughed.

"That wasn't *my* mother," I said.

"It was my mother," Dorothy explained with a groan. They all laughed very loudly at this.

One of the girls — her name was Sandy — said, "Well, is your mom, like, totally bizarre, or what?"

More laughter. I raised my glass to signal the bartender I wanted another beer.

"So," Sandy asked, "did you go to college, or what?"

"I never finished," I said.

"He was an English major too," Dorothy said.

I put my arm around her. "You see, we're both interested in the same things."

"English is sooo hard," the girl next to Tod said. Her name was Rebecca. She had long red hair and beautiful emerald-green eyes. Her eyelashes were prominent and white, and when she blinked her eyes looked almost evil. "I like English," she said. "But I don't understand a lot of the books I read. Especially when it's not even, like, this century, you know?"

"Aren't you an English major?" I asked.

"I'm more interested in, like, the twentieth century. I'm much more comfortable with that."

"I notice you and Sandy are from California."

"They just sound that way," Tod said.

"How come?" I really wanted to know. There was general silence. Tod studied his beer, thinking.

The conversation drifted after that. I ordered another beer and gulped it down. Then I had another. And another. In spite of the beer, I could not relax. I kept looking for an approving gaze from Dorothy, but she was engaged in the conversation and did not pay much attention to me. They talked about classes, papers, and quizzes.

There was a pause at one point, and Sandy said, "So what do you do?"

"I sell cars."

A long silence followed this. Dorothy sipped a glass of white wine. Then I said, "I manage Shale Motors, in town."

"Oh yes," Tod said. "I've been by there."

I turned to Dorothy. "You've never told these people what I do?"

She shook her head slowly. "The subject just never came up."

"I can well believe that," I said.

Tod said something to Sandy I didn't hear. Then Rebecca laughed. I had the feeling they were talking about me. I might have begun to concentrate on each of them, to know their thoughts and what they said to one another, but then Dorothy said something about one of her professors, a man named Peabody. Tod looked at her and said, very seriously, "He had no idea, you know."

"No idea of what?" I said.

Dorothy patted my arm. Tod said, "It's the goddamnedest thing. You're going along minding your own business, and then suddenly you find out your wife is schizophrenic and a klepto."

"His wife went crazy?" I said.

"Like, totally," Sandy said. "My psychology professor's wife is schizoid. I heard she's got something like fifty different personalities."

They all thought it was pretty sad, but I started laughing. "She's a group," I said. "An association. A collection."

Rebecca smiled.

"A regular accumulation."

"It's not funny," Dorothy said.

I could not stop laughing. "I mean, we're talking an assembly here. A conclave, a caucus, a conference. It must take her a long time to read her mail."

Dorothy wouldn't say anything, and I couldn't get her to look at me. Tod said, "I really do love Professor Peabody."

"So do I," Dorothy said.

"He's a psychologist and he didn't know his wife was a platoon? What sort of psychologist is he?" I said. "Does he work with animals?"

Tod said, "He's the finest man I've ever known."

"Well, you're not very old yet."

"I feel sorry for him," Sandy said.

"I wouldn't want a democratic household if I were him," I said. "Imagine voting on dinner, or a movie. You'd always lose."

I couldn't believe no one was laughing. I felt wonderful. It was too bad about Professor Peabody. But think about it. He lived with a woman who was fifty different people, and he didn't know it. Now there's an alert fellow for you.

"How did he find out?" Dorothy said.

"I don't know," said Tod. He was ignoring me now with a kind of passion.

"Hey," I said. "Hey, maybe he found her arguing with herselves about what to wear one morning. If they all disagreed and decided to wear what each one of them wanted to wear, she'd look like Orson Welles. She'd be a bit warm, too."

"Apparently she got caught shoplifting, and when they called him she was hysterical," Sandy explained.

"Maybe she was just not herself," I said.

Tod took a drink of his beer. "Everything just unraveled after that."

"If you trained each personality on a different instrument, she'd be an orchestra."

Rebecca laughed, but Sandy frowned at me. "You're very cruel," she said.

Tod said, "Perhaps it's not cruelty."

"Like, totally," I said. "I'm just into laughter. It's a kind of self-actualization. I'm getting in touch with myself. I mean, it's like laughter is a good thing, you know?"

There was a pause. Nobody would look at me, but I noticed Rebecca staring at the table, trying not to laugh.

I said, "Poor old lady Peabody will need a party line to get in touch with *herself*. That's a goddamned conference call, you know?"

"Let's go," Dorothy said. She was angry. I was being insulted by her friends and all she could think about was how sorry she was that I had showed up. I made a few jokes, for God's sake. What's wrong with that?

"Let me finish my beer," I said.

"You've had too many already."

"I have not."

Tod looked at me and said, "You should let Dot drive when you leave. I can follow you home in her car."

"I'm fine," I said.

He shook his head. Dorothy turned toward him and shrugged her shoulders.

"Look, old bean," Tod said. "Why don't you —"

"I'm not a bean."

Rebecca smiled. I think she felt sorry for me.

"You got a calculator?" I asked her.

"No."

Somebody else had one and passed it down. I handed it to Sandy, then I turned to Dorothy and said, "I'll show you how sober I am."

"What should I do?" Sandy asked.

"He wants you to test his mathematical skills," Tod said.

"Right."

Sandy and Tod leaned over the calculator. Tod said, "Okay, you really want to be tested?"

"He can't even balance the checkbook," Dorothy said. "I'm going home."

"Wait," I said. "Watch this."

She started to get up, but I grabbed her arm. "Come on, sit down."

Tod recited six numbers, each four digits long. He went so fast, Sandy had a hard time keeping up with him on the calculator. I had the answer for him faster than she could get it.

You should have seen the look on Dorothy's face.

Tod couldn't believe it either. "Let's try another one," he said. "What's 3565 plus 858 times 643 divided by 16 plus 533?"

I said, "178,282.31."

Sandy punched away on the calculator. "He's right! Jesus Christ, he's right!"

Tod's face seemed to open up. "That's fucking amazing."

The girl who had moved when I sat down called out from the end of the table. "What's the square root of 53 times 85 divided by 4 —"

"You're going too fast," Sandy said.

"154.7023," I said.

Everybody but Dorothy laughed. She was looking at me as if I had developed wings and might fly up and perch on one of the ceiling fans.

160

"I never knew you could do that," she said.

"Oh, I can do almost anything," I said.

For a while there I had a good time. They kept throwing numbers at me until I told them I was tired. By that time, all of them were pretty much mesmerized by my talents.

I had a couple more beers, then I noticed a dartboard on the back wall. I suggested we play darts and strolled over there, leading the entire crowd. The bartender turned the light on above the board and handed me six darts. I threw six straight bull's-eyes.

Tod said, "Hit the number twenty."

I threw six straight darts into the number twenty, right in between the two and the zero.

I hit the bull's-eye forty-seven times straight.

You should have heard the cheers. The last two darts I threw, I turned my back to the board and heaved them over my shoulder. I held each dart by the fins and just flipped it without looking. But I willed a center hit in the bull's-eye. Everybody egged me on, but as I was getting ready to throw the forty-eighth dart, I noticed Dorothy gathering her things at the table.

So I went back over there. It seemed as though the entire populace of the bar had one will, and it was mine. They all followed me as though I were a major celebrity, a modern-day prophet. As we all approached the table, Dorothy sat down. I held my hands out and signaled for everybody to have a seat, and they moved almost reverently to their places.

I think being so popular might have been enough to help me regain my waning confidence in the power, if Dorothy's reaction had been different. I felt like a rock star.

Sandy said, "You should have been a math major."

"He flunked math all the way through school," Dorothy said.

"Math," I said. "Eeuuh. I hate it. Like, totally."

Dorothy leaned over and whispered, "They know you're making fun of them when you do that."

"Naah."

"It's not funny."

"Oh, you mean it's, like, totally rude, right?"

"It's getting late," she said. "I'm going."

"Aww, come on."

"Stick around, Dot," Tod said.

"Her name is not Dot," I said. "Not Dot. Can you remember that?"

He had this surprised look on his face. "Hey. Okay. I'm sorry, man. Not Dot." He laughed way too loudly.

"You've had too much beer," I said.

Dorothy slung her purse over her shoulder and picked up a pile of books from a chair at the adjoining table. "I'm tired. Goodnight, everybody."

"Wait for me," I said.

"You stay," she said. "You're having quite a time."

"No. I came to be with you," I said, but she didn't hear me. I watched her weave her frosty way through the tables and out the door.

I said goodbye to everyone and followed her. We drove home in separate cars, which gave her time to cool down. She was quiet but civil when we got back. I didn't think she'd hold anything I did that night against me, but I figured I had pretty much nullified any progress I might have made with the family outing.

10

Near the end of April I came home late one night and found Dorothy already snoring in her room, which didn't surprise me very much. I was shocked, however, to find Norm waiting for me, sitting in my black chair with his hands resting on the arms like Lincoln in the memorial. He was not reading or eating or sleeping or watching television (his entire arsenal of possible activities).

"What's the matter?" I said.

"It's very late," he said numbly. "Yes, it's very late and there's nothing for it." He sat still while he talked, as if he were wired to the chair and feared tripping a fuse. "Something's happened."

"You don't say." I took a seat on the couch, loosened my tie, and stretched out with my feet on the coffee table.

"First, do you believe in God?"

I felt very strange answering him. "Yes."

"Do you pray?"

"I used to."

"But you don't anymore?"

"Well, I don't have to."

"Why?"

"What's the matter, Norm?"

"Why don't you have to?"

I couldn't think of anything else to say: "Because I'm saved."

I thought I saw the faintest glimmer of a smile struggling for eminence around the corner of his mouth. "You think you're saved, huh?"

"I guess so."

"What makes you think so?"

I wasn't in the mood for one of his quizzes. "I've met God."

He stared at me without blinking. "I'm not laughing. I wanted to know." He almost whispered this. Something was troubling him, but he wouldn't let it into his mind, so I couldn't figure out what it was. He did not react the way I had expected.

I felt foolish. "Tell me what's happened."

"Nobody's saved," he said. Then he moved his head down further toward his chest. You'd have thought he was about to nod off for a minute.

"Are you all right?"

"Nobody's saved, in the end." He looked up, met my eyes. He'd been crying.

I sat up. "Hey, come on. What's wrong?"

In a voice so wounded and slight it passed me like a soft tone in a dream, he said, "Herta's dead."

I found myself standing in front of him, fists clenched, as if I'd just knocked him into the chair. "What's happened, Norm?"

He told me, in that faltering, lost voice, that Herta kissed him on the cheek and went to bed right before Dorothy got home. The evening had been absolutely normal. He read late, sitting in the black chair. I saw him in my memory turning crisp white pages with the sort of contentment only a book could lend him. When he went up to join Herta, he did not hear her breathing as he crept into their room, and he knew before he touched her that she was gone.

"I didn't hear her," he said. "I knew I was alone in the room."

"Did you touch her?"

"She's dead." He looked at me, watery-eyed and helpless. "She was as cold as a sink."

"How long?"

"She went to bed early."

"No, I mean how long ago did you find her?"

"I just came down here and sat down, then I heard your car."

164

"And you haven't told anyone else?"

"I was going to wake Dorothy."

"Did you —"

"I waited for you. I didn't call anyone."

I did not even consider that Norm was sitting there watching me. I flew into action just as I had at the fire, only this time I remembered what particular gifts I possessed. I clattered up the steps so fast I think he thought he was dreaming. He'd never seen a human being move like that except in science fiction movies or cartoons. I burst into Herta's room and shot the power to her full force. I wasn't taking any chances, either: I restored her brain function as completely as the limits of my power would allow. I said, "Let her be the same. Let her come back to life and be the Herta Herrmann who died, minus what killed her."

When I got to her side, I whispered, "Herta! Wake up!" She was already beginning to moan.

"Herta," I said. "Are you all right?"

She opened her eyes. "What are you doing in here?"

"Nothing," I said. "Go to sleep. Sorry." I patted her hip and started to back out of the room. Then I was overwhelmed with pride and an intense, sweeping elation that threatened to knock me unconscious. "Goddamn, Herta. You're alive."

"What?" She was not yet fully awake, but her eyes bulged and moved in little circles, as if she were watching somebody play tetherball, and I knew she was terrified.

"Go back to sleep."

She tried to sit up, but her flabby muscles failed her. There was a panting pause while she appeared to stare at the ceiling and consider her predicament. Then she let out this tiny, almost inaudible syllable, a high-pitched, birdlike cry: "Help."

I gave her sleep. Made her believe, even in her sleep, that she was dreaming. Then I leaned over and kissed her warm cheek. "Sleep well," I said. "And wake up feeling like your old self."

When I came out Norm was crouched at the top of the stairs, his legs slightly bowed, his arms extended in ugly parentheses to his baggy shirt and pants. He looked like an old wino.

"Norm. You scared me to death."

"What?"

I waited a bit, to lend the moment proper gravity. "There's nothing wrong with Herta."

He looked down at himself. His hands shook. His body seemed to shrink a little, as if the bones had suddenly turned soft. "She's — she's alive?"

"She's just fine. Got mad at me for waking her."

He tottered by me, hesitating at the door. "You mean she's okay?"

"Go on in," I said.

He did not turn away. He looked into my eyes, recognizing something for the first time. There was a pause while we both stood outside the room listening to Herta's steady, rhythmic snore, and it occurred to me that Norm actually wanted to thank me. For a very brief fraction of time he understood that I was his savior, and it moved him in ways that were both frightening and terrific. Here was his life, and it had been redeemed by this man he could not respect, a car salesman, his irritating son-in-law. He was not yet convinced of what had happened, yet something told him that he had witnessed a miracle and I had performed it. But he told himself that he was only feeling grateful that I was there and had shown him that in fact Herta was just sleeping.

"I must be losing my mind," he stammered as he pushed open the door.

"Everything's all right," I said.

"Thank God." He disappeared inside and quietly closed the door.

Of all the activities I had pursued, this one miracle did more to confirm me as an active, hands-on sort of God than any other. I was without fear when I went to bed that night. I knew that in spite of all the problems I had inadvertently created, I *was* in fact creating. That was the important thing. God is the creator, and that means he creates. As acting God I had been doing that, first with anticipation, then with timidity and fear. Only very gradually had I won any sort of confidence. Now I would be absolutely fearless. I had begun to have luck with my consequences, and that helped, of course. I knew I had fixed Brad's life, and I'd begun a serious effort to renew Dorothy's interest in the family. I had managed perfect weather for our outing, and although it did not have the immediate effect I had hoped for, it had been a very fine day. Dorothy said it was fun. I knew in the weeks ahead I could regain any losses I had incurred the night she missed the cookout. As the weather naturally improved, so would I. I had pretty much settled the problems between Dottie and Mr. Shale. After all, he pursued her with the stubbornness of a starving wolverine. Now that I had a resurrection under my belt, I knew that when I turned the power on Dottie, made her love him the way he loved her, I'd be creating a marriage made in heaven, literally.

I had only one other problem to worry about before I turned to the world and settled some things there. Only one other problem. If I listened closely, I could hear her in her room; I could almost see the slightly restless dreams that swayed in her sleep like a sheer curtain blown by a soft night wind.

※

The next morning was gorgeous — cut from mid-June — and since I had not willed it, I figured perhaps God or Chet approved of my recent behavior and this beautiful day was a kind of reward. When you save a person's life, it truly enlarges your soul, gives you a sensation that diminishes the distinction between spiritual and physical things. I felt as though I could walk through walls if I wanted.

I got out of bed before anybody else and left the house early. I went to Dottie's place. There was no need to go in. I just stood in the parking lot and willed for her a tolerance of sexual quirkiness and a nearly insatiable passion for Mr. Shale.

Then I went to Crystal Lake Park to be alone and think.

At that hour of the morning, on a Thursday, the place was empty except for the ducks. I wanted to concentrate on Dorothy, to think about our life together and what I could do about our problems. But as I walked along the shaded pathways around the murmuring lake, I found myself listening to the birds and the wind-blown water slapping against the stone barrier at the water's edge. It was a lovely, almost wondrous sound, and I could not concentrate on much of anything, save the odd question of whether it was me enjoying it or the God in me.

And that got me to thinking about the Creation — about God, in a new suit, beginning the world. Imagine what fun that must have been. Picture God designing the simplest thing, the most elementary thing.

Try this: Get a bucket and fill it with water. Stand in front of a sink and pour the water out of the bucket. Pour it slowly at first, then gradually increase the flow. Notice how the water forms a long and slender sort of V, and at the place where it begins to be a single stream, it seems to twist a bit like a rope. See the fine, straight ripples in the V? They appear to be a pattern superimposed on the water, almost like a double exposure. As you increase the speed of the flow, the rope seems to twist more, and the ripples get farther apart. This is the way water flows. It's part of the design.

Imagine God designing that. Imagine him thinking about water and deciding what it will look like when you pour it out of a bucket or a glass or whatever you pour it out of. Have you ever wondered why he didn't design it to fall from a bucket like a big W? Or maybe have it drop out with a square edge, like this?

At any rate, I sat by the lake and studied the water and tried to imagine how *I* might have designed it if I had been God at the beginning. It was not good for me to think about such things, because I was reasonably sure I would never even have thought about water, much less how I wanted it to flow, and I didn't want to be thinking about anything negative. I knew I would probably have forgotten to create water, and life on earth would never have happened. Or perhaps I might have invented life on earth that didn't require water. I had to admit that if I had God's power, I ought to be able to do that. Imagine making a world, and putting fifty million different species of life on it, and remembering to give water particular properties when it's poured. It all seems so incredibly complex. Yet if you think on the matter a bit, it becomes clear that in spite of all the variety and splendor, there is also a goodly measure of duplication on earth. After all, water isn't the only thing that has those properties when it's poured. It seems contradictory but nonetheless true that God took some short cuts in the Creation. I mean, virtually every creature has an alimentary canal of some kind, and a terminus for it — a place to get rid of dross, to put it politely. Imagine God designing the anus.

Doesn't there appear to be something contradictory in all that? I kept asking myself why he would be so specific in the particular design of things and yet so consistent in the overall picture. It seemed that I should have answers to such questions simply by thinking them. I hated it that I still didn't have the complete command I needed to make the answers clear to me — especially the answers to why he would bother to create such things as brilliantly sunny days, or the sound of water lapping against a wall, or rain, or even a child's smile, at the same time he was creating rabies viruses and ticks and wart hogs.

Across the lake I saw a loon rise and disappear into the trees, and it reminded me of what I had come there for. I walked down to the water's edge and stood in the soft dirt by the stone wall. At my feet a small toad leaped toward a tuft of high grass. Its back presented an extraordinary array of colors, a spiny disguise against predators it could not know. If I wanted to, I could easily make it aware of me. I could put obstacles in its path and make it seek some other stand of grass. I could step on it and kill it. But I didn't. It hopped again, slipped in the slick, wet sand around the roots, and disappeared in the grass. I knew it would never acknowledge my existence if I didn't tamper with its path.

I picked up a small black stone and skimmed it across the smooth water. Another loon rose toward a tattered willow. It was the sort of morning that creates silence in people. You walk in it a while, feeling almost religious, as if you have stumbled into a great church and should observe the proper decorum. *This is a gift*, I said to myself.

A voice behind me said, "It's a fine day."

I turned and saw Chet smiling at me, his arms folded across his chest. He was dressed in red slacks, a white short-sleeved shirt open at the collar, and a straw hat dipped low over his brow. Oddly enough, I wasn't even slightly surprised to see him. It was as if we had come to the lake together and he was only making conversation in this cathedral of a lovely June morning in April. He bent over, picked up one of the stones, and skimmed it across the water. It bounced and bounced and bounced and bounced and bounced and bounced and bounced until it disappeared on the other side of the lake.

"You cheated," I said.

"No. If *you* did that it would be cheating."

"Why?"

"You're human. The best a human can do is six, maybe seven bounces. I'm not human." He picked up another one.

"Then tell me, what are you? You look human."

"Looks are deceiving."

"Are you an angel?"

"I'm your friend. You don't have to have a name for it, do you?"

"Some friend."

He turned the stone a few times in his fingers, then bounced it across the lake.

"What if somebody sees you doing that?"

"There's nobody out here but you."

"Well . . ." I felt interrupted and thwarted. I wanted to question the God in me about Dorothy, and, failing that, to enjoy the warm breeze and the sound of the water. I had come to the lake to think, and I did not wish to have a conversation with my benefactor right at that moment. I guess you could say I was also a bit nervous about why he had suddenly come to see me.

"I'm not going to heaven today, am I?" I said this with real fear. I wanted very badly to visit heaven, but I was also absolutely horrified at the idea. Even when you tie yourself to the railroad tracks and pray for a train to come, you get scared when you feel the tracks tremble.

"Soon. Not today," Chet said.

"Is there something you wanted?" I asked.

"Well, why don't we sit down." He searched a bit, then pointed to the stone wall. "Over there."

"Something wrong?"

He motioned with his hand, moved me toward the wall. When we were seated, he took off his shoes and socks and dangled his feet in the water. "Wow! Is that cold!"

"The air thinks it's June, but the water knows better."

The lake appeared black under the trees, but in the middle, where clouds danced along, it was almost white. There was a long pause while we both surveyed the reflections in the lake, and I came to wonder if I would see something there that he expected me to see. But then he said, "Is there anything you need?"

"What?"

"Anything you want?" He gazed out at the gorgeous lake.

"You mean money? Talent? Vitamins? What sort of thing might I need?" I was not trying to be difficult. His question seemed completely opaque.

He still was not looking at me. "Anything at all."

"I don't know what you mean," I said. "I need my wife to come back to me. Of her own free will."

"You want that. You don't need it."

"Oh yes, I do. I need her. I need her to be my wife again."

"I said any*thing* you need. Not anyone."

"What could I need? You say that like I'm defending a fort here and I might be running out of ammo or the artillery isn't going to show up."

"Such unhappiness."

"Oh, I'm not unhappy. Actually, I'm feeling rather wonderful."

"Good."

"But I'm also sometimes very frightened."

"Of what?"

"Of everything. So much can happen."

"To you?"

"No, not just to me. So much can happen to everyone."

He smiled, apprehending some irony I was not aware of. "So you find yourself without any significant needs at the moment?"

"I didn't say that."

"What do you need?"

"I need answers to questions."

"Ah." He raised the straw hat, wiped his brow. It was only a gesture, for he was not even slightly damp. "Well, now. Questions of what sort?"

"Why was I given this power? How about that?"

"You don't mean questions that can have correct answers or incorrect answers, such as who played Doc Frail in *The Hanging Tree?*"

"No, I don't."

"Those sorts of questions are more fun, I think."

"That's not what I asked."

"I like it that with that sort of question, you can check to see if the answer is correct."

"I don't want to play trivia games."

He leaned toward me, placing the hat back on his head very carefully. "Gary Cooper."

"What?"

"It was Gary Cooper who played Doc Frail."

"I didn't ask that question."

"I figured secretly you wanted to know, so I told you."

"What I want to know is —"

He put his hand on my shoulder, and for a moment I thought I felt something change in me, as if some new organ had sprouted in my abdomen.

Then he said, "You're not the first to have this offering. Nor will you be the last. It's a sort of mission." His voice was very gentle, and seemed to originate in my head. When he took his hand away, I felt my body return to itself, and whatever had grown in me dissolved.

"That felt terrible," I said.

"Some have liked it."

"What was it?"

"It was nothing."

"I felt something."

"Let's just call it a spiritual hug and forget about it."

"I don't understand any of this."

"Read Job. You'll get some idea of how God reacts to questions about why he does what he does. Some questions I simply can't answer, and you shouldn't ask."

There was a pause. The ducks noticed us and moved in their purposeful way toward us across the lake. They gathered in our shadow, searching for food. I looked at Chet and felt like one of the ducks, nattering at his feet for a handout.

"I wish I had some popcorn to give them," Chet said.

"Why don't you just create it?"

"Then I wouldn't have the wishing."

"Oh."

"I like wishing."

"I wish I knew what I can ask you."

"Why don't you just ask me? If I seem to evade things, you'll know."

"Okay. Can I ask you about . . . Is there something I've done that's brought you here?"

"No."

"Am I doing all right?"

"So far."

"Do you know about Herta?"

"Of course."

"I brought her back."

172

"She didn't get far." He smiled and swished his feet in the water. The ducks quacked indignantly, then gathered again at his feet.

"Why did you let her die?" I asked.

"I didn't have anything to do with it."

"Why did — why was it ordained that she die?"

"Her heart stopped. She had a myocardial —"

"That's not what I mean."

He shook his head. "She is getting old. That sort of thing happens to old people."

"It doesn't happen only to old people."

"True."

"Why is that?"

"Not every heart can be perfect." He seemed to rock slightly, like a man who'd been drinking. "This might make you sad," he said. "Perhaps you should pursue some other line of questioning."

"Why can't every heart be perfect?"

"Why can't every heart be imperfect?"

"Is that an evasion?"

"It's a lateral transfer." He smiled again.

"Who made cancer?"

"You already have the answer to that."

"I do?"

"Certainly. Everyone does."

A loon called, then dipped out of sight in the black water under a tree.

"Refresh my memory," I said.

He looked at me with deep brown eyes that seemed dead. "Who made that loon?"

"I see."

"Well," he said, adjusting his position on the wall, slapping his feet in the cold water. "These are certainly easy questions."

"*Why* did he make cancer?"

"You'll have the answer to that soon enough."

"An evasion."

"You know, the world isn't the way people want it to be. It never has been." He lifted a foot and took a small shred of green weed from between his toes. "What you value, your vision of things, it's just — well, you'll see. The universe can be described by human beings, and some

173

things that human beings name do exist. You might say human beings discovered them. Things like triangles and atoms. Other things humans invented, like time or goodness or . . ." He paused, looking at me again with those lusterless eyes. "I'm sorry to be inarticulate about all this, but I am not very good at describing what is true in human terms. Forgive me. I'm not talking down to you."

I watched for the loon, wondering where it would come up. For a brief moment it seemed that Chet wasn't really there at all, that I was alone, merely thinking.

Then Chet said, "You've been very active the last few days."

"Yes."

"On a personal level."

"Not completely."

"You're feeling confident about yourself?"

"Now you're asking the questions."

"And you're evading." He leaned toward me and studied the side of my face.

The loon came up near the middle of the lake, then dipped down again — only this time its tailfeathers remained above water. The ducks at our feet appeared to be discouraged about food and started to disperse. I could not escape Chet's frowning gaze; the tone of his voice made something drop in my chest, and I realized I was absolutely terrified. If I could have hidden my head like the loon, I would have.

"No need to be frightened," Chet said.

I was shaking. "I don't know why I'm so — so nervous."

"You're afraid of disapproval. Of *my* disapproval."

"Yeah." I took a deep breath.

"You're afraid of disappointing somebody very important."

I didn't say anything. He bent over, his elbows on his knees, and peered into the water at the base of the wall. "Little fish," he said.

"I've been active," I said. "On the personal level, yes."

"Sort of a micro perspective." He was not looking at me. "You haven't been involved in the big picture too much, but you've educated yourself." He winked at me. "You've prepared very well."

"Thank you."

"You need more macro activity."

"I expect I'll be getting to that. I've been planning it."

"So, do you need anything?"

"I feel like you expect me to have an answer to that — a particular answer."

"No." He turned to me. His eyes were absolutely lifeless. "We were just . . . I was only concerned that you had everything you needed from this end of things. That there's nothing we're doing to hold you up."

"I'm getting more and more comfortable with this — this situation."

"Good."

"I plan on more large-scale operations."

"Remember consequences."

"Of course."

"Remember who you represent."

"Is there something I'm expected to do?"

"You're expected to make a bit of a mess."

"That's what you want? I think I've already done that."

"It's not what we want. It's what we expect."

"Well, why? I don't understand."

"You will. What we want . . ." He paused. "I want you to be careful — very careful. Thoughtful. And active." His eyes seemed alive again; they were animated. "Especially active."

"Why especially active?"

"Because that would be interesting." He got up and brushed his pants with brown, chubby fingers. "Don't make a mess we can't clean up."

"I won't."

He tipped his hat, turned to leave.

"Wait," I said. "I have another question."

He stood there under the green trees, the morning light exploding around him as if he held the sun in his hands.

I said, "Are there any other things I've done that I don't know about?"

"You mean like the fire?"

"Yes."

"One thing."

I felt sick. "What'd I do?"

"You don't like religious fanatics."

"I don't even think about them."

"But you don't like them. Especially the ones on TV. You gave most of them gout."

"You're kidding."

"It was the unconscious God in you."

I remembered an afternoon weeks before. I had caught Norm watching some television salesman with slick hair preaching about God and goodness and how if you only believed in the goodness of the "Lard Jahezus he would transfoworm yer laf." This barely educated, silver-haired clown was speaking of God and promising that faith would get every viewer a better job, a raise, or even a boat. I hated the man's eyes. But I did not know that I had taken any action against him.

"For God's sake," I said. "This is just horrible." I felt cruel and life-less, like a weapon in somebody's hands.

"It's a relatively harmless thing," Chet said. "No need to fret about it."

"No need for *you* to fret about it."

"Or you."

"What's the point of all this if I can't know what I've done?"

"We know what you're up to."

"And half the time I don't."

"Just concentrate on the other half." He started to leave again.

"One more question," I said. "You remember you told me once that God doesn't often make absolute conditions — absolute laws?"

"Yes."

"Has he made one in my case?"

"What do you mean?"

"Has he decreed anything like — well, like nothing I do will be per-manent, or that I can't make any absolute laws?"

"You have the power," Chet said. "It's yours while you have it."

"I know, but —"

"It is not absolute."

"I've already seen evidence of that."

"I will tell you this." He paused and seemed to consider something, to be working out a problem in his head. Then he spoke as if he wanted to test his conclusions out loud. "I will trust you with this: God has not set any limits to your power that are not already there when he owns it. He does not like to use his power in such a way that it ends up being self-limiting." He smiled broadly and waved at me like a politician standing up in a convertible. "God almost never says never."

"I guess I won't either, then," I said.

176

"So long, Goodman Wiggins." He strolled up the path toward the road and the parking lot beyond it. I realized, as I watched him amble out of view, that he had come to see me for a specific reason. Chet's purpose had been to prod me into greater action, to encourage me to engage in something other than the minor shocks and pains of my own life.

It had always pestered the back of my mind that I had not yet involved myself in any of the world's problems. Every time I picked up a newspaper I noticed something I might have prevented. A few days before the fire a seventeen-year-old kid had shot and killed his mother and father, his three sisters, his teacher, and his doctor. Then, when the police arrived on the scene, he put the gun to his own head. The authorities said he was headed for his car when the police caught up to him. "Who knows where he was going next?" one of the policemen said. Imagine being that kid's next appointment. Wouldn't you feel as if you just swerved out of the way of a semi at seventy miles an hour?

Of course, I knew that intervening in that young man's misery would not truly address the cause of the problem. I'd need to intervene in the whole human propensity for such behavior for my work to have any impact on the scheme of things. But how was I going to do that without creating a permanent change in the whole race? Without using my will in ways God didn't seem to have the nerve for? What might happen to men and women if I removed murder and mayhem from the human heart? If I subtracted malice from the arsenal of human feelings?

I tried for some time to imagine what sort of alterations I'd make in the world when I began to pursue "macro activity," as Chet put it. But the lake seemed to beckon me, and I lost interest. Before long I was studying the black water, listening to the impatient ducks, and thinking about Dorothy.

I still believed in making her see the value of family life, but I had to admit my plan was not going to work all by itself. That night when I had amazed everybody with my mathematical skills, she had been astonished and truly impressed. In spite of her anger, she had not looked at me like that in a very long time. What I needed to do more than anything was pursue Dorothy — become her suitor all over again. It was clear that no matter what I did, if she did not come to the conclusion, on her own, that being married to me was good for her life, for her blasted fulfillment, she would leave me.

But then I asked myself, what if I put the idea in her head? Couldn't I, as God, simply stick that notion in her mind? Make her believe that being married to me was a fulfilling thing?

As I'm sure you remember, I had already toyed with the idea of sticking notions in her head and had pretty much dismissed it. On the day of the snowstorm, when I thought she was leaving me, I made her love me with enough passion to burn a few cities. The problem with inserting fulfillment in there as well, you see, was if I put *that* in her head, I would be creating a new wife. The Dorothy I knew would cease to exist, because the woman I wanted to win wouldn't need winning anymore. I didn't see much difference between creating a new Dorothy and buying an inflatable doll, to tell you the truth. I still felt I needed at least some part of her to come to me as herself, without my divine intervention. Otherwise it wouldn't be *her* loving me, it would simply be *me* loving me. You see my dilemma? I needed her, not some replica of her created out of my own psyche, for my happiness. Yet I wanted her to be a particular Dorothy — the one who loved me so completely early in our marriage. It was tempting to create an end to the whole thing, but I couldn't do that and have Dorothy's love be truly hers.

No, I would have to win her back. If I courted her, if I pursued her like most men pursue women, I might be able to find some way to make myself more lovable in her eyes, and then maybe she'd want me again, the way I always wanted her.

❀

Imagine what it means for a man to have to woo his wife of almost a dozen years. She knows you. She's seen you in every possible circumstance — in bed, in the bathroom, in the shower, in the kitchen at three o'clock in the morning with your hair standing up like an Indian headdress, in the first waking moment of a thousand cold mornings, when your eyes are caked and your mouth is thick with feathers. One morning early in our marriage, Dorothy touched me very gently on the shoulder to awaken me, and I had been dreaming that a giant yellow moth had perched on my shoulder and was preparing to suck blood out of my ear, so when I opened my eyes and saw her leaning over me in her yellow robe, I screamed so loudly she fell off the bed laughing. I pictured myself, that frightened man with sleepy eyes, grabbing the covers like a five-year-old, trembling like a terrified squirrel at the gentle touch of my wife. That man, whom she knew so well, was now going to woo her and win her? I might as well try to impress a fire hydrant.

As I'm sure I've made clear, I had never really been very skillful around women in the first place. I had originally attracted Dorothy because I was not thinking of trying to win her — I was trying to sell her a car. I guess my charm as a salesman wore into her natural resistance to rutting males, and things blossomed from there. It was never a conscious choice on my part to make any sort of overt gesture toward her in the beginning; we just ended up together. At least, that's how I think she'd describe it.

So now I was faced with the problem of attracting Dorothy all over again, even though I did not know — well, there's no better way to say it — how to *be* in front of a woman. That's what it amounts to when you get to the heart of things: some men know how to behave in front of women, and some men, like Mr. Shale and me, do not.

Of course, it didn't help any that the whole idea of being a man had changed. I might have developed a capacity for shooting game animals, or practiced the art of skinning rabbits or casting a fly. I might have learned how to flex my jaw muscles and stand around with my legs two feet apart like I might leap into a speeding car at a moment's notice. The trouble was that attracting women seemed a whole new enterprise. Anyway, isn't attraction a product of the unfathomable in new people? Isn't attraction fed by strangeness and anticipation? How could I attract a woman who knew everything about me?

I came back to the house after my talk with Chet and found Dorothy getting ready to hit the pavement for a five-mile run. (She'd quit smoking after the Blake exam, and as the weather had improved she'd started running again.) She was wearing purple tights, a black headband, and a bodysuit so tight it made her breasts look like solid muscle. I wasn't ready to see her so soon after my decision to court her, so naturally I felt fairly awkward standing in the path of her intrepid blue eyes. And, I have to admit, I was afraid she might be harboring a small residue of resentment from that night in the bar.

"Where have you been?" She was tying her running shoes.

"I went to the park."

She didn't say anything.

"I was thinking."

"The children are up," she said. "They've had breakfast."

"Good."

She looked at me, her expression puzzled. "What happened last night?"

"What do you mean?"

"Dad's acting real weird this morning."

I was tempted to say, "Your mother died and I brought her back to life." But I only frowned and acted concerned. "Your dad is always pretty weird, if you ask me."

"He pulled me aside this morning — he was half naked, wearing only his briefs. I said, 'Dad put some clothes on.' And do you know what he said to me?"

I waited. She moved closer to me and whispered, "He said he saw a miracle last night."

"Maybe he did."

"He said *you* performed a miracle."

"Oh, I can explain that. He thought your mom was dead."

"Dead?"

"I came home and he was sitting in my black chair grieving over his loss."

"For God's sake."

"I went into her room and touched her and she rolled over. Scared the daylights out of me."

Dorothy laughed, throwing her head back as if she were standing beneath the shower. The sound of it relaxed me, gave me confidence.

"Yeah," I said. "I went up there and imitated Christ in a subtle way, and your mother woke up from a deep sleep and told me to get the hell out of her room."

"My father has lost his mind."

"It's wonderful to hear you laugh," I said.

"Thank you."

At that moment she seemed almost perfect — her long legs slightly bent at the knee, leg warmers around her ankles, the body suit accentuating the shape of her waist and hips. I couldn't help myself. I reached out and took her in my arms.

"I love it when we're like this, friendly and happy."

For a brief moment I thought she would let me hold her, but then I felt her hands crawling up my sides like tarantulas, working their way between us. She tried to push me back.

"Don't," she said.

"I just want to —"

"Stop it."

"I wanted to tell you what I was thinking at the lake today." I said this in a hurry, struggling to hold her. "I thought about us, and I think we — I believe we can make a new stirt."

I couldn't believe I said "stirt."

"Let me go!" She was getting loud, so I stepped back. She ran her hand through her hair, adjusting her headband.

"Start," I said.

A smile tried to gain a foothold. "Don't be silly, Charlie."

"Charlie? What happened to 'honey'?"

She shrugged, staring at the floor.

"You've been calling me Charlie a lot lately."

"Do we have to have this now? I'm on my way to —"

"I want to go out with you."

There was a very brief pause, then we both spoke at the same time. She said, "*That* would be a miracle," and I said, "It would be a date." I felt my face ripen like an apple.

We stood there facing each other for a while. Then she reached out and touched my sleeve. "I'm sorry. I didn't mean to say that."

"I know it was just a joke."

"You're so funny."

"Will you go out with me?"

She went to the back door and opened it slowly, concentrating on something in front of her. Then she turned and I realized she was beginning to cry. "You're so funny," she said, and went out the door.

It took me a while to compose myself. I might have started crying too, but I went into the kitchen and washed my face. I stood in front of the sink, gazed out the window at the bright morning, and willed a certain confidence and alert affability in myself so I could face the rest of the day and my family. Shortly after that, Herta shuffled in, her feet tucked in little pink fur slippers. She was slightly dazed and seemed intent on touching things to make sure they actually existed. She stood by the sink and peered out the window too.

"Good morning," I said.

"I feel like I've died." She rubbed her forehead.

"Bad night, huh?"

"I had a dream about you."

"Well." I went to the refrigerator and got some eggs, a hunk of cheese, some milk and butter.

"You pushed me off something very high," she said.

"Feel like a cheese omelette?"

She turned around, looking directly at me for the first time. "Then you caught me somehow — shook my shoulder as if you were trying to wake me." She coughed, placed her hand over her breast. "It was frightening."

"I guess I'm a nightmare."

Norm came around the corner timidly, as if he were suffering from stage fright and somebody held a gun on him to get him to come in.

"Morning, Norm."

Herta said, "The fall scared me so, my chest hurt."

"I haven't told her," Norm said.

"Oh?" I said.

"About last night."

"What about last night?" asked Herta.

"As it turns out, I *was* in your room last night." I put a frying pan on the stove and got a few pats of butter sizzling while I stirred the eggs and milk. Norm stood next to his wife, and both of them watched me.

"What's wrong with you two?"

Norm said, "What did you do to bring her back?"

"Did you say you were in my room?" Herta said.

"I didn't do anything but wake her."

"She was . . ." He paused, looked at Herta. "You were dead last night."

"I was very tired."

"No," he said. "I mean dead. Dead."

I put a little thyme in the egg mixture, then poured it into the pan.

Herta still didn't understand what her husband was trying to say. "Okay," she said. "I get the point. I'm sorry I was so tired." She turned to me. "But why did you want to wake me?"

"Herta," Norm said. "Last night you passed. I saw you with my own eyes."

She frowned, looking up at him. "Are you —"

"It was no dream. You passed. Don't you see? It was death."

Herta turned to me. "What is he talking about?"

"Maybe he had a dream too."

"It was no dream," Norm said. "I saw you. I saw you." He moved closer to Herta and took her elbow in both hands. "Last night when I told him you were dead, I saw him fly. He went up the stairs and his feet weren't touching anything."

Herta removed her elbow. "Brush your teeth."

"It's the truth," he said.

"The older you get, the worse you get," said Herta.

"Who wants eggs?" I said. "I'm making a big omelette."

Norm's expression was absolutely priceless. He was not sure if the floor would stay where it was, if *any* of his senses could be trusted. He might have been in a stalled ski lift, 1500 feet above a frozen canyon. "Herta," he whimpered, "it's the truth."

I would probably have given him some relief if I had liked him more. When he first started talking I thought I would have to erase his memory, since he remembered so much about my behavior the night before. I never considered how hard it would be for him to get anyone, even his own wife, to believe that he'd seen what he'd seen me do. If you actually met me in person and somebody told you I could work miracles and fly, you wouldn't believe it either. At any rate, I was very happy to discover that I could leave him with his impressions, even though they caused him considerable distress. It didn't take him long to commence wondering about his mind. In spite of his terrible bodily habits, he was a smart, introspective, and perhaps even sensitive man. As everybody knows, such people are given to anxiety, mental disturbances, and even madness.

"I thought you were dead last night," he whispered, moving closer to Herta.

She patted his head. "Brush your teeth, honey."

"You want some of these eggs?" I asked.

Herta sat down at the table. "I don't want anything. I don't have the energy."

"I've made quite a lot."

She nodded in a distracted sort of way. Norm went out of the room moping. "I guess we're getting old," she said.

I piled half the eggs on my plate and sat down across from her. She watched me eat for a time, then she said, "Did you make coffee?"

"No. Do you want some?" I could tell she was hungry, and when I examined her thoughts I realized she was trying to figure out how to go ahead and eat some eggs without having to retract what she'd said earlier about not having the energy. She was worried about appearing to contradict herself. She'd already said no to the eggs. What she wanted was for me to make the offer one more time.

"Go ahead and have some eggs," I said. "I make a good omelette."

"That's your breakfast," she said. "You enjoy it."

"Nooo. I'll just throw away what's left, if you don't eat it."

"Are you sure?"

I pointed to what was still on my plate. "This is all I can eat. There's enough left in the pan for you and Norm."

"Well," she said, "I don't want you to be wasteful." She struggled to her feet and went for a plate. "Norm probably won't want any. He's never been much for breakfast, you know."

"No, I didn't know that. I didn't know Norm ever missed a meal."

She spooned the rest of the eggs onto her plate as she talked. "No, he never liked a big breakfast. Not like me. I could eat a ton in the morning, and then the rest of the day I eat like a bird."

"Birds eat five times their body weight in a day."

"I just nibble at bits of things all day. Never a regular meal, even dinners for Norm when he was working. I'd just be nibbling." With two chubby fingers daintily pincered before her, she picked at tiny slivers of what was left of the omelette in the pan, holding aloft in her other hand the heaping plate of steaming eggs.

"So you eat like a bird," I said. "Five times your body weight. That's a lot of food, isn't it?"

She sat back down at the table, a look of puzzlement on her face. She was out of breath, and I noticed sweat beaded on her broad forehead. "What'd you say?"

"Nothing."

"You were talking about body weight?"

I had not meant to, but I had reminded her that she was fat. "Just making a bad joke." I scraped up the last of the egg on my plate. I could tell that she had finally understood what I was saying and her feelings were hurt. I don't know why I made such remarks to her, except it made me slightly angry that she was taking the rest of the eggs for herself when she and I both knew that if we offered them to Norm, he'd eat them.

"I'm so overweight," she whispered, more to herself than to me. Then she said, "A lot of things happen to you when you get old, young man."

"I know," I said.

"And there isn't much you can do about them."

I sat back, trying to pretend I had not insulted her. "I'm really full."

She ate slowly, staring out the back-door window. Tears were condensing in the corners of her eyes, and I really did feel terrible. At one time she had been lithe and beautiful, like her daughter. Now she looked like a stuffed chair. *Maybe*, I thought, *when I get to macro activity, I'll do something about that sort of problem.*

When Dorothy came back, soaking wet from her five-mile run and shuddering like a horse, I asked her again if she'd go out with me.

"You never give up, do you?"

"It'll be fun."

She shook the sweat out of her hair and considered for a moment.

"I don't have any expectations," I said.

"What do you mean?"

"I'm not going to try and seduce you."

"Really."

"Not like your other dates."

"I don't have other dates."

"I didn't mean that like it sounded."

She went to the linen closet under the stairs and rooted around in it for a while. Herta had been taking care of the laundry since she and Norm had moved in with us, so I felt no pangs of guilt when Dorothy could not find a towel. "Shit," she said.

"Use a sheet or a pillowcase."

She was startled to see me still behind her. "Please."

"Please what?"

"Let me get cleaned up."

"I just want to . . . you know, take you out and talk."

"We can talk here."

"Not with the children and all."

"I don't have time."

"Just because I think of it as a date is no reason for you to see it that way." I inserted in her cerebral cortex an intense feeling of potential loss and the tragic finality of missed opportunity; also, I admit, I gave her a powerful jolt of pity for me and my pathetic little request. The more hard-boiled reader may regard this as a desperate act, but I didn't see how I could woo her if I couldn't even get her to go out with me.

"Look," she said. "You want to go out, we'll go out. Just leave me alone now, okay?" She ran upstairs to the shower. I felt like a freshman getting his first date.

My elation didn't last long. Before Dorothy was out of the shower, I was frantically flipping through the folds in my brain looking for the perfect place to take her on our date. I wanted indirect lighting, perhaps a terrace, with white furniture, candles, and a slight, pulsing breeze. Willows swaying in the darkness before a dim streetlamp. A beach in the distance, the hiss and roar of the ocean providing a sort of passionate background music.

Hard to find a place like that in Champaign, Illinois.

Even God couldn't do that. I knew I was going to have to give up the ocean, and probably the soft breeze and the terrace. I might be able to find the white furniture and a few candles.

Of course, the setting was not my only problem.

I didn't see how I could impress Dorothy without showing her ever-larger portions of my new education and power. I didn't want to use the power on her as much as I wanted her to see more of it in action. Not enough for her to guess that I was the acting deity or anything like that. Just enough to impress her with my — I hope you'll pardon this expression — male prowess. I could, after all, do just about anything. If I thought it might bring her back to me, I'd discover a cure for cancer while we sipped our after-dinner drinks. Or I might singlehandedly lift a car off a child's crushed toy and put it back together again. It didn't matter whether she was impressed by intelligence or physical strength, or both. I could do all of it with the power. I don't look like much, but you see the irony here? I was *everything*. As the early manuscripts say, "In mundo erat, et mundus eum non cognovit." I was in the world, and the world knew me not.

I had to somehow orchestrate things so situations that demanded my prowess would arise in her presence. And I was still incredibly aware of the problem of overcoming all her experience with me — the days and weeks of marriage that accumulate in the bottom of a soul like lint in a laundry sack, and tatter it at the seams.

So my elation quickly turned to anguish. My only comfort was that we were not going out on our date right away, so I'd have time to examine Dorothy's thoughts to see what she might expect and what she was really hoping for. You might think that having such knowledge would be an unfair advantage over her, but believe me, it wasn't. You must remember, she knew quite well what *I* was hoping for.

II

Near the end of May we had our dinner date. I decided to take Dorothy to Jolly Roger's, a restaurant with a pirate motif a few blocks from Shale Motors. It had white wicker furniture, a gigantic picture of a pink sunset on the wall behind the bar, and a few discreetly placed speakers that echoed a continuous and fairly loud recording of the ocean and sea breezes and even an occasional whale song. Great twisted fishing nets hung from the ceiling, and one wall was draped with thick ropes and a tattered sail. The bar looked like a crow's nest, with rigging hanging from it. Each table had two candles and a tiny basket shaped like a Spanish galleon, full of little toy pirates and tiny swords.

"Have you eaten here before?" Dorothy said.

I told her I hadn't but I'd heard good things about it. Actually I had used the power to find the best working chef in the city, then I had decreed that tonight would be his best night in years.

I borrowed one of Mr. Shale's limousines — a huge Chrysler New Yorker that he normally used only for special occasions and that he leased every now and then to the local funeral home. Dorothy was stunned when she first climbed into the front seat and got a look at the ornate wood-paneled dash. When I started the engine we couldn't hear it, and the noise of other cars in traffic was only a very distant whisper.

"You really went all out," she said.

"I thought you'd get a kick out of it." I tried to be especially careful about what I said, since this was going to be the beginning of our new courtship. I have to admit, I also had the feeling that if things didn't go well on this night, it would be my last chance.

On the way to the restaurant, I poked around in Dorothy's mind and realized that she was slightly nervous. Although she thought I looked attractive — I wore a new charcoal gray suit, a white, stiffly starched shirt, and an absolutely gorgeous navy blue, burgundy, and gray pais-ley tie — she was worried about the best way to reject me. She kept picturing me crying all over my tie, making a last-ditch effort to get her to stay with me. It was odd the way her mind worked. Behind the pic-ture of me crying, like a projection on the back wall of a movie theater, another scene played itself out: her mother and father settling into a new house, and she — young and dressed in the bright, pied garb of youth — stepping resolutely into her own apartment. As soon as her parents could move out of my house, she would be on her own. She didn't resist this thought at all, although it's true she didn't let it get into words.

I tried not to let such a horribly selfish and mean-spirited little pic-ture of things get me down as we cruised along Kale Street in Mr. Shale's limo. It took all of my power not to feel slightly used when she let herself wonder if she would have agreed to this date with me if she hadn't needed to stay with me until her parents were properly housed and happy. But she resisted such thoughts, and I came to see that it was only her naked, unfettered id working on her. She felt bad for what played in her mind.

"You're awfully quiet," she said after a while. "What did you want to talk to me about?"

"Lots of things," I said.

Her pulse quickened. She studied the streetlights, expecting me to start some sort of rambling plea for mercy. She imagined me breaking into song, begging her to come along and be my party doll.

"We can talk during dinner," I said.

She couldn't help hearing that old song now, and she hummed the damned thing without realizing it.

"That's an old song," I said.

"Yes."

"I can't remember who sang it. Was it Buddy Holly?"

"I think so." She looked at my hands gripping the wheel and thought about how tender I could be. She wished that we were better together, that we did not have to have this talk.

"You know," I said, "I wish we didn't have to have this talk."

She laughed. "I was just thinking that."

"I sensed it," I said.

"You did?"

"Sometimes I just know what you're thinking."

"That's a scary idea."

"I like it. It means we know each other so well that —"

"I never know what *you're* thinking."

"Yes, you do."

A sliver of resentment dropped into a small open space in her mind. It wanted to make a sentence for her memory about how I like to tell her things about herself that she knows are not true, or that she does not want to be true, and how she really hates that.

"I'm sorry," I said. "You really don't like it when I do that, do you?"

"When you do what?"

"Tell you things I've observed about you."

"Who knows?" She shifted in the seat.

"I dictate things too much."

"No, you don't." She was thinking, *He's right about that. All men dictate too much.*

I said, "Probably it's a character trait most men share."

She moved closer to the door. "It's a lovely evening, isn't it?"

"I don't want to talk about the weather," I said.

"Well, what do you want to talk about?"

"Whatever's on your mind."

She concentrated on the windows we passed, trying to get some idea of the decor of each house by what she could see through sheer curtains or a half-opened shade. She remembered our house when we first moved into it — how it was suddenly important to her what it looked like from the outside. Her house, her home. She always liked the way it looked in winter, at night — the soft lights in the windows, white smoke rising toward a flat, lustrous moon.

"Right now," I said, "you're thinking about our first year in the house."

She turned back to me, almost frightened. "I am not."

"Remember how happy we were then?"

"I remember we were only going to stay temporarily."

"But we were happy. And we can be happy again."

"You think so."

"I remember going for long walks with you in the neighborhood, talking about the children and people and the whole world." It was difficult to keep my voice steady, thinking of all those lost words and days. "I loved those times under the shade of the trees on our street. I remember the children's voices. I was sublimely happy."

She smiled a bit.

"It was a kind of bliss, you know? Maybe the only bliss we know on earth. What could ever surpass it? We have so few periods of unshackled time." My voice broke, and I paused to get control of my emotions. Then I said, "I just want those days back. That's all."

She was thinking, *Here come the tears*. I really could not control my voice.

"Don't you just love, even now, the way our house looks at night in the wintertime?" I said.

"It's just a suburban neighborhood." She picked up her purse, brushed her dress under it, then placed it more carefully in her lap. "I always wanted to move out of there."

I watched the road for a while. She made this promise to herself not to anger me, but not to humor me to the point of surrender, either. *He is a person you care about*, she told herself, *even if he is stubborn and childish*.

I waited for a few blocks, then I said, "I'm sorry if I seem stubborn and childish to you."

She looked like somebody had spilled icewater down her back. "Why did you say that?"

I didn't hesitate. "Sometimes I feel like that's what you think of me."

"Why?"

"I just do."

"You felt that way just now?"

"I thought you might be thinking that."

"But why? You were being a perfect gentleman."

"I don't know. It just felt that way."

"This is eerie," she said.

I didn't answer her. I studied the taillights of the car in front of us and tried to see her thoughts as clearly as possible. She was definitely confused now, so I couldn't arrange any of it in coherent order. It worried me that she was beginning to discover that she didn't like having a person know her as well as I apparently knew her. And, I confess, I was slightly apprehensive that perhaps she was jamming her signals on purpose so I couldn't find out what she was thinking.

In the city lights, she looked like an apparition. Her hair was pulled back above her ears, and a white scarf was tied in it; she wore a thin gold necklace with a single stone in it, and a matching stone in each earring. (There was no trace of the ring I had gotten her for Christmas.) She had on a low-cut white dress, one I bought for her right after Jody Beth was born, and white, high-heeled shoes. I hadn't seen her in a dress since she went back to school. It was very warm, even for the last week in May, but she wore a burgundy sweater that made her lips look dark red. Her skin seemed almost incandescent, like polished ivory.

"You really do look beautiful tonight," I said.

"Thank you." She was picturing herself, feeling quite satisfied with the image. A shadow crossed her mind — not words or sentences, but with the same distinct meaning and impact. It would have looked like this if it had been words: "He loves me, and it is terrible to lose someone you love. I understand his suffering." The whole thing went through her mind like a remembered film, with no sound but with subtitles that you understand even though you cannot recall a single word of it.

"When a person looks like you do," I said, "it must be difficult not to love yourself too much."

"You're being very bizarre tonight." She tried to read my face, to determine my mood.

"I'm sorry."

"One minute you tell me I look wonderful, the next you insult me."

"No, I didn't intend . . . I was only commenting on how beautiful you are."

She shifted in the seat again. It consoled her to think that we would be having dinner soon and then the date would be over. I knew I wasn't getting very far toward attracting her back to me, but it was early, and I forced myself to remain confident that I could begin to turn things my way once we got to the restaurant.

※

I think she liked the decor. We picked a table near a window and one of the speakers — or I should say I picked it. I lit the candles on the table before the waiter could do it. He came over to us with the sedulous and inescapable friendliness of an insurance salesman and told us that his name was Randy and he would be our host tonight. The poor kid was dressed like a buccaneer, with a red scarf over his head, a wide black belt, and knickers. His shirt bloused out at the sleeves, and it was open from neck to navel. He seemed to shrink a little bit when he noticed me looking at his pink, absolutely hairless chest. "They make us wear these," he said.

"They?" I said. "You mean the great make-them-suffer-and-do-it-the-hard-way-or-they're-fired they?"

Dorothy sent me a discreet frown.

"Would you like cocktails?" Randy said, passing out rolled-up treasure maps that contained the "bill of fare."

We ordered a carafe of white wine, and when Randy snapped his heels and disappeared into the captain's cabin, I said, "I wonder if all restaurant managers go to the same college and take the same courses."

"What do you mean?"

"Look at this." I held up the menu. " 'Bill of fare.' "

"So?"

"Treasure map. It's all such a cliché."

"You might enjoy it if you weren't so critical of everything."

"It's just something I noticed," I said. "I'm not being critical."

"You always do that," she said.

"Do what?"

"Criticize everything."

"I'm sorry. I hadn't realized."

She was quiet for a moment, then I said, "Is that one of the reasons you want to leave me?"

She didn't answer. I studied the menu for a moment, trying to get into her head, but she was only feeling a little dissatisfied with my apparent bad attitude about everything.

"What are you going to have?" she asked. She was very hungry but did not want to engage in any sort of gluttony unless I was going to join her.

"You're hungry, aren't you?"

She looked over the top of the menu. "Will you stop doing that?"

"What?"

"Telling me things about myself as if you've read my mind or something."

"I think I could read your mind."

"No, you couldn't."

"Want to try me?" I wasn't serious, but if she had challenged me I might have given her a slightly flawed demonstration just to intrigue her a bit. It irked me that I *had* been reading her mind and she had noticed how accurate what I'd been saying was and was continuing to deny it anyway.

She frowned. "Just look at your menu."

While I read, I noticed a man lighting a cigar at the table next to us. He was an incredibly big, powerful-looking man with huge arms, a tiny waist, and a chest like the back end of a compact car. He had a gray, rocky jaw, a walrus mustache, and wiry hair that scattered down from his bald pate like pine trees falling off a great rock. He sat across from a younger man who wore a brown leather jacket and one of those giant cowboy hats that looks like a caricature of what it's supposed to be.

Dorothy's nose gave a twitch, and then she looked up from her menu. If you've seen a deer at the water's edge when it gets the scent of man, or a bear, that's what she looked like.

"What *is* that?" she said.

"A cigar."

She turned around, looking for the source.

"Over there," I said, pointing to the next table. I was disappointed about the cigar at first. Since I had had to compromise on most of the crucial features of the setting I thought we needed, it didn't seem fair to have to contend with some slouch with a cigar. But then I realized that here was an opportunity to impress Dorothy, and I didn't even have to create it. It was blind luck staring me in the face, and I almost didn't notice it.

Dorothy said, "Well, it's going to be awfully difficult to eat with that." She had the expression on her face of someone who'd just risen out of a septic tank.

"It's just tobacco," I said, trying to appear reasonable. "But if it bothers you . . ."

"I just won't enjoy my meal."

"Do you want me to say something to him?"

"Well," she said, "you did pick the table, didn't you? And this *is* the smoking section, isn't it?"

I pointed to the nonsmoking section, which was five tables to our left. "You think we wouldn't get a whiff of it over there? Besides, you just quit smoking yourself. How can it bother you?" I couldn't believe she was peeved at me for not requesting the nonsmoking section.

"Cigarettes don't bother me. But *that* . . ." It truly made her angry that she had to smell the big man's horrible stumpy cigar. "Some people," she said.

"You want me to do something, I will."

She put her menu down and looked into my eyes with a challenging fierceness that surprised me. "All right," she said. "Do something."

I rolled up my menu and turned my chair so that I was facing the big man with the cigar. "Excuse me," I said.

He looked up.

"Have you ever heard of Murad the Cruel?"

"You talking to me?" He puffed on the cigar. The young man in the hat across from him turned to me.

"Yes," I said.

"Murad the what?"

"Murad the Cruel."

"Never heard of him."

The younger man said, "Sounds like some lousy medicine for your eyes."

"Oh, he was bad medicine all right."

"What about him?" said the man with the cigar.

As I spoke, I observed, out of the corner of my eye, Dorothy staring at me as if I were the hero in a movie. I said, "Murad, sultan of Turkey in the seventeenth century. A little-known bloodthirsty figure who killed people for smoking."

Neither man said anything. I waited for a few moments, staring at both of them, then I said, "He was fourteen years old when he became sultan of Turkey. Once he had the power, he made smoking a crime. He'd sneak out at night and wander around the city looking for taverns and inns, then he'd creep up to the windows and watch some poor fellow smoking a cigar over his coffee. The next day Murad's troops would come around, cut off the smoker's ears and nose, and then nail a piece of paper that said NO SMOKING to each wound."

"Is that a fact," the big man said.

"It said NO SMOKING in Turkish, of course."

"No shit." He puffed on the cigar again.

I looked right into his little piggy eyes. "Murad the Cruel. Look him up." I crossed my legs, sat back in the chair. "Sometimes he'd crush the offending smoker's hands and feet." I paused briefly, smiling. "I'm a direct descendent of old Murad."

The younger man laughed and pointed at me with his thumb. "You believe this guy?"

I stood up, very slowly.

Dorothy said, "What are you doing?" Her astonishment was gradually turning to fear.

"Relax," I said.

The big man pushed his chair back. "You see that sign?" He pointed to the wall behind me.

I didn't take my eyes off him. "I think you should douse your cigar, sir."

"It says SMOKING SECTION."

"You got cigarettes, light up." I felt like a gunfighter in an old western. "But *that* —" I pointed to the cigar. "That is offensive to my wife."

Dorothy whispered, "Sit down." I knew she was afraid. But I did not think she actually wanted me to sit down. Though I did not read this in her mind at that moment — I was too busy orchestrating my heroic scene to pay much attention to her thoughts — she seemed very definitely excited by my forcefulness.

"Just ignore him," the younger man said.

The big man shook his head, stared at me for a moment, then got out of his chair. "What do you say we go outside and discuss this?"

I threw my head back, opened my arms in a sort of benediction, and said, "Ah, I thought you'd never ask."

"Stay here," Dorothy said.

The big man moved toward the door, hitching up his pants. From behind he looked like a sack of tractor tires. The younger man came over to me, smiling. "That's Ned Hines," he said. "Big Ned Hines. Maybe you've heard of him?"

196

"Never have."

"State champion, arm wrestling. That's all." He opened his mouth in a wide smile, and I noticed a tiny bullet-shaped shred of spinach on his left eyetooth. "He's going to break your little ass in two, you go out there."

"You come on out and watch," I said.

He started for the door.

"I didn't even know the state had a championship for arm wrestling," I said.

Dorothy gritted her teeth. "Stop this."

When I looked at her, it hit me that she truly did not want me to go outside. As a matter of fact, she was actually getting angry at me for starting the whole thing. I was amazed to discover that I wasn't impressing her at all.

Go figure. One minute I'm dazzling her with my willingness to stand up for her, and the next she's thinking I'm some sort of bushy-haired gibbon that needs a chain around its neck.

"I have to go out there," I said.

"Why?"

How could I answer her? I had a true dilemma now. I couldn't go out and put on a display of my power for her without creating disgust in her heart — she'd see me as a failure of evolutionary progress. If I sat back down meekly and let the big man wait for me outside, she'd never believe it was her words that had convinced me. She'd remember what the younger man said to me about Ned Hines the great arm-wrestling he-man. I'd be fairly low in her esteem either way: a Cro-Magnon or a coward.

I moved toward my fate, watching her the whole time. "I have to get this settled, but I promise to do it without violence."

"Men!" she said.

"Come see," I said. "I'll do it with logic and reasoning."

I was backing slowly away from her, thinking about Ned Hines, and I didn't know the waiter had come up behind me. He touched me on the shoulder, and I almost leaped into Dorothy's lap. I think I let out this little deep-throated scream.

"Is everything all right, sir?" the waiter asked.

Dorothy laughed.

"No, everything's not all right," I said. Even when you're acting God you can be scared witless when somebody jumps you from behind.

"I'm sorry, sir." He had a tray with two glasses and our carafe of wine.

"I've got to go," I said.

Dorothy reached for my hand. "Wait." She felt sorry for me.

"I don't need you to feel sorry for me," I said. "I was just going outside for a moment."

"I don't feel sorry for you."

"Order us a salad," I said.

"If you go out there, I'm leaving." Her face was absolutely expressionless. The waiter cleared his throat, set the glasses down, poured the wine. Then he whispered, "I'll come back for your order."

When he was gone, Dorothy said, "I mean it." Her voice was completely without emotion. Just three flat notes.

"Come with me," I said.

"No."

"Just come watch. I promise you I won't do anything violent."

"Why do you have to go out at all? He's out there with his cigar." She gave a brief smirk of triumph. "That's what I wanted in the first place."

I stood there for a moment, looking into those stony blue eyes, and I understood that she would very definitely leave if I went outside. My date would be over almost before it began. Only God knows what might have happened if I had turned the power on her and willed her to go outside with me. So I sat back down in my chair, in a way that I hoped would display considerable disappointment.

"Thank you," she said, taking up her wine.

"He'll just come looking for me."

"Then we'll get the manager and he can call the police."

"Women!" I said.

She smiled, twirling the glass in her hand as if it were the stalk of a flower.

"If you didn't want me to do anything, you shouldn't have asked me." As I said this, the door opened and Ned Hines came back in. "Here he comes," I said.

Dorothy turned and saw him, then she set her glass down and got up. "Christ."

"Where are you going?"

Hines came up behind her.

She said, "I'm going to get the manager."

"Sit down, little lady," Hines said.

I stood up, walked over to the big man, and punched him on the cheek. As I did this, I closed off his carotid artery for a few seconds. He dropped to the floor like a bag full of apples.

Dorothy screamed.

"Step away from him," I said. "He might vomit."

There was a lot of confusion. Our waiter came tripping through the small group of people that gathered around Hines. I heard somebody say, "Call an ambulance."

"There's no need," I said. "He'll be all right."

"Goodness," the waiter said.

I winked at Dorothy, then I said, "Randy, do us a favor and remove this." I pointed to the mound of gradually recovering flesh on the floor between us.

Dorothy disappeared behind two people. I couldn't see what she was doing, but she was so confused and embarrassed and angry, it was entirely possible that she was getting her things and planning to leave.

"What happened?" Hines sat up, rubbed his bald head.

His friend tried to help him up. "You got cold-cocked."

Hines massaged his jaw. "I didn't feel a thing."

"Take him out of here," I said, "or he'll feel the next one."

They both glared at me. They looked like children that had just been spanked — hurt and frightened and swallowed up with impotent rage.

"Run along," I said.

Dorothy may not have been proud of me, but I sure was.

Of course, after everything had settled down and Randy had brought our dinner, Dorothy came back to the table and reluctantly sat down. I noticed that she was employing the procedure she usually used when she was unhappy with me: she stopped talking. She was so angry, the only reason she didn't leave the restaurant right behind old Ned Hines was that she didn't want to be alone outside the restaurant with him and his friend.

In spite of her anger, I assumed we would be able to get on with our date once I worked on her a little bit. But then something extraordinary and final happened. As I tried to get a sense of her mood, I was stunned to discover, growing in her heart like a black, poisonous flower, a truly pure and focused distaste for *all* males — for maleness. I don't mean males as she had come to know them through her daily experience, but males as she had come to see them through her struggles with me. She saw me with eyes that would not ever see me for who I was, because I had come to symbolize everything in men that she hated. At the same instant, I knew this was something beyond even God's power. How could I alter her sense of me when it had come to represent everything she could not abide in *any* man? It was not something she would ever put into words. This was not a stereotype, a mere prejudice. It existed in her like her bloodstream. I had become representative, without wanting to. And there I was, sitting across from her like a lit cigar, stinking up her meal. It is no consolation to see, as I do now, that she could not hate me in particular, she could only hate me in general.

So it came to pass on that fateful night — a night that I had believed would be the beginning of our renewed courtship — that I understood suddenly and with certainty that I had nothing more to say to her. It hurt terribly that she would not see me anymore, only my sex. The fact that I had created intense, heart-crushing love for me in her soul only made her hatred for my maleness all the more acute and intractable. Imagine that.

When it hit me how permanent her condition was, when I realized I would have to rearrange her personality and mine ever to have a chance to get her back, I was so sad that I couldn't bring myself to say anything. I knew, once and for all, that I would have to let her go.

She noticed me sitting there with tears in my eyes. She stared at her food and said nothing. She was ruinously attractive, and so much of my living had been buoyed by the fact that she loved me that I didn't see how I could descend to whatever my life would be without her. She had been lover, wife, mother, daughter, sister, aunt, and friend — one woman and all women to me. In giving her up, I felt as though I were giving up the company and companionship of women altogether.

I got up from the table in the middle of dinner, leaned over to her, and said, "I guess I'm finished with all this."

"What?"

"Maybe we *should* call it quits."

She sat back, wiping her mouth with a napkin. "Are you —"

I put a hundred-dollar bill on the table by her plate. "This ought to cover dinner and cab fare home."

"What is wrong with you?"

I shrugged. What could I say to her?

"You — I've never seen you like this."

"Maybe you've never seen me at all."

I didn't even think about what the disintegration of my family would mean for Claire and Jody Beth. Before the bold, stubborn eyes of their mother, I turned on my heels and walked out of Jolly Roger's, defeated and frustrated and angry.

❋

When I got outside the restaurant, Ned Hines and his friend with the cowboy hat were waiting for me.

"I figured I ought to have another chance," Hines said. He hitched his pants up around his flat, hard stomach, licked his fists, and then started moving them around in little circles in front of his face.

"Don't bug me now," I said.

"Knock him on his ass, Ned," the cowboy said.

"Please, just leave me alone." I started toward my car.

"Wait a minute," Hines said, beginning to dance now.

"Look," I said, "you wouldn't believe the kind of trouble I could give you if I really wanted to."

"Who do you think you are?" the cowboy said. "Bruce Lee?"

I said, "No, I'm God."

Hines executed a sloppy jab that missed.

I stepped up, intending to lay him down again, but he hit me with the palm of his right hand flat on my nose and mouth, and I went down at his feet.

"Waahoo!" yelled the cowboy.

"Now *you* get up," Hines said, his fists still circling.

The only way to describe what happened next is to say that I literally became action. I was not even remotely conscious of what I would do or how. I found myself instantly behind him; my body moved there so fast I wrenched my neck. He was still bobbing and weaving toward the spot where I had landed when he hit me. With the palm of my hand

201

flat on his smooth, bald skull, I deadened the synapsing activity of all the nerves to his arms, which dropped to his sides like white plastic bags full of water.

"Hey," he said.

I tried to slow down a bit, still moving around him like a humming-bird circling a hibiscus bush. I clipped him with a rapid-fire series of blows that went so fast I couldn't give an accurate count of them. I didn't hit him hard, I just smacked him thirty or forty times to impress his friend, then I touched his back with my index finger and removed all the air from his lungs. He let out this tiny sound, a brief syllable that sounded like half a note on the high end of a flute. For a few shocked seconds all three of us stood there in the moonlight looking at one an-other. Then, with a high-pitched, squeaky, little girl's voice, Hines said, "God." Whereupon he lurched forward, swerved a bit, and dropped to the pavement.

"You got it," I said.

The cowboy backed away.

"Don't worry," I told him, "your friend's not dead."

"Jesus Christ, you're fast," the cowboy said.

"You want some of me?" I asked. I bobbed and weaved at a more reasonable pace, moving toward him. "I'm Charles Wiggins, almighty boxer."

"Not me," he said. "Get away."

"You should be thankful I didn't kill him," I said.

"Don't kill anybody."

I stepped right up to him and peered into his frightened eyes. "I'm *God*, you stupid sonofabitch!"

He watched me in absolute and complete human terror. I felt sorry for him, to tell you the truth. But I couldn't help myself. "Don't ever mess with me," I yelled. "Got it?"

"Yessir."

"Because I'm pissed off. Do you read me, cowboy?"

"Yessir."

"I'm *God*, and I'm real pissed off."

"Okay, your holiness," the cowboy said. I could have told him I was Dangermouse and he would have pretended to believe me. It really was sort of funny. He knew I was crazy, but I was the toughest little wiry sonofabitch he'd ever seen. He didn't want any part of me — just like Dorothy.

It didn't take me long to feel guilty about what I had done to Ned Hines and his friend. Imagine God in a street brawl. I don't know if I can describe the complex mixture of emotions I experienced riding away from Jolly Roger's that night. I knew that I was going to have to get on with my life without Dorothy — that I was going to have to begin some sort of macro activity in the world, and I was going to have to do that without the benefit and comfort of the woman I loved. At the same time, I realized that I had engaged in the lowest form of human conflict, the everyday, common alley fight. I had let my emotions run away with me. This by itself might not have been so disturbing, but when I jumped on Ned Hines I did not know I was going to do it. Like my victim, I never saw it coming, so I wasn't sure if it was really me who jumped him. I had no time to think about what I would do. My body reacted instantly, like a ricocheting bullet. Afterward I did feel the most profound anger at the notion that two such complete failures of human creation would have the temerity to assault me, the acting deity, in a restaurant parking lot. So you tell me, was it the God in me who was pissed and who threw me into the fray? Or was it really just me losing my temper? When I told the cowboy I was God, I felt as if I were a third person commenting on my behavior. I might have just as easily said about myself, "He's God. He's pissed off."

As I drove away in the limo, I tried to force myself to think about what I was going to do for the rest of my term as God. I knew it would help me live through the ending of things between Dorothy and me if I simply cast myself into the currents of God's work — if I began, once and for all, the macro activity I had promised Chet to undertake that day at Crystal Lake.

My nose was sore. It felt frozen, and I could not forget the faint oily odor of Ned Hines's meaty hand. *Someday*, I thought, *I will be proud of the way I handled myself*; the power gave me a kind of physical prowess I might never have known. Thinking about having the power made me remember the days when I didn't have it, and that led me to the revelation that soon I would be without it again. My year would be finished, and God would be himself again.

It is difficult to express the terror that followed close on that thought. I think the marrow of my bones might have boiled. *I would no longer be acting God.* I would just be me again. Good old Wiggins, car salesman and general manager of Shale Motors. Even being the best general manager in the history of the business and having an attic full of crisp cash could not dissolve the furious anxiety that now bubbled hotly in every bone. It didn't matter what sort of life I made for myself when it was all over. I would simply be a person again, an ordinary person, just as helpless and weak and benighted as everybody else.

And I would not have Dorothy.

I pulled the big Chrysler into a vacant lot next to a dry cleaner's and turned off the engine. I wasn't sure I could continue to drive, the way I was feeling. I watched the street behind me in the rearview mirror. Hundreds of cars passed, each carrying other ordinary people. My mouth was so dry it felt like my tongue was buried in sand. What would I do? I couldn't get the question out of my head.

12

I let the days go by, the rest of May and part of June. Dorothy came and went courteously, busy with final exams and preparations for summer school. She seemed to pay a little more attention to the girls, but something that had the taste of finality had happened between us, and it made her oddly uncomfortable. In spite of the fact that it was a movement toward what she wanted, she was very nervous about it.

I went through the motions at Shale Motors. Dottie was back on the job and happy as an oil sheik. Mr. Shale pursued her like a schoolboy, and she walked around behaving as though she were actually attractive. Somehow, once she was in love with Mr. Shale, his curious sexual demands became less intolerable, and her ability to refuse him when she needed to was developing into a high art.

I spent a lot of time in my office reading the newspapers, looking for something about the world and my problems as if they were one and the same. I might have been trying to find a macro activity that would influence my situation with Dorothy.

It seemed to me that if I decreed that humans would remain faithful to the people they love and never want to leave them, or if I willed that all women would come to see aggression and possessiveness as a necessary outgrowth of primitive existence, as the thing that allowed the race to survive, perhaps that would affect Dorothy in positive ways. I might create a new woman and a new man. Make men and women glad to be in each other's company without ultimately getting sexual with each other. Not that I'd eliminate sex. I'd just eliminate the tendency in men to relate to women only in sexual ways.

I might actually make men and women like each other. Maybe that would reawaken something in Dorothy.

But then I had the problem of messing with God's design. That was what I would have to do. Though I was still not very good at getting human beings to do what I wanted, it hardly mattered, since choice certainly doesn't play much of a role where the design is concerned. The problem is, there's something wrong with the design. Women are different from men. I'm not just speaking anatomically, either. Women and men are different in their souls. It's really a sort of miracle that they have anything to do with each other.

At the least, a man can impregnate more than three hundred women in a single year. At most, if the circumstances are right, a man can impregnate two or three women a day for a year. That's over a thousand different women. If you give most men the chance and tell them it will be okay, they'll be happy to make the effort at a thousand. Only culture, religion, women they love, and their own limitations and fears keep them from it.

Except in extremely rare cases, a woman can bear only one child a year. When she is pregnant, nature conspires against her attractiveness. She may be beautiful to the man who loves her, but not many men are sexually interested in a woman once she's fully pregnant.

This creates a significant difference in the nature of men and women. Men have the sexual loyalty of cats and dogs. They can engage in sexual intercourse with such things as sheep and chickens and even apples. Oddly enough, a man does not have to be in love, or in any way emotionally involved, with any of the thousand women, or the sheep, or the chicken, or the apple. A man does not care whether the room is dimly lit, whether there is soft music, or whether the ewe or chicken or apple is comfortable. Now, a lot of men go against their sexual nature, their biologically determined polygamous soul, and allow social conditioning to change them into faithful husbands who are loving and loyal. These men find other outlets for their true nature — outlets such as playing aggressive sports, racing boats, or studying the campaigns of

Napoleon. Some men take up an intricate hobby, like building model airplanes, fly-fishing, or carving little wooden cathedrals. These outlets require hours of concentration and effort, and effectively allow men to escape the knowledge that what they really wish they could do is find a new woman in whom they can, as they might crudely put it, "bury the bishop." A lot of these men — and I count myself among them proudly (I have never, in eleven and a half years of marriage, been even slightly tempted by another woman) — die very young of heart attacks if they are not careful about what they eat and drink.

Women have an interest in such things as love, emotions, the value of tenderness. If it were not for women, human beings would still squat with the other apes and pick ticks off one another all day. The world would be much less developed, and probably much more beautiful. Women gave birth to civilization and continue to influence it every day. Women were the first humans to think of the idea of peace. They invented caresses and soft pats. They helped pioneer the embrace, which, before women put it to good use, was a form of mortal combat. Women created such things as blankets, bandages, pillows, mattresses, perfumes, cradles. They were the wind that blew the cradle down out of the tree. They needed love. When they were eight and a half months pregnant, they simply could not hunt down an antelope and choke it to death. It was difficult to stand up, much less sprint after a rabbit. Mastodons were out of the question. A woman needed a man in order to survive. So she invented love and fidelity so she could keep whatever man she attracted. It was easy enough to attract a man, because women possessed what every man wanted, what every man would wait in line to get. And women are, after all, easy to love. They are tender, usually, and when they are cruel you often don't find out about it until it's too late to hurt them back. Their violence is more subtle, and hence more lasting. Still, they definitely prefer kindness, even when they have to be kind to people they hate. They usually love each other, and when they don't they pretend to. They do not want a man to be feminine. No. They love a very strong, masculine man who — and here's the part they love — contains underneath his coarse exterior a warm, sensitive, articulate, caring person. In other words, a woman.

The truth is, women are responsible for all that is good in human creation — and, since humans would never have risen upright and stopped dragging their knuckles along the ground if it were not for women, they are responsible for all that is terrible in human creation. You can therefore blame all the parking lots and factories and oil slicks and strip mines and paved green fields and murdered trees on women. You can also thank women for love, tenderness, charity, the idea of peace.

Of course, women do create some evil themselves, and men create some good. Mozart made beautiful music. Catherine the Great built fake cities. Lincoln freed the slaves, and the Beast of Buchenwald collected odd lampshades. But generally speaking, the race is controlled by the male, and the male is especially prone to such things as violence, murder, torture, butchery, and high-rise development.

When a man desires a woman, his feelings are mostly biological. Some men desire a woman because there is the potentiality for love there, but this is rarer than anyone would be willing to believe. Frequently a man's first attraction and his first thought have very little to do with love. Usually love develops later in the relationship, but love can nonetheless be passionate, as my early years with Dorothy attest. When a woman desires a man, her feelings are mostly spiritual, and have little or nothing to do with her sex drive.

Now, sexual *desire* is not the same thing as sexual *drive*. Most women, once sufficiently aroused, have the same intense sexual desire as any man. In fact, some have considerably more. A young woman whose interest is piqued can rival in real action the sexual lies and fantasies of the seediest and most loud-mouthed male. The sexual *drive* of the average woman, however, since she is concerned more with matters of the heart than with matters of the body, can be represented by the following graph (see Figure 1), in which the dark area represents that part of the female brain taken up by sexual drive.

In contrast, the sexual drive of the average male is not necessarily creature-specific and is not influenced by other parts of his brain. The male sex drive is represented by the graph in Figure 2.

A male can be ready to make love in fifteen seconds or less. He can be done with it in less than a minute. It takes a woman a good half-hour to remember that sex exists. If the atmosphere is not right, or if she's been thinking about something fairly complex and vexing, like the killing of whales or getting the little bones out of canned salmon, you can forget it. She won't be ready ever.

■

Figure 1. The sexual drive of the average female

Figure 2. The sexual drive of the average male

What on earth could God have had in mind? Why would he create such significant differences between men and women and then expect them to remain happy throughout fifty years or more of married life? If the design is in favor of love not happening, if love is only born out of biological differences that have long ago been subdued in men and women, and if there is nothing in the nature of men and women that is truly compatible, then what is the point of love at all? Why engage in anything so certain to cause sorrow?

I didn't spend much time thinking about these questions. I was terrified of the mess I'd make if I should tinker with God's design even a little bit. The problems between Dorothy and me were not sexual, anyway. As I've said, I would have had to change the entire psychological makeup of men and women to get at what was troubling us. And to tell you the truth, until that night at Jolly Roger's, I would have had a difficult time identifying what our problems were. Once I knew, it was very difficult to accept, even though I realized that Dorothy had been telling me over and over right from the beginning of our troubles. I was simply not what Dorothy wanted; I was simply not what Dorothy believed she needed. Not that she coveted some other sort of fellow. She didn't want me or anyone. She just wanted to be herself, by herself. Imagine that.

❋

Without wishing it consciously, I began to follow Dorothy around. No matter where I was or what I was doing, I would conjure her and watch everything she did: from class to class, from cafeteria to library, from library to home. I did not often let myself get distracted from her.

Don't get me wrong; this was not surveillance. I would not have intervened in her life in the slightest way. I was as defeated as I've ever been.

One unseasonably cool afternoon in late June, as she was taking a stroll around the campus, I caught her thinking of me. She had just eaten in the campus hangout, a greasy, thoroughly white-tiled little room called Big Pink's, and as she came out into the clear day and bright sun, she remembered being with me on just such a day, in fall, in the mountains. She remembered how fine and sanctified and permanent she felt that day, as if only she and I knew what love really meant, and we might not ever tell anyone else or we might announce it to the whole earth.

It tempted her to remember us that way, and as she walked across the shade-splattered lawn she began to feel exquisite fear. She felt as though she were standing on the balcony of a ten-story building, looking over the edge. There was no sadness in her face, no fear or anxiety measuring her walk. She seemed to know exactly where she was going. She was all business and purpose, as if she were on her way to a board meeting. As I watched her, I realized she was crying. I was sitting in my office when I conjured her, so I could join her in tears without embarrassment. I never knew sadness could be so physical and lasting. I thought my heart might explode from the weight of it.

She stepped to the curb, looked down the street. She was thinking about how badly everything between us had gone; her whole mind was occupied by every sentence, every word of the last few months. She felt lonesome and mean, as though she were friendless and wanted to be friendless, in spite of the unhappiness it caused her. She made up her mind to resist this sorrow with all her strength, although by degrees she became aware of a particular sort of impression that she would not have been able to describe adequately. It was very much like satisfaction. In some ways, it provided her with the kind of pain she needed to feel good about giving up what she was certain she needed to have done with: her life with me.

She wanted to deny how she felt to someone. This was very much like grief. Yet as she made her way up the street she kept reminding herself that leaving me was also the most necessary thing in her life. The tears on her face seemed to freeze in the cool air and the cold tracks on her cheeks intensified her anguish. It took everything in her to resist sobbing out loud. There were so many things she was sorry for. She had taken years to think of what she might become. And in all that time, while I loved her, she had seen me as an end. I was what happened to her when she grew up. The children were what happened to her after she met me. Our family was what became of her. The only choice left to her would be deciding what retirement community to move into.

This, too, heightened her sadness.

She stopped under a dogwood tree on the boulevard. A young man, probably a student, approached her and asked if she was all right.

"I'm fine," she said.

"Are you sure?"

"Yes. I'm not unhappy. I'm just feeling sad."

The student nodded and patted her arm.

Dorothy smiled. She had a handkerchief in her hand, and she touched it to her eyes. If the student had asked her what was wrong, she would have told him all of it. She wanted so badly to say everything. She felt trapped in her hot mind, overwhelmed by grief and thoughts of me and change and loss.

For a few minutes I thought she might sit down right there and lose control, but then she straightened herself. Her face registered a decision, a new resolve. She wiped her nose with the handkerchief, put her hands in her pockets, and began a regal walk across the street.

She was so beautiful. As she stepped up onto the sidewalk on the other side, she tilted her head and shrugged her jacket higher on the back of her neck. Something in the turn of her head, in the way she closed the collar of her jacket, touched me deeply, and suddenly, as though I had been there with her and lived it, I remembered her when she was a little girl — just like one of my own children — standing in front of a mirror with a white bonnet on, hoping for happiness. She turned herself, smiling gaily and studying the curve of the bonnet and the curls in her hair.

Then something very strange happened. I was surprised to find that I felt sorry for that little girl, and for unwittingly hurting so many things in her. I realized that time had swallowed her, and now she was once again seeking the future. The look of expectation on little Dorothy's face, her innocence of everything yet to come, made me wish we had never met. For the first time, I saw Dorothy and me as I believed God must see us all: as earnest, helpless, hopeful, disconsolate, and erratic victims of our own lies and dreams.

I opened my desk and took out a handful of tissues to wipe the tears from my face, and as I did this I willed that Dorothy's pain be short-lived. *Perhaps*, I thought, *I am now finally learning to act like God, and to give up my personal life altogether.* If I had not been fighting tears so hard, that notion might have made me happy.

At the end of the day I drove my car over to the lake again. I was afraid to go home — embarrassed to face my wife so soon after she had discovered the pain of her estrangement. I think I was hoping that Chet would come to see me again so I could tell him how terrible I felt. In spite of the new charity spinning in my breast, I did not see how I could hurl myself into macro activity as long as I felt this gnawing sense of loss.

I don't know how long I stayed at the lake. It was dark when I got there, and I stayed by the car and watched the moon rise in the chilly sky. When it was finally too cold, I got back in the car, intending to drive on home. I didn't have a chance to start the engine. The car was just suddenly propelled out of that parking lot as if it were fired from a cannon. It lurched around the corner on two howling tires. I screamed, grabbed the steering wheel, and slammed on the brakes, but the wheel spun in my hands. The view in front of me whirled like a bad film, and suddenly I was looking directly at the rear end of a parked dump truck.

I didn't have time to draw a breath. I went into that truck so hard and so fast, I'm fairly amazed, even now, that I had time to recognize what it was before I hit it.

Thus, unexpectedly, and without warning or time to prepare, began my prearranged guided tour of heaven.

13

I swear I didn't feel a thing when I hit the back of that truck. The world just seemed to explode, and then it was instantly very dark. I heard a siren, far off. People seemed to whisper in my ears, and they pulled at my flesh until I started begging them to stop. Or at least I tried to beg them. Then I saw a bright light and realized I was in an operating room. I heard somebody say, "We don't have a pulse."

It was cold. Everything around me seemed to be made of metal, and it touched my naked skin and stuck fast there. I couldn't move. I felt a hand place itself over my nose and mouth, then I heard another voice — a different voice — say, "We're losing him. Come on, goddamnit!"

A deep-throated voice whispered, "Come now, let's go."

Then I was free. As light as the husk of a cicada, moving above the table where my body lay. Yet I felt like a body; I had the same shape and structure but without substance, like a hollow version of myself, fragile and with absolutely nothing I could touch or brush off or scratch. I don't think anybody could have seen through me, but I don't think I would have filtered smoke or air very much. It was definitely odd, and not at all like you often see it pictured. I had the feeling that I was highly flammable, and that a good wind might decompose me. And I was above the room, looking down into it like a child staring into a soap bubble. My body was on the operating table, and seven people worked over it with almost sexual intensity. They were trying to bring me back, but I watched them with a bored and even detached sort of amusement. I was lying on air above them, and gravity seemed reversed. I could not have climbed down to that table any more than a person can levitate himself from a bed to a ceiling. I felt as if I had fallen to this place above the room. I didn't know if I could still hear, because it was so quiet. But then I heard the whispering voice say, "Come now. Come."

I turned and saw what looked like a narrow passage — it had textured walls, so it took on the appearance of a magnified version of an esophagus. The walls seemed to move. I tried to ask if I were being swallowed, and although I heard what I wanted to say, much in the way that you and I hear our thoughts, I don't know if I actually made anything we might rightly call sound.

The passage gradually lit up, until it became so bright I could not see the walls anymore. I was just moving down a corridor of light toward even brighter light. I was no longer cold, and I felt the most excruciating happiness. I can't describe it in words anyone would understand. It was both wonderful and painful. It seemed to be a mixture of all the possible intense, wondrous, and desirable emotions. If there was a drug that could make you feel that way, it would be illegal, and everybody would use it.

At the very center of the brighter light in front of me, a shadow seemed to swirl and gather like a cloud of wispy smoke. It gradually took on the shape of a man, and the light stopped filtering through it. The figure grew, but I did not think it moved toward me. Rather, I was propelled toward it, without volition.

When it seemed I would pass right through it, the shadow reached out and stopped me.

"Well, here we are." It was Chet. Or I should say it was Chet's voice. I could not make out any features because of the extraordinary light behind him.

"This will all subside," he said. "Or most of it will. After you've made the transition. We've had to put you into a sort of coma to bring this little visit off, so there will still be a certain dreamy quality about everything."

"This is heaven?"

"Not quite. Not yet." He started to move back from me, and I felt myself set again into motion.

"This is extremely odd," I said.

Chet laughed. "Human language is so inadequate."

"Sometimes."

"It can describe only human things."

"That's all it needs to describe." I was next to him now, and the light seemed to collect in him and glow back at me. "You look so different here."

"Oh, I'm sorry, will you feel more comfortable if I do this?" Immediately he evolved into the Chet I remembered. He was still wearing the hat, bright shirt, and red slacks.

"You can go around in here dressed like that?"

"Sure. You can pretty much dress any way you like."

I reached for the fabric of his sleeve. It surprised me to actually feel cloth. "That feels as if it's real."

"When you die," he said, "you bring all your senses and apprehensions with you. Memory. Desire. Longings and fancies. Everything."

"So this is really cloth?"

"If that's what you feel when you touch it."

"*Is* it cloth?"

He laughed — a short "heh-heh" kind of laugh. "It's as much cloth as you think it is."

"I mean like on earth."

"How do you know it's real cloth there?"

"I can touch it."

"You touched it here."

"Okay. I can put a match to it."

"There could be fire here." He smiled, and his teeth glistened in the light.

"Real fire?"

"I don't suppose you go around touching fire, now, do you?"

"Would it burn me if I did?"

"I don't know. Nobody here wants to find that out."

"Does it give off heat?"

He pointed to the light ahead of us, which seemed to shimmer and pulsate now. It might have been the source of the northern lights, the way it swirled and danced above us in what I suddenly realized was a dark, ethereal sky. "If we feel warm, perhaps it is best to attribute our comfort to the light," he said. "Though as you can plainly feel, it does

217

not really put forth any heat. We feel warm because we are not cold, and we are not cold because we feel no chill, and we feel no chill because we are warm. If we were hot, we would need a chill. If we were cold, we would need heat. Since we are neither hot nor cold, we don't need either heat or chill. You see?"

"So what do you do up here for ice cubes?"

He seemed slightly exasperated. "You see?"

"Seems like you went a long way around —"

"To make a point. Precisely. I've always preferred the oblique approach to important questions." He put his arm around me, and I felt the weight of it.

"I might as well be alive," I said.

"And so you are."

"But would it be like this if I were *really* dead?"

"You have no right to ask that question."

"Tell me anyway." I felt like his chum, like we were headed for a saloon to lift a glass or two.

"Yes. It is almost exactly like this when you die."

I felt more relaxed. After a pause I said, "Heaven's not so bad — what the hell."

He laughed again. This time it was more genuine. "What the hell," he said.

"And everybody's so afraid of death."

"Yes, human beings are an odd lot." He squeezed my shoulder. "They fight just as hard to keep from being born as they do to keep from dying."

"I wouldn't mind dying at all if I knew about all this."

He didn't answer me. We kept moving toward the light, and though it didn't decrease any, it seemed to grow more diffuse, as if we were actually walking away from it. I couldn't feel any sensation in particular, although a powerful euphoria still possessed me. Gradually I began to notice objects I recognized, except that they were somehow disembodied and appeared to float in the air as we passed. I'd see a tree go by, all by itself, surrounded by the light. Then a daffodil, a blue stone, a puddle of water. It was all so eerie that I almost reached out and tried to snatch one of the objects from the light.

"This is really strange," I said.

Chet took his arm off my shoulder and moved a little in front of me. "Remember, you are only a visitor."

I laughed. "You're going to tell me to mind my manners in heaven? I'm already here — how am I doing?"

"I told you, this isn't heaven yet," he said, and there was a decided change in his voice. "I don't know if you're going to be allowed to see that."

"Well, what *is* all this?"

"It's the entrance."

"No, I mean why have I been brought here?"

"You're going to see the part of heaven that all human beings who are intended for heaven see when they die. But actual heaven I'm not so sure about."

"Why?"

"What you're going to see is the vestibule or parlor."

"You're kidding."

"That's what you would probably call it." His voice was softer now, more human.

"When will we get there?"

"You'll see."

I cannot say I had any consciousness of time, so I don't have any idea how long we moved along in the light. Objects passed us like luggage on a conveyor belt, and by degrees things began to take on a more fixed position. Chet fell into a studied silence, as if he were checking each object for punctuality or accuracy. Before I could ask him what was happening, the movement stopped and we were standing in the middle of a very long street. All around was the odor of trees, and the sound of a breeze brushing through leaves.

This is going to shock you, and I don't know if God will let me set this down on the page — if he won't create a blank right here after I write the words — but do you know where we were? It was a giant suburban neighborhood, with cars and telephone poles and black driveways surrounded by green, well-trimmed hedges and shrubs. In the distance, looming in what looked like soft, benevolent morning sun, I could see the spires of a vast city, and beyond that solid white clouds that rose as high and straight as any I'd ever seen. They looked like huge doors at the end of the earth.

"It's beautiful," I said, only half meaning it. To tell the truth, I was a bit disillusioned. I almost said, "I had to be smashed into a coma to see this?" But I realized it was, after all, Chet's home. And you wouldn't be impolite enough to walk into somebody's house and say, "Gee, it isn't decorated like I thought it would be. Kind of disappointing."

Chet said, "You might say it's morning here."

I saw a dour, sad-faced man emerge from one of the houses, pick up a newspaper, and retreat inside.

"There're newspapers here?"

"Everything humans wish to have is here."

"What's it called, the *Heavenly Times*?"

"No."

"Let me guess. The *Paradise Post*? The *Eden Enquirer*? *God's Gazette*?"

"You're going to have to stop doing that."

"What?"

"Making wisecracks."

"I'm sorry. You've got to admit, from a certain point of view it's kind of funny. I expected to see seraphim performing canticles at a cloudy gate or something." I put my hands in my pockets, feeling extraordinary pleasure because I could do that. I gradually became aware of weight on my feet, the hard surface of the street beneath me. My senses came swimming back, and with them a consciousness of body that was no different from being alive on earth. Only a slight blurriness on the edge of my vision seemed to persist, but I got used to it fairly quickly, and after a while I didn't notice it any more than a person notices the rims of his glasses.

A Toyota went by. Then a Buick. They made the same sound cars always make, but there was no odor of gasoline or exhaust.

"Lots of cars," I said.

"And trucks, planes, and trains." Chet pushed his hat back, rubbed his chin. "I told you, everything humans have is here."

"Cancer? Is cancer here?"

He frowned.

"I'm sorry."

"There's no need for such things here. People are already dead."

"But don't they wreck their cars once in a while?"

220

A professorial smirk adorned his face, letting me know I was once again being the inadequate student, asking the wrong questions. "I'm going to give you a brief tour. After that I will answer any questions you have."

"*Any* questions?"

"Any question I *can* answer."

"And you won't be enigmatic and mysterious?"

"I will tell you the truth. Once you've seen everything, there won't be any need for me to be subtle."

"Now I'm *really* looking forward to the tour." As I said this, Chet stopped next to a blue Ford van parked at the curb.

"Here's our transportation."

"Doesn't anybody drive a Dodge up here?" I was thinking, *After I die I can open a dealership.*

❊

The tour lasted most of what we would probably identify as a day and a night. It never got very dark, but there was a time there when I thought it might — the sky looked like a washed-out version of our own evening sky, but then the light started to intensify again and it was as bright as ever. I saw so many things I don't know where to start. If you came to earth for the first time, what would you say about it? The place was like earth. Chet told me, in the first few minutes of the tour, that there's a lot of development going on.

"Even here," I said.

"Oh yes. Whatever evolves on the earth happens a little bit here. Except for violence — wars, earthquakes, and such." He drove the van as if it didn't matter if he touched the steering wheel or not. He turned to me when he talked, letting his hands rest on the wheel as if we were sitting in a parking lot getting ready to open our brown bags and have a sandwich.

"No tragedy?" I said.

"Not like on earth."

"No accidents?"

"Oh, of course not. That would involve chance."

"Ah."

"Nothing happens accidentally here."

"It's all determined, then?"

"Most of it. Everything but what we do."

"You and I?"

"No, the people here. They can affect certain things by choosing to."

"Give me an example."

"I'd rather save that until later." He turned his head away, watched the passing trees. "Right now I just want you to see everything."

"If everything's determined, I guess there aren't any racetracks or roulette wheels, right?"

"Oh, yes." He smiled. "I guess you got one of your examples."

We were headed toward the city. The road seemed to go straight for it. We didn't make any turns, though there were plenty of side streets and adjoining roads. The stop signs were huge, and it seemed that to the left of the road, in the far distance behind tall green trees, there were high, blue, shadowy mountains. As we moved along, the landscape got more and more filled with houses — larger, more substantial homes. "This is one of the better neighborhoods," Chet said.

"Some people are lucky here, right?"

"No, everybody lives in the sort of house they want."

"That's one of the choices, then?" I felt very important and smart. I wondered if the people we saw knew I was the acting deity.

"Well," he said, "I wouldn't put it that way."

"Do they have families?"

"Most do. At least *some* of their family." He seemed slightly unnerved by the question. He answered it too quickly, and I perceived that he was trying to make an answer that would not lead to any more questions.

He parked on the side of the road near a great arch that curved over what appeared to be the entrance to the city. There were more people now, moving busily about in the same purposeful way you'd see in any city. It might have been St. Louis, except that it appeared clean, almost washed out, like an architect's idealized drawing. I wondered if there were police departments or law offices or hospitals in this city. If perhaps one might find a brothel, or a drug parlor, or a street devoted to pornographic bookshops and peep shows.

"We'll get out here for a while," Chet said, opening the door.

As I got out of the van, I saw a dog running along the road to my right. "There are animals here?"

"Yeah, some people have to have them." He closed the door. "Not many insects, though. Butterflies and a few lightning bugs." He went around behind the van and opened the door there. When he emerged, he carried a pair of binoculars. "Here," he said, handing them to me. "You might need these."

We walked a few blocks to a bridge overlooking what appeared to be a rapid transit terminal. There were tracks going in all directions.

"This is where people make lots of choices," he said.

"Where do the tracks go?"

"Other neighborhoods, the countryside."

"There's a countryside?"

"See those tracks over there?" He pointed to a brightly shining pair of tracks that disappeared deep into the city. "Take a look at those."

Close up, through the glasses, I saw that the tracks were silver, and absolutely clean. Trains moved on the other tracks, but there was not even a freestanding car on the silver ones.

"Those are the tracks to heaven," Chet said. "If you go there, you'll ride on them."

"I hope I get a chance to see it."

He didn't say anything.

"It'd be hard for it to be better than this, though. I like it here."

"A few come to like it," he said. "This is the biggest place you'll ever see. Absolutely. Except for heaven. Heaven is bigger."

"It's difficult to believe this isn't actually heaven."

"Well, it isn't," Chet said.

"I know, I know."

Through the glasses I saw colossal silvery clouds that seemed almost painted on the dome above us.

"I'm afraid I won't understand all this," I said.

"Don't worry. You'll understand," Chet said. "I'll see to that."

⁂

We went back to the van and drove into the city. Chet showed me movie theaters, restaurants, clothing stores. I tried to feign great interest, but I have to admit I was growing bored. I felt like I was getting a tour of the earth by someone who held a less than realistic vision of what it contained. I saw no police cars, no fire engines or rushing ambulances. There didn't seem to be any launderettes or pawn shops. No alleys full of trash, empty cans and bottles, and slumping street people grasping brown paper bags.

But the most curious feature of this city was the people I did see. If you've ever noticed the way mourners behave at a funeral when the speeches are over and everybody has to leave the gravesite and return to somber black limousines, you have some idea what everybody looked like. I don't think I witnessed a single human smile on the whole tour. Chet talked cheerfully enough — in fact, his enthusiasm sometimes grated on my nerves because of the way it contradicted the visages we passed in every corner of the city. I came close to asking him about it more than once, but I had resolved to contain my gathering doubts about everybody's willingness to occupy this space in "preheaven," as I had come to think of it, until Chet was ready to answer my questions. Since he had promised me the truth, I didn't see any reason to push him into anything until he was ready. Still, it was very difficult after a while to resist the temptation to ask why the vestibule to heaven seemed so heavily populated with sourpusses.

After our visit to the rapid transit terminal, we returned to the van and drove for most of the tour up and down the perfect streets of the city. Then we drove to the airport, and I got a magnificent view of things from the cockpit of a smooth-riding, almost silent helicopter.

This is what I saw:

The vestibule is laid out like earth in almost every way. There is only one city, but it is large enough to contain most of Asia, and probably North and South America as well. Surrounding it on the east, west, and south are a thousand broad and extensive suburbs, with millions of homes sprawling in regimental order. To the west, where I saw the mountains, is a great plain, mostly empty, with an occasional small town or village sprouting along the highway like a weed in a badly tended carrot patch, and beyond that the mountains, blue and majestic, with great snowy peaks that pierce puffy white clouds. To the east, as far away as the moon from earth, is a body of water that seems endless. Along its shores are more towns and villages. To the north, the track to heaven winds its way across another empty plain, a treeless expanse of barren land that finds its terminus at the base of the high white clouds

I mentioned earlier. Chet told me those were the doors to heaven and not clouds at all. I realized, once I had a chance to view them directly, that the bright light that illuminates everything perpetually and without heat emanates from behind those doors and seems to leak out through their cracks and hinges.

Virtually every sort of earthly climate, landscape, and locale is represented in the vestibule to heaven. Or I should say every sort of *desirable* climate, landscape, and locale. Though there are great plains, I saw no desert and no steamy jungle. Even the body of water had only a thin strip of sand along its edge. Kids from California would be very polite if they called it a beach.

Chet told me that what people wanted, generally they could have here. Even if they had not verbalized it, or had not lived when or where it was possible to have it on earth. So even the Bedouins ended up living in verdant pastures. He emphasized that there was very little bad weather in the vestibule, since that usually meant struggle for somebody, and then he said something that really puzzled me. He said, "There's only one struggle here."

We were in the helicopter, high in the light — you might call it a sky, though I felt no wind, and at that altitude there was very little color to it. He flew the craft the same way he drove the van: inattentively and without much care.

"Only one struggle?" I said.

"Only one."

There was a long pause while I surveyed the vast green surface below. I wanted very much just to say, "Which struggle is that?" But I was getting curious signals from his demeanor that made me suspicious: at times his voice was heavy with drama and he'd stare at me as if he were expecting some specific reaction. I had this vague notion that perhaps I was being manipulated a bit, that Chet's words were calculated to elicit a particular response. And as you've probably figured out by now, a very large portion of the sap that feeds my bark is basically contrary.

Chet pointed to the blue water far in the distance. "People who liked living by the ocean? When they taste that water, it's salty."

"No kidding."

"Fresh-water people taste fresh water."

"Even if they do it at exactly the same time?"

"Right."

"So the water's not really salty? Or is it that it is not really not salty?"

He smiled and turned the craft toward the mountains. As we passed over some of the smaller villages along the way, I noticed an extraordinary variety of architectural designs. Apparently people who preferred the living style of other centuries could have it.

"Whatever people prefer," Chet said. "If they want to live in the thirteenth century they can."

"I guess most people prefer the city or the suburbs, then?"

"They eventually come around to that sort of thing. That's what the tracks are for." He seemed to wait for me to say something. Then he said, "You see, some of these people have been here a very long time."

"I guess."

"They come here. The earth goes on, revolves, changes. Developments on earth gradually make their way here because of the wishes and dreams of the constantly gathering dead. People who died in the thirteenth century get to see what the new dead bring with them, and gradually they want those things too."

"But not everybody lives like this on earth now. There's poverty and —"

"Oh, but the earth is so — so cross-connected, what with TV and radio and satellites." He let out a short laugh. "You should see the faces of some of the primitives and deprives when they get here, though."

"Primitives and deprives?"

"People not generally exposed to the current earthly delights. Even the savages give in to all this eventually."

"And they can just have it?"

"Sure."

"They don't have to work for it?"

"That would be struggle."

We passed over the first range of mountains, and I saw below a blue-green valley with a river snaking through it like tinsel on a bough of a Christmas tree. Along the path of the river, tiny houses seemed bundled together as though they had come to rest there after falling down the mountain. On the other side of the valley was another mountain, taller and bereft of trees, which glistened in the light from the doors of heaven.

For a while my companion surveyed everything calmly, without comment. I thought we might continue westward and discover more valleys and high mountains, layer after layer of them, but when we had nearly reached the other side of the valley, he turned the helicopter around and headed back for the city.

"The tour over?" I said.

"The visual part of it, anyway."

"It was breathtaking." I felt really stupid for saying such a thing, since I was definitely not breathing. Body or no body, all of the functions you and I recognize as part and parcel of physical existence were simply missing. To some degree, I think that might have been a reason for the incredible feeling of euphoria I felt in the beginning — a sensation that had diminished since my arrival, but that nonetheless continued to run in me like blood. I am telling you the truth about this: I was entirely myself, I had my body with me, I could see my face in the glass of the helicopter windshield, but I did not have to breathe or eat or sleep or ask to go to the men's room. So perhaps I had not experienced euphoria at all. Perhaps it was only the first rush of the soul's release from the stuffy chamber of the body and its thousand little pains and nagging unfulfilled wishes. Like when you get out of a hot shower in the summertime and you feel wonderfully cool. You're not really cool at all. You're just not so hot anymore.

As we were descending I happened to mention that I had not seen any children.

"None of them are here," Chet said.

"Why not?"

"The little ones went on." He moved his head as if to show me the direction.

"Went on where?"

"There," he said, pointing toward the light. "Through the doors."

"Oh. Heaven."

"They gave up the struggle. They didn't have enough of life to ruin them, so you couldn't really call it much of a struggle."

He faced the instruments as we settled to the ground, but he was not really doing anything but watching. Then he said, "Others, they didn't deserve this."

"Other children?"

"They didn't make it," he said. "They were not worth . . ." He turned to me. "They were not worth saving."

This struck me very hard, and immediately my mind reeled with questions. I might have stammered trying to ask them all at once. Before I could get a single one of them articulated, Chet reached up and turned off the engine. There was an uncomfortable pause while he appeared to regard me with a critical eye. Then he said, "Heaven is not what you think."

I did not realize it at the time, but I see now that Chet was given to understatement.

To some degree, heaven is what humans have dreamed it to be. Or at least the vestibule is. Life does continue, and it continues in ways that most would probably not find entirely disagreeable. You bring yourself with you to the vestibule of heaven, if you make it to heaven at all. Chet said not everybody gets to heaven. Fewer than three out of ten survive the catastrophe of death, and their final reward is not contingent upon any earthly behavior. Salesmen and senators, harlots and heathens, philanthropists and fanatics — the selection process includes them all. Some beautiful and some ugly, some with perfect physiques and some so disfigured it is hard to determine race or sex.

"Hitler is here," he said. "Ivan the Terrible. Idi Amin. Every shambling, brutish, and hairy creature in the history of the earth is represented. And there are saints: Aquinas, Anselm, Augustine."

He went on listing people, both saintly and sinister. "It is only with a peculiar blend of self-righteousness and blindness that a man or a woman can say, 'I belong here,'" he said. "The truth is, no one knows why he has survived death and been allowed to wait here to enter heaven."

And that is what all of them were doing. Waiting in the vestibule to enter heaven.

"Why don't they just go in?" I said.

"They can't." He got down out of the helicopter, and I did the same. I had the feeling he wasn't ready for my questions yet. We walked back to the van, silently. When we were seated in the front seat and he had started the engine, I said, "Why can't they?"

"No one can. Not anyone. Any *one*. You understand?"

"No. I don't."

He was actually driving now, turning the wheel as though he had to keep the van on the road.

After a while I said, "Is it because they can't enter heaven that everybody's so . . ." I stopped, looked at him. I felt as if he knew what I was going to say. "Is that why everybody seems so sad here?"

"No," he said, looking out the window at the great white doors and the scattered light. "No. Everybody is sad because eventually they *have* to enter heaven."

If I'd had breath, I'd have lost it at those words. As it was, I felt as if I had just begun a long fall from a great height.

"Good Lord," I said.

※

Sometimes, when one has a choice in the matter, one chooses to remain innocent just a trifle longer than necessary. On the drive back into the city, Chet and I did not speak. I believe I was afraid of what I was about to learn, and he sensed that. He took me to a great silver fieldhouse next to the mass transit terminal he'd shown me earlier.

"Thanks for the grand tour," I said.

He waved his hand. "Follow me. Now you'll get your questions answered."

I was surprised to see that the fieldhouse had turnstiles and ticket machines. Inside was an immense stadium, with red seats and a yellow wooden floor like a tremendous, oversized basketball court, except there were no baskets or white lines. Chet walked to the middle of the floor and sat in a black leather lounging chair. In front of the chair was a small table with a chessboard on it, set up and ready for play. There was a small folding hard-backed chair for me. Chet pointed to it. "Sit," he said.

"Is this a gym?" I tried not to notice the difference between his chair and mine.

"You might say that."

"For what sport?"

"Whatever anybody wants. You and I are going to play chess."

I sat down. "You mean —"

"It's an all-purpose court. Whatever sport people wish to see here, they see. Football, basketball, track, baseball, hockey —"

"Hockey?"

"Even hockey."

"And you charge admission?"

"Well — it wouldn't be authentic without the turnstiles."

There was a long pause while I tried to shuffle my questions into some sort of coherent order. I could feel Chet's eyes on me and understood that he might be getting impatient, but I wanted to be thorough and certain about what I asked him. I admit I was also somewhat apprehensive.

My chair was close to his, and I found it difficult to appear comfortable before his unblinking eyes. "I guess I'm ready," I said.

"Your move."

"Are we really going to play chess?"

"Why not? It will help limber your mind."

"I've never played this game very well." The last thing I wanted to do was engage in a complex board game with God's emissary.

"You have God's power. Just look at the board, study it."

I studied the pieces in front of me. Without much effort I calculated that there were 169,518,829,100,544,000,000,000,000,000 possible combinations in the first ten moves. To avoid making the right move, I chose pawn to king's bishop three.

Chet frowned, shook his head. He moved his pawn to king four.

I moved my king's knight pawn to knight four.

"Very funny," Chet said. He moved his queen to rook five. "Mate." He was very disappointed. "You're going to keep doing things like that, aren't you?"

"I told you I don't play very well."

He sat back and folded his arms. "Go ahead. Ask me anything you want, but remember, there are some questions to which, you may be displeased to find, one does not want the answer."

He could not have known how right he was. Nothing he had ever said to me could have prepared me for what I was to learn from him that day. When it was all over, I understood perfectly why everyone in the vestibule seemed so demonstrably sad.

I did not think I would ever be able to reveal this to a single breathing soul. It was only after a momentous decision I was to make later — a decision that prompted the writing of this narrative — that I determined to disclose, once and for all, what Chet said to me. Even so, I have suffered searing anguish over whether I should reveal any of my conversation with Chet in that empty, all-purpose stadium, under the sunless sky of the vestibule to heaven. I simply cannot keep it to myself, though, since it is at least partially responsible for the predicament in which I now find myself. Thus I have chosen to set it down here in the hope that the ultimate purpose of my story might be fulfilled.

The conversation started innocently enough. I said, "Why have I been given this tour?"

Chet said, "So you will understand heaven better."

"I've never given much thought to heaven, to tell you the truth."

"You haven't really seen it."

"Will I see it?"

"You've no need for that. The vestibule is enough."

"Why?"

"It's all your human senses will allow. To see the rest you'd have to . . . well."

"Have to what?"

He leaned forward and moved the pieces on the board back to their proper places. Then he turned the board around. "I'll be white this time."

"I'd have to what?"

"You'd have to *not* see it."

"I thought you said you weren't going to be enigmatic."

"I'm being as truthful as I can be."

"As truthful as you're allowed?"

"As truthful as I can be."

"Okay. I can ask you anything I want?"

"Anything." He moved his pawn to king four.

"What's the only struggle in the vestibule?" I moved my pawn to king four.

"It's not so much a struggle as it is a sort of . . . let's call it resistance."

"To what?"

"To the light." He moved his bishop to bishop four.

"Is the light God?"

"No. The light is the light. God is God."

"Are *you* God?"

He laughed. "Of course not. Do I look like a god?"

"Have you seen God?" I moved my bishop to bishop four.

"No." He leaned forward and studied the board, rubbing his chin with a puffy hand.

"Have you talked to him?"

"I know what he wants." He reached over and moved his queen to rook five.

"If you've never seen him, how do you know he exists?" I said.

"You've been sullying the earth with his power for the better part of an earth year. Where do you suppose that came from?"

"But how do you know this power giver is God?" I said.

"Who else would it be? When you say the word *God*, what do you mean? He's the source of everything and the effect of nothing. Humans call that God. It's a word we've gotten used to here. So that's what we call him."

"And does he answer?"

"He lets me know what he wants."

"Why does he want Dorothy not to love me anymore?"

"He has nothing whatever to do with that."

"What does he want, then?"

Chet smiled and pointed to the board. "Right now he wants you to make your move."

I calculated that the worst move I could make would be knight to queen's bishop three, so I did that.

Chet shook his head again, then used his queen to take my bishop's pawn. "Mate."

"That's two games," I said.

"You're not going to take this seriously, are you?"

"Well, it isn't limbering me up, let's put it that way."

He pulled on the collar of his shirt, then picked up the white queen. "You throw away power when you play like that."

"Power for the game," I said. "Nothing more."

"But you see, you're playing badly because you don't want to play."

"That's true."

"There's a lesson in that."

"I guess I don't see it."

He arched his brow slightly.

"What is God's business?" I said. "I mean, how does he operate?"

"It's not like he dresses up in the morning and goes to work."

"You know what I mean."

"All of your questions impose a certain limitation on my answers. You are human, and your response to things is naturally human. You would not believe how limited that is."

"Tell me."

"Look. God created the earth and put humans on it so they might move him by their entanglements. He is a great artist. He is also a celestial artist. The idea of art is the only human creation that mirrors God himself. This accident — you may call it coincidence if you wish — has pleased him mightily. Humans actually invented something that God is gratified to recognize in himself. It *is* himself. He is the creator, the maker of all things."

"Most of the artists I know are fairly weird."

"Precisely." He was smiling now, delighted at the thought. "Of course you would think God was weird. But you're pretty odd yourself."

"So why is everyone so unhappy here?"

"This is the vestibule. It isn't . . ."

"Why do some people get to the vestibule and some not?"

"God is an artist. Some of his work is worth saving, and some of it just doesn't satisfy him. You say you've known some artists. Have you ever been able to figure out why they like a certain piece of work and wish to destroy others? There's no understanding it. That's simply the way it is."

"So it doesn't matter how a man or a woman lives?"

"Not in the least."

"You mean I could commit a mass murder and still get to the vestibule?"

"Or you could commit no crime at all. What you do doesn't matter, except to you and others like you."

"I could barbecue a child?"

"It would matter only to you and your race. It would not matter to the animals, the insects, the viruses, or God." He pointed to the table, and now there were cards and poker chips there. "Let's play poker."

"I don't want to do that." I was pretty emphatic about it. His head tilted down a bit, and I had the feeling I had been too sharp with him. "What is it with these games, anyway?" I asked.

"Well, you play them, you see, by the rules." He pointed to the cards. "You don't play *any* game until you learn the rules. They mean something to you, am I right?"

"Yes."

"And you play by those rules, but you don't know who made them?"

"No. I don't."

He seemed satisfied. "Just so."

"Just so, what?"

"It's what we're talking about here."

"If you don't mind, I can't focus on what I want to know and play parlor games too."

"You showed yourself to be a pretty good darts player," he said.

I shrugged. "I was showing off."

He picked up the cards and shuffled them.

"Please," I said. "I don't want to play."

"Fine. I'm just fiddling here."

After a pause, I said, "I can't believe the suffering of innocent children doesn't —"

"Is there such a thing as a *guilty* child?" His tone was different now. I had the feeling I'd touched a nerve. "It is really quite amusing to me, these human ideas about innocence and guilt and the suffering of the children. If the human race does not wish its children to suffer, why do people make so many of them do it? You refuse to let a puppy suffer because it does not know what is happening to it. What does a child know of its suffering? There is innocence that implies one has done nothing wrong, and there is innocence that suggests one has no knowledge of the world and its delights and defeats. Children are innocent on both counts, but you make them suffer anyway. They starve on sun-warmed African plains, burn in Middle Eastern terrorist raids, fester and twitch in hospital wards where doctors administer painkillers and make them hold on until the last agony. Even the subtle suffering your own children have endured while you and Dot —" He noticed the sudden frown on my face. "I'm sorry — Dorothy. While you and Dorothy work out your problems, have you ever considered asking yourself how much they are suffering?"

"I sure have. I think about it all the time."

"I'm sure that's a big help to them. You can't blame God for the suffering of the children. He made the earth, and he made things that cause earthly terrors. Human beings make suffering happen and continue. They make it with such regularity and conviction that I'm surprised your education has not enlightened you in the matter."

"But God *did* make the earthly terrors."

"Yes."

"And it doesn't matter to him that those terrors afflict and destroy us?"

"No."

"Why? What's the use of — of being good? Why should a man try to do the right thing?"

Chet laughed. "Excuse me. I'm sorry if I offend you, but I can't help it. You really think it matters to God what one of the tiny creations in this whole vast universe does? When you were a kid playing in the sand, did you give a damn one way or the other how each of the ants underground behaved? Do you truly believe a beekeeper is interested in the life of one bee?"

"Then what's the point of . . . Why should we resist . . ."

"Evil?"

"Yes."

"You won't play poker with me," he said. "What if I tell you a story?"

"All right."

"Two human beings are riding in a car and they're running out of gas. They are on a country road, and they haven't seen a gas station for miles. Let's say it is late at night and they don't want to run out of gas in the middle of nowhere. So they begin to pray. 'Oh God, please let there be a gas station around the next turn.' What do they think? That God changes the topography as they drive? That suddenly he reaches down his great benevolent hand and a gas station simply pops up out of the barren ground, complete with bright lights and surly, soiled attendants?"

"I guess they hope for the unknown to be what they want it to be."

"Right. And the unknown is precisely where humans got the idea of evil and good. Let me finish my story. Say these two humans in the car think the road will lead them home. And let us say they see home as the place they need to be. They have things there they value: love, warmth, charity, compassion, companionship, cold beer — all those things human beings crave and need. So they seek them by continuing down the dark road at night. Now, they believe going on down that road will be good. It will get them home. But unbeknownst to them, the road leads instead to a great chasm — a sixty-foot drop at a blind curve. Continuing down the road will end in crippling injury or even death for both of them. Would that be good or bad?"

"It's not good."

"Exactly. They might *think* going down the road is good, but it is *not* good. Or at least it is not good for them. It would be bad for them. One might even say evil."

"Why evil? There's nothing moral in that."

"Why does it have to include a moral component? If you came upon several children buried in a pile of rocks, suffering horribly, would you think that was good?"

"No. Of course not."

"What would it be?"

"Bad."

"Would it be evil?"

"Well . . ."

"What if you found out a farmer had put them there to suffer?"

"*That* would be evil."

"And if it was a rock slide? Or an accident?"

"It would be . . . unfortunate."

"Ah, what games you humans are capable of. The outcome's the same, isn't it? You would want to prevent it somehow, wouldn't you? Why? If it is only evil when a person brings it about, what is it that makes it evil? It can't be the suffering of the children, because you've said it is not evil if it happens accidentally."

"I said it was unfortunate."

"Why, though?" He was growing impatient. "Why do you insist on these semantic games? Evil is anything that harms human potential or causes needless suffering. Don't you see? The whole idea is a human one. Only humans, on earth, know who and what they are. Only humans can even consider what might be around the next bend, and then choose a path in the hope that it won't be bad for them. Bad is what hurts or hinders or destroys them. Good is what does not. The rest of that nonsense, all that whimsy about morality and sin, is merely a result of human attempts to impose what each of them values on their fellows. The universe is completely indifferent to all of it."

"And God? He didn't make evil so we would have a chance to

choose goodness? What's the point of our will? Why do we have the capacity to make moral choices?"

He laughed again. "You have the capacity to make choices. Morality is your idea."

"*My* idea."

"Human beings. The human race. God created the earth, and he put on it millions of competing things — viruses, bacteria, insects, plants, beasts and fishes, and men and women. He created the need of all things to subsist by destroying and eating other things. The competition amused him in some way, perhaps. I can't say. But that's what he made. He did not give humans the capacity for *moral* choice. He gave them memory, and let them develop the capacity to conceive of the future. Human beings could remember where they'd been and they could picture what might be ahead of them. Everything else followed from that. The ability to imagine the future led to a highly developed sense of survival. The dinosaurs didn't know how to hide their eggs and they stumbled into huge pits that kept them from eating. There might be five brontosauruses struggling in a tar pit, and the sixth one, since he could not conceive of the future, since he could not imagine himself in the same predicament, would wander into the pit himself. This turned out not to be good for dinosaurs. Humans did not fall prey to such a thing because God gave them the past and the future. But humans could imagine that a particular act would be good for them, do it, and discover that it was bad. A primitive man might think fire would be good to drink, and after he finished picking the blisters from under his nose, he might come to the conclusion that fire is definitely *not* good to drink. Thus developed the notion of good and bad, and when our caveman wanted to warn other cavemen about fire, or keep them from burning his children, he labeled the bad 'evil.' The notion of evil, of forces in contention for humanity's well-being or ill-being, led to the idea of God as this great father figure who follows the personal lives of each and every human being, even those who never heard of him. I suppose it was inevitable that humans would nurture this idea of morality. But, I assure you, morality is a completely foreign idea to God. In fact, I think it is safe to say that God is fairly insulted by the idea that he ought to abide by some moral code humans have invented for themselves. Every time a human being says, 'God is good,' there is a rumble behind the doors."

237

I was considerably upset after this somewhat lengthy oration. Chet did not seem to need air, but when he was done he looked at me and blinked, as though he had surprised himself with what he had to say. Though he was not loud, there was vehemence in every syllable.

I stammered, "I wanted to be a good acting God, and God is — he's not . . ."

"Good? That's right. He's not evil either. Those words belong to you, to human beings. Not to God. They mean nothing to him except that they reflect, in some ways, the curious nature of his most interesting creation. Believe, me, he spends more time fooling around with the earth than any other place."

"There are other places?"

Chet's voice was softer now. "Earth satisfies and frustrates God in ways I don't yet understand. Perhaps there is some secret thing about men and women that draws him there. Perhaps he can't avoid it because everybody spends so much time talking about him and addressing him. And he does save more humans than any other thing. You've seen the size of the vestibule. That's for humans alone. Of course, other forms of life would never require such a thing."

"Why?"

"They don't have consciousness. It's the consciousness that made a mess of everything."

"Everything's a mess?"

"Well, the vestibule keeps growing. You saw it. The doors to heaven are rarely opened anymore. People just don't want to go through."

"What's *wrong* with heaven?"

"Nothing. It's what everybody wants. It's bliss."

"I'm really confused now," I said. He had touched on a subject very close to my heart: the idea of bliss. I had sought, all my life, as much unfettered happiness as I could gather. "If it's so wonderful, why doesn't anyone —"

"Do you know what bliss is?"

"Yes. I think I do."

"Tell me."

"It means happiness. Absolute happiness, without a single — with no pain. No woes. No fears or worries or . . ."

"Or grief, or sorrow, or misery?"

"Yes."

238

"Or even a tinge of sadness or regret?"

"Yes. I've had one or two days like that on earth with my family." I was thinking of our trip to the park back in March.

"Well, there you are."

"There I am what? That's what I mean when I say bliss. Isn't that what *you* mean?"

"That's what bliss is, yes. To a human being. And to me. Now you take a happily married fellow who comes here. He's going to get here alone. Maybe his wife is still alive, or perhaps she doesn't get saved. Let's say she's one of the seventy percent or so that God decides not to keep. This man's going to be unhappy. He remembers his wife. He loved her deeply. She's gone, for eternity. A destroyed soul is simply lost to us all, even God. Maybe this fellow also remembers his dead children, three of whom made it to the vestibule but soon thereafter passed through the doors. They are gone too. He cannot see them again except in his memory. Now, how does this man gain bliss from such a condition? He mourns them every day, thinks of them with great affection and sadness almost every waking hour. Even on the best days, when he forgets them momentarily, he still loves them and wishes he didn't have to do without them. Do you think a man can find bliss as long as he has that sense of sadness and loss?"

"I don't know. I never thought about it. Can't he simply pass through the doors and be reunited with —"

"No! No!" He almost shouted this. Then, in a softer tone, he said, "Don't you see? Through the doors is bliss, and you've already agreed that bliss does not include anything like grief or sorrow, or even a little sadness. He cannot pass into heaven until bliss is possible for him. That's why we have the vestibule, and also why there is so much development here."

"How can such a man pass into heaven, then?"

"He must give up love."

"But isn't God love?"

"God is *law*. Love is a human idea. And people cling to it with such incredible stubbornness that even God can't break them of it. After thousands of decades and countless calamities and misfortunes attributed to it, the idea of love has not lost even a fraction of its luster in the human mind. You'd think it was a biological need, like thirst or hunger. But don't let that mislead you — hate's a very popular and sturdy notion of human beings, too. Both are probably a product of an overzealous affinity for selecting preferences. What a man does *not* prefer he learns to abhor, and what he prefers — well, you get the idea."

You wouldn't think it could be possible, but I was sitting in the vestibule of heaven feeling sick to my stomach. "What you've told me is . . . it's just horrible," I said.

"Well, I expected you to say that. You can't even give up a woman who needs to be away from you very much."

"I love her."

"Yes, you love her. In your own selfish way, I suppose you do. But you hate her a bit, too."

"I'm beginning to hate a lot of things now," I said. I stared at the table in front of me. There was a game of Trivial Pursuit there.

"Perhaps this has all been too much for you," Chet said tenderly.

"How does a person give up the idea of love?"

"It's not just love. It's everything. To be pure spirit, one has to surrender all *things*. As soon as a man stops missing his wife or his lost children, as soon as he surrenders everything of himself that he clutches in his breast so tenaciously, he will stop being that particular man and pass through the gates."

"But who's going to enjoy the bliss, then?"

"Bliss is not possible for any single soul who retains any part of what he or she once was. This is not a condition set down by God. It is a product of memory and desire — the very things that distinguish humans from animals and amoebas. The other living things that God wishes to save enter heaven almost at the instant of death. Only humans remember loved ones and fret and worry over them. Only humans make bliss nearly impossible. You should see some of them when they get here — they've left *everybody* behind, you see, all the people they love. It's so ironic — while a man's family gets together and wails over his death, the one who has died suffers from indescribable grief for everyone and everything he has ever cherished. Some of them are so miserable it is easy to see where human beings got the idea of hell."

"What you describe is terrifying," I said. "It makes me sick to think of it. It isn't heaven to me, or anyone I know."

"That's also ironic. Human beings covet love and family so blindly, and yet they picture heaven as this blissful place where they will not

240

miss people they have loved very deeply. I can see you'll probably be loitering in the vestibule with everybody else when your time comes."

"Yes. I will. I can tell you that right now. It's preferable to nothing."

"Heaven is not nothing. It's bliss. Just what you and every other human being claims to crave."

"It sounds like a sort of Alzheimer's disease of the soul, if you ask me." I think I was beginning to feel angry. My stomach churned with it, and that is what made me ill.

Chet said, "There aren't any complaints from behind those doors."

"I don't hear any cheers or laughter or music either."

He gave me a paternal smile. "It's all spirit, and spirit is bliss, and bliss is silent."

"Still, I'd want to stay here. I like noise. This place isn't that bad, and I think a person could get used to it after a while. Grief lasts only so long, and then there are fond memories, and the busy task of continuing to li— of continuing to be a person."

"Ah, but don't forget the struggle."

"You mean the resistance? To what, the bliss? I could resist that."

"That's not all of the struggle. You must imagine being here. It's a pretty monstrous boredom. That is another reason why so many are unhappy here. Shall we play just one round of Trivial Pursuit?"

"So the struggle is boredom?"

"It grabs like a spiritual hug. You've felt it, remember?"

"Yes." I was suddenly terrified that he would demonstrate it again. I braced for it, but he picked up the dice and rolled them.

"Five. Good." He moved his little circle five spaces. "Sports and Leisure."

"I don't want to play," I said.

Still looking at the board, he said, "Everyone in the vestibule is finally beaten down by intense equanimity. It's the terrible struggle against not struggling that gets everybody finally. It will even get you someday."

"And then I'll know bliss." I was being sarcastic, but he didn't seem to mind it.

"Oh, of course you will know it. But it's not like we force anything on anybody. It's just what happens."

"Is it possible to go somewhere other than heaven when we die?"

Again he thought I'd said something funny. "How delightful you are."

"I'm serious."

He frowned slightly. "The twenty or thirty percent he saves, he saves for here."

"Am I saved?"

"Yes."

"And Dorothy? Claire? Jody Beth?"

"I can't tell you."

"You can't or you won't?"

"I won't."

"Why was I given the power? Tell me that."

"I've never understood why God lends his power to mortals. I can guess about it, but I really don't know. He has not given me to know, only to help carry it out. Perhaps it has something to do with his desire to understand better what humans seem to value. The universe is pretty much governed by laws he set in motion at the beginning, when he hurled the rocks and scattered the lights, but the earth still presents the possibility of mutation and revision of the laws — humans keep altering things. I can tell you that Homo sapiens is the only creature in the universe who has actually brought about the de-creation of one of God's creatures. Only human beings can cause extinction."

"What about the dinosaurs? Humans didn't do that."

"No. God did. God does it all the time, through various means. But so do people, accidentally and without the same deliberation and purpose as the deity. You will admit that?"

"Yes. But —"

"So it is perhaps a consideration of God's to see what a human being will do with the world when it is all his."

"I never felt like the world was all mine."

"Oh, but it is. God's power is absolute, in a limited sense."

"Isn't that a contradiction?"

"No. I've already explained it to you. Only those laws that God has decreed cannot be changed, cannot be changed. Everything else is mutable."

There was a brief pause. He sat with his hands on his knees, watching my face.

"So," I said, "if I decree that my family is saved, will they be saved?"

"You've tricked me."

"No, I haven't. I merely want to know."

"You are wiser with the power, and I neglected to remember that. I will not answer you, but in doing so, I presume you have your answer, anyway."

"If I willed that my wife and children would all live healthy lives until their early hundreds and that no one could ever change that, would that become immutable?"

"I don't know why it concerns you. If you live to be ninety or a thousand, it won't reduce by a single millisecond how long you're going to be dead."

"I know," I said. "But it will increase how long I'll be alive."

"And when you get here, you'll probably hang around like everyone else."

"Why doesn't God simply wave his hand and dissolve this problem in the vestibule? You know, make love and identity unimportant to the dead?"

"Why don't you just wave your hand and make Dorothy be what you want?"

"I've thought of it. I'm not —"

"Don't you see? It wouldn't be what he created anymore. It would be something else. He wants to work with what he created, watch it strive and turn and stumble amid the stars. He doesn't want to start over. Believe me, God can be extremely stubborn."

I thought of my own stubbornness, then pictured myself here after I died, looking for Dorothy. "Do people fall in love here? In the vestibule?"

"I suppose some do, but it doesn't develop in the same way."

"Why? How is it different?"

"Affection that develops here is unfettered by the threat of calamity, suffering, and loss. There's no way to express love physically, since there is no birth here. There's no need to care for or nurture or encourage or inspire a loved one, since people here can have whatever they want. After a while lovers get to talking about earth, where they felt *real* love — where love was necessary for them."

With ill-disguised awe and sadness I said, "I thought it was necessary everywhere."

"Nah."

"For everyone."

"If it were not for the love affair human beings have with themselves on earth, the vestibule would wither away very fast. It isn't the love that develops between souls here that keeps the tracks to heaven unused and shiny."

I was afraid that what Chet had told me would ruin me for earth.

"You asked for the truth," he said.

"Will I remember all this when I go back?"

"Absolutely. If you ever tell anyone, I want you to get it exactly right."

"Why?"

"It's important to me."

"Does it have anything to do with why I've been chosen for this?"

His voice was very soft, as though he were offering absolution. "I really *don't* know God's reasoning. But I think you were chosen for this offering because you might have some impact on the overcrowded situation in the vestibule. It would be like God to see if he could bring about some important revision by delegating his power and allowing for random responses to it. Perhaps you will inadvertently change something in the nature of human beings that will make love less important. You see, love is weaker in you than in most humans."

"It is not," I said. "It most definitely is not."

"I don't expect you'd recognize it, but it's true."

"How can you say that?"

"You don't really love Dorothy, or even your children. What you love is *believing* you love them. That's what you love."

"I love them inexpressibly." I was never so sure of anything in my life.

"Yes, but not inexpressibly well."

I didn't know how to look him in the face. I studied his brown shoes, the smooth wooden floor. I think he noticed that I had lost interest in asking him any more questions.

I said, "I have never felt anything so powerful as my love for Dorothy and the children."

"I believe you believe that," he said flatly. "In any case, you might say your gift is part of a design. I am only guessing at the purpose of it."

I was almost in tears. "How can you know what I feel for my children?"

"I've observed you. From that I've drawn what I think is an accurate conclusion."

"Tell me, what makes you such an expert on love?"

"I've been watching it for eight thousand years. It's an action. A verb. A behavior. It's a thing one *does*. You're one of those who thinks it's a feeling."

"No wonder Dorothy doesn't love me," I said.

"Don't be so dejected." Chet leaned forward and put a hand on my shoulder. "Your attitude toward love is the best thing about you, and probably why you were chosen. Love is feebler in you than in most humans. If you'll excuse this theft from your own terminology, that's a *good* thing in heaven's vestibule."

14

The trip back was sudden. Chet leaned forward in the black chair and placed his hands on my bowed head, and the next thing I knew, I was lying on a hard bed in a hospital room, and I could hear Dorothy's voice. My senses weren't dulled or distorted in any way, although my eyes were closed and I felt as though I had been sleeping very deeply. I might as well have appeared in the room like a ghost, and I suppose that in a way, that is precisely what I did. The room was an odd shade of green, like the underside of a northern pike, and bright sunlight cut through half-open venetian blinds to my right and made striped patterns across the bed cover. I was extremely pleased to feel the sun's warmth. Beyond the end of the bed, where my chart dangled from the metal frame, Herta was standing like a mound of clothing, her hands in her pockets, her head nodding ever so slightly up and down. Dorothy stood in front of her, and to her right, facing me, was Norm. They were whispering, although, as I said, I could hear Dorothy's voice very clearly. Their tone was so reverential I thought at first they were praying for me. But then I came to see that they were comforting one another, talking about what a fine man I had been and how terrible it would be for the children to lose their father at such a young age. They were discussing when the doctors would want to unplug me from my life-support system and let nature take its course.

I looked out the sliced window, watched cars and trucks pass a stand of sycamores, and thought about the birdless trees I'd seen in the vestibule of heaven. I couldn't remember any particular kind of tree — ash, or birch, or oak or spruce or maple. I couldn't recollect a single dogwood or pine tree. The trees of heaven had green leaves, and there were plenty of them, but I couldn't name a single one. Nor could I recall a shrub or a flower. There were few clouds in heaven — not much weather to speak of. I had seen the whole vast vestibule of heaven, viewed the great door to eternal bliss, and yet, lying there in that hospital bed, I could not resist a vague, gnawing sensation that I had been cheated by grandeur. I was in the grip of a higher presentiment of things familiar and drab, of a heaven without splendor or beatitude or grace.

How would you feel if you'd just had a tour of heaven and you came back feeling as if you'd just visited a bowling alley?

I felt horrible.

I found myself hoping it was really only a dream that had quickened me while I was in a coma, but then I remembered the way the steering wheel had spun in my hands before the crash and the terribly disturbing conversation I had just had with Chet. I knew it was true, and I was back on earth, with God's power for just a few more months.

It surprised me how consoled I felt by the presence of Dorothy and her mother and father. I watched them whispering together in the slotted light from the windows and realized a powerful sense of belonging to them and with them. But I might have felt the same way if they had been a custodial crew at the foot of my bed. You see, although I liked it that these people were my family, it wasn't that relationship that moderated my fevered sadness over what I had seen and heard in heaven. It was merely the fact that these were human beings, and they were alive. I had been outside Fortress Earth, in the other camp. I had seen the enemy. And now I was back with my fellows, under siege.

Herta said, "We should pray at a time like this."

I watched Norm get a grip on himself, nodding his head gravely.

"Sometimes," Dorothy said, "you get to thinking a person is always going to be there. You never think a person so young is going to be taken."

Herta embraced her. "I know, honey."

Dorothy sobbed.

I sat up and said, "Hey."

After a frozen pause, the three of them came at me as though I might disappear if they didn't grab hold of me. "You're awake," Dorothy said. Norm laughed and hugged me so hard I felt my ribcage shift. All of us were gasping with such relief and happiness, anyone in the next room might have thought we were having group sex.

"Where are the children?" I said.

"They're in the waiting room with Mr. Shale," Dorothy said. "They aren't allowed in here."

"I want to see them."

"How do you feel?" said Herta.

"I can't believe it," Dorothy said. "You're alive."

There was a long pause while we let go of each other and rearranged ourselves a bit. Then Dorothy said, "Mr. Shale's been wonderful. He stayed with the girls every afternoon so I could be here."

"I wrecked his car."

"No need to worry yourself about that," Norm said. "He's got plenty of insurance."

Dorothy put her arms around me again. "I just can't believe it," she said. She must have recognized my gathering confusion over her joy. I didn't understand yet why she was so affectionate, since the last time I saw her, I was reasonably sure it was going to be the last time I saw her.

"We thought you were a goner," Norm said.

"Let's leave them alone." Herta pulled her husband's sleeve.

I watched them shuffle out, Herta clutching Norm's arm as though she were afraid she'd lose him if she let go. Herta's sudden death and resurrection had intensified their love. I soon came to see that Dorothy was similarly moved to tenderness and warmth by the miracle of my recovery. The desperate prayers she had muttered during the long vigils by my bed appeared to have been answered.

As soon as her mother and father were gone, she took my hand in hers and said, "Darling, I know now."

"I know some things too," I said.

"I know what's — what really matters. The thought of losing you . . ." Tears rimmed her eyes. She truly believed she was feeling a flowering desire to be with me. But I knew better. What she was experiencing was actually only a surface reaction to crisis, a sort of coverlet. There was no depth to it, and underneath, still festering, was her essen-

248

tial need to be on her own. Indeed, a large part of her wild sentiment at that moment was fueled by her sense of surrender and loss. She would have to bend her will to mine. She would do it gladly — sacrifice herself on the fiery altar of her unyielding love for me.

I did not think she would burn very well.

"Look," I said. "Something's happened to me. I understand a little bit more about life than I did before."

"So do I." She rubbed my hand, tears running down her cheeks.

"The earth's not such a big place."

"What?"

"It's not so very important, either — except to us."

"Are you quite awake yet, darling?"

"Yes, I'm fine. I mean, I'm not in any pain."

She lay her head down on my hand, sobbing again. "I'm sorry for what I've put you through, honey."

"We put ourselves through things," I said.

She looked up. I swear her eyes could light the vestibule of heaven.

"But I've learned about it," I said. "I've learned a lot more than I bargained for." Now I found myself fighting tears. But it wasn't because of what Dorothy and I had lost. I wasn't even thinking about Dorothy and me just then. To tell you the truth, I felt terribly sad for us all, for you and me and every last one of us.

She put her arms around me. Her hair smelled like fresh pine, and it was so soft on the side of my face that I felt as if I had rediscovered all my senses at once. I was a body again, held by a woman who loved me but who did not know that her love was mostly my creation. I had failed her in ways she could never put into words.

No. We had failed each other. What I expected from her was more than she was willing to give, and I had nothing to offer but my expectations. I could see now why Chet might think that love did not run too deeply in me. He was wrong, of course. I would not have allowed my eyes to open again if he had been right. What he seemed completely unaware of was a truth I came to know without having thought of the words. I write them for the first time here: *a human being can make up his mind to love a person better.*

I put my hands on Dorothy's shoulders and gently moved her back from me. "I see it all more clearly now."

"I'm sorry."

"No, I mean I *really* see."

She didn't say anything. I realized she was suffering extraordinary anguish over what we had been through in our marriage; she understood that I would not necessarily believe that she loved me.

I said, "Something has happened to me."

She looked worried.

"No, listen. I'm not talking about the accident."

"I just want us to be together again."

"I know you do."

"I want us to be — to be a family." She took out a pink tissue and wiped her nose. She wasn't crying anymore, but her eyes were still bathed in tears.

"You should take some time to mull things over."

"No. I've had the last five days to —"

"Five days?"

"You've been out five days."

"It didn't seem nearly so long."

"They didn't give us much hope. They said you were brain dead."

"Then . . . I'm a miracle."

"Yes," she whispered.

"The whole staff will be crashing through the door any minute, with tests and cameras and lights and newspaper . . ."

"I don't care. You're fine. You've come back."

"Yes, I've come back."

"And *I* want to come back too. I know where I need to be now," she said. "I promise."

"It's not the sort of thing you make promises about. You either know or you don't know. Take some time and think about it."

She sat on the bed and stared at her hands, fiddling with the tissue in her lap. "I guess I deserve this."

"What?"

"You don't believe me."

"Oh, I believe you," I said. "But it's too important to decide right here."

"Nothing's more important than how I feel about you."

In spite of the tubes and wires hooked to me, I rose from the bed, and as I did this I clasped her hand. She stood too, and I took her by the shoulders and held her in front of me. She thought I was going to kiss her. Instead, I gazed into her exquisite blue eyes and said, "Look, honey. I haven't loved you the way I know I can. You see? It would be wrong for me to take advantage of — for me to use all this . . ." I looked around the room still fighting back tears. "Take some time. Decide when you're calm and you think I'm going to be around for decades — into my hundreds. Then decide."

She looked down and whispered, "Okay."

"Fine," I said. "And when you decide, I'll accept that."

She smiled, reached up to kiss me. "I'm going to get the children and take them home."

"Good."

"I'll be back tonight."

I shook my head, moving unsteadily back to the bed. "You won't have to come back. I'm getting out of here right now." I removed the tape from the IV in my arm.

"Don't." She took hold of my wrist.

"I'm fine," I said. "I want to see the girls. I'm not going to hang around here for all the hoopla, if you don't mind."

"You might be hurting yourself."

"Nah." I pulled off the dressing and took the needle from under the skin. Then I yanked the tube from my nose. I was a little stunned to see how far into me it went. You should have seen Dorothy's face.

"Sickening, isn't it?" I said.

"Are you okay?"

"It doesn't hurt."

"Please don't leave me," she said.

"I won't. And I hope you decide to stay with me."

"I will. I have."

"We'll see," I said. "Right now, help me get dressed. I'm real stiff."

Of course they wouldn't let me out of the hospital. The nurses came in just as I was bending into my shirt, and the clatter that followed was enough to arouse the interest of most of the ambulatory patients on my floor. They wandered down the hall to my room, some of them dragging IV stands. Doctors came in and out like grocery clerks unloading a produce truck. They poked and prodded and listened to my interior so often, and with such amazement, you'd think they were picking up Mahler's Fourth Symphony through their stethoscopes.

Later that evening they put me in a tube and gave me a complete CAT scan. Then I was treated to an EEG and an EKG. I told a nurse I was getting hungry and could I please have an EGG! She didn't even smirk. Apparently she'd heard that one a thousand times.

"I really am hungry," I said.

"I'll see if I can get you a biscuit."

Through it all, I could not get heaven out of my mind. Nor could I escape a creeping realization that if I did not do something to change the temper of love in the human heart, my tenure as acting God would be a failure. It simply didn't matter to anyone in heaven what good I might do. How could it matter in the scheme of things what one of the ants did underground, to quote Chet's apt description of the role of human beings in the universe? And Chet said that I was not to make a mess that could not be cleaned up.

What Chet feared was that I might destroy the world. I had the power to do it. Any other mess would not truly *be* a mess — could not be, since the idea of a mess is foreign to the greatest mess-maker of them all.

But the thing that really troubled me, that stuck in my heart like a hot knife, was that I could not be a good acting God no matter what I did or didn't do. Good was my idea — our idea. Think of it.

Thus I made the momentous decision I spoke of in the beginning of this narrative. It came to me while the doctors and nurses pinched, rattled, rubbed, and jostled me, while the miracle of my recovery was set down and recorded for all time.

I had been sadly reflecting on the God I felt I had lost — a God who cared about me and mine, who gave me, and all of us, the world and wondrous love, a God who suggested order, purpose, and a painless, ecstatic, and eternal future. And suddenly it was clear what I had to do.

Absolutely clear.

❋

You know, I was never a very popular person. When you are afraid of people — when you spend your time avoiding embarrassment or awkwardness around people — it is easy to miss the fact that your reticence has been misperceived as unfriendliness. The normal result of that perception is that you are often left alone, and you begin to see the world as an outsider. When that happens, anything you get from people that betokens affection takes on the importance, ironically, of a miracle. I had spent my entire life observing human beings trying to be kind to one another, and it wasn't until my return from heaven that I understood the truth about our little group. It *is* a miracle that we care for one another, because virtually everything in the universe resists that notion.

I simply could not let God have his way with us any longer.

So I finally turned to the earth and all of its problems. Sitting alone at last in my hospital room, staring through half-open blinds at the now darkened street, I engaged in the sort of macro activity that Chet had never dreamed was possible for me.

With the power and authority of God, and in the order that things came to my mind, I ordained:

1. that no one will ever suffer from any of those diseases that strike insidiously and give you months to think about the fact that you're going to die.

2. that everyone will be saved after they die and no one will be bilked into leaving the vestibule, nor will future generations have to mourn loved ones who did not make it there. Everyone will have a choice about whether or not to spend eternity in the vestibule of heaven, but since everyone's loved ones will be there, probably no one will choose otherwise. (For myself, I am unable to distinguish between nothing and bliss. It's the vestibule for me, permanently.)

3. that death will be quick, painless, in a bed, and completely unembarrassing right before old age gets to be too much to bear — probably when you are in the early to mid-nineties.

4. that since death can only take place as described in #3 above, there will be no more kidnappings, muggings, beatings, rapes, or any other sort of human violence against other humans. There will be no more torture, mental, physical, or otherwise. Malice and sickness will disappear from the human heart.

5. that starvation will stop. No one will ever again be too poor to feed his or her children. The earth will be plentiful and big enough for all of us. Population growth will slow just enough to keep us from being uncomfortably crowded.

6. that no one will ever again suffer from a heart attack, stroke, or any sort of arterial accident.

7. that no one will suffer from cerebral palsy, liver disease, blindness, pellagra, or any nervous disorders — especially those that make you bark like a dog or slobber or wet your pants or decide to take a garden hose and water a library in the middle of the night.
8. that all babies will be born normally and without pain and every child will flourish without violence or neglect or mental anguish.
9. that all accidents, earthquakes, and other natural or manmade disasters will be harmless. No one will be crippled or marred by life or any of its misfortunes. Life's misfortunes will be only minor disturbances and will not inhibit human potential or welfare in any way.
10. that war, terrorism, and other nobly motivated human calamities will cease to be the instruments of love. Since human beings will no longer feel malice, the world will finally know, and come to enjoy, peace.

I created all these things.

When I reflected on this list, I felt an odd sensation in my soul. A sort of deeply moving, almost spiritual variety of satisfaction gripped me, although I was swallowed up in alternating storms of fear and giddiness because I was not quite finished yet. You see, I figured that once I made changes that God couldn't abide, he'd have to undo them somehow. But if I ordained that he could not change them, then he would have to either get me to do it or find some way to get around me. The only way he could undo anything I had done was if he had foreseen everything and set the power against such things in advance. That's where I knew I had him.

So I decreed that no one except me could ever even slightly change my creations in any way. I followed that with a conditional decree: if anyone negated any part of what I had created, including the decree that no one could change what I had already decreed, that being's power would be diminished to the level of the weakest, most physically helpless species of amoeba. Having insured myself and the rest of us against God's wrath, I ruled that he could not take the power back from me unless all that I had decreed came into being permanently. In other words, he could not have his blessed power back unless he was willing to accept what I had done. Period.

Thus I covered all the possibilities. If God wanted to be the deity again, he would have to agree to everything. Even if he had preserved some measure of the power before he gave it to me — even if he had preordained that I could not make any permanent distasteful changes in his grand design — when I surrendered this earth to him, as soon as he tried to alter any of my creations, he would immediately become as harmless as a wildflower.

And that's pretty harmless.

❊

Of course I got an immediate response from Chet. In fact, we had a terrible argument about it that very night. When the doctors shook my hand and told me I could go, Chet was waiting in the white hallway like a dissatisfied ghost. He gave me a blank look and said, "I'll give you a ride home." Despite his relative calm, I knew he was steaming. Anger was a completely new experience for him, an earthly emotion he didn't quite know how to handle. His words contained an extraordinary variety of stressed syllables, and he wore a look of shock on his face, as though his demeanor alarmed him. We walked to his car, a bright red Porsche 924, and I thought once he got me in the parking lot he'd try to make me change my mind by putting my head in a heavenly hammer lock or giving me a great big spiritual hug. But he got in the car without saying anything. I settled into the seat next to him, and he put his hands on the dashboard, stared off across the moonlit parking lot, and said, "What do you think you're doing?"

"I'm fixing things."

"Oh?"

"That's right."

As soon as he spoke I knew I had created more than a minor problem in the corridors of paradise. I had created things neither Chet nor his employer had expected. You should have seen his face. If you've ever worked in an office for a short time and been promoted over a man with thirty years' experience, you have some idea what he looked like.

"You have to undo all of it."

"I won't."

"God's not going to let this situation —"

"He should have known what I'd do."

"How could he, when you didn't even know?"

"He knows everything, right?"

"He knows everything that's knowable."

"Well?"

255

"The future is only knowable to you when you're the one making it. When somebody else is making it, it isn't." He started the car. "Anyway, this isn't about God. It's about earth."

"It is?"

"It's the earth I'm worried about."

"Me too."

He pulled out into traffic, shifting the car as if he wanted to cause it pain. Since this was his first experience with anger, I thought it was fairly heroic that he was working so hard to keep it under control.

After a while he said, "You're tinkering with things you don't know about."

"It seemed okay when I was unwittingly setting fires and crippling the toes of religious fanatics."

He seemed to flinch, then he took in air and hissed like a puff adder.

"I know you're angry," I said. "You don't have to try and hide it."

"I'm not hiding anything."

"That's a normal human reaction to things ordained. How's it feel?"

"You don't know what you're talking about."

"I know about a lot of things. You told me, remember?" Outside in the rushing lights of the city I could see so many strange and yet familiar faces — apparitions of people whom I'd never seen before but whom I now felt I knew quite well. I cared about all of them. Every one of them. I said, "I want to see what will happen on the earth when there is no suffering."

"You'll create a boring, deadly existence. Nothing to struggle for."

This accusation sparked something in my spleen. For the first time I felt embittered toward Chet, a sensation that astonished me. "You can't get me with that silly argument. What would you call what's been going on between me and Dorothy, mutual encouragement and support? There's plenty of struggle just to find happiness between two people."

"That's not struggle. It's — it's nothing but sloth. The human desire for affection and all that rot."

"It means a lot to us, as you've pointed out."

"Do you actually think there will be anything worthwhile in your perfect world? What will you watch on TV? What will writers write about? Doing the laundry? Trimming hedges? Picking apples? What will the painters paint?"

"What do they paint in heaven?"

"It is clear from this that you simply do not understand the concept of the spirit."

"Yes, I do. It's a glorified nothing. I don't want to go anywhere I can't take my self. Whatever it is, if I have to stop being me, I'm not interested."

"You're small. You're earthbound. You're —"

"Fine," I said. "That's what I want."

"You will despise perfection. It will ruin living."

"Have you ever looked at the wild imagination of a child? Children don't know yet about the possible horrors of this place, and for them, if they're left alone, the world is perfect. I haven't noticed that a perfect world has adversely affected the creativity or beauty of children. I want to explore the unlimited potential of unthreatened human beings."

Chet turned to me. "You couldn't stand it. You don't even like people."

"I don't much like them when they're pestered and terrorized and frightened." I could not keep my voice down. "I want to see what happens when the strings are pulled on earth by somebody who cares about it, somebody who cares about persons. God has never shown much interest in persons."

"As it should be. God is God."

"No, he's not. Not now. I am."

"You're irrational."

"No, I'm not. I'm sane, sensible, and enraged. That's what I am."

"You have defied the order of this creation, and it will not be allowed."

"I'm not defying anything," I said. "I'm revising things."

"Call it what you want."

"I'm finally answering the prayers of the human race. How about that?"

"You are recklessly defying the laws of God."

"I'm improving the laws."

"No."

"Making them more humane. It's the will of the people. You've heard of that?"

"It will not be allowed."

"Well. We'll see, won't we?"

I tried to control my anger, or at least to direct it. I think I managed as well as Chet did. To some degree, we both felt betrayed — I by his reaction to my creations, and he by what he considered my misuse of his great heavenly offering.

Believe it or not, God did not worry me. I was certain that he would not be able to punish me for my earthly revolt; in order to do that, he'd have to take the power back, which would cost him too much. He'd either have to accept everything I had changed, which would limit his influence on earth extremely, or he'd have to alter my work in some way and immediately lose all of his power. My decree left no other possibility.

And I would not give up. There was no way I was voluntarily going to surrender earth back to him, because I truly believed — and still do — that I could do a better job.

epilogue

I have been the acting deity now for three years, and as I'm sure you know, nothing on this earth has changed. Apparently God has some way to prevent what I ordained, as long as he does not take his power back. Although I can still perform some pretty extraordinary tricks, the world remains a treacherous and troubling place. And now, whenever I try to use the power, the voices that nearly destroyed me that day in front of the hospital break through again and torture me. I have no control over them. The horror of that thunderous noise in my skull is worse than anything I have ever felt. I find myself cringing at the thought of a single human prayer.

Chet dropped me at the house after our argument — it didn't take me long to convince him that I was not going to back down — and I found Dorothy and her parents getting ready to come to the hospital to pick me up. We truly had a fine celebration that night, with drinks and laughter and repeated tales of reprieve and canceled doom. They had no idea, of course, what I had just done for them all. It made me happy just to see them rejoicing over my miraculous recovery.

What I remember most about that night, however, is seeing my daughters for the first time after heaven: when I held them in my arms the floor seemed to drift beneath me, and I felt my heart tremble like an injured bird. I could not look into their eyes. I was weakened by their innocence, and although I felt an electric thrill at the notion that I had made for them a better life, it terrified me, nonetheless, that they would grow up in a world *I* made.

I decided to quit Shale Motors. I figured if I was going to be in some sort of tug of war with God, I didn't need to be battling salesmen and Mr. Shale about floor plans and car orders.

There was an extravagant and loud tribute to me upon my arrival when I went in to make this announcement. Mr. Shale gave a tearful speech in which he told of the sad eyes of my children when they thought I was going to die. Everybody slapped me on the back and told me I was lucky and I should thank God I had been saved. Dottie seemed so peacefully happy, I found myself envying her. When the festivities dwindled, before I went up to tell Mr. Shale I would be leaving, I called her into my office.

"I'm glad things worked out for you," I said.

She smiled. Her hair was arranged in an odd profusion of swirls across her forehead, and she wore a sleeveless lavender sweater over a white blouse and black skirt. She looked incredibly sure of herself. Her arms were crossed in front of her boyish chest, and I noticed she was holding a pad of paper in her hands, and there was a pencil over her ear. She stood there watching me try to think of something else to say.

Finally I said, "I'm leaving, you know."

Mr. Shale ambled around the corner and leaned on the doorjamb, his hands in his pockets, a look of absolute satisfaction on his chumpy face. It mush have been what Caesar looked like after Pompeii.

"Come on in," I said.

"Well," he said to me, "I see you've met the new president of Shale Motors." He put his arm around Dottie. "And the future Mrs. Shale."

"I'm very happy for both of you," I said.

Dottie looked at me as though she knew what I had done for her. There were tears in her eyes. "Thank you."

Mr. Shale rubbed her back, then seemed to study something in her ear. He smiled at me and went out.

Dottie said, "You're really leaving?"

"Yes." I didn't know what to do with my hands.

"I'll miss you."

"Well," I said. "As it turns out —"

Before I could finish, she put her arms around my neck, and though she was crying, she kept saying, "I'm happy, Charlie. Can you believe it? I'm happy."

"That's good." I patted her on the back. "That is very good."

As I held her there in the office, I realized it was the end of our friendship. Mr. Shale would not brook any prior attachments in his bride, and I was probably going to be busy battling God. Oddly enough, I found myself fighting back tears. I would not want to say whether they were tears of sadness or of joy. I knew Dottie was happy because of me, and this made me remember how unhappy I had made Dorothy.

So I resigned. Mr. Shale was very sorry to see me go; he offered me twice my salary to stick around and continue ordering cars and making deals. He knew a good thing when he saw one. He was convinced I was resigning because my feelings were hurt that Dottie had been promoted over me. I let him go ahead and think that, since it was easier than making up a reason to quit.

Cherry was ecstatic. "Now some doors will open for me," he said, patting me on the back.

"Yeah, I was always in the way."

"You got some *great* job, right?"

"Yeah, a great job."

"Well, good luck."

"The same to you," I said. He was going to need it. I wasn't going to be making any more sales for him, and he'd finally be on his own. He believed Dottie would fail and then, with me out of the way, he'd rise to the top, where he belonged. When I walked out the showroom door, the smile on his face was as broad and proud as a new father's.

Shortly after I left Shale Motors, while I was still waiting and worrying about what God would do, I reaffirmed my intent to let Dorothy think about things before she decided to come back to me. She hung on for a while — nearly five months. But finally, after her parents moved back to Dunkin, into a beautiful Victorian house, she once again saw the need to be on her own. This time my resistance was private — I fought a tremendous battle with myself over what I knew was right and what I wanted.

The day she left was a bright, blustery October afternoon full of wind-swirled leaves and the smell of wood smoke. I stood in front of her, looked into her sad blue eyes, and touched her cheek with my hand.

"I'm sorry," she said. "I'm just not happy like this."

I told her I understood.

She moved toward me and paused on the verge of a kiss. "Are you all right?"

"I hate it," I said. "But I'm not going to fight it."

"You'll find happiness," she said. It was more a flat statement of what she hoped than any sort of prediction.

"Don't take this wrong," I told her, "but if I had loved you better, maybe this wouldn't be happening."

"You loved me too much, Charlie."

"I'm doing my best to love you now. That's what matters to me."

She frowned, trying to understand but unwilling to ask for an explanation.

"Maybe when I've finished my —"

"No," I said. "There's no need to say that. Whatever happens, happens."

I was certain, after she picked up her bag and started down the walk, that she would not remember anything I had said to her. She turned to wave to me — an attempt to give some sort of finality to her departure — but I just closed the door. It took all of God's power not to ask her to stay.

I still wish she had found some way to continue with me and the girls. She's in graduate school now, studying the early Romantics. She plans on beginning a career in teaching at the university level. She sees Jody Beth and Claire frequently, and in spite of the terrible break in their childhood, I think they are happy. Dorothy and I talk about how they are growing, almost as if we were still together. There is a shared pride there that even time can't tatter.

In our own way, and without expectations and demands, we might come to care for each other again. In spite of what has happened between us, I still love her, though I don't spend much time thinking about it.

I've lived the last three years playing with my children, making home mean something to them, and reflecting on this earth and all the old imbalances. I have not been very active at all — nor have I wanted to be. I simply cannot stand the horror of those voices rattling in my head. Oh, I intervened in a few major events — I increased the level of reason in Eastern Europe and the Soviet Union, created a mess in China, saved a few lives here and there. God only knows what I've subconsciously stirred up in this world.

Chet almost never comes to see me anymore, and when he does we only argue. He's gotten calmer as the months have passed, so our arguments are fairly dispassionate. I think that until I told him I planned to write this narrative, he believed I was going to be as inactive and indifferent to human suffering as God has always been. Although it took some time, I gradually came to understand that if I didn't do something about this stalemate, the earth would remain exactly as it was, in spite of my revisions. So I have written all of this down. If this story has no impact, at least it will serve as a record of my term and the revisions I have tried to make.

God has been very stubborn, and so have I.

I think I am stuck with his power.

I couldn't give it back if I wanted to.

Unless I revoke all my decrees. Unless I put suffering and misery back into the scheme of things. Back where Chet says they belong.

What do you think I should do?